Falling For the Ace

A Grumpy Sunshine Military Aviation Romance About Forbidden Love and High-Stakes Flight

CK Franco

Blurbs

Two pilots. One forbidden spark.
One academy where secrets can kill.
Love was never part of the mission... until now.

Astra Flight Command is where legends are made—and where falling in love can destroy everything.

Captain Blaze "Falcon" Arden returns with scars no one sees, determined to keep every cadet at arm's length.
Then there's Lyra Vale—brilliant, relentless, and the one woman impossible to ignore.

When a string of dangerous "accidents" threatens the academy, Lyra uncovers a trail of buried truths—and Blaze becomes the only one she can trust.
Their chemistry is undeniable. Their connection is catastrophic.

CK FRANCO

*But in a world ruled by duty, loyalty, and survival...
loving each other may be the most dangerous risk of all.*

"Some hearts learn to fly long before the wings ever do."

Prologue

The sky burned the moment the jet broke through the clouds—
a streak of fire carving across the horizon,
a warning that came too late.

Captain Blaze Arden had felt this moment before.
The tightening of the air.
The silence that swallows a cockpit right before everything goes wrong.

And now, standing on the cracked runway of Astra Flight Command,
the memory slammed into him with the same merciless force as the crash
that stole his wingman and almost broke him.

Engines roared overhead, rattling the steel frames of the hangar
behind him.
The ground vibrated.
The wind tasted like metal and ghosts.

And then—
footsteps.

**Lyra Vale stepped onto the flight line, chin high, eyes locked
on him—**
a spark in human form, daring him to look away.

He didn't.

Because deep down, in the place he never let anyone see,
Blaze knew what this moment meant.

The sky was about to catch fire again.
Only this time, he wasn't sure he'd walk away from the flames.

Contents

Fire in the Sky

The first light drapes across the tarmac in bruised hues—orange molten into purple, fading like a slow burn on the horizon. Distant thunder mutters under the vault of dawn, a low, warning growl that stirs the heavy air. Captain Jareck "Blaze" Arden moves alone, his boots tapping a steady rhythm on the cracked concrete. The scent of jet fuel hangs thick, sharp, and metallic, cutting through the coolness of early morning. Each cadence of his steps echoes past the lined-up warbirds—sleek fighter jets parked with disciplined precision, their gunmetal skins shimmering in the dim light, silent sentinels waiting. He passes row after row, the shadows of the past curling in those empty cockpits, the ghosts of missions etched in every gleam, every whispered engine growl that once was.

His shoulders stiffen; breath shallow as a familiar ache curls behind his ribs, tightening like a noose. The loss is physical—a weight that presses against his chest and won't lift, no matter how many hours he logs in the sky. Three weeks since the last sortie. Three weeks since Rodriguez didn't come back.

Not a single word crosses his lips; only his eyes, hard and steady, scan the horizon beyond the runway where sun and storm wrestle. The sky's slow bleeding of light unfolds in quiet rebellion against the gathering clouds, mirroring something inside him—a fracture neither sun nor rain can heal.

The dormitory looms ahead, an angular block of sterile gray that swallows warmth. Astra Flight Command has a reputation: a crucible where the best pilots hone their edge, where discipline is religion and danger is the price of excellence. Those who walk these halls carry a weight that civilians will never understand. Those who don't make it home leave ghosts in the barracks.

The door sighs open under his grip, his polished uniform catching the first indigo shafts slicing through the windowpanes. Inside, silence is a living thing—hushed steps in a place caught between rest and rally. The corridors stretch, walls gleaming with antiseptic sterility, the faint hum of fluorescent lighting threading through the stillness. His boots sound heavier than expected—deliberate thuds. Each footfall is designed to mask the ache in his bones, the fatigue that clings to him like a second skin beneath his calm exterior. Discipline. That's what it is. Years of command and loss carved into every step.

He threads through the maze of halls, past empty rooms and lockers lined like soldiers in wait. The air smells faintly of cleaning solvents mixed with the distant tinge of ozone from overhead flare tests—cold and clinical, a stark contrast to the fevered heat of flight. The dorm breathes quiet respect for those who live by strict codes, but also whispers secrets of lives interrupted mid-flight.

At the end of the hallway, the weight in his hand grows heavier—the duffel bag, scuffed and softened by travel, swings at his side. The door to his shared quarters stands unmoved, an unspoken boundary. Past battles lie on one side, while uncertain days await on the other. He halts, his fingers tightening around the worn strap until his knuckles blanch white against the coarse fabric. Time thickens for a moment, and the world narrows to the thin veneer of that door.

He lets his gaze drift over the chipped paint and scuff marks, each flaw a testament to passage—fleeting moments, hard decisions, and the quiet collapse of control that war leaves behind. The morning chill pricks at the skin beneath his uniform, a subtle reminder of vulnerability beneath the armor.

Somewhere beyond, the first calls of waking birds struggle against the rumble of engines starting on the far side of the base. Yet here, in this narrow corridor, time seems to stall—the heavy silence swelling, waiting for the lock to yield.

A slight tremor runs through his fingers as he reaches for the handle, a ripple beneath the calm, a whisper of the man caught between battlefields, duty, and shadowed loss. The breath he draws is measured, steady as a pilot's approach to touchdown.

I'm home. The thought tastes hollow.

Two voices suddenly spill into the sterile corridor, breaking the spell—a muted quarrel between cadets just beyond the stairwell:

"You're seriously backing off already? You always bail when things get hot, Jareck. I thought you were tougher."

Blaze's jaw twitches slightly, but he remains motionless, his gaze fixed on the door. The words sting with familiar heat yet do not pierce the hold he has so carefully wrapped around himself.

"It's not about toughness. It's about surviving to fly another day. Do you think I don't remember?"

A sardonic laugh, low but edged with frustration.

"Survive or fade away. You can play it safe, or you can live."

Silence swallows the echoes, leaving only the distant storm and the tightening grip on the door. Blaze doesn't answer. He doesn't move.

The lingering energy of those words melds with the faint hum of thunder beyond the walls, a challenge and a warning mingled in the charged air. He breathes in—cool, damp, and electric—letting it settle like an oxygen mask steadies a pilot before the dive.

This morning, the sky writes its first line in fire and shadow, and Blaze stands ready to face the unwritten chapter beyond that door.

The metal groan of the door hinges sighs under Blaze's touch as the lock clicks open. He slips inside the shared quarters. The faint scent of stale boots and recycled air greets him like a ghost. The room wears the same stillness it held when he left—no dust disturbed, no sign that time has marched forward.

Across the narrow space, his wingman's bunk stares back, untouched by absence. The blanket is folded with military precision, and the helmet is perched atop it like a silent sentinel, gleaming under the dull overhead light. That helmet—never moved, never dusted—holds the shape of a man who no longer breathes the recycled air of this base. Blaze lingers on that side, the air seeming to thicken with the weight of memory.

Then he hears it: easy laughter—sharp, unguarded. His wingman's quick, confident bark cuts through the engine's roar, moments before their last sortie. The ghost rides the stale air, threading through the empty bed and knotting tight in Blaze's chest. It feels as if the room holds its breath alongside him.

Blaze lowers his duffel, the weight of it unfamiliar after days in the combat zone. He moves to his own bed—the one still layered with the scent of home amid the sterile base. The chill in the recycled air prickles his skin like a bad memory he can't shake. He sits.

His fingers work mechanically, unpacking essentials: a dog tag, a small journal, and the worn photograph taped crookedly to the wall just above his pillow. He stares at it. Two grinning faces, both dirt-streaked and sunburned, flushed after a victorious mission that felt like it might be the one that saved them. His wingman's eyes gleam with reckless joy, matching Blaze's own half-grin—a fractured moment of victory before everything cracked open.

His eyes close, light fading behind lids heavy with unshed grief. He breathes deeply, trying to empty the weight lodged in his chest, but the silence presses in, unyielding.

His hand twitches uncertainly before brushing away a trail of moisture he can't admit to, fingers trembling as if grief had a weight he could feel. He smooths his jaw, forcing the thin line of control back into place. No cracks. Not here.

The room's faint hum—a mix of distant engines and muted voices in the hall—fills the void as Blaze rises. The practiced stillness slips back into his bearing, a mask fashioned over raw edges.

His gaze flickers once more to the empty bunk beside him, the ghost of camaraderie lingering in the sharp crease of the blanket and the matte finish of the helmet's visor.

Without a word, he steps toward the door, the resonance of loss anchored behind him like a shadow he cannot outrun.

"I keep thinking I'm going to hear you laugh again," Blaze says softly, his voice low, almost swallowed by the quiet.

A pause. Almost silence.

"Yeah? Maybe I'll surprise you someday."

Another pause.

"Until then... keep flying like I'm right beside you."

The words echo in his mind, fractured and incomplete—a conversation held just beyond reach.

He turns away before the weight breaks through, sealing his sorrow behind the calm front he has mastered over years in the sky.

Blaze shoulders the silence, folds it tightly inside, then crosses the threshold—leaving the room exactly as it is, frozen between then and now.

The automated message chimes through the silence—sharp, edged with urgency. *Report to Hangar B for cadet orientation.* Flat. Unyielding. An order wrapped in command code.

Blaze's fingers twitch. He sets down his duffel without ceremony.

The basin's cold steel catches his tired face—a ghostly echo. He bends, cups his hands, and splashes water against skin parched by too much unspoken grief. The cold bites. It helps.

His starched uniform demands a fresh appearance. He works his jaw as he washes, scrubbing the exhaustion from the lines of his face. His fingers find the crease of his collar, pressing the edges into place as if the fabric itself can bolster his resolve. Just breathe. One breath held tight between his teeth. Build the wall between the past and duty.

In the mirror, his reflection blurs. Sorrow warps into something steely and unreadable. The weight behind his eyes lingers—a storm behind frozen glass. But there's no time to melt beneath the surface. He pulls the arm of his jacket with a precise tug, letting the motion steel his shoulders straighter.

The silence hums heavily, broken only by the creak of old pipes. Beyond the walls, engines thrum to life.

He steps away from the basin. Detergent mingles with the lingering ghost of jet fuel—a stubborn remnant clinging to these quarters. His boots strike the floor deliberately, and hollow clicks echo through the narrow hallway.

The dormitory stands sterile and unchanged, a quiet shrine to routine discipline. These walls have witnessed promises made under adrenaline-filled skies—some kept, some lost in the haze of combat.

One hand tightens on the duffel strap as he nears the door. The chill of early morning slips under his collar, brushing against skin raw from nights spent wrestling with shadows. His breath forms a low mist in the cavernous air. The door's cold metal handle presses into his palm, causing his knuckles to pale.

He pauses and lets the silence root itself. The weight of history folds into the present moment, leaving no room for hesitation. His form straightens, and his mask settles back into place. The comms crackle again—a reminder that the past waits behind closed doors, but the future demands attention.

Blaze steps into the corridor, his boots syncing with the distant roar of waking jets.

Outside, pale light stretches thin over glossed concrete. Puddles from the night storm catch the glow. The air tastes sharp—ozone and damp earth. His resolve tastes the same.

His shadow stretches long beneath the harsh fluorescent hum, fractured by steel beams framing the narrow walkway. Each step carries him further from the quiet room where memories lingered, toward the open expanse of Hangar B. The hangar's vast doors yawn like the maw of a sleeping beast, swallowing light and promises alike. This place—Astra Flight Command—does not tolerate weakness. It never has. It demands excellence or exile. Today, Blaze becomes its instructor. The thought settles cold in his chest.

He pulls his collar tighter against the chill, scanning the horizon where the sky strains to lighten. The distant murmur of voices and mechanical growls rolls across the base—a steady pulse, a rising tempo. The nervous cadence of a new class stirs life into the battleground of wings and wills.

Every motion is taut with purpose as he approaches. His jaw tightens, the faint tremor of weariness buried beneath iron resolve. The brief wash has scrubbed away the night's heaviness but not the weight beneath it. His eyes narrow slightly, hooded beneath a brow that bears the scars of hours spent in hard silence.

A voice breaks the calm—clipped, distant, looping through comm frequencies.

He does not say a word, just nods—a silent agreement. The day's script plays on.

With the duffel swung over one shoulder, he strides beyond the dormitory's shadow, his limbs powered by habit and necessity rather than ease. The wind lifts the hem of his jacket, pushing him forward as if the very air urges him to claim this new chapter—however unwelcome it may be. He moves with the cold exactness of someone wound tight against relentless pressure.

"Still hanging in there, Captain?"

Sarge's voice, low and steady, cuts through the cold air. No answer is needed—not yet. The words hang between them like morning mist—loaded with unspoken fears and reluctant hope.

Blaze keeps his focus masked, his gait unwavering. The world narrows to the runway lights flickering faintly in the rising dawn, to the jets idling patiently—armored beasts waiting for their pilots to awaken the sky.

With one last glance toward the dorm's dim outline, Blaze steps fully into the deepening light. The scent of aviation grease, hot metal, and distant rain mingles into a familiar cloak. The academy breathes around him—a living, pulsing reminder that the rules remain immutable even as new stories are forced to take flight.

His hands find the straps of his bag again as he enters the flow of activity. The thrum of preparations swells, with orders exchanged in clipped tones and boots pounding in unison. His role beckons—cold, unyielding. The weight of leadership settles in his spine like a harness forged from steel and shadow.

The day's first assignments whisper through the air. Blaze's eyes lock on the horizon—sharp and unflinching. The past waits behind closed doors.

Ahead, the sky beckons.

The flightline hummed with early activity. Cadets clustered at its edge, silhouetted against the swelling dawn, their bodies tense with anticipation. Engines whispered beneath their breath. The sharp tang of jet fuel cut through the damp morning air, mingling with the salty bite rolling in from the coast. Around them, the low murmur of voices and the distant clatter of gear stirred the quiet, edges fraying under the weight of what was to come.

Blaze stood apart, arms folded across his chest. The morning chill bit through his thin jacket, but he didn't feel it. His thoughts lingered elsewhere—on missions past, on failures that still burned. His gaze locked upward anyway, tracking the sky as it bled violet and molten gold.

A solitary training jet cleaved through the air above. Its silver skin caught the first light, gleaming sharply. It arced gracefully, banking with precision—like tracing an invisible thread from cloud to earth.

Below, cadets stirred. Eyes followed the sleek machine's descent, a mix of awe and competitive hunger written across their faces.

Lyra Hale's Mark-9 dropped smoothly. Her mastery showed in every flick of the controls. The jet's nose tilted just so, skimming the runway with a whisper before she pulled back. The wheels kissed the asphalt in a landing that was tight and textbook-perfect. Then came the final touch—a sharp snap to the left, aligning her craft dead center on the designated mark. Tighter than most instructors expected from a first-timer.

She popped the canopy with a fluid motion, exposing windswept hair and a grin that gleamed brighter than the jet's polished frame. Without missing a beat, she saluted the ground crew. But it wasn't an ordinary salute; it was cocky—a flash of defiance and pride wrapped in a smooth flick of her wrist.

Heads turned among the onlookers, and instructors exchanged raised eyebrows. Some cadets scowled, annoyance writ plainly across their faces, as if her flamboyance burned too brightly against the disciplined dawn.

A whisper curled through the gathering: "Show-off." "Too much gumption." "Not here to play nice."

Blaze's jaw clenched, a dull ache settling behind his ribs. His eyes—haunted and sharp—tracked Lyra as she strode away from the jet. Each step rang like a challenge along the concrete. The salute lingered in his vision like embers against the soft morning light—bold and unyielding.

"Impressive landing for your first Mark-9 flight."

Jazz's voice cut through the heavy rhythm of the morning. She slid up beside Blaze, a teasing lilt warming her words as she nodded toward Lyra, who was still basking in the afterglow of applause and glares.

Blaze glanced down, meeting Jazz's warm, knowing smile.

"She flies like she owns the sky," Jazz added with a light chuckle, shaking her head.

"She'd better back it up with discipline." Blaze's voice was quiet, edged with the storm he kept carefully contained.

Jazz's eyes flickered toward Lyra again. "Oh, the flair is there. I just hope the ego doesn't get too high."

Lyra's head snapped around, her eyes gleaming with mischief. She caught their words and smirked, stepping closer.

"You boys are scared she'll outfly you all, huh?"

Blaze didn't flinch. He met her with icy calm. "Skill without discipline is just luck."

Lyra's grin widened, sharp and fearless. "So is fear."

Murmurs rippled through the gathered cadets: surprise, unsettled amusement. Jazz masked a nervous laugh, though her eyes remained steady on Lyra, unwavering in support.

Blaze's scowl deepened. The line of his mouth hardened like chiseled stone. Without a word, he turned away. His boots thudded against the concrete, the echo swallowed by the rising roar of the base waking around them.

Lyra watched him go, her shoulders squared and unbowed. The sharp blaze of rebellion burned in her gaze.

Blaze paused for just a moment, catching one last glimpse of her—the sunlight glinting off her helmet like a halo of defiance—before he steeled himself. The collision of grief and fire simmered beneath his skin, unresolved and as dangerous as the storm clouds gathering on the horizon.

The new cadets snapped into formation on the tarmac—a neat grid of uniforms and helmets against the vast stretch of concrete. Dawn's early colors bled across the sky, casting long shadows beneath stern faces.

Astra Flight Command's reputation preceded every cadet here. Few survived the first week with their pride intact.

Captain Jareck "Blaze" Arden stood before them, rigid and unreadable. His jaw was a hard line, and his eyes were sharp and cold as the steel jets waiting like silent sentinels behind him. The air hummed with the scent of warm jet fuel and distant ozone—a smell that quickened heartbeats and sharpened focus in equal measure.

His voice cut through the dawn: low and clipped. Each word was measured like a command dialed into cockpit controls.

"You want to fly with the best." He paused, letting the words settle. "That's the truth. There's no room for error. No margin for arrogance."

His gaze swept slowly across the rows—icy and unforgiving.

"You will be tested in ways that break most people." Another pause. He could see the swallowed breaths and the tightened grips on helmets. "But before that happens—before any of you earn a stripe or a call sign—you'll learn this: nobody here is exceptional yet. Not one of you. Not until you prove it."

He can't let pride blind him. He's seen what that costs.

A ripple passed through the formation—quick glances, swallowed breaths, fingers tightening on gear. Eyes darted to one another, hunting for reassurance that wouldn't come.

In the center of the formation, Lyra Hale stood with relaxed poise, her helmet tucked under her arm. The dawn light caught the curve of her stubbled jaw and the faint sheen of sweat. Her posture radiated something dangerous—reckless confidence that hadn't yet learned its limits. She let her gaze roam lazily over the disciplined lines, aware and utterly unbothered.

Blaze's eyes flicked toward her. His jaw tightened. A quick blink. Something flickered behind those cold eyes—frustration, maybe begrudging respect—before he exhaled and squared his shoulders, slipping back into command.

"Flying isn't a game." His voice dropped lower. "It's precise. It's brutal. And it can kill you in a heartbeat if you think you're above the rules. Here, you'll learn to answer to more than just your gut or your pride. You'll learn to listen to your training, your team, and, above all else, the machine beneath you."

The metallic clang of helmets being locked echoed suddenly. Cadets secured their gear. Whispered conversations wavered beneath Blaze's unwavering gaze. Somewhere behind him, an idling engine hummed steadily and raw.

A sharp gust cut through the formation. Jacket collars tugged, and papers scattered from clipboards.

Each cadet's breath fogged in front of them, fragile ghosts against steel and dawn. Their eyes remained fixed, lungs filled with cold air and unmistakable dread.

It was the kind of silence that crackled louder than any engine—waiting, watching, measuring.

Blaze's hand sliced through the air in a sharp gesture. "Dismissed. Check your equipment. Stay sharp."

Steel-trap. No softness. No room for second chances. Not today.

The cadets scattered with muted footsteps, rippling like wind-blown leaves. Tension still tugged at the edges of their nerves.

Lyra moved casually with the pack, tossing a quick glance back toward Blaze, her eyes smoldering with silent challenge.

Somewhere deep in his gut, a stubborn spark kindled, refusing to be snuffed out.

Blaze remained still for a moment longer, his eyes tracking the squad as they dispersed. Muscles taut as a snapped cable, his posture locked—precise, unyielding. The weight of the morning settled around him like a second skin.

No one here is exceptional yet.

He repeated the words silently. The cold truth settled in alongside the relentless buzz of fate hovering over Astra Flight Command's runway.

Lt. Marcus "Sarge" Sullivan stepped forward as Blaze dismissed the new cadets to conduct equipment checks. The air hummed with jet fuel and the crisp scrape of heels on concrete. His voice dropped low and deliberate. "You good?"

His gaze pins Blaze, searching the taut lines of his face as if scanning for a fracture.

Blaze freezes. Tension coils in his shoulders—tight as a drawn wire. His lips press into a firm line. Without a word, he nods once—slow and deliberate—but tight enough to lock anything deeper beneath the surface. His green eyes flicker—restraint, perhaps—then reveal nothing.

Sarge's gaze hardens, shadowed by worry he won't voice. This isn't mere exhaustion or routine strain. He senses the heavier weight Blaze carries, the ghosts folded tightly beneath that quiet exterior. The remnants of yesterday's mission bleed through in the set of his jaw and in the way his fingers flex and still. But for now, Sarge remains silent, letting him bear the burden alone.

Sarge shifts his stance, stepping back into his role as supervisor. His boots scrape softly against the tarmac as he moves toward the scattered groups of cadets gathering around the gear racks. The distant rumble of engines and the clinks of metal fill the space. Sunlight streaks the sky with sharp edges, casting long shadows across the flight line.

At Astra Flight Command, mornings like this pulse with contradiction—fresh ambition crackling like electricity before a storm, yet weighted with the academy's relentless demand for perfection. Every cadet intake represents new beginnings and impossible pressure, a crucible where dreams sharpen into steel or shatter. Sarge has watched it for years; Blaze lives it differently now.

From the corner of his eye, Sarge tracks Blaze. The captain's posture is rigid, a steel spine carved into the morning haze, but something about the way he exhales is less certain. His jaw tightens whenever a cadet's energy flares too brightly—a defiant glance, a restless shift. Low grumbles ripple through equipment checks, mingling with sharper commands.

Sarge lets his gaze slide along the line of cadets: varying heights, mixed nerves, and swagger. The buzz of fresh ambition tastes electric in the air. He smooths his palms on his dark coveralls and surveys quietly, a sentinel tethered between duty and the flicker of unease beneath the surface.

Blaze's eyes glide over the assembly like a hawk scanning for movement: battlefield calm, hard-earned discipline. But Sarge sees the fissures—brief shadows crossing behind those sharp green eyes. Cracks that reflect a tension the others don't sense, though Sarge feels it in the tightening air and tastes it like metal on his tongue.

His voice breaks the silence beside Blaze, low and almost casual but laced with genuine concern.

"Don't let the weight choke you, Jareck."

Blaze blinks, startled. A ghost of fatigue flickers behind his eyes before they close. He draws a breath to steady the storm beneath his skin. When his eyes open, the steel has returned. "I'm in."

Sarge exhales through his nose, his eyes narrowing beneath the brim of his cap. "Good. You're not alone in this. Remember that."

Blaze offers the barest nod, the smallest crack in his stoic armor, before he turns away to address the waiting cadets and the day's demanding rhythm. The hum of preparation swells—the rattle of harnesses, the thuds of boots in line, and the sharp clatter of flight helmets snapping into place.

Sarge steps back, scanning the deck with a practiced eye. Polished jets line the tarmac like predators under the awakening sky. Sunlight catches their surfaces, and a distant roar of engines fires up. The earth trembles faintly beneath his feet.

The academy pulses like a living thing, all taut muscle and breath held tight.

He lingers near the fringe of the cadet line, his eyes flicking from Blaze to the restless new faces. Even among the disciplined ranks, uncertainty simmers—unspoken challenges in every exchange, every sideways glance.

Sarge's fingers curl into loose fists. The calm of morning belies the storm barely contained beneath the surface—between the cadets, inside him, and most of all, within Blaze.

His voice slips out again, quieter this time, meant for no ears but his own.

"Hold steady. We'll get through it."

The breeze picks up, carrying the sharp tang of salt and fuel. Somewhere overhead, seagulls call—fractured cries scattering over the tarmac. The morning stretches thin, pulled between orders barked and nerves strung taut like wires.

Sarge stands rooted, a lone watchman on the edge of a restless dawn. The cadets move through their checks, bright faces shaded with tension—a promise of fire beneath their skin.

For Blaze. For these pilots-in-training. This morning marks the first line drawn in the sky—a boundary between what was lost and what could still catch flame.

Sarge's gaze flicks back to Blaze. The man stands a quiet sentinel amid the stirring chaos. Unmoved. Unyielding. But fought for in every breath.

As the cadets absorb the day's call to action, Sarge's watchful presence remains a tether—a silent vow to guard what—and who—matters most.

The clatter of boots on concrete fades as the cadet formation splinters into clusters drifting toward the equipment racks scattered along the flight line. The sharp scent of lubricants and ozone swells in the cool air, blending with the salty bite carried from the nearby coastline. Blaze stands rigid, arms crossed, gaze fixed ahead even as voices buzz around him.

A smooth voice breaks through the ambient hum. Jazz slides up beside him, her stride easy, a half-smile playing on her lips. "Welcome back, sir," she says, nodding toward Lyra, who stands a little apart, helmet tucked under one arm, radiating barely contained energy.

Blaze doesn't meet her gaze. The corner of his mouth twitches—almost a smile, raw and fleeting, like a crack in his usual armor.

Jazz's eyes sparkle with easy mischief. "That landing? First time in the Mark-9. She's already making it hers... total show-off, no doubt." Her words dance lightly, tinged with both admiration and a teasing edge.

Blaze's green eyes flick toward Lyra. She shifts her weight onto one boot, tilts her chin in the sunlight. She pulls his attention despite the chill he works so hard to maintain. He can't look away.

The rumble of a distant engine drones, mingling with quickened breaths and the clink of gear being adjusted around them.

Lyra catches his glance. She lifts one brow, a sardonic smirk curling her lips. Confidence buzzes off her like static—almost tactile. An electric charge ripples through the crowd nearby. Everyone feels it: the spark of a fire, daring and untamed.

Jazz glances at Lyra, then back to Blaze. A soft chuckle escapes her. "She's got that look, right? Already plotting her next move."

Blaze's jaw tightens imperceptibly. The weight of unspoken history presses against his chest beneath his crisp uniform, mixing with that flicker of respect he is loath to admit aloud. Jazz steps back quietly, slipping into Lyra's orbit.

Lyra's laugh rings out—a brief, bright burst of sound. Jazz gently catches her arm, pulling her toward the racks, their chatter low but lively amid the sharper percussion of boot heels striking metal cases.

Blaze's gaze lingers where Lyra stood moments before. The early sunlight catches the edge of her silhouette—a mix of fire and shadow, daring and reckless. The faint smell of jet fuel clings to her flight suit, sharp and alive.

His fingers curl briefly around the strap of his duffel bag, his knuckles pale under the weight of thought. Tension tightens at the corners of his eyes, a hesitation buried beneath years of discipline.

But the morning doesn't wait. Neither does the flight line.

Blaze turns back toward his own path, but not before throwing one last glance at Lyra—animated now, her spirit flickering like wildfire beneath the cold gaze of the academy. A promise of turbulence, cloaked in sunlight.

Lyra steps forward, sunlight catching the gleam of her helmet cradled effortlessly in one arm. The usual hum of subdued chatter and shuffling equipment hushes like a drawn breath. Her voice slices through the morning air—crisp and unfiltered. "Sir, just tell me when the real flying kicks off. I'll leave everyone here eating my contrails."

Blaze's dark eyes locked onto hers. His jaw tightened, the chill of discipline hardening his posture as a cold frost seemed to seal the spark in his eyes. His hands clenched briefly at his sides. When he spoke, his voice was steady, sharp as a razor's edge. "Skill without discipline is just luck. Luck runs out."

The words hung between them like a challenge and a warning. A ripple stirred through the assembled cadets.

Lyra shrugged, that same smirk curling at the corner of her mouth—half defiance, half amusement. She had spent her whole life proving that she belonged in spaces that hadn't asked for her, hadn't wanted her. This moment was just another stage, another chance to show them all exactly what she was made of. "So does fear," she shot back, a flash of lightning in her gaze.

Gasps bloomed unexpectedly.

Several cadets blinked wide-eyed, uncertain, caught off guard by the raw audacity. Jazz snorted in disbelief, a nervous chuckle escaping her lips.

Blaze's expression crystallized: icy, unyielding. He turned without another word, his back a solid wall of authority. The sharp slap of his boots against the tarmac punctuated the silence settling over the crowd.

No one breathed for a heartbeat too long.

Murmurs threaded through the formation like a whispering wind—curious, shocked, unsettled. Lyra stood her ground, chest lifted, unbowed beneath the weight of gazes. Her eyes flickered once to the retreating figure of Blaze, unreadable yet fierce. The morning sun cast her shadow long across the concrete—a dark slash breaking the ordered geometry of the flight line.

The equipment checks paused momentarily, leaving the cadets caught between awe and uncertainty. Yet Lyra didn't waver under the scrutiny. Instead, an unspoken promise rode the hum of whispered words: she was here to rewrite the rules.

The air tasted faintly metallic with jet fuel and tension, mingled with the sharp tang of ozone carried on a cool breeze drifting in from the runway. The scent clung to her skin and uniform—a reminder of the stakes buried beneath bravado.

Lyra's fingers tightened briefly on her helmet's smooth curve. The polished surface was cool to the touch, grounding her in the swirling storm of expectation and defiance. The sun warmed her back like a mantle she had chosen, not one given.

Blaze's departure left a vacuum—rigid, charged—his silence louder than any command. The class watched, caught on a razor's edge between discipline and rebellion, with the line between respect and challenge blurred.

"The real flying," Lyra murmured under her breath, her voice low but steady. There was barely a ripple through the growing hum.

A half-turn glance drew the shadow of a smirk from Jazz—a silent vow between friends. The murmurs swelled into a restless buzz.

Blaze's silhouette retreated toward the hangar—sharp and solitary. The rumble of distant jets stirred, their engines waking like beasts roused. But the tension hanging over the tarmac was thicker than any storm.

Lyra exhaled slowly, steadying her breath against the weight of countless eyes. She planted her feet firmly—unshaken, unwavered.

In that moment, the line was drawn clear. This wasn't orientation; it was a battleground from the very first word.

No one dared move to break the silence. The clash on the tarmac set a new rhythm—one that demanded more than skill. It demanded fire.

And for Lyra, the fire was just beginning to burn.

###

The tarmac stretched before him, a broad expanse of concrete scarred by countless takeoffs and landings. The smell hit first—bitter jet fuel heavy in the crisp morning air. Blaze's boots thudded in a steady rhythm, the hollow echo cutting through the dawn.

The sun, still low, poured caramel light across the runway. The metal skins of parked jets ignited into fiery mirrors. But beside him was only emptiness—a cavern where his brother's shadow once stood. Now it was vanished, gone silent.

He squared his shoulders, his jaw clenched tight as a knot twisted low in his gut. His gaze locked onto the horizon, where the sky bruised from violet to molten gold. The harsh clang of distant hangar doors and the murmur of voices faded to nothing—a cold backdrop for the tempest churning inside him.

The exchange with Lyra still burned sharp and unyielding, fire and frost colliding beneath his skin and igniting something new he wasn't ready to name.

Blaze's stride slowed, a flicker of unrest appearing behind his emerald eyes. He tilted his head—a slash of movement against the glowing dawn.

There she was: Lyra, backlit and defiant, her silhouette framed by sunlight—a restless flame against the cooling air. She shifted beside Jazz, whose easy laughter floated on the breeze like bright sparks. They moved toward the cluster of cadets, and already, eyes curved in their wake. She moved with a magnetism he couldn't quite name—wild yet coursing with purpose.

"I'll burn through their ranks in no time," Lyra said, her voice smooth yet edged. She caught his glance without flinching.

A shadow flickered across Blaze's face, and his fingers tensed at his sides—just for a moment. "Your kind of fire won't light the way. Control it, or it will burn you up."

Jazz threw a sidelong grin at Lyra. "Don't mind him. Blaze just remembers how quickly the flames can turn."

"And what if I don't mind burning?" Lyra's voice folded into a challenge that hung between sun and shadow.

Their sparring words vanished with the wind as Lyra and Jazz marched on, unbowed. Their presence cracked the quiet like thunder's first murmurs before a storm.

Blaze exhaled. His breath misted cold in the dawn air. He stopped in the wide emptiness between the sprawling horizon and the echoes of past missions.

A flicker at the edge of his vision—the ghost of a smile, a laugh—pulled at him, just beyond reach. His wingman. An unbreakable tether to a loss too raw to ignore. That ghost had weight. It pressed against his chest most mornings, especially here on the tarmac where the engines hummed and the day stretched ahead, full and relentless.

Yet something else flickered now, too. Something alive. Something dangerous.

The runway hummed beneath his boots. Distant cadet chatter scraped against the rising song of warming engines. Duty called, relentless and unyielding. His jaw tightened, catching the morning light. A faint scar along his jawline caught the glow—a permanent mark of battles fought both in the sky and within.

His eyes found Lyra again. The morning light sculpted the determined tilt of her shoulders and the confident arc of her back as she strode with Jazz through the ranks. She moved not with hesitation but with the reckless grace of someone who flew on instinct rather than fear. The air between them crackled with unspoken truths—a collision of grief and fire, a dangerous balance he wasn't sure he could trust.

Blaze stepped forward, the hard surface of the tarmac solid beneath his feet, grounding him as past and future converged in this moment.

"Why do you always have to be the brightest flare, risking burning out?" he muttered. His voice was a husky undercurrent beneath the morning chorus.

Lyra's voice returned, clear but tethered with something softer and elusive, though she was already moving away: "Because if you don't risk the burn, you never really glow."

Her words lingered, fading into the hum of the day waking around them.

Blaze watched her go. The sun haloed her in defiant light. The runway stretched on, endless and waiting. He knew the battles ahead wouldn't be fought alone.

The collision between his old ghosts and this new blaze hummed beneath his skin—unresolved, a furious promise etched across dawn's canvas. He inhaled sharply; the tang of fuel and heat rose with the sun.

Then he turned. His boots kicked up faint dust as he stepped into the relentless flow of duty—the weight of yesterday and the fire of tomorrow locked together beneath a burning sky.

The Ace Meets the Wildcard

Astra's flight line stirs with early morning murmurs. The sun brushes the horizon, casting long shadows across sleek, waiting jets. Cadets in faded flight suits cluster beside their assigned Mark-9s, their fingers busy over instruments and gauges, whispering final pep talks like secret incantations. The air smells faintly of burnt ozone and grease, mingling with the metallic bite of cold machinery warming to the day.

A breeze carries the distant call of seagulls. Their cries circle over the runway—an eerie calm before the engine storm. The coast beyond the tarmac stretches gray and restless, a reminder that even here, hemmed in by steel and protocol, the world breathes wild and untamed.

Near the tarmac's edge, Jazz bounces on the balls of her feet, a spark of sunshine amid the muted hum of preparation. Her smile stretches wide, and her eyes are bright with that contagious energy that could snap the tensest nerves. She nudges Lyra's helmet strap, her fingers flicking a quick double knot with practiced precision.

"C'mon, Hale," Jazz grins, her voice low but fierce. "Today's the day to make 'em eat your dust. Just—don't go burning rubber too soon, yeah?"

Lyra fingers the helmet strap, drawing it tight. Her knuckles blanch with the pressure she refuses to show. A tremor quickens beneath her skin—unseen and electric. She tilts her head back, and a small smirk tugs at her lips, the kind that dares the day to try to outfly her. Her eyes glint sharp and steady, ready to throw down the gauntlet.

Sarge moves down the line, clipboard in hand. His gaze cuts across faces like a hazel searchlight in thick fog, catching every micro-expression of doubt and every clenched jaw.

He nods slightly here and taps a note there. He's the calm in the eye of the storm, deeply attuned to the cadets' unspoken stories, catching frayed nerves before they fracture.

Blaze follows closely behind, his jaw clenched tight enough to reveal faint creases along his hard jawline. His eyes sweep over the jets and the checklist pinned to his clipboard, scanning each cockpit's readiness with surgical precision. With his hands folded briefly before a jet's fuselage, he steps forward, his voice clipped in quiet commands that disappear beneath the hum of engines and whispered affirmations.

Between the rows of aircraft, the tension feels like static—an invisible charge threading through the morning haze.

Above, on the catwalk that arches over the tarmac like a sentinel's perch, Major Voss stands unmoving, arms crossed. Her sharp gaze slices through the low light with the weight of authority—the kind cadets feel as pressure in their chests. Around the base, her name carries the weight of uncompromising standards and evaluations that can remake careers or end them. Her presence alone chills the air.

When she watches, cadets know the stakes have shifted from routine to reckoning.

The curve of her mouth tightens—a wire pulled taut. Watching with unwavering attention, she embodies the weight of expectations and the unforgiving gravity of high-stakes command.

Slowly, the murmurs dim. Like the slightest shift in atmospheric pressure, the cadets sense the impending moment. Engines wake with low growls, jets cradled by the morning mist, steel birds restless on their perches. The first aircraft begins its slow, deliberate taxi, wheels grinding against the tarmac with measured, mechanical breath.

The flight line falls into a brittle hush. Every heartbeat seems magnified, every small sound swallowed by the vastness of the runway. The tension curls and coils, ready to snap.

Jazz leans toward Lyra, her voice dropping to a whisper but vibrating with fierce conviction.

"You ready to burn this place down?"

Lyra's eyes flash with fire as she nods, her voice calm but charged with a promise.

"More than ready. Let's show them how the sun rises."

At the far end of the runway, Blaze's expression remains unreadable, shadowed by the dawn. But beneath the surface, the flicker of something fierce—anticipation, perhaps, or a warning—shimmers before hardening back into stone.

The day's reckoning has begun.

Cadets move toward the runway in quiet, measured footsteps. Their uniforms are crisp, but their shoulders are taut with anticipation. From the hangar's heavy metal edge, instructors lean over clipboards and glowing panels. Their eyes scan more than numbers—they catch the flicker of nerves hidden on young faces.

The first name sliced through the buzz over the comm.

"Cadet Sato, you're up."

Sato's chest tightened for a fraction of a second. Fingers trembling, she stepped into her cockpit. The hum of hydraulics and switches filled the space as she snapped her helmet into place. Her hands moved over the controls with practiced precision—fuel gauges, throttle checks, avionics calibration—all the rituals that wove routine into readiness.

The crackling voice of an instructor ushered her forward. The low rumble throbbed through the concrete underfoot, vibrating in her chest like a physical drumbeat syncing with her accelerating pulse.

One by one, the cadets slid into their cockpits and sprinted through pre-flight checks beneath the hangar's cool overhang. Outside, the sun baked the tarmac. Jet fuel cut sharply through the dry air, mixing with the salty breeze from the coast. A distant roar lifted as Sato's Mark-9 rumbled to life, spinning up like a coiled spring ready to launch.

"Clear for takeoff. Execute pattern one."

The cadets peeled off in a disciplined queue. Engines hummed sharply, slicing through the azure sky. One after another, fighter jets traced elegant arcs—wheels leaving grooves against the wide strip before wings tilted, banking into tight formations.

They stitched the sky with practiced maneuvers: crisp takeoffs, tight formation holds, and standard rolls that tested reflexes under G-force pressure. Down below, instructors scribbled meticulous notes. They tallied the nuances invisible to untrained eyes—wing angles not quite exact, minor drift in formation, and radio calls clipped too early or too late.

A sudden wobble disrupted Cadet Harper's aileron roll. His jet jangled mid-rotation like a brittle leaf caught in a gust. His voice flickered over the comm, tense and rushed.

"...uh, stabilizing... corrections—"

Another cadet snapped a terse radio response. Tension bristled beneath the surface.

Sarge's jaw tightened as he watched the screens flicker and pulse. His voice cut through the comm like tempered steel.

"Formation hold at a thirty-degree bank, not sixty! Cadet Simmons, maintain radio clarity. Cadet Harper, smooth those rolls—predict, don't react."

Blaze's voice sliced through the static next. Not sharp with anger, but precise as a scalpel. Each word was measured and unyielding.

"Discipline is the only thing keeping you alive out there. Forget the flair. Stick to procedure."

Harper's pen moved furiously across his clipboard. His eyes never left the telemetry feeds coloring the wall of monitors—heart rates creeping upward, yaw deviations, flap timings. He mapped subtle mistakes like a forensic artist, noting inconsistencies where instinct overwhelmed training.

Major Voss stood tall on the catwalk above, arms folded. Her gaze was a hard lens.

The ritual continued. Jets darted through the pale blue, engines humming, wings cutting silence into fragments. The tension tightened like the strap of a harness. The air thrummed with the unspoken promise of scrutiny and the weight of expectations.

From Blaze's vantage point, hesitation was a virus. It spread. One cadet's doubt infected the formation, and from there, disaster branched into a dozen trajectories. She had seen it before—the moment confidence cracked, the moment instinct took over, and procedure became secondary. That's when pilots died.

"Cadet Hale, you are next."

A ripple of unease threaded through the ranks as Lyra's name vibrated across the comm frequency. The baseline of the morning's performances crystallized—a canvas painted with disciplined precision, smudged here and there by hesitation and fragmented confidence.

The sky waited, patient but charged. Every sensor and eye was trained upward, ready for the next act in this deadly dance.

###

Lyra stood by the sleek Mark-9, its metal skin catching the pale morning light, cool beneath her fingers. Her helmet rested snug under her arm, polished and humming faintly with intercom static. The horizon stretched wide and endless—a canvas streaked with faint pinks giving way to brightening blues.

The sharp, salty tang of sea air curled in her nostrils, mingling with the faint diesel sting from nearby vehicles. She closed her eyes for a fraction of a moment—a fleeting calm before the storm.

Around her, cadets chattered softly, checking gear and running through mental run-throughs. But Lyra's focus cut through the hum. When her name rang sharp over the PA, she straightened, chin lifting and spine unwinding. A curl of a sharp, confident smile brushed her lips, flickering like a signal flare. Heads turned—some with curiosity, most with cautious respect.

She steps forward with long, purposeful strides, the soft thud of her boots against the tarmac echoing across the morning stillness. Her heart hammers beneath her ribs—not from fear, but from the electric charge of knowing exactly what she is about to do and precisely how well she will do it.

Jazz perches just beyond the yellow line, bouncing lightly on her toes, her eyes gleaming. They have flown together since basic training. Jazz knows every hesitation and every doubt Lyra has ever harbored. She also knows that none of those things reside in Lyra now. Not on days like this.

Lyra catches her gaze, winks with a flash of mischief, and then keys the radio.

"Mark-9 going up, folks. Try not to blink, or you'll miss it."

Her voice is light and teasing—too casual, a thread of rebellion wrapped in a joke. Over the comm, the usual clipped responses give way to a few flickers of amusement and surprise.

Lyra tugs on her helmet, the padded straps pressing close. She slides into the cockpit with a grace that belies the raw energy coiled in her muscles. The canopy seals with a hiss—a breath stolen into the gear-filled chamber.

Her hands move quickly, a storm beneath calm waters. Switches click. Gauges hum. Lights pulse in precise order, as if conducted by an unseen orchestra. She does not rush. There is method in her speed, a steel-edge certainty that fills the air like an electric charge.

Engines murmur deep and steady beneath her, a tune crafted for precision and power. The Mark-9's nose lifts, coaxed by confident hands as the wheels gently slip from the earth.

The joy of flight rushes in: cool wind roaring past, the faint metallic tang of hydraulics, and the steady vibration against her palms. She carves the sky with textbook precision—flawless takeoff, wings slicing through the air with no hint of hesitation.

The first aileron roll leaps from the jet, smooth as silk and rapid as lightning. The Cuban Eight follows, a near-perfect figure tracing against the blue canvas. Each move aligns with crisp strategy and skill.

Eyes flicker beneath helmets across the line. Other cadets murmur—some caught between admiration and the steady burn of challenge. Jazz's grin widens, sharp and proud. Her voice crackles over the airwaves, vibrant and alive.

"Look at her go... Damn, Lyra."

Whispers ripple through the ranks. Unease flickers in tight glances, as if Lyra's confidence unsettles more than just their ease. She's rewriting the script in real time—each maneuver a statement etched in quiet defiance and blazing competence.

Lyra leans into the wind, banking hard into the final leg of her run. Her smile curls wider, sharp as the razor edge of a cloud cutting through the sun's rays. Adrenaline drums a wild rhythm beneath her ribs. The sequence races beneath her fingers like a heartbeat picked up too fast—careful and thrilling all at once.

"She's on fire," Jazz murmurs, his voice alive with awe and something fiercer: anticipation.

Lyra's hands dance across the controls, each movement fluid and deliberate. The world outside shrinks to this moment: the hum of the engine, the salt-tinged air slipping past the canopy vents, the endless sky folding open. Everything tightens—the sequence, the stakes, the silent watch of every eye below.

Her head snaps slightly toward the formation, a spark of challenge in her gaze. The pressure tugs at her—not as a weight but as fuel, lighting something fierce inside. This is more than evaluation; it's a performance, a test, a reckoning.

"Bet you're gonna eat my dust, Jazz," she says into the comm.

Jazz's laughter crackles through the speakers—light and teasing, a thread of warmth amid the high tension.

"Not a chance, Hale. Unless you want me to buy you a drink when you crash."

Lyra's fingers tighten once, precise and steady. The Mark-9 dips and rolls into the next maneuver, as steady and wild as her grin. In this sky, she's not just surviving the game; she's rewriting the rules.

The air thrums with the pulse of engines as Lyra's Mark-9 slices through the sky, racing toward the final segment of her run. Beneath her, the quilted tapestry of clouds stretches endlessly and taut. Ahead, a slower jet crawls stubbornly through her airspace—a problem with teeth.

Lyra's eyes dart with sharp calculation, her fingers twitching against the throttle. The timing of the sequence teeters on the edge. Every second bleeds into the next. She needs this window, and it's closing.

Her breath tightens behind the visor, a barely audible hiss swallowed by the cockpit's roar.

She clicks her teeth together. The rulebook feels as thin as paper at thirty thousand feet. Clearance is protocol. Protocol is safety. But safety doesn't always win races, not in her sky. Not today. Lyra's fingers blur across the switches—cutting the throttle and diving the nose into a sudden, breathtaking plunge.

The world tips.

The horizon pitches and spins. She twists the joystick, and the Mark-9 folds into a precise, velvet-smooth roll that flips the world inverted. Her heart hammers—a drumbeat synced with the roaring engines and the rushing air hammering against the canopy. Then, in one fluid motion honed by instinct and reckless hours, she pulls hard on the stick. The sky curves around her as G-forces press her deep into the seat.

The slower jet slips down her field of vision. Her silhouette eclipses it as she cuts dangerously ahead.

On the ground, the morning's rhythm halts tautly. Instructors freeze mid-step, their eyes glued to the dizzying maneuver overhead.

Major Elena Voss perches rigidly on the cold metal catwalk, her lips pressed thin. A spark—sharp and unreadable—flickers in her eyes. Her composure thins just enough to betray a calculated interest. Voss has seen raw talent before; she has also seen ego burn bright and fast. Lyra Hale straddles that line like few pilots ever could.

Flight Officer Harper's pen clatters sharply onto her notepad. Her fingers race feverishly across the page, marking every instance of Lyra's unauthorized maneuver.

"Lyra Hale, where the hell are you on comms?" The voice crackles over the static—breezy, defiant.

Blaze clenches his jaw behind his headset, his green eyes hard as tempered steel. Every muscle is taut. The sharp line of his profile is a quiet storm. He doesn't speak; he doesn't broadcast the fury brewing behind his gaze—not yet, not while she's still airborne.

The Mark-9 wheels toward the runway. Thin clouds blur past as sunlight hardens to steel.

Lyra's hands move without missing a beat, coaxing the jet into a graceful descent. Her focus is absolute—her eyes sharp as cut glass, every input measured and precise. The cold rush of air prickles against her skin, matching the edge in her chest.

The tires kiss the tarmac with a crisp, purposeful shush. The jet glides in smoothly, a final bow to a dance performed on the edge of rules and recklessness.

Breaths are held. The world waits.

The engines purr down, like a dying beast settling into the early morning stillness. Lyra taxis in, the thin line of her smile tightening into something fierce and full of promise. The air around the tarmac crackles with the unspoken. A brittle hush hangs heavier than fuel vapors.

Jazz's voice breaks through the tension, almost a whisper over the comms. "Did you see that? She just rewrote the damn rulebook."

Blaze's throat tightens. He presses his hand against the cold metal rail, grounding himself. The moment stretches—a raw wound of whispered awe and hushed warnings drifting like smoke across the ranks of cadets and instructors.

"No call for clearance," Blaze finally cuts through the static, his voice low and brittle. "You risked us all."

Lyra's response shoots back, her voice laced with equal parts defiance and dare. "Sometimes you gotta fly like someone's gunning for you."

The line goes silent. A collective breath is suspended in disbelief and grudging respect.

Harper's pen hovers, still jotting. Her eyes narrow as she weighs defiance against skill.

Major Voss folds her arms tighter, the hint of a smile trapped behind the discipline in her gaze.

Blaze clenches his jaw again, forbidding himself to unravel. This fight is far from over.

Lyra swings open the cockpit canopy with a sharp metallic scrape. Ozone and warmed leather flood her senses as she lets the harness clicks fall away, her muscles uncoiling. Boots thud against the tarmac. The sun warms her face, casting sharp shadows beneath her cheekbones, and her grin feels electric—wild and unrestrained.

Around her, murmurs ripple into a swell. Eyes drawn by her swagger gather like moths to a flame.

Cadets close in—a spectrum of reactions. Some break into spontaneous applause, hands slapping her back in rapid-fire high-fives. Others gape silently, brows furrowed with unease. A few exchange subtle, worried shakes of the head, their lips pressed into tight lines. The social hierarchy shifts beneath the surface—admiration and envy twisting around each other like smoke. Some cadets orbit Lyra with grudging respect, while others simmer with the sharp sting of competition, watching someone break the rules and soar.

Jazz is a blur, bouncing up like a hyperactive sparrow. She slaps Lyra's shoulder hard enough that the impact echoes off the concrete. "You're insane. And amazing," she hiss-whispers, her eyes flashing with pride and disbelief.

Lyra's grin widens. Her gaze locks with Jazz's—shared secrets passed in a storm. The tension hangs thick in the air, mingling with exhaust fumes and the underlying hum of jet engines cooling in neat rows.

A sharp bark cuts through the charged air. Sarge materializes from the shadow of a jet, clipboard clutched tightly. His voice pulls everyone upright.

"Enough of the festivities. Listen up."

His gaze slices through the crowd, anchoring their scattered focus. "Today's runs exposed more holes than expected. Missed checklist items—unacceptable. Radio comms clipped as if you're scared to speak. Formation drift is sloppy enough to get us killed in combat."

Cadets shift uneasily, their shoulders tightening under his scrutiny. His eyes find Lyra's briefly—an unspoken warning flares there—then move on.

"Discipline. Precision. That's what saves lives. Not stunts."

The words land like cold steel, hanging in the rising wind.

Blaze steps forward from the edge of the tarmac before the echo dies, boots grinding softly on gravel. His jaw is a hard line, his expression carved from years of battlefield rigor. Green eyes scan the cluster, sharpening as they settle on Lyra. Something flickers beneath the surface—a flash of reluctant respect, perhaps concern—before the steel door slides shut again.

"Cadet Hale." His voice rings clear, icy and sharp as a blade drawn in silence. "Your radio breach and that unauthorized maneuver risked more than just marks on your evaluation sheet. At Astra, flair comes second to protocol. If you can't respect that—" He lets the sentence hang, chilling the space between them.

The gathered cadets stiffen. Whispers fall silent beneath the weight of his tone.

Lyra matches his stare, unwavering. For a fraction of a second, her jaw tightens—a shadow crosses her eyes, vulnerability flickering beneath the defiance before she banks it down. Her lips curl into a smirk that straddles the line between challenge and redemption. "I was saving time. Flying as if the field is actually contested," she fires back, her voice steady but laced with irrepressible fire.

Breath hitches. Stifled laughter ripples through the crowd. Jazz's fists clench at her sides, biting back a proud smile.

Blaze's eyes narrow. His face betrays nothing more than controlled disappointment—a wall of cold discipline unmoved by charm or challenge. The air tightens, thick with unspoken tension and reluctant respect.

Around them, the runway holds its breath. The sharp scent of jet fuel mixes with something more intangible—the electric charge of rebellion sparking against authority. Radio static crackles faintly in the distance. Boots scrape against concrete. Overhead, the distant drone of engines powering down hums through the heat shimmer.

The cadets absorb the twin forces—Blaze's steely rebuke and Lyra's insolent grin—like twin stars locked in orbit. Neither yielding. Both burning bright.

The silence drags taut. An uneasy pause precedes the next command, before the day's next test of skill and will.

Blaze's gaze doesn't waver—sharp as shattered glass catching the sun. Lyra's teasing grin flickers; he won't bite. The wind tugs at his flight suit, carrying the faint clang of jets cooling down. A sharp tang of spilled hydraulic fluid cuts through the air. He steps closer, his voice low and steady like the rumble beneath a jet's roar.

"You'll be held to the highest standard," Blaze says. Each word slices through the low murmur spreading across the tarmac. "This isn't a circus. Discipline, not flair, wins at Astra."

Lyra's eyes narrow for a heartbeat; a spark of challenge flickers before she lets it go, her lips tugged into a taut line. She retorts, her hand shifting to her hip, but her voice softens under the weight of his stare. Blaze doesn't blink.

Nearby, Flight Officer Harper stands with her tablet cradled against one wrist, her fingers tapping out a careful rhythm. Her brow furrows, sharpened by the morning light filtering through the hangar's glass walls, and her gaze flicks between Lyra's defiance and Blaze's controlled fury. She scribbles notes about the unauthorized split-S—sharp, precise, dangerous—and logs the breach of radio protocol. Her fingers tighten on the stylus, then resume with clinical precision.

From the catwalk overlooking the scene, Major Voss leans forward, her arms folded. The sharp lines of her face catch the last golden rays of dawn. Her eyes narrow just the slightest fraction—a silent appraisal, a ledger being made in her mind. Two names are already etched by the morning's fire: Lyra Hale, whose brazen skill threatens both safety and status; and Blaze Arden, whose barely restrained storm promises consequences. She presses her lips into a thin line—neither approving nor condemning, simply calculating.

Below, the throng of cadets ripples with whispered currents. Gossip spirals, lightening the shadows.

"Did you see that split-S?"

"I thought she was toast."

"Blaze didn't hold back. That reprimand was ice."

Voices dart between clusters like nervous sparrows. Tension hitches their steps as they edge toward the hangar. The corridors will buzz for days.

Jazz weaves through the shifting crowd, staying glued to Lyra's side. Her grin is wide and fearless—someone daring the world to say no. She tosses quick jabs over her shoulder, masking concern beneath mock bravado.

"Girl, you're nuts—flipping without clearance? You've got half the squad thinking you lost your damn mind."

Lyra's breath comes steady, her cheeks flushed from raw adrenaline pushed to the limit. She shoves a loose strand of hair behind her ear. "Better nuts in the cockpit than stuck in a slow spin, right?"

Jazz snorts, elbowing her playfully as they stride together. "Yeah, well, some of them think you're insane—and maybe rightfully so. But damn, you've got their attention. That move? Legendary." She glances over her shoulder at the tight-lipped instructors standing stiffly by the hangar's edge.

Lyra shrugs, a spark of defiance gleaming in her restless gaze. "Let them whisper. I'm here to survive Astra, not babysit their egos."

They pass rows of sleek Mark-9s parked like soldiers—cold metal gleaming under the pale sun. Jet fuel hangs thick in the air, mingling with the distant honk of a horn. A sudden clang—a dropped wrench somewhere nearby—snaps the fragile calm.

Blaze remains rooted at the edge of the tarmac, the sun casting his long shadow over the concrete. His hands tighten into fists at his sides—contained. But the storm beneath his stoic face churns like fuel igniting. Lyra's defiance isn't just a breach of protocol; it's a challenge to his grip on control and to the fragile structure he's trying to impose in this world of speed and danger.

He hears snippets: the quiet crackle of radios, murmured speculation. He feels the weight of eyes that are no longer just watching training; they are witnessing the start of a war between two different kinds of fire.

Jazz leans in closer to Lyra as they near the hangar doors, his voice low, eyes scanning the growing crowd of cadets buzzing with speculation and awe.

"People like Blaze don't forget this stuff. You just made a whole lot of enemies."

"Or allies," Lyra replies.

"Mostly enemies."

A flicker of steel threads through Lyra's tired smile. "Good."

No one notices the subtle exchange of glances between Major Voss and Flight Officer Harper, who stand apart under the shadow of the catwalk. Each carries the quiet burden of judgment and the looming pressure of consequences. For them, the day's events signal not merely a protocol broken but tectonic shifts beneath Astra's carefully balanced order. They bear the weight of knowing that reputations, once carved into the academy's stone, reshape everything that comes after.

Between whispered rumors and loaded stares, the atmosphere thickens—electric, like charged ions gathered before a storm. Lyra's name hums through the ranks like a challenge thrown down. Blaze's enforced coldness hardens their standoff, carving their rivalry into the academy's rough stone.

The tarmac stretches wide and barren ahead, sun-bleached and shimmering. Once, cadets stepped as one; now, fissures split the ground beneath their feet. The social landscape shifts as definitively as the wind drags at their uniforms.

As they disappear into the hangar's shadowed interior, the echoes of today's collision ripple on, setting the stage for battles yet to come—painted not in smoke trails but in spoken words and hardened glances.

"You ready for the storm, Lyra?" Jazz asks.

She smirks, her eyes blazing with promise. "Born ready."

Jazz's chuckle carries them down the flight line—a shield and a spark amid the swirling currents of academy life. The day has ended, but the fight has just begun—between rules and rebellion, between discipline and daring. The fissures spreading beneath Astra's feet will only deepen from here.

Sarge's voice cuts through the crisp late afternoon air—clipped, steady, sharp as a snapped cable. He crouches over a battered clipboard outside the briefing room. The steel door stands ajar behind him, catching the low sun's amber light. Around him, the other instructors lean in, their faces tight. Notebooks and tablets scatter across their hands like battlefield maps. Beneath their murmurs, the faint hum of distant jets thrums—a mechanical heartbeat against the rustling of pages and the scratch of pens.

"Listen up," Sarge begins. "We're experiencing communication breakdowns during formation changes: clipped responses and delayed acknowledgments. This won't cut it when lives depend on it." His gaze sweeps across the group and locks onto Blaze. "We will tighten protocols immediately. No exceptions. We can't afford to let this slide."

Blaze nods, his jaw clenched. His fingers tap the edge of the clipboard—sharp and restless. Tension stiffens his stance, rigid as steel.

Beside him, a shadow shifts. Harper slips into the briefing room, her footsteps silent on the polished concrete. She folds a stack of crisp papers with clinical precision, placing them into the dropbox marked "Operational Reports." Her eyes flick toward Blaze—steady and unreadable. The accusations in her report—Lyra's unauthorized split-S and her brazen radio breach—are etched in black and white, despite the quiet that fills the room.

Major Voss stands off to the side, her arms crossed like a fortress. Her dark eyes scan the runway's afterglow beyond the windows. She watches the cadets disperse casually, but her mind is already elsewhere, filing mental notes and preparing to brief Commander Reynolds on the firebrand Lyra and the tightrope Blaze walks between discipline and risk management. Voss's lips press into a thin line, the kind of challenge that promises to disrupt everything.

Outside, on the runway's edge, Blaze stands alone. His gaze is fixed on the empty tarmac stretching endlessly, cracked concrete reflecting a blood-orange sky. Jet engines have reduced to a dull echo.

He breathes in deeply: jet fuel, sun-baked asphalt. The faint whisper of wind threading through the metal skeleton of parked fighters fills his lungs.

His face remains unreadable, but behind those emerald eyes, a tempest churns—calculations of risk, flashes of defiance, and caution drowned by a reckless edge he won't admit aloud.

The memory of Lyra's split-S cuts through his thoughts: a slash in a rigid sky.

Perfect. Too perfect.

Beautifully dangerous. The kind of recklessness he's sworn to crush, even if it means fighting his own respect for her skill.

Behind him, footsteps crunch on gravel—quick, light. Lyra and Jazz make their way back toward the barracks, their march sharp against the stillness surrounding Blaze.

Lyra's cheeks burn with adrenaline. Her uniform clings damply to her ribs, rising and falling with quick breaths. Strands of wind-whipped hair cling to her skin, and a faint smear of cockpit grime ghosts across her jawline. She carries the bruised weight of reprimand like war paint, her chin lifted. But her eyes betray the flicker of hurt beneath the defiance. Jazz walks close, a protective grin tugging at her mouth.

"You're mad, I swear," Jazz murmurs, fingers flicking Lyra's arm in a quick high-five. "But damn, you're good."

Lyra lets out a short laugh—sharp and wild. The kind that carries both challenge and exhaustion. "Yeah, well. I might as well be amazing if I'm going to get noticed." She glances over her shoulder as the barracks come into view, bathed in deepening gold.

Jazz nudges her, teasing. "You've got their attention. Now you just have to survive it."

Lyra's lips twitch into a crooked smile. "Surviving is just the start. Let the games begin."

They reach the barracks—a long rectangular building silhouetted against the blazing horizon. Warm light spills from the windows, cutting through the chill that sneaks in with dusk. The scent of aged wood mingles with laundry soap and early evening rain. Lyra hesitates before stepping inside, her fingers tightening around the strap of her flight bag. Then she strides forward, her spirit unbowed.

Back on the runway, Blaze remains rooted. The last remnants of daylight paint sharp shadows across his weathered features. The roar of unseen engines thrums faintly in his chest, matching the turbulence in his mind. His jaw tenses—frustration and fierce admiration swirling behind his controlled exterior.

The sun dips beyond the horizon. Night gathers. Neither can cool the fire in his gaze.

"You think she'll last?" Sarge's voice cuts through the silence, rough with concern as he approaches.

Blaze doesn't answer at once. His eyes track the last glowing streaks of light before settling into a hard-set line. "She flies like she owns the sky," he finally says, his voice low and tight. "But the sky doesn't bend for anyone. Not even her."

Sarge smirks wryly. "Sounds like you're already in trouble."

"Maybe." Blaze turns away from the empty runway. "Or maybe it's just beginning."

The fading twilight swallows the runway whole, leaving only shadows and the promise of storms yet to come.

Forced Pairing

The briefing room buzzes like an eager swarm as cadets gather around the bulletin board nailed to the cinderblock wall. Its metal frame feels cold beneath the shafts of morning light slicing through the high windows. Fresh sheets taped in neat columns flaunt names and numbers—High-G assignment lists. Each printed letter is a promise or a setback. For cadets fighting their way through the academy's most punishing flight program, these pairings could forge them into elite pilots or wash them out in a single brutal semester.

Murmurs thread through the crowd, rising in tense waves. Boots scrape against worn linoleum. Elbows nudge for better views.

Lyra slips through the tightening mass with practiced ease, a comet weaving past straining bodies. But beneath her pressed uniform, her muscles twitch. Her chin stays high, though her fingers curl into restless fists at her sides—grinning, yet her heart thuds like a warning siren.

Jazz bounces beside her, eyes gleaming with contagious mischief. She leans in close, her voice barely audible over the nervous chatter.

"Bet they throw you to the ghost squad, huh?" Jazz whispers, a sly grin tugging at her lips. "Or maybe the old man finally gets his wish—us flying straight for once."

Lyra shoots her a sideways glance, her lips tugging upward despite herself. "If by 'old man' you mean Captain Arden, I'd rather learn to fly blindfolded."

Jazz snorted. "Oh, you and your wild cards. Just keep your head down... or, well, don't."

The double doors scraped open.

A quiet ripple moved through the room. The air sharpened. Blaze strode in last, shoulders squared like a wall bracing against an incoming gale. His jaw was a tight line, and his green eyes flickered beneath dark brows as he zeroed in on the bulletin board. His fingers closed around the clipboard he carried, knuckles paling. The paper crinkled in silent defiance.

The room hummed. Voices dropped to urgent whispers. Cadets exchanged hushed bets over shoulders. Fingers darted. Eyes flicked between names and faces—who has the luck, and who bears the burden.

Freshly milled paper filled the air, mingling with the metallic tang of jet fuel clinging to uniforms and skin—an invisible reminder of what waited beyond these walls. In this room, partnerships meant survival or collapse. Friendships fractured under G-forces that could crush the unprepared. Some cadets watched with barely concealed hunger; others with dread.

"Who's pairing with Voss's protégée? I heard she flies like a mech in a blender."

"Bet you five credits she snaps under that pressure."

"High-G is unforgiving. The wrong coach means bruises you don't get to heal."

Lyra edged closer, the rough fabric of uniforms brushing against her as she shouldered her way toward the front. Jazz stayed close, a steady pulse beside her quickening heartbeats.

Blaze never took his eyes off the list. His sharp gaze traced the lines of names, like a surgeon dissecting the anatomy of duty and promise. A slow breath settled in his chest. His fingers tightened around the clipboard—a silent promise to maintain control, even if the terrain twisted beneath him.

The murmurs crescendoed, a tide swelling as more cadets pressed forward. The energy crackled, electric and taut. Bets hatched like fireflies flickering in the dusk—who would rise and who would falter.

Lyra caught a glance from Jazz. Her eyes sparkled with the rush of what was to come.

"Whatever happens..." Jazz whispered, a teasing edge beneath the tension, "try not to burn him alive on day one."

Lyra's chuckle came quickly, her confidence a fragile armor. "You think Blaze even knows how to catch fire?"

The crowd thickened. Everyone leaned in as the sheet unfurled fully, the last names revealed in stark black ink under the glare of sterile fluorescents. Silence locked in—anticipation hanging thick like ozone before a lightning strike.

Cadets squeezed closer. Breath fogged in the cool air. Hands gripped the bulletin board frame, eyes sharp with hunger and dread.

Every name held a story, but one line alone fractured the room's breath. Its weight fell like the distant thrum of jet engines waiting on the runway—cold and relentless.

The printed pairing sat unveiled in black ink: Capt. Jareck Arden (Blaze) – Cadet Lyra Hale.

A thread of silence spiraled first, subtle and stunned, like the crack of distant thunder before the storm fully breaks. From there, a ripple emerged: suppressed cheers, stifled groans, and the sharp edges of disbelief carving across faces.

The room pulsed with raw electricity, rewriting futures in a single line. Each cadet was frozen in a moment framed by whispers and shifting shoulders. The inevitable question burned silently beneath every gaze: what comes next?

The sheet of paper clung to the bulletin board under the harsh fluorescent glare—a stark white rectangle holding futures in crisp black type. Eyes scanned it like code, searching and calculating.

Then it leaped out.

"Capt. Jareck Arden (Blaze) – Cadet Lyra Hale."

The air shifted. Half a heartbeat of stunned silence followed, then a swell of muted cheers and grudging groans threaded through the recycled air.

It's the kind of pairing nobody expected: a seasoned combat pilot turned instructor paired with a cadet who flies as if rules are mere suggestions. Whispered speculation rippled through the crowd, tension and excitement tangled together like smoke.

Jazz weaves through the cluster of cadets like wildfire, energy bright and close. Lyra stiffens, chin lifted, lips teasing a smile as Jazz pulls her into a quick side hug.

"You just broke the Ace," Jazz murmurs, low enough that only Lyra catches the edge of mockery wrapped in pride.

Nearby, laughter bubbles—sharp and eager. "Blaze and Lyra? This is going to be one hell of a show," mutters a cadet, nudging his friend.

Lyra's eyes flicker with smug satisfaction and something tighter beneath—a crackling challenge.

Across the room, Blaze's jaw clenches with slow, grinding tension. His shoulders stiffen; fingers curl so tightly around the clipboard that his knuckles blanch. Every inch of him holds rigid—military steel forged into silence—hiding the storm that flickers behind his sharp green eyes.

A steady presence slides to his side. Lt. Marcus "Sarge" Sullivan moves with practiced ease, no fanfare, only a low murmur meant for Blaze's ears alone.

"Trust me, Jareck, you could have landed worse. She's a blaze all her own—don't douse that flame."

Blaze nods, a barely perceptible twitch at the corner of his mouth betraying his tension. Sarge steps back, melting into the crowd, leaving Blaze suspended in the quiet storm.

The room fractures—groups breaking apart, voices snapping like static on a radio. Gossip bubbles up in pockets, swelling fast and engulfing the cadets like wildfire. Some bet on chaos; others on something thrilling and uncharted.

Blaze lingers near the board, his eyes scanning the lines beneath the names. The buzz of voices feels distant—soft thunder rolling under his skin, a counterpoint to the rigid calm he projects.

Jazz skips past, pulling Lyra in her wake, their laughter bursting into the heavy air like a bell jar shattering. The knot of onlookers begins to thin. Yet Blaze holds his ground, suspended a moment longer in the wake of the storm.

The first pulse of a story unfolds around him—electric, charged, and alive.

At the back of the packed briefing room, Major Elena Voss leans against the cold, gray wall, her arms folded tight. Her jaw twitches almost imperceptibly as her eyes never leave Blaze and Lyra. The bulletin board behind her, now stripped of lists, seems to pulse with the weight of what she is calculating. She drags her fingertips across her chin, then jabs a terse note into her datapad. The screen glows faintly under her steely gaze—a flicker of calculation, then back to those two names lingering like a spark in the charged air.

Major Voss knows the politics. She knows how a single pairing can ripple through the academy's hierarchy. She knows that Blaze and Lyra together represent a risk—not because they can't handle it, but because they will handle it too well. Too visibly. The academy thrives on control, on predictable hierarchies. This isn't that.

Near the opposite side, Flight Officer Harper tilted her head, her brow rising in subtle surprise. She held a tablet, her thumbs poised above the screen. Her sharp eyes caught every twitch, every whispered wager, and every half-smile exchanged across the room. She filed her mental notes with procedural precision: pairings, personalities, and potential pitfalls. Her fingers tapped briskly as she logged another detail, her eyes narrowing with professional focus.

Amidst the murmurs, a cluster of cadets huddled near the center, their voices low but animated. A tall cadet with shoulder-length hair let out a dry chuckle.

"So, what do you bet?"

"Blaze and Lyra? It's like mixing gasoline and a spark," a second voice replied, thick with amused skepticism. "You know the rules: no fraternizing. This one's gonna blow up—mark my words."

"I'll throw five creds on them surviving the first week without a fist-fight." Another cadet's eyes glittered with challenge. "Call it disaster or drama, but it's gonna be a hell of a watch."

Laughter rippled through the group.

"'No fraternization,' they say." Someone wryly shook their head. "Like that ever stops anything."

The words hung—half jest, half warning. Most cadets understood the academy's unspoken truth: the no-fraternization policy was less about actual enforcement and more about creating a pressure cooker. Break the rule quietly? Acceptable. Break it publicly? Career-ending. Blaze and Lyra together meant someone would break it. The only question was how spectacularly.

A few feet away, Jazz slinked into view, her eyes bright with spark and wit. She exchanged quick, conspiratorial glances with a cluster of Lyra's closest supporters. Their smirks never quite reached their eyes—shimmering with a knowing gleam and silent promise. This pairing was more than a roster entry; it was a story about to unfold—a spectacle.

Jazz leaned in. The small group hushed, as if they were sealed into something sacred—betting on every move and every word yet to come.

"The fire meets the ice," one cadet muttered, nudging another as they both grinned knowingly.

In the corners, instructors shifted their weight. Some exchanged glances heavy with unspoken concerns, while others barely suppressed the flicker of grudging respect. Even in this charged atmosphere, discipline coiled beneath it all, waiting.

The hum of whispered gossip began to swell—soft undertones of excitement, nerves, and speculation. Like shifting gears before a launch, the room vibrated with anticipation.

A sharp glance from Major Voss sent a ripple of quiet through the space. Cadets straightened, and smiles tightened. Plans for the upcoming orientation rippled beneath the surface as everyone absorbed what the pairing might mean for their futures.

Harper's voice drew a brief thread of words between two nearby cadets—clipped and analytical.

"Do you notice the body language? Arden's jaw is clenched tighter than a hydraulic seal."

"And Lyra Hale? She's grinning like she just lit a fuse. This isn't just another assignment; it's a test."

Jazz grinned, elbowing Lyra lightly. "Are you ready to throw a wrench in his well-oiled machine?"

Lyra smirked, her eyes gleaming with fresh fire. "I was born ready."

Jazz winked. "Then let's watch the fireworks."

Across the room, faint laughter trickled through the buzz. The pulse of rumors began to tighten into something resembling social gravity. The name pairing had done its work—fueling hopes, fears, and endless debate.

The hum of pre-flight energy rippled into the halls as instructors and cadets began to move toward the orientation briefing. Steps shuffled, papers rustled, and weighted glances were exchanged. The air tasted sharp with possibility, electric with the promise of disruption and daring.

Whispers trailed behind them like contrails.

No one dared to say it aloud, but beneath the bravado, the entire room leaned in.

Waiting.

The voices thinned. Cadets filed out, their boots striking polished concrete in sharp staccato bursts. The sound mingled with the faint hum of filtered daylight spilling through narrow windows—thin slivers of pale gray light that seemed to drain warmth from the hallway. Blaze stepped forward, his silhouette knife-sharp against the sterile walls. The scent of jet fuel lingered faintly beneath the recycled air.

His voice cut through the lingering buzz—clipped, final.

"Lyra. A word."

She turned, one eyebrow already raised.

"The High-G program doesn't tolerate shortcuts," he continued, his green eyes locked on hers. "I expect you to follow protocol—exactly. Instincts come second, especially when the pressure's on. No exceptions."

His jaw was tight; that was all the warning she'd get.

Lyra's grin spread slowly and brightly—like sunlight breaking through storm clouds, dangerous and defiant. She leaned into the moment, her voice smooth but edged like fractured glass.

"Discipline. Cozy." She stepped closer, the drag of her boot against the scuffed floor deliberate. "But maybe sometimes the sky doesn't care about your procedure checklist before it throws a curveball at you."

Her eyes glinted with challenge, that smug smile part dare, part secret. Nearby cadets caught the tension building between them; their eyes flickered with interest, static crackling in the air where the two stood.

Jazz perched a few steps back, flashing a silent wink. She mouthed the words, her lips curving with delight: *Don't burn him too badly.*

Sarge stood like a sentry, arms crossed but posture open. He watched them both, his eyes narrowing with thought before shifting into a small nod aimed at Blaze—an unspoken message laced with trust. He knew the war raging beneath that smooth exterior—knew the fire and the frost they both wielded, and believed in both.

The hallway stretched cold and orderly ahead. Between Blaze and Lyra, tension snapped tight—a taut cable strung between caution and temptation. Their steps fell in sync yet hesitant, each one measured, each one charged.

Blaze's jaw muscles tightened imperceptibly. His fingers flexed at his sides as unspoken rules collided with the raw edge of instinct that Lyra embodied. There was a rhythm in their proximity—a hesitation that spoke louder than any command.

Lyra's eyes flicked over his profile: rigid, controlled, but undeniably alive beneath the armor. In that glance lived a silent promise: high stakes, no margin for error.

Their shadows stretched and merged with the dimming light filtering through the paneled windows as they walked side by side toward the orientation briefing—the next battlefield where rules would be spelled out and the true tests would begin.

Major Elena Voss's voice cut through the briefing hall like sheared metal: sharp and unforgiving. The room—a cavernous space of cool steel panels and rigid rows of chairs—seemed to swallow her words and hold them suspended, hanging on the edge of each syllable. She stood poised at the front, the building's ventilation system humming its low, steady pulse beneath the restless shifting of cadets: eager and uncertain.

"This program demands more than muscle," Voss began, her eyes narrowing under the harsh fluorescent glare. She paused, and the silence stretched. "High-G means extreme physical strain."

Another beat passed.

"It crushes lungs, blurs vision, and fractures concentration. You won't just fight gravity—you'll fight your own body." Her tone was clipped and uncompromising. "Trust isn't optional here. You must rely on your partner and your training without hesitation. Fail one, and both of you pay the price."

The weight of her words rippled through the room—quiet but electric, like a storm pressing against reinforced glass. Cadets straightened; some tightened their grip on their uniform fabric, while others stole glances sideways, measuring the resolve in their neighbor's jaw. The air tasted of polished floor wax and recycled oxygen, tinged with the faint metallic bite of steel and the soft scrape of notebooks opening.

Voss shifted her stance, her gaze sweeping toward the front row and zeroing in on two cadets sitting side by side but occupying entirely different worlds.

"Discipline," she said. The word could cut iron. "Will be enforced without exception."

Her eyes lingered on them—Blaze and Lyra—and when she spoke again, her voice dropped lower but lost none of its lethal precision. "Your failure is not a failure of one; it is a breach in the entire line."

Blaze sat rigid, every muscle locked beneath the crisp fabric of his uniform. His fingers pressed so tightly against his thighs that his knuckles whitened. His jaw clenched with the slow, aching intensity of a man born to order—green eyes scanning the major but mostly fixed on Lyra, a storm gathering behind that fortress of discipline. When Voss fired a rapid volley of questions at him—protocol steps in emergency G-LOC situations, recovery sequences, communication drills—his answers came without hesitation. Each word was clipped and precise, switches flipping in a flawless machine.

Lyra, meanwhile, wiggled in her seat. The hinge of her boot tapped sharply against the metal strut of the chair. The edge of her notebook peeked from her lap, a jet sketched in quick, loose strokes dancing across the page. When Voss invited her to explain emergency procedures, Lyra's voice rippled through the silence with a bold, almost theatrical twist.

"Yeah, you follow the checklist. But what happens if the comms go dead or the system craps out mid-stack?" She leaned forward slightly, her eyes bright. "Sometimes you just gotta trust your gut, flip the script on the rulebook, and improvise fast. A quick heads-up, maybe pulling G off-angle to catch the wind pocket—that sort of thing could save your skin when the manual's worthless."

Laughter and gasps sliced through the room—some cadets amused, others disbelieving, and instructors frowning with thinly veiled skepticism. A few exchanged glances, their eyebrows arching like question marks.

Blaze's gaze sharpened, and his lips pressed into a thin line. When he spoke, his voice was quiet but carried the weight of a counter-strike—measured and brisk. "Improvisation has its place—after strict adherence to protocol. Deviating too soon risks losing control. Instinct without discipline isn't survival; it's a gamble you can't afford up there."

Lyra's eyes flashed—defiant, bright. "And discipline without instinct? That's just a slow death. If you're too busy watching the checklist, the sky will sting you for ignoring what's obvious."

The debate hovered between them—electric, taut. Voices were low but sharp enough for the packed hall to catch every word.

Murmurs bloomed among the cadets, a ripple of tension and fascination spreading like wildfire.

The instructors' faces hardened. Major Voss's jaw tightened imperceptibly, while Lt. Sullivan shifted in his seat, unwilling to interrupt but visibly bracing for what came next.

The room simmered with the aftereffects of the exchange, the air thick with anticipation. Whispers gathered in clusters—some cadets laughing, some betting silently on who would break first, and others already drafting mental playbooks for the clash of wills that was now inseparable from the assignment.

Lyra flipped her notebook shut. She shot a smirk at Blaze—cocky and deliberate—before settling back, her posture relaxed yet defiant. Blaze's eyes lingered on her for a flicker longer. His gaze held storms and hidden things. Then he shifted back to the front as Major Voss began to wrap up.

"As you enter the High-G program, remember," Voss said, her voice sharp and carrying into every corner, "it's more than flying. It's survival. Trust. Hard, unforgiving discipline. You break the rules, you break the team—and failure is a cost none of us can afford."

The final words bounced off polished surfaces, silencing the room. A weight settled over the gathered cadets like a held breath.

A low buzz of conversation ignited almost immediately. Quiet at first, then building steadily. Speculation laced with awe, judgment tangled with curiosity.

Blaze sat still, his green eyes steady but shadowed. The storm inside him breathed quietly—controlled and contained. Lyra stretched her hand as if she were itching to take off, a restless flame trapped behind a cool facade. Around them, whispers grew. Their names became the focal point of murmured commentary and tentative bets, the latest spectacle seared into Astra Flight Command's unwritten history.

The briefing hall doors swung open with a hollow clang, spilling a flood of cadets into the corridor. The air tasted faintly of recycled coffee and sweat, thick with the residue of tension and too many simmering nerves. Blaze stepped out first, his boots echoing a precise rhythm on the polished floor. His eyes locked on Lyra, who was lingering near the edge of the group, her fingers tracing the rim of her notebook. Her expression hadn't dulled since the briefing; that stubborn spark still lit her gaze.

He crosses the space between them in a few measured strides, the scent of jet fuel clinging faintly to his uniform. The frustration coiling through him isn't just about her answers—it's the recklessness wrapped in them, the way she speaks as though protocol is optional. He's seen what happens when discipline frays at the edges. He's scraped the consequences off the tarmac. Protocol isn't red tape; it's the difference between coming home and not. Yet something in her defiance makes him want to shake her and listen to her all at once, a contradiction that tightens his jaw.

His voice cuts through the murmur, crisp and pointed. "Your answers back there? Way too cavalier, Hale. Undermining protocol in front of the entire cohort isn't just reckless—it's dangerous."

Lyra meets his glare without flinching, the defiance in her stance barely hiding the quickened pulse beneath. "Danger is part of flying, Captain," she replies, her voice low but steady, the edge sharp as a razor. "Sometimes you can't wait for a checklist to save your life. You fly on instinct. You improvise when the rules don't fit the moment."

Blaze's jaw tightens, shadowing his usually guarded face with a flicker of frustration. "Chain of command isn't a damn suggestion. It's the lifeline that keeps everyone alive when the pressure's crushing. Improvisation without discipline is a damn good way to get someone killed."

"So you'd rather fly by a rigid rulebook than react to what's real in the sky?" Lyra's smile is a dangerous tilt, half challenge, half tease. "Because when this place starts choking you with regulations, it's going to be gut instincts that pull you through the worst."

Their voices drop lower, the tension weaving tighter between them like an electrical current. Blaze's tone remains clipped and controlled, but it hums with the fire of conviction. "Discipline creates order. Without it, you've got chaos — and chaos doesn't care how bright your instincts are."

Lyra leans in fractionally, enough that the scent of her—earthy, with a hint of citrus—brushes against his senses. "And sometimes order suffocates you. Sometimes you *need* to break free to survive."

Jazz loiters just out of earshot with a small cluster of cadets, grinning as if she's watching a live show. She nudges a nearby cadet, whispering with amusement, "Looks like the Ace finally met his match. This is going to be one hell of a ride."

Nearby, a few other cadets mirror the sparring stance, mock whispering back and forth with sly smirks. The buzz builds—half amusement, half anticipation—a chorus of eager whispers laced with bets on who will crack first.

Blaze studies Lyra with narrowed eyes, his posture rigid but betraying the faintest hesitation, like a fortress shaken by a persistent wind. Then, without a word, he pivots sharply and strides away, the sharp slap of his boots fading down the corridor.

Lyra watches him go for a brief moment, her chest rising and falling slightly faster, curiosity threading beneath the remnants of irritation. When the crowd begins to thin, she trails behind at a measured distance, the thin space between them charged with an unspoken challenge.

"You think you're the only one who's ever flown blind through a storm?" Her words hang in the air, almost to herself, wavering between a challenge and a confession.

Blaze doesn't turn back. Instead, gravel edges his voice as he finally breaks the silence between them.

"Flying blind doesn't mean ignoring the rules that keep us alive. You want to rewrite the book? Prove you can do it *without* wrecking the squad."

The memory flickers through him—Torres bleeding out in the hangar, the rookie's chest rising and falling in those final moments, all because someone decided the evacuation protocol was too slow, too bureaucratic. They had improvised. They had paid for it in blood and silence. That's what Lyra doesn't understand yet: discipline isn't about control; it's about the ones who come home.

Lyra's grin quirks sideways, sharp and bright as a flare. "Watch me."

The cadence of their exchange pulls the attention of the last stragglers. Jazz sidles closer to Lyra, eyebrows raised in impressed disbelief. "Girl, you just signed up for a whole season of fireworks."

Lyra shrugs, pocketing the challenge like a secret prize. The corridor empties, leaving behind only their echoing footsteps and a buzz of murmurs drifting from the briefing hall.

Blaze's jaw remains clenched as he walks on, muscles tight beneath his uniform. Lyra follows, her gaze flickering briefly to his retreating figure. Neither of them admits it aloud, but the edge between them feels less like a barrier now and more like a thread ready to pull taut, unraveling everything they thought they knew.

The corridor smelled faintly of worn leather and stale sweat, with footsteps fading into low murmurs that clung to the cold fluorescent glare. Sarge intercepted Blaze, placing steady hands on his shoulders and pulling him aside with a firm grip.

"Ever think about how you flew back in the day?" Sarge's voice rumbled beneath the hum of the lights.

Blaze didn't answer. The silence stretched.

"Not just by the book," Sarge pressed on, his gaze unwavering. "But on gut. Instinct. You were an unorthodox ace, Jareck. Hell, you *ran* risks that no one else had the guts for."

Blaze didn't move. His jaw tightened, and his shoulders pulled rigid like coiled springs. His fingers curled into fists at his sides as he stared ahead—eyes dark pools reflecting the sharp white lights above. The weight of those words settled between them, an echo from a past life and a challenge hanging in the air.

"You see that cadet?" Sarge gestured subtly toward the clusters of younger faces just around the corner. "Lyra Hale. Bright, reckless, dangerously alive. She's already turned heads—and not all of them are pleased. She's the kind that either burns herself out or burns bright enough to light the whole academy." He paused, letting the words sink in. "If you snuff that fire out, she dies silent. But if you channel it... maybe that fire can burn clean. You don't need to break her. You've been where she is. You know what it takes to fly sharp."

Blaze's lips twitched—a momentary crack in his stone-cold armor. The glance he cast toward the cadets was guarded and calculating.

"Discipline is the backbone," Blaze murmured, his voice clipped like broken glass. "Talent without it is just chaos."

"True," Sarge nodded. "But sometimes discipline has to flex. You can't cage what is alive and expect it to thrive."

Blaze's eyes flickered. Annoyance tightened his jaw, but something unspoken flickered beneath—a reluctant recognition. The tightness in his chest loosened just a fraction, though the edge remained as sharp as a blade.

Not far off, Jazz rounded the corner, her voice a spark cutting through the corridor's quiet. She hooked an arm around Lyra, pulling her in with a grin that was half amusement and half challenge.

"Girl, you just set the whole academy on fire," Jazz whispered, her eyes gleaming with mischief. "They're going to be gossiping about this pair for weeks. You? Paired with the ace himself? It's like watching a live wire and a flamethrower get tangled."

Lyra's laugh was bright and reckless, echoing off the concrete walls. She shrugged, self-assured and daring.

"Let them talk," Lyra replied, her voice husky with defiance. "If I'm going to crash and burn, I might as well light up the damn sky first."

Jazz nudged her playfully, her eyes scanning the corridors as whispers bloomed into murmurs, swelling with the pulse of cadet wagers and predictions.

"I've already heard bets," Jazz said with a sly smile. "Half say Blaze will tame you within a month. The other half swear you'll rattle his entire command." Her voice dipped conspiratorially. "Either way, this is the show of the season."

The hallway rippled with anticipation. Cadets cast sidelong glances, their voices dipped in excitement and speculation. Somewhere in the undercurrent, alliances formed, friendships tightened, and rivalries flared just beneath polite smiles.

Sarge watched the scene unfold, then nudged Blaze gently toward the exit, back to the flight line that awaited with its endless sky and unforgiving horizon.

"Remember what I said: fire is a tool, not a threat." His gaze held steady, unwavering.

Blaze walked away, his clenched jaw loosening just a fraction as his mind churned beneath the disciplined exterior. The weight of command pressed heavier, but beneath it, the spark of reluctant curiosity ignited—a dangerous thing, kindled by a girl who burned too bright to ignore.

Behind him, Lyra and Jazz exchanged a knowing glance, their laughter low and shared—two wildcards ready to shake the rigid order, with the promise of a combustible partnership simmering like a storm on the horizon.

Blaze stands motionless in the dim dorm hallway, the steel-framed window beside him framing the fading glow of twilight over the sprawling flight line. Jets rest like silver ghosts on the tarmac, their forms blurred by the humid haze rolling in from the coast. The hum of distant engines fades into silence, replaced by the soft whisper of a coastal breeze brushing through cracked glass panes. His fingers curl into fists at his sides, knuckles pale beneath worn leather gloves. In the brittle quiet, memories surface—sharp and unyielding: the final sortie, the sudden flare of tracer rounds, the wrenching boom when his wingman went dark.

The weight of that loss crouches deep in his chest, a familiar pressure that tightens whenever he is alone. Control had been everything then—every calculation, every split-second maneuver—but in the end, it slipped through his fingers like smoke. Now the ghosts trace invisible wings beside him, reminders of a precision he once mastered but now battles to reclaim.

A flicker of movement outside the corner of his eye fractures the reverie. Her grin—bold, unapologetic—rises unbidden. Lyra's quicksilver wit, the spark in her eyes when she bent rules as if they were paper airplanes. That answer during the briefing, that daring weave of instinct and intellect that raised the room's hackles and laughter in equal measure. Blaze's jaw twitches, a flash of irritation crashing against an unfamiliar tide of reluctant intrigue.

Her defiance, impossible to ignore, gnaws at the hard edges of his resolve. She is precisely the kind of reckless individual he has learned to fear—the kind that costs lives—yet something within him recognizes a hunger beneath her rebellion that mirrors his own fractured desire for flight. She does not bend to authority the way most cadets do; she bends authority itself, and that terrifies him as much as it compels him to watch her more closely than regulations demand.

Meanwhile, half a wing's length away in the barracks, Lyra sprawls on her bunk, her limbs tangled in the rough-knit blanket, the scent of worn canvas and faint jet fuel clinging to the fabric. Jazz leans beside her, a mischievous glint dancing in her dark eyes as the soft murmur of distant footsteps ebbs behind the barracks walls. The hum of the base settles into a distant lullaby.

Beneath Lyra's confident exterior runs a current of doubt she would never voice aloud—the academy has a way of grinding down ambition, of whittling natural instinct into approved patterns. Every rule she bends is a small rebellion against becoming what they want her to be: a pilot who flies by formula rather than conviction. Blaze's criticism stings precisely because part of her fears he is right, that her defiance might one day cost her everything. But the alternative—surrendering the wildness that makes her feel alive—represents its own kind of death.

Lyra's voice slips into the quiet room, half confession, half challenge.

"I don't hate him—he just makes me want to fly harder."

Jazz throws back her head and laughs, the sound rich and warm, a welcome pulse in the dorm's quiet rhythm. She nudges Lyra playfully, the gesture like a tether anchoring them amid the swirling chaos of new alliances and old rules.

"He's lucky you're not burning him down to ash by now. You've got that wild fire, no doubt."

Lyra's lips twitch with a grudging smile, shadows of the day's clashes flickering in her eyes—sharp flashes of frustration mixed with sparks of something unknown.

Back in the dorm hallway, Blaze's gaze locks onto the runway lights, twin beacons burning bright against the encroaching night. The steady pulse of the lamps mirrors the beat of his own chest—calm exterior veiling the tempest beneath. He exhales slowly, muscles unwinding by an infinitesimal fraction. The interplay of discipline and instinct, order and chaos, spins in his mind like a reluctant enemy to be mastered.

Across the barracks, Lyra's fingers trace idly over the coarse blanket, her thoughts tangled with the morning's sparring—her toss of rules against protocol, his rigid tether to the past. She lingers on the memory of Blaze's clipped, precise words, the tension that electrified the air between them like a live wire.

The silence between thoughts hums with unspoken admission: neither of them can quite shake the other's gravity.

"You think you're just going to snap your fingers and I'll fall in line, instructor?"

"I don't expect you to fall in line. I expect you to fly like you want to live."

Lyra's grin surges, daring and sly.

"Well, then maybe it's time you stopped breathing down my neck and started watching how I actually fly."

Blaze's reply is clipped but steady.

"Flying isn't a game, Hale. It's war."

"War isn't all about rules. Sometimes it's about guts."

Their words hang in the empty corridor, a taut thread stretching between order and rebellion.

Jazz's laughter bubbles again from the bunk.

"You're a handful, Lyra Hale. Just don't let him clip your wings."

Lyra nudges her back, a spark of gratitude hidden beneath the bravado.

Blaze turns from the window, the cold metal frame pressing into his back as he steps away, the first slivers of understanding piercing the armor he has crafted. Lyra exhales deeply, the weight of the day giving way to a pulse of anticipation beneath the fatigue—two hearts tethered by friction, poised on the edge of something neither dares to name.

Night settles fully over Astra Flight Command, the shadows folding in like a quiet promise as pilot and cadet retreat to their separate sanctuaries, each carrying the fragile embers of connection that might yet ignite a storm.

First Flight, First Collision

The locker room sits shrouded in half-light before the first trace of dawn touches the windows. The concrete floor hums faintly with distant echoes—footsteps, the click of boots, and the occasional rustle of gear. Lyra slips inside, the cool metal of the locker door biting against her palm as she yanks open its dull gray face. Her flight suit hangs neat and fresh, the fabric smooth beneath her fingers. She pulls it free, lets it fall slack in her hands, and then slides it on. The fabric smells faintly of ozone and synthetic fiber, a scent she's beginning to crave.

Jazz bounces in place beside her, practically glowing with energy despite the hour. "Lucky pairing, huh? Blaze and you." Her voice is low, grinning, and challenging, like a hand shoved into the heat of a poker game.

Lyra's smirk tugged up an edge, but her fingers trembled slightly as she tightened the Velcro strap. A ripple of nerves brushed beneath her ribs, sharp and electric. "Yeah. 'Lucky.' Like a black cat crossing a runway in a hurricane." She worked through the remaining tabs with practiced ease. "Let's just say the stars don't always align for me."

Jazz laughed, bright in the quiet room, and clapped her on the shoulder. "Well, you're flying high today—don't let the 'grumpy instructor' put you off."

A door thudded open.

Blaze stepped in last. His presence carved a shadow along the floor, and the air tightened in response. His gaze swept over the posted simulator rosters that cadets crowded around like moths to a flame. The frustration from yesterday's simulation still simmered beneath his disciplined mask—a tension threaded through the set of his jaw, muscles taut and still as steel wire. Those piercing green eyes, sharp as blades, surveyed the room with unyielding focus.

Sarge moved smoothly to the front, his voice cutting through the low buzz like a well-honed blade. "Listen up," he barked, firm but steady. "Simulator day means precision—no shortcuts, no stunts. Safety comes first. You rely on your wingman here. Teamwork isn't just a buzzword; it's survival." He let the words hang, then steepled his fingers. "This day marks a rite of passage for you—it tests both skill and survival instinct. Protocol exists for a reason. Break it, and you pay the price."

The room shifted. Cadets adjusted, some meeting eyes anxiously, while others bristled with barely repressed eagerness.

Blaze stepped forward. His voice came out clipped, cold like frost biting bare skin. "Hale." His gaze pinned her, public and unblinking. "You'll follow orders. Trust breeds survival, not hotshot moves." He paused, letting the weight of his words settle. "This is not a playground. Your recklessness endangered more than just yourself during the last run."

Lyra held his stare, her chest tight against the weight of his scrutiny. Her jaw clenched. Around them, cadets exchanged looks—half shock, half something akin to fascination.

At the back of the room, Harper stood with Major Voss, the two statuesque figures quiet and alert, pens scratching against paper, eyes taking in every gesture and every exchange. Neither moved to intervene—observers in a delicate dance, measuring risk against discipline, ambition against control.

Whispers rippled through the ranks, threading like static beneath the authority's voice.

Jazz sidled closer to Lyra, a mischievous gleam sparking in her dark eyes. She poked Lyra sharply in the ribs, her grin wide. "So, what's it like being saddled with the human embodiment of a thundercloud?"

Lyra shot her a glare sharp enough to cut through the fog of pre-dawn nerves. "Keep it up, Jazz, and I'll hand you off to Sarge for a solo ride."

Jazz laughed, unfazed, tugging her gear tighter as the cadets loosened their formation. Footsteps clanked down the corridors. Voices faded into the anticipation stirring beneath the hum of the base waking.

Metal clanked, and boots echoed against the cavernous hangar as cadets streamed inside, shedding the last traces of civilian life like a second skin. The air buzzed with the sharp scent of lubricants and polished aluminum, mingling with the faint tang of sweat and anticipation. Rows of lockers stood like silent sentinels under harsh fluorescent lights, each square a vault of secrets: dog-eared manuals, worn patches, and keepsakes fastened against the relentless regimen. One by one, the cadets peeled off their jackets, stowed away their phones and trinkets, and donned the flight suits that promised immersion into a world where the sky was both playground and battlefield.

Lyra slid into her gear with practiced ease, the coarse fabric snapping snugly against her lean frame. The oxygen mask hung loosely at her side, with the helmet soon to follow. Beside her, Jazz's grin was an electric charge.

"Lucky pairing, huh? Blaze and Lyra. This just became everyone's favorite front-row show."

The flight gear wasn't mere equipment—each buckle, each seal, and each precisely calibrated component represented a threshold between the living world and one where a single miscalculation could unravel everything. The simulator demanded absolute faith in these tools and absolute precision in wielding them. Donning them meant accepting that the next hours would strip away any margin for error and any room for hesitation. This was the armor of the unforgiving.

Lyra smirked beneath the dim lights, fighting the flutter pressing low in her stomach. Lucky or not, being paired with him felt like stepping into a pressure cooker sealed tight. Jazz's teasing edged a flicker of nervous excitement.

Blaze appeared like a shadow folding into the frame of the hangar's mouth, jaw clenched tight, eyes narrowed as they swept over the room. The air thickened against his lean silhouette—six feet of silent warning. With hands shoved into his pockets, he moved at a slow, deliberate pace that carved space between him and the restless cadets milling beneath the cavern's steel ribs. Murmurs hushed as he passed; some eyes darted, others fixed—but no one met his gaze for longer than a moment.

The restless clatter gave way to a sudden crispness as Blaze moved toward Lyra. His fingers, rough and sure, checked the mechanics with military precision: the helmet nestled firmly over her brow, the oxygen hose clicked into place without slack, and the harness straps tightened, threading snugly around her torso. His touch was methodical yet careful, like adjusting delicate machinery that could fail in an instant if misaligned.

Her hands, surprisingly steady, did not betray the storm behind her gaze. No tremors, no fluttering nerves—only the hard gleam of focus.

"Gloves secure?" Blaze's voice cut through the hum—flat, clipped, an order more than a question.

"Secured," she replied, her voice steady as the tightening grasp of gravity.

They moved in near silence toward the narrow corridor leading to the simulator wing. The concrete beneath their boots echoed like a cold metronome against the muted drone of distant engines. Other cadets drifted past, casting sidelong glances like furtive sparrows eyeing a hawk. Whispers threaded through the hangar—half admiration for their prowess, half wariness of what their pairing might ignite. Blaze's reputation for flawless execution met Lyra's known hunger for the edge; together, they were either a masterclass or a collision waiting to happen. The speculation kindled something electric in the air, a current of anticipation and mild dread that followed them both.

Lyra broke the taut silence with a tentative grin, searching for a crack in Blaze's armor.

"Guess the simulator's about to see fireworks today. Hope you're ready to keep up."

His eyes met hers briefly, sharp and ice-chiseled, before relenting with a slow but firm shake of his head.

"No improvisation. Follow protocol." His tone was knife-edged beneath the cold surface, slicing away the warmth she tried to lure out.

She flinched behind the mask of her smile; the unspoken challenge in his silence was heavier than any words.

The weight of expectation pressed against the fluorescent-lit walls and concrete floors. The corridor narrowed, transforming from hangar vastness into a stifling passage where tension pooled like thick oil.

Lyra's jaw twitched, a flicker of irritation burning just beneath her composure—a spark she bit down on hard as they neared the entrance to the simulator bay. Her fingers twitched at her sides, craving release but locked tight within. The buzz of ionized air from the threshold promised steel and synthetic skies, a realm where instincts and rules clashed beneath flickering neon.

A voice cracked through the corridors as Jazz trailed behind, his voice low but pointed.

"With Blaze? You're either going to crash or take off like a comet. Either way, I can't wait to see the fallout."

Lyra spared Jazz a sharp glare over her shoulder, her eyes narrowing just enough to warn but softening with the ghost of a wan smile. The brewing storm between her and Blaze felt almost tangible in the tight, humming space. The doors loomed ahead—glass and steel barred like the airlock to another world.

The moment they crossed the threshold, the stale weight of the hangar faded, replaced by the antiseptic chill of the High-G program simulator. But the tension lingered, coiled tight between them like compressed air, ready to explode.

Lyra climbed into the simulator pod first, squeezing through the narrow opening of the armored glass shell that encases the cockpit.

The seat cradled her with cold, calculated precision—black leather harnesses waiting to wrap tightly around her torso and thighs. She breathed in the sterile air, feeling the weight of the machine's expectations settle over her shoulders. The simulator offered no mercy, no margin for hesitation—only the promise of exposure, of every mistake laid bare on the telemetry screens. It thrilled her, that razor's edge between control and chaos, though she'd never admit the flutter of nerves in her chest to anyone, least of all to the pilot slipping into the pod beside her. Adjacent to hers, Blaze's form slipped into the neighboring pod with unmistakable ease. His lean frame barely seemed to disturb the tight confines, every movement efficient and minimal. Between them, the transparent wall gleamed, a fragile boundary holding two volatile forces side by side.

Inside, each instrument panel is a symphony of blinking lights and tactile switches, with every dial calibrated to mimic the unforgiving machinery of real jets. The cold metallic scent of the simulator mixes faintly with the sharp tang of disinfectant, lingering in the recycled air. Lyra's fingers brush against the smooth surface of the throttle, cool and unyielding under her touch. Blaze's hands hover over his controls, his jaw clenched and green eyes narrowed on the displays in front of him.

Above, a massive dome of screens flickers to life, casting an ethereal blue glow over the room. The simulated sky stretches wide—a sculpted digital expanse of jagged mountain crags, sloping valleys veiled in shifting mists, and roiling cloud banks curling like restless beasts. In the distant horizon, snow-dusted peaks pierce a sky painted with the creeping hues of dawn. The technicians move silently, their headsets glowing faintly as they perform last-minute checks on the array of cables fastening the pods to the hydraulic arms.

A steady hum rises as Blaze's voice cuts through the comms, clipped and unyielding.

"Preflight checklist, start. Flight controls, tested and green."

Lyra answers, her voice tight but steady.

"Flight controls, green. Instruments, aligned."

Blaze ticks down the list with measured precision.

"Hydraulics and hydraulics. Oxygen supply, hooked and functional. Communications, secure. Ejection system, armed."

Lyra has never been good at following scripts. Her instincts run faster than protocol, sharper than the rulebook—impulses that have saved her in tight spots and gotten her called to Sarge's office just as often. She knows better; she technically knows the checklist by heart, but there's always that voice in her head that whispers she can optimize, streamline, and cut through the redundancy. It's dangerous thinking in a military context, the kind that gets pilots grounded. But it's also what keeps her alive when things go sideways.

Lyra's tone shifts—snappier, less rehearsed—a flash of boldness bleeding through as she slips into the launch sequence, tweaking a step without freely announcing the alteration.

"Launch sequence initiated. Auxiliary power checks complete. Ready for ignition."

A pause clamps the room into charged silence.

Sarge's voice emerges from the operator's desk—calm but authoritative.

"Ten seconds to go. Ten... nine... eight..."

Hydraulics surge to life; pistons groan under pressure. The pods shudder; the feeling is mechanical yet eerily lifelike—as if the skin-tight cockpit can now hurl them into the physics of a real High-G maneuver. Vibration ripples through the seats; the soundscape shifts to the roar of engines and wind slicing through mountain passes.

"Seven... six... five..."

Lyra's breath catches just before the pods tilt forward, the simulation lurching into the climb.

"Four... three... two... one... launch."

Together, in virtual tandem, the pods fire forward, the projected landscape rushing beneath a canopy of storm-hardened clouds. Simulation displays envelop their vision—the virtual jets skimming razor-thin ridges as distant valleys open like waiting jaws. The cockpit panels flood with data streams; speed, altitude, and G-force indicators climb with breathtaking immediacy.

Blaze's eyes sharpen on the heads-up display as he slides the throttle forward, his hands firm and his voice steady over the comms.

"Maintain formation. Eyes sharp."

Beside him, Lyra's lips press into a line, the faint twitch of a grin betraying her excitement. Her fingers dance over the controls, coaxing the artificial aircraft into smooth, sweeping arcs. The simulators settle into the relentless hum of flight, a taut rhythm pulsing through metal and muscle.

Outside their pods, the chamber's lights dim to a cool blue, heightening the illusion of altitude and exposure. The air grows thinner with the synthetic quality of mounting altitude, and the pressure on their chests is perfectly mimicked by the harnesses tightening, whispering promises of crushing Gs to come.

Between the cockpit walls, an unspoken tension hums, each pilot attuned not just to the simulated jets but to the volatile electricity flowing in the narrow space between them.

"Ready to lock formation?" Blaze's voice cuts sharply.

Lyra shoots a glance toward the dividing glass, her eyes alight with restless energy.

"Born ready."

The digital mountain course sprawls beneath them, jagged earth and shadowed valleys creating a perfect, treacherous playground for the High-G trial about to unfold. The simulators pulse, alive now, carrying the promise of danger cloaked in virtual safety—a battlefield where every heartbeat counts and trust must be earned with precision.

They lean into the climb, instruments flickering under the weight of altitude and expectation as the virtual jets surge forward, carving a path through the dawn-lit peaks, eyes locked, muscles taut, ready for the dance that will decide everything.

Blaze's fingers flick over the controls—precise, with a scalpel's grace. The simulator cockpit hums, alive with synthetic power.

Outside the glass, a digital mountain range unfurls—jagged peaks clawing at cloudbanks that shift like living things. Simulated winds tremble through their flight instruments, carrying the weight of unforgiving terrain.

His voice cuts through the static, clipped and sure.

"Maintain tight formation. Precision is your safety net—no deviations."

Lyra shadows him closely, her avatar a streak of raw color against icy grays. She matches his every line, her controls flowing with textbook precision, yet something pulls at her—instinct nudging her craft wider, testing angles Blaze hasn't sanctioned.

The simulator vibrated beneath her as she banked further out. A low mechanical thrum rippled through her bones, mingling with the sharp tang of recycled air caught in her throat.

"Formation's slipping, Hale. Pull it in," Blaze snapped over the comms.

Her fingers clenched the controls, knuckles whitening. A flicker darted through her green eyes—distant lightning beneath the visor. She banked hard, skimming the simulated canyon face. Overheated circuitry stung her nose. The pod shuddered with every calculated tilt, each movement a negotiation between protocol and what her body screamed to do.

"No way I'm flying this close like it's some drone swarm," she muttered, her voice low but cutting through the channel. "Feels like I'm dancing with ghosts, not pilots."

Nervous laughter rippled through the comms. Tension crackled like a sudden storm, sharp-edged and electric.

Jazz's voice burst through, teasing and sharp as a whip. "Hale, you planning to fly us all off a cliff with those fancy dance moves? Need a tracker beacon or what?"

Lyra's lips twitched despite the pressure. "Keep talking, Turner. I'll pass when you're not glued to autopilot."

Blaze's grip tightened. His tone carried the weight of stifled frustration, cold as the cockpit around them.

"Cut the chatter. Focus up. This ends with a fail report if you don't."

The jets glided in strained harmony, weaving through narrow valleys where shadow and light fractured like broken glass. Each maneuver demanded a razor's edge. One slip, and the virtual cliffs would close in like a predator's jaws—unforgiving and absolute.

Lyra's breath came in measured rhythm, her mind torn between two truths: protocol and instinct. The kind of instinct that made or broke pilots in the unforgiving sky. She pressed forward, her avatar skimming rocks and mist, threading a needle of blue light between barren stone.

The High-G course simulator demanded everything—no margin for hesitation, no room for compromise. Formation integrity meant survival; every pilot knew it. The mountainous terrain existed to cull the careless, the slow, and the half-committed.

Blaze's voice softened just a fraction, a ghost of grudging respect cutting through.

"Wider turns kill formation integrity."

"Maybe," she fired back, her eyes flashing with fire. "But tighter's how you choke out every bit of life." She dipped beneath a simulated ledge, threading through barren stone with reckless grace.

The map pulsed ahead; the mid-course waypoint was approaching.

The formation groaned under pressure—a fragile thread between discipline and chaos. Every heartbeat pounded like thunder in the sealed cocoon of the cockpit. Static flickered with nervous energy, as pilots balanced in that terrible space between control and collapse.

The digital horizon blazed with storm light, waiting to break.

The sudden, shrill screech of alarms jolted the air inside the simulator pods—a cacophony that slammed into both pilots with violent intrusion.

Harper's fingers flew over the console, her eyes sharp and unblinking as she triggered the simulated missile lock on Lyra's jet. Red warning lights pulsed wildly, bathing the cramped cockpits in an urgent, flickering glow that danced across the instrument panels.

Lyra's breath hitched. Her fingers gripped the joystick with raw intent. She snapped her head to the left, her eyes locking fleetingly on Blaze's lead jet just ahead. But instead of following the prescribed evasive vector outlined in the drilled protocol, she veered sharply off course. Her gut screamed a warning as the tight confines of the canyon terrain closed in relentlessly on all sides.

"Break left! Break left, Hale! Regroup!" Blaze's voice sliced through the comm, razor-sharp and clipped. His jaw clenched so hard that she could almost hear his teeth grinding through the headset.

Lyra's fingers twitched over the controls, but her mind rejected the standard playbook.

"No time for that," she muttered, her voice tight as wire-framed steel.

Her jet pivoted hard. The pod shuddered as she kicked into a corkscrew barrel roll—an impulsive dance against the rules etched deep in her training. In that split second, her instinct overrode every classroom lecture about formation integrity. The maneuver twisted her through the narrow canyon like a flash of fire, the simulated landscape folding dizzyingly around her. It was a desperate gamble to shake the missile's lock by breaking its line of sight.

Her flight path arced dangerously close to Blaze's formation, piercing the thin margin of airspace they shared. The radar displays on both pods blurred into near overlap, and her wingtip brushed the invisible line.

"Damn it, Hale!" Blaze snarled through the comms. "You're way too close!"

Lyra didn't respond; there was no space for words in the rush of adrenaline and tight control. Her palms were sweaty against the harness straps, her muscles taut as a drawn bowstring.

On the operator deck, Sarge hunched forward, his mouth tight as he watched telemetry spike from the near collision. The air felt thick with anticipation, suspended on the knife-edge between disaster and salvation.

The cockpit alarms dwindled, the frantic blaring fading to a tense hum. Then, silence.

A single display screen spun, a missile indicator cycling through colors before settling on cold, final green: "MISSED."

Both jets surged forward, hurtling through the canyon's narrowing gap before peeling out toward the next waypoint. The simulated G-forces pressed the pilots deep into their seats, their hearts pounding wild praises in their chests as the hydraulics rumbled the pods with a steady vibration.

Lyra exhaled slowly and deliberately, trying to uncoil the tension cramped beneath her ribs. She exchanged a glance with Blaze's jet—distant and untouchable behind the shimmer of glass—uncertain whether defiance or relief would hold sway when they finally met again.

"Thought you said to break left," Blaze snapped, frustration scorching the silence.

"Not when zigzagging through a canyon might save your ass." Lyra's chin lifted in hard defiance, fire blazing in her eyes. No regrets.

"Rules exist for a reason, Hale." Blaze's voice dropped low, slicing cleanly. "You just gambled with formation integrity. If you'd clipped me, that flight would have been over."

"And if I hadn't done *something*, that flight would have ended with a simulated explosion," Lyra retorted sharply. "Instinct trumps your checklist today."

The radio flickered with murmurs from other cadet pods. Jazz's whispered voice broke through, filled with breathless disbelief.

"What was *that*?!"

"Risky as hell," another cadet murmured over the comm channels.

Harper's quiet voice cut in from the operator desk, firm and methodical as she logged the incident. "Telemetry flags a near collision. Missile evasion was successful but noncompliant with protocols. An incident report is required. Both pilots are accountable."

The pods' hydraulics ground to a halt, shuddering under the weight of decelerated motion. Blinkering screens dimmed from the high-strain simulation to the sterile glow of lockdown.

Silence settled in the bays like thick fog. The simulator pods held them in stillness, while somewhere in the academy's cold corridors, protocol violations were being logged. The kind that didn't get overlooked. The kind that turned promising cadets into cautionary tales.

Their jets are frozen mid-flight on the displays, still streaking toward the next waypoint while the simulators' internal logs silently etch the near-miss into cold digital memory.

Lyra's breath comes sharp and ragged over the comms. "Missile lock broken. Maneuver shook it off. Sortie's alive."

The cockpit hums around her. Recycled air sits thick in her nostrils, a metallic tang coating her tongue. Her fingers hover tensely over the controls, pulse hammering in her temples as she waits for confirmation. Telemetry blinks back on the monitors—missile missed, threat neutralized.

Relief floods through her. Then something else. Something restless. Harder.

She knows what she did. She knows it bent protocol past the point of reason, that survival instinct had overridden the manual evasive's deliberate pace. But improvisation kept them alive. It always did.

Blaze's voice slices across the channel, taut and cold-edged. "Lyra—damn it, what were you thinking?" His tone snaps like a whip. "You risked the entire formation with that stunt. Did you even consider the consequences?"

"It wasn't a stunt." Her fingers tighten on the sticks, knuckles bleaching white. Low and fierce. "The manual break was too slow. I did what was necessary."

Static crackles. Sarge's commanding voice cuts through the tension like a blade.

"All pilots, stabilize vectors. Regain formation immediately." His fingers fly over the operator panel, and his eyes scan the flurries of telemetry. Red flags bloom across the screens. "Telemetry has flagged a near-miss breach—both pods, tighten protocol now! This isn't negotiable."

Around them, the simulated sky jerks and shudders. The metal arms of the pods groan under strain, matching the violent twists their bodies imagine—mountains, clouds, the knife-edge between control and chaos. Hydraulic pressure presses Lyra firmly into her seat. Sweat slicks her skin beneath the flight suit. Commands echo harshly off the hull.

Adrenaline churns in her veins, numbing the caution she tries to clutch.

Jazz's voice crackles through her earpiece, breath barely a whisper but alive with awe. "What was *that*? Seriously, what the hell was *that*?"

Murmurs ripple through the other cadet channels—shock caught in speechless gasps, adrenaline crackling through the airwaves like electric current. Lyra catches the excitement beneath the worry and feels it like static against her skin.

Blaze's glare would have seared her through the glass. But they are locked in separate pods—worlds apart physically, yet tethered by voice and data streams. His discipline is iron, and beneath it, edge-to-edge tension hums.

Lyra's chest heaves, her ribs straining against her harness. Her jaw clenches tight enough to taste copper. Sweat traces cold rivulets down her temples.

"End simulation," Sarge orders sharply.

The pods respond. The violent gyrations slow. Hydraulics sigh down to a gentle vibration. The cockpit lights mellow to a quiet pulse. The illusion of battle retreats into stillness.

Silence follows, thick and loud in the empty space between them.

Both pilots remain strapped in, their bodies trembling from exertion and the aftershocks of adrenaline. Lyra's palms press flat against the worn controls as she steadies herself. Blaze clenches and unclenches his fists inside the cockpit, his jaw flexing as if he wants to grind every last word into the console.

Jazz's voice, hushed but buzzing, breaks the quiet again. "That corkscrew? You came damn close to taking Blaze with you."

Lyra's smirk is invisible but felt—just a pulse in her chest as the pod settles fully. An edge of ice settles beneath her skin, fierce and unyielding.

"Saved us both," Lyra mutters back, grounding herself against the hum of the cooling machinery. Her muscles remain tense from the wild, forbidden dance of their near-catastrophe.

The fluorescent lights hum overhead, stark and unforgiving. Cadets shuffle into the briefing room adjacent to the simulator bay, their faces flushed from adrenaline, oxygen masks stripped away moments before. The metallic scent of sweat and recycled air hangs thick, mingling with the sharp tang of jet fuel that lingers faintly from the pods.

Sarge steps forward, and the murmurs die instantly. The room snaps to attention—rows of folding chairs creaking under eager weight. His voice cuts low and measured through the tension. "Settle in. We'll review the critical moments from today's run."

The projector flickers to life, casting jagged shadows across the white screen. The near-collision replays in heart-stopping clarity. Two jets thread razor-thin through simulated canyons, wingtip to wingtip, with barely inches separating them. The room exhales collectively as telemetry lines flash across the display, and digital readouts pulse like a racing heartbeat.

Sarge's voice returns, tempered yet firm. "What you saw wasn't a routine error. Formation integrity was compromised. Control was lost—plain and simple. Blame is assigned where it is due."

He bears the weight of those words. Part of him recognizes Lyra's instinct as the kind of split-second thinking that keeps pilots alive. But instinct alone isn't discipline. Command demands both.

From the rear, Harper stands with a notebook in hand and eyes ice-cold beneath furrowed brows. She has investigated three safety breaches in her career and has seen two pilots dead because someone thought protocol was optional. Her words slash into the thick air, clipped and precise. "Cadet Hale executed maneuvers in direct viola-tion of academy protocol. The barrel roll was unauthorized and intro-duced unnecessary risk not only to herself but also to her wingman."

Her gaze shifts to Blaze before she continues with clinical impar-tiality. "Captain Arden failed to maintain formation oversight, allow-ing this breach to escalate. Responsibility is shared."

Whispers bubble through the room like static. Some faces tighten with judgment, while others flicker with reluctant respect. Lyra plants her feet, squares her shoulders, and lifts her chin just enough—a hawk refusing to blink. No apology trembles on her lips; her eyes blaze steady and fierce.

"My move disrupted the missile lock and kept us in the fight," Lyra states plainly, her voice unwavering. The cadets exchange looks—some skeptical, others intrigued by her sheer audacity.

Blaze remains silent, his hands clenched at his sides and his jaw tight enough to shatter. The distance between them hums like a taut wire charged with unspoken conflict.

Jazz leans forward from the middle row. Never one to soften blows, his voice comes out clipped but sincere. "I don't care what the regs say. Lyra's reflexes saved us from a mess none of us saw coming. That roll? That took guts."

Sarge narrows his eyes at Jazz. "Innovation is no excuse. Recklessness endangers us all. Rules exist for a damn good reason."

Harper nods, adding with unyielding precision, "Creative tactics within protocol are mandatory. Breaking it isn't an option."

The room tightens, a collective holding of breath as the debrief spirals toward its close. Formal notes tap out on keyboards nearby. Responsibility traces blot the official record against both pilots—a stain neither can easily scrub away.

The silence that follows hangs thick. Only the soft rustle of gear and the scraping of chairs break it. Eyes flicker between Lyra and Blaze—each locked in a battle neither has verbalized yet. The space between them hums with grudging admiration, simmering frustration, and the fragile tension of unwritten futures.

Amidst the clatter, cadets whisper in hushed tones. Speculation threads through the room like wildfire. The fallout from today's flight settles like dust, refusing to be disturbed anytime soon.

Blaze's boots thud hollowly against the polished corridor floor. He emerges from the shadows near the briefing room, eyes hard and jaw locked tight like a drawn bowstring. The chatter and nervous rustle of flight suits fade into a low hum around them as he corners Lyra against the bare metal wall. The chill of the steel presses against her spine. Fluorescent lights buzz like distant thunder overhead, slicing across his face in sharp angles. His voice drops—flat and sharp, like the hiss of jet exhaust.

"You jeopardized both jets today," he says, the words pressing out like a cold gust. "Not just yourself, but the whole program. Do you understand what you did?"

Lyra squares her shoulders, fists tightening at her hips. Her breath remains calm, but her voice cracks just enough to warn him that he isn't dealing with a scared cadet. The faint scent of ozone and sweat clings to her flight suit, her pulse hammering beneath the fabric.

"I saved us. When the manual would have lost us, I kept us alive. Do you think protocol means anything when a missile is locked on your tail?"

His gaze narrowed, tension coiling in his shoulders like a predator's spring. The corridor felt smaller somehow, the walls pressing in as witnesses to the electric charge between them. A cadet passed, stealing a quick glance before hurrying on. The narrow space isolated the two pilots in something fragile and dangerous.

Blaze stepped closer, his voice low and biting. "Does instinct matter? This isn't some street race. Protocol exists for a reason—our instinct isn't enough to keep us alive out there."

"So what, would you pick obedience over survival?" Lyra snapped, her words sharp-edged with the raw adrenaline still tangled in her nerves. "Try telling that to a flak-shredded wing or a blacked-out engine."

Their eyes locked—his piercing green against her fierce, unyielding brown. Blaze's jaw clenched, and the muscles in his neck stood taut.

The silence after her words hung like smoke, heavy and thick with unspoken truths. Neither looked away. Distant voices faded beneath the weight of their standoff.

Then Blaze pushed away from the wall, the tension peeling from his frame like shed skin. His voice dropped, dark and final.

"You don't get to skate by calling reckless moves 'instinct.' This isn't a guessing game. That's not how this program survives."

His boots echoed sharply as he strode away, shoulders rigid, silhouette stark against the sterile lighting. Before he disappeared around the corner, his eyes flickered back—brief and almost reverent—a grudging respect quickly masked by hardened resolve.

Lyra exhaled, the air tasting faintly of burnt ozone and frustration. The hum of the academy threaded back into her awareness. The corridor settled around her, still charged, as she watched the tail of his retreating form vanish into the shadows.

Jazz cornered Lyra near a row of scuffed metal lockers. Her eyes glinted with awe and mischief. "Alright, spill. Was that pure adrenaline? Recklessness? Or just trying to watch Blaze blow a gasket?"

Lyra shrugged. The tension eased from her shoulders—just a fraction. Her flight suit creaked softly as she shifted her weight, worn fabric stretching with the movement. "Honestly? I didn't think about protocol. I just flew." Her lips twitched into a half-smirk, muscles taut beneath the fabric. "Saved us both, didn't I?"

She hadn't thought through the academy's rigid rules. She hadn't weighed the consequences. Flying was instinct for her—raw and true—and that instinct had paid off. But she knew better than most that the protocols existed for a reason, even if they felt suffocating.

Jazz's laugh breaks the silence—sharp and quick. But her eyes flicker—uncertain and sharp under the harsh fluorescent glare—before she steps closer, her voice lowering. "Bold move. But the fallout is coming faster than you think."

Around them, the locker room pulses with murmurs and sidelong glances. Groups of cadets drift through the haze, their voices dropping to whispers that snake around corners and bounce off concrete walls. A cluster near the main exit bets quietly, syllables punctuating the tension.

"Bet you a prep ration that Lyra breaks Blaze before the day's over," one mutters, fingers tapping a rhythm on a scratched bench.

"No way. Blaze doesn't fold easily."

"They always say that until someone shakes the cage. I heard Lyra's got fire."

Lyra catches snippets—words slicing and soothing all at once. The cacophony settles into a low buzz, admiration entwined with apprehension. Jazz sidles closer, lowering her voice. "Don't let it get to you. You flew like hell today."

Not far off, Sarge steps from the shadows near the corridor, his gaze sharp and measured. He pulls Blaze aside, his voice rough but guarded. "She's wild, no doubt. But that means you have to draw a line. Firm." He glances toward the sim bay, his eyes narrowing. "You saw what she did up there. High risk, high reward—and you can't ignore that."

Blaze understood the weight of that responsibility. Sarge had been steering him since day one, teaching him how to channel volatility into leadership. That is what separates good pilots from broken ones: control, discipline, and the ability to rein in someone else's fire without losing your own.

Blaze's jaw clenches tightly. His green eyes darken for a moment—hard to read—before he nods and turns away. Beneath that rough exterior, a grudging respect pulses like a steady undercurrent, hidden yet definitive.

The locker room hums around them, alive with speculation. The air tastes metallic—gear stacking, uniforms brushing past, and the sharp tang of sweat and lingering jet fuel clinging to everything.

Lyra and Jazz exchange a glance. A spark of understanding flickers between them; no words are needed. The day's upheavals have marked their territory, and whatever comes next, they are ready.

Blaze sits on the edge of his narrow bed, the pale glow of the tablet casting stark shadows across the angular planes of his face. The room smells faintly of ozone and leather—a mix held over from the day's gear, stubborn and sharp against the quiet hum of the night.

His fingers tap the screen. Rewind. Again.

There she is—Lyra—twisting her jet into that illegal corkscrew barrel roll. A precise spiral of defiant grace sends the missile chase spiraling uselessly away. The telemetry overlays blink insistently, logging the razor-thin margins: twenty feet from his formation, less than a second to collision, alarms screaming in digital fury.

The cockpit vibrations thrummed through the speakers. He could almost feel the lever under his palm and the strain in his arms as the hydraulics groaned beneath simulated G-forces. His hands had moved like that once, years ago, before discipline carved the recklessness clean away. Before he learned that control was the only means of survival.

His jaw tightened. Anger flickered—storm-lit beneath calm. She had broken every rule in the book. Every. Single. One. And yet there was something in that reckless precision that grabbed at him, stirring a reluctant fascination. Raw. Untamed. Unmistakable. A pilot who wouldn't bow. A flight instinct sharpened on adrenaline and guts.

He set the tablet aside with a quiet grunt, his eyes fixating on the dark windowpane where city lights twinkled weakly against the cloak of night. Somewhere beyond the glass, the base breathed in its steady rhythm. Engines rested but restless. Blaze's mind didn't rest.

The thread of irritation wove tighter against an unspoken thread of respect. Damn her for flying like she owned the sky. Damn him for wanting to watch her do it again.

Across the compound, light filtered diffusely through the narrow window of the cadet barracks. Lyra sprawled across the rigid cot, her flight suit a crumpled heap beside her. The ceiling stared back blankly—an unyielding canvas for the restless murmur of her thoughts.

Her fingers traced the cracked paint, following the fractures like a map of all the ways she could still fail. The instructors' voices echoed in her mind—warnings steeped in discipline and distrust. Fallout loomed like clouds pregnant with thunder. Every mistake, every rule bent, felt like another notch in the cage tightening around her dreams. The academy would be watching now, waiting for her to crack.

A faint buzz pulled her from the swirl of tension. Jazz's silhouette leaned into the doorframe, framed by the dim amber glow of the hall beyond.

"Not how anyone wanted the morning to go," Jazz said, her voice slipping out quietly, practical and steady, "but you held tight. They'll be watching harder now. You ready to dance their dance?"

Jazz's eyes flickered with a dry kind of fire—a mix of humor and hard-won wisdom.

Lyra snorted, the sound rough but unbroken. "As ready as I'll ever be. That doesn't mean I'm apologizing for saving our skins."

Jazz stepped in, settling onto the edge of the cot, her voice dropping to a conspiratorial whisper. "Just keep your head down. Play smart. Show them you're not just reckless, but damn good at the game. That's how you shift the rules without breaking in."

Lyra nodded slowly, the tension in her jaw softening just enough. "Yeah, I get it. Protocol's a cage, but wrecking the whole thing?" She exhaled. "Not my style."

Jazz smiled, her hand brushing a stray lock of hair from Lyra's forehead—a gesture tender and grounding in the shadowed room. Outside, a low murmur returned to the corridors—the distant soundtrack of boots and muted conversations blending with the steady night. On the wind, the scent of rain teased at the edges of the compound. A coming storm brushed close.

Back in his quarters, Blaze's gaze drifted to the far corner of the room, where a battered flight jacket hung, its leather worn like the map of battles past. His fingers stroked the tablet's cool surface—her image frozen in a perfect moment of defiance. Hands steady on controls. Eyes sharper than any instructor's gaze.

"You flew like hell today," he murmured to the empty room, his voice barely a rasp. "Too fast. Too wild."

The words hung in the silence.

"But damn if you didn't save us."

That flicker, buried under layers of discipline and scars, refused to burn out. He could see it in the frozen frame—the fearlessness, the refusal to accept limits. Maybe she was the partner he never wanted, the wrench in the order he guarded, the one who made the rules feel brittle and small.

But she was the one he couldn't ignore—not now, not ever.

He leaned back, the weight of the day settling into his bones. The tablet screen faded to black as the last light died. Somewhere in the dark, a shift hardened—the uneasy truce between fire and ice, between the rules and the rebel.

The night closed in, and with it, a promise unspoken but searingly clear: the sky ahead would never be the same.

Breaking Points

The sky before dawn is a bruised canvas, streaked faintly with the first promise of light. Blaze stands solid on the edge of the tarmac, the gray concrete slick with last night's mist, a clipboard clasped tightly against his forearm. The wind claws at him, slicing cold fingers beneath the collars of flight suits and across exposed necks, flinging stray hair across faces flushed from early rising and lingering tension.

His voice shreds through the shivery air—sharp, calculated, a blade cutting through murmurs and scattered footsteps. "Formation, now." The call bounces off the empty hangars like gunfire in a canyon.

The scent of jet fuel and cold metal permeates the morning, mingling with the wet chill that seeps into boots and bones alike. Blaze has stood on this tarmac a thousand mornings before. But the smell—it used to mean something different. Years ago, it meant possibility. Now, it means ghosts.

From the gatherings of cadets trickling into stiff rows, Lyra meets Jazz's eyes. The brief exchange is electric, a current sparking in the half-light. Lyra's lips curl into a smirk, but her knuckles whiten on her flight suit as her jaw tenses. The stubborn knot of irritation from yesterday's simulator clash twists deeper. Jazz's response is a whispered tease, low and sly, intended to cut the tension, but Lyra swallows it down, locking the amusement behind her bright eyes.

Somewhere in the distance, a faint clang—metal striking metal—carries on the restless wind.

On the sidelines, two figures stand still, like statues carved from decision and duty. Major Elena Voss is rigid and commanding, even in the shadows, her angular silhouette marked by the sharp crease of a pristine uniform. Lt. Marcus "Sarge" Sullivan is calm and watchful, his eyes scanning the lined cadets with quiet intensity.

Voss's gaze lingers on Lyra and Jazz for a fraction longer than necessary. The High-G program is her credential, her gamble. Blaze's unconventional methods—his tolerance for cadets like Lyra—make her cautious. Everything here carries political weight. Neither officer makes a sound; their silence is louder than any command, a weight that presses on the shoulders of those assembled.

Blaze steps forward, the clipboard's edges rough against his knuckles. He flips it closed. His gaze roves over the line of cadets—cold and precise beneath the glow of dim runway floodlights. The world feels tight here, compressed into sharp angles: boots on concrete, leather gloves scraping straps, engines humming softly, resting in slumber.

"My orders," Blaze's voice cuts through again, clipped and brisk like a metronome, "start with endurance sprints, followed by timed push-ups. Then, the obstacle course. Full run-through. No exceptions. Keep pace. No heroics."

His green eyes flicker from Lyra's steady stare to Jazz's subtle nod, narrowing slightly where rebellious sparks lurk. Without waiting, he lifts his arm in a strict gesture, signaling forward movement toward the obstacle field adjacent to the tarmac.

"The mistakes from the earlier sortie aren't flaws to ignore. They're a warning. You fly as if your choices matter. Let's see if your legs and arms follow suit."

The murmurs ripple briefly—quiet whispers threading through the ranks—but none break formation. Even Lyra's smirk fades, replaced by something sharper. Her jaw tightens against the cold, against something more fragile.

Jazz leans slightly toward her, his voice dropping once more. "Are you ready to run circles around them all again?"

Lyra's smile is a flash—quick and guarded. "Just wait and see."

The shifting wind carries away the last ghosts of night as boots hit the cracked concrete in measured cadence, rolling forward as one, climbing toward dawn. Blaze's silhouette cuts a lone, unwavering line against the growing light, with the cadets arrayed like a battle-ready flock behind him.

The cold air curls between them, carrying the echo of unspoken challenges and the charge of a day that will be harder than the last. This is Astra Flight Command—where steel nerves must outmatch the biting wind, and every breath tastes of grit and gasoline.

No glad handshakes. No hollow greetings. Here, only precise orders and the rough music of readiness. The day beckons with a cruel edge, and Blaze's voice slices through the air, clear and unyielding. "Move out."

Blaze's boots hit the gravel in a steady, unyielding rhythm, setting the cadence for the squad forming behind him. The cold air bit sharply through their flight suits, raising goosebumps beneath the taut fabric. He didn't flinch as sweat beaded along his temples, turning to mist with each exhale in the near-frigid dawn. His clipboard hung at his side, fingers curling around the edges with quiet authority.

"First drill: fifty-meter sprints, three rounds. Move out."

The cadets snapped to attention. Lyra's lungs pulsed, sharp and eager. Blaze was already ahead—muscles coiling and uncoiling with effortless precision, a man forged by countless hours in the cockpit and on the field. The ground thudded under his feet, each stride clean and controlled, never faltering.

At the start line again, he dropped to the ground without hesitation. Fingers splayed, arms straightened. Push-ups began—steady, relentless. The cold air stole warmth, but his sweat was a quiet furnace. He counted each repetition with an internal metronome, cadence locked into a rhythm that brooked no slack.

Cadets followed, some gasping by the second round, muscles quivering. Blaze's form remained perfect. Not one wobble. Not one break. The unspoken challenge hummed in the air: keep up or fall behind.

Next, they stormed the obstacle course—a tangled maze of walls to vault, nets to crawl beneath, and pipes to jump. The scent of damp earth mingled with lingering sweat. Sharp pine needles pricked the air.

Shafts of golden sunlight pierced the clouds, dappling worn wood and weathered steel. Every wall vaulted and net crawled was not just about muscle—it was survival training reimagined for the sky, demanding split-second decisions and relentless grit.

Jazz's face flushed with exertion as she leapt toward the towering wall with a determined grunt. Her fingers slipped just as she reached the crest. A heartbeat's falter sent her sprawling onto the ground. A sharp breath hitched from somewhere in the throng.

Without a pause, Lyra twisted on her heel, her steel-gray eyes locking onto Jazz. She doubled back, her feet pounding hard against the muffled earth. The pulse in her throat thrummed louder as she crossed back through the maze.

Jazz's fingers scraped at the cracked wood of the wall, her muscles trembling.

"You good?" Lyra asked, crouching beside her, her voice calm but edged with something softer beneath the grit. She shot Blaze a brief glance—the silent sting of reprimand laced in that look—and reached out a hand.

Jazz grasped it with warm desperation, gripping tightly as Lyra hauled her up over the edge, muscle and resolve intertwined.

"Got you," Lyra said, her voice low.

But Blaze caught the moment, feeling the undercurrent of defiance beneath Lyra's kindness flicker like a flare. His gaze pierced through the quiet buzz of camaraderie erupting in the otherwise rugged field.

"No," he barked, his voice cracking with authority over the muted chatter. "This isn't about heroics."

The last word clipped like a whip. The cadets halted mid-motion, brows furrowed, breaths catching in their lungs against the cold.

Beneath the bark lay a deeper fear—of mistakes that cost lives, of lessons learned too late. He couldn't afford to let her—or himself—forget that.

Lyra's lips pressed flat, a faint tremor in her fingers as they curled tightly at her sides. Her breathing remained steady despite the biting cold and the ache in her legs. She met his glare with a dangerous calm, her eyes holding their own storms.

Whispers spiraled around them, a weaving buzz of speculation splintering the air. Why was Blaze harder on Lyra than on the others? What did he see that they didn't?

The rest of the run became a blur of grunts, thuds, and stinging muscles. Cadets vaulted, crawled, scrambled, and sprinted—every last ounce poured into the timed course that felt endless under the rising sun. Faces shone crimson with heat and effort. Lungs, ragged with unsteady breaths, tore through the chill.

As the final pounding steps carried them across the finish line, the energy collapsed. Ragged sighs and murmurs rippled through the cadets. Bodies swayed, leaning against weathered rails or each other, hands gripping thighs or chests, attempting to still the wild drum of their heartbeats.

"He doesn't cut anyone slack, but with Lyra—"

"Feels like he's waiting for her to break."

"Or maybe he's just expecting too much."

Lyra wiped a sheen of grime and sweat from her brow with the back of her glove, pushing a stray lock of hair from her face. She glanced over at Blaze, whose jaw was set and brow furrowed deep. He stood like a sentinel at the edge of the field, his eyes holding storms—both in command and something more personal—against the biting cold that clung to them all.

Jazz exhaled loudly beside her, nudging Lyra's shoulder. "You've got a target on your back, you know that, right?"

Lyra's smirk was quick and sharp. "Tell me something I don't know."

Jazz grinned, but the brightness was thin. "Still, maybe he has a reason."

Lyra looked at the course behind them—the scattered footprints, the smudges against the wood, the quiet surrender of the land after their assault. Her mind replayed Blaze's glare and the hardness of his words.

It had never been about heroics.

It was about survival.

And if she wanted to fly through his walls, she'd have to stay sharp, no matter the cost.

The cadets shuffled out of the biting wind, rubbing their hands together as they stepped into the High-G simulator wing. The contrast hit immediately: ozone and disinfectant replaced the tang of sweat and cold air. Fluorescent lights hummed overhead, casting a clinical blue-white glow on polished steel.

Pods rose like metallic beasts from their docks, cables and hydraulic arms clicking and hissing as operators worked the controls with practiced precision. This was where elite cadets proved themselves—where the simulator's crushing G-forces separated the gifted from the exceptional, the survivors from the broken.

Lyra moved through the line with fluid confidence, her helmet tucked under her arm. Her eyes gleamed bright with the morning's adrenaline spark. Her boots clacked softly against the metal floor as she stepped into her pod. The cockpit swallowed her whole, snug and close, but she smiled. The challenge ahead wasn't a threat; it was a game she'd already won.

She reached out, her fingers brushing the cool glass canopy. The pod sealed with a hiss.

Firm controls pressed against her palms, tactile feedback humming softly beneath her touch. Small screens flickered to life, washing her face in a cascade of digital readouts and green indicator lights. The operators cued the pre-flight cognitive checks—quick mental taps designed to calibrate her responsiveness and situational awareness.

Lyra's eyes darted from prompt to prompt. Her mind raced through threat assessments, prioritized targets, and calculated vectors before the system finished its sequence.

From the raised operator gallery, Blaze watched from above, clipboard in hand. His jaw clenched as Lyra's initial scores flashed across the display—reaction times slicing past those of most other cadets, and threat evaluations precise and swift. His fingers drummed an impatient rhythm against the clipboard's edge. Something dark flickered across his face—grudging respect, perhaps, but something deeper too: an urgency to test her limits.

"Load the variable suite Delta-M six and eight into her next run," he ordered, his voice low but sharp enough to cut through the buzz of the room. He made a subtle motion to the technician at the console.

The operator nodded briskly, fingers flying over the keyboard. The pod's hydraulics groaned softly as the simulation parameters shifted, priming for the harder iteration.

Back in the cockpit, the air hummed to a different cadence. The pod's vibrations deepened—a mechanical heartbeat entwined with electronic whispers. Lyra readjusted her harness, her breath steady despite the tightening knot of anticipation coiling in her stomach. The recycled air lingered faintly metallic. She leaned forward, her fingertips trembling only slightly as she dug in.

A distant murmur filtered up from the observer gallery. Lyra's world narrowed to the glow of her displays—a digital battlefield alive with shifting threat arrays and flashing warning sigils.

Blaze shifted on his feet, his eyes narrowed. His presence weighed like gravity. The clipboard in his hands threatened to slip, clenched too tightly as his pace slowed into deliberate stillness. A crease deepened between his brows—years of experience etched into the lines of his face. His expression hardened to steel.

The pods' mechanical whir rang louder now, hydraulic arms adjusting with precise tension, mirroring the rising pulse in Lyra's veins. She instinctively jammed the thrusters forward as the simulated sky twisted and folded at impossible angles, testing not just reflexes but also endurance, wit, and raw nerve.

Around her, fellow cadets sat tense in their pods, their faces illuminated by flickering readouts. Some bit their fingers, while others remained blank-faced in concentration. But all eyes flickered to Lyra's section—half out of admiration, half out of wavering apprehension.

When the operator called out the sequence initiation, crisp and clear, a faint bead of sweat slid down Lyra's temple. Her pulse quickened, and her muscles tautened beneath the flight suit. The pod rocked gently, sensory inputs flooding her nervous system.

Blaze's gaze never wavered from the data scrolling across his screen. His lips pressed into a hard line. He jerked a thumb toward the console again. "Let's see how she handles the real tests."

Lyra's hands danced across the controls, weaving through complex arrays of simulated threats with a rhythm that was half-learned and half-instinctual. The digital battlefield pulsed with artificial chaos, and each moment demanded split-second decisions. Her breath caught as warning alarms buzzed faintly beneath the wet roar of her own heartbeat.

The pod's metallic chassis vibrated against her skin, with pistons flexing with deliberate force to mimic the crushing G-forces that twisted cadet pilots in actual flight. Synthetic gravity pulled at her limbs and spine—a constant pressure she both fought and welcomed.

Outside the cockpit, the operator room glowed with pulsing telemetry and system diagnostics. Lyra's status feeds flickered across every screen in sharp streams of data, and her scores climbed to staggering heights.

Still, Blaze's expression tightened, hardening like cooled lava. His eyes skimmed the readouts but saw beyond the numbers—the lurking dangers of pushing too hard and flying on instinct instead of training. His finger hovered above the intercom button, and the decision weighed heavily on him. What challenge would come next?

A buzzer sounded, and the pod doors sealed tighter, with hydraulics locking in place. Lyra fastened her helmet, and the visor clicked down with a smooth mechanical whisper. Warmed circuitry and recycled air swirled close, mingling with the faint metallic bite of adrenaline lingering in the pod.

With a final glance upward through the glass canopy, the room tilted imperceptibly as the pod moved into position for the loaded run.

Blaze exhaled, sharp and steady. Every risk was cataloged, and every variable accounted for—his world measured in exact calculations, even now. The simulations hummed louder, the high-octane digital storm about to break loose around the determined cadet straining inside.

He tucked the clipboard under one arm and stepped back, his eyes dark with anticipation. Every muscle coiled in readiness.

The sim chamber hummed, mechanical and cold, its steel walls reflecting faint streaks of chilled light as Lyra slid into the cockpit pod. The harness clicked tight against her chest and shoulders, snug enough to press into her skin like a second layer. Her fingers danced over controls already alive with data streams. Ozone and plastic—sterile, sharp, undercut by the tension coiling in her gut.

The operator's voice counted down. Targets flashed to life before her eyes—complex arrays of enemy drones weaving deceptive paths, bursts of false threats bleeding across her display. The challenge ratcheted upward with each split second. Her world compressed to incoming fire vectors, threat assessment warnings flickering in her peripheral vision. The simulators' hydraulics whispered impending shifts in gravity. Her body readied for the surge.

Her heart pounds fiercely. She watches a target disappear behind a phantom cloud—too fast, a trick to bait her. Her mind catches a ghost of movement out of sync with protocol. She abandons the checklist, trusting the sudden gleam of instinct instead.

A twist of the joystick. A sharp turn.

Then a brutal jolt shudders through the cockpit. Red alarms scream across the panels. A warning light flares crimson—simulated systems are failing.

The pod registers a crash.

Lyra's breath catches. For a split second, disbelief floods through her, hot and sharp. Outside the pod, the world buzzes with dry data and murmurs.

Blaze emerges immediately from the shadows of the operator gallery, his sharp gaze locking onto Lyra like a hawk focused on prey. His reputation precedes him—unyielding, merciless, a captain who never lets failure slide. That public rebuke carries weight. Everyone in this bay knows it.

His voice cuts through the charged air: "Flying with your heart gets people killed."

The words slam down in the debriefing area, harsh and public. Around him, cadets stiffen. Some gazes drop to their boots. Others exchange cautious glances. The operators lean forward over blinking consoles, their screens pulsing with telemetry reports—kill ratios, reaction times, and now, failure markers glowing ominously red.

Lyra's jaw clenches. Her fingers twitch near the controls—barely restrained fire simmering beneath her skin. She pulls her gaze from the floor and slings it back across the room, uncaring of the gazes fixed on her like cold spotlights.

Her throat tightens. The words come sharp as a razor:

"Maybe if you actually felt something in the cockpit, you wouldn't fly like you're already dead."

Whispers hitch in the room. Stunned silence cracks the space between them.

The room suddenly feels too small. The hum of machines fades beneath the seismic weight of that retort. Blaze's jaw tightens. His green eyes glitter with something just beneath control—anger? Hurt? The lines on his face deepen, shadowed by memory more than rage.

Without another word, Lyra unclasps the harness with a practiced flick. The straps peel from her shoulders with a soft rustle. Her boots hit the cold steel floor, heavy and deliberate, as she strides toward the exit. The pod's consoles blink insistently. Digital echoes of the clash replay in cold light.

Cadets exchange hushed conversations behind her back—a steady ripple of speculation and divided loyalties threading through their ranks. Some admire her guts, while others are wary of the trouble her defiance marks her for. The faint hum of the hydraulic arms retracting the pods echoes before the door clicks shut behind Lyra.

Blaze stands rigid, his gaze tethered to the flickering monitors for a desperate moment. Then the tension in his shoulders snaps taut. Around him, the simulators' sterile blue light casts jagged shadows across the room—shadows that seem to stretch longer where his control cracks.

The silence holds. Thick. Biting. A silence that hums with unspoken truths and battles far from the safety of simulations.

A door slides open down the hall. Footsteps recede.

The cadence of whispered speculations swells softly—chaos in quiet.

The sim bay exhales a steady mechanical sigh.

The locker room door swings open with a crack like a rifle shot. Blaze's boot slams against the steel locker hard enough to send a shudder through the row. His palms tremble, fists clenched tight enough to whiten his knuckles. The echo reverberates across the metal walls. Sharp silence snaps over the scattered cadets who have been changing out of flight suits. Heads lift. Breaths pause. No one dares to break the stillness.

A step follows—firm, unflinching. Lyra slips inside, shoulders squared beneath her uniform jacket, eyes blazing despite the lingering sting from earlier. Her jaw sets, lips pressing into a hard line. She moves forward anyway, pushing past the fear that claws at her ribs, refusing to let Blaze's authority cage her again. She crosses the room with measured strides, slipping past the lockers as murmurs clamp shut like a drawbridge.

When she stops facing him, her voice cuts clearly through the charged air.

"You punish me for improvising," she says, her voice tight but steady, "but you don't trust a single damn cadet who wouldn't stick to your exact checklist."

The words hang between them, charged with more than defiance. There's a dare—a challenge wrapped in that tremor of frustration. Blaze's mouth twitches, as if the weight behind her accusation forces a flicker of unexpected recognition. Then the tension breaks loose.

"Some mistakes..." Blaze rasps, his voice raw and brittle like crushed glass. "You don't just walk away from them."

His gaze drills into hers, fierce and haunted. For a moment, something cracks behind his eyes—a memory surfaces, sharp and unwelcome. The weight of a past failure presses against his chest, stealing his breath. He pushes it down and locks it away.

"I don't have room for yours."

It's not anger—not the usual burn of discipline or authority. There's something darker, something fractured beneath the surface that shivers through his eyes, the barest flicker of pain laid bare in the jagged lines around them. The words slice through the room's stale air, biting sharper than any reprimand.

Lyra's jaw slackens for a heartbeat before she clamps it shut. The fire in her eyes flickers, faltering, caught off guard by the sudden weight behind his words. The scent of liniment and sweat mingles with faint traces of jet fuel clinging to the stale air. Around them, cadets watch. An invisible bubble of tension presses down on the room.

She swallows. Her anger doesn't vanish; it transforms into something quieter and more complicated: understanding.

Finally, she steps back. The tension drains from her shoulders as the fire in her eyes dulls to a flicker. Without a word, she pivots and moves toward the exit, her footsteps light yet purposeful against the cold concrete floor. Behind her, the metal of the lockers groans softly as the door slams shut.

Blaze remains motionless. His hands shake slightly as they fall to his sides. The echo fades. The room hums with quiet whispers and the soft shuffle of boots, but his world narrows to the afterimage of her retreat and the weight of unspoken wounds left smoldering in the silence.

The sky stretches out, a bruised canvas of thinning light as the sun dips low, reluctant to leave the day behind. At the edge of the barracks, the small recreational field lies quiet, save for the restless whisper of the wind stirring the tall grass like restless fingers.

Lyra sits alone on a battered wooden bench, the coarse grain biting through the worn fabric of her sleeves. Her gaze drifts vaguely toward the distant runway, where amber lights blink steadily through the gloom—tiny sentinels guarding the night's approach.

A tight knot settled low in her chest, squeezing with every shallow breath she dared to take. She replayed it again—the confrontation, the way Blaze's eyes had hardened into something unrecognizable. The last time she had defied him, weeks ago, he had gone silent for days. Cold. Distant. She had wondered then if she had pushed too far. Now, sitting in the gathering dusk, that doubt crept back like frost spreading across glass.

From the shadowed path, Jazz's boots crunched softly on dry leaves as she stepped closer. The familiar cadet laughter and chatter had already silenced inside the barracks walls. She stopped a few feet away, waiting just long enough for the silence to deepen before breaking it.

"You're pushing hard, huh?" Jazz's voice came low and steady, a tether pulled from the tension hanging in the air. "But what if he cracks? I mean, I saw it—he snapped. Worse than I've seen before."

Jazz's eyes flicked away, dark with concern she rarely let slip. It was the tell that gave her away every time—the way she masked her deeper fears with that casual tone, her protective instinct fighting against the walls she had built around herself.

Lyra's fists pressed flat against the rough wood, knuckles paling as her fingers twisted. Her jaw clenched. Blaze's harsh words scraped through her mind like cold steel. She inhaled the cool evening air, a sharp bite filling her lungs, and wondered—briefly and uncomfortably—if maybe Jazz had it right. Had she crossed a line she couldn't come back from?

"I didn't want it to go down like this," Lyra finally admitted, her voice barely more than a whisper. "But he doesn't trust anyone who doesn't follow his damn checklist. And I..." She bit her lip, pushing away the sting creeping up her throat. "I can't be that."

A pause stretched between them.

"Maybe I did go too far."

Jazz slid down to sit at the other end of the bench, close enough to catch the hum in Lyra's silence but careful not to crowd her space. The grass bent low around them, the scent of earth and faint ozone—left-over breath from high-altitude jets—mingling with the cool dusk air. Her eyes caught the fading light, softening as she offered quiet reassurance.

"You didn't." Jazz's gaze turned honest and solid. "Not really. What you did—that was survival. You fought to make it out the other side." She shifted, her boot scraping against the packed earth. "Yeah, it made enemies. It probably ruffled feathers. But it was real. What's out there—" she nodded toward the dim runway lights, "—is not about playing by every rule. It's about who's still standing when the smoke clears."

Lyra exhaled slowly. The tension in her shoulders finally loosened. She let her fingers trail over the splintered bench, grounding herself in the rough, worn texture. The wind stiffened, carrying a low, urgent whistle that wove through the grass like a forgotten ghost.

They sat together then. Words faded into the quiet evening, wrapped in the fragile bubble of shared understanding.

"Sometimes I think he's just scared," Lyra murmured, her eyes locked on the horizon where the clouds gathered shadows like secrets. "Scared of losing someone again."

Jazz's fingers twitched at her side, a restless energy barely held at bay. "Yeah. Me too." She chuckled dryly, the humor a thin veil folding over deeper fears. "But that doesn't mean you step back. It means you watch out for the cracks. Don't let him fall alone."

Lyra nodded. The faintest smile threatened to appear at the corner of her mouth, fragile as a breeze-lifted leaf. Somewhere far beyond, a distant engine droned—a steady heartbeat in the silence. The air tasted faintly metallic, tinged with oil and ozone, an imprint of their world that never quite let go.

After a moment, Jazz pushed herself to her feet. The dry grass snapped beneath her boots. She cast a quick glance toward the darkening barracks and then back at Lyra, her eyes sharp with promise.

"I'm keeping watch," she said simply. "You don't have to face this alone."

Lyra remained seated, her shoulders squared yet slackened by the quiet companionship. Her gaze stayed fixed on the runway's pale, blinking lights—each one a pinpoint of hope in the vast dusk. The wind ghosted through the grass again, whispering faint encouragements that only the night could understand.

The fading light stretched long shadows across the cracked concrete outside the med office. Blaze leaned against the cold wall, a paper cup nestled between his hands—his fingers curled so tightly that they creased the rim. His flight suit shivered in the cold breeze, his shoulders pulled tight as if trying to hold himself together beneath the weight of the day. Beneath the dusk, his skin carried a ghostly pallor, marked by adrenaline spent and battles fought within his mind.

Soft footsteps approached—methodical and unhurried.

Dr. Calloway emerged, her presence calm and steady against the sharp edge of twilight. She exuded a quiet grace, a gentle authority reflected in the measured way she closed the distance. The scent of antiseptic clung faintly to her—a subtle reminder of the clinic inside, where hope and healing battled constantly with injury and loss.

Her eyes settled on him, narrowing just slightly, attentive to the signs others missed. She stepped closer, her gaze flicking to the tight grip on his cup and the tremor in his clenched jaw. She heard the silence that spoke louder than commands.

Gently, her fingers reached out, brushing along his forearm as if measuring the weight he carried. The slight warmth of her touch contrasted sharply with the evening chill. Her voice broke through softly and deliberately.

"How's the sleep, Jareck? Are the nightmares still keeping you tethered to that last mission?"

He stiffened, muscles coiling tight. The name tasted sharp on his tongue, deflecting her concern. His answer came clipped, stripped of vulnerability.

"Fine. Sleep's the same as always."

Calloway's eyes didn't waver, tracing the taut lines of his face and the haunted flicker hidden there. She knew better than to buy into the shield of stoicism.

"You bury it deep, but it's restless," she said, her voice steady as the hum of distant engines over the base. "Fight all you want, but you can't outfly your ghosts, Jareck."

His jaw snapped shut, a hard line etched under his cheekbone. He shifted his gaze away, staring down at the cracked pavement as if willing the shadows to swallow the words whole. The paper cup crumpled in his grip, sweat slick beneath his calloused fingers.

"Those ghosts don't have a seat," he muttered, his voice low and distant. "I keep the line. That's what matters."

"But fighting alone doesn't keep you whole. It doesn't keep you safe."

"Safety's a luxury, Doc." His voice hardened, each word a deliberate barrier. "I'm not here for sympathy. Just clearance."

Calloway's lips pressed into a thin line. She didn't push harder, but her expression softened—a glimpse behind the professional filter to the understanding beneath. The understanding of someone who had watched too many soldiers break in silence.

"Clearance isn't enough if what's under the surface breaks first."

He straightened, his shoulders rising in a controlled exhale. The faintest tremor betrayed the war beneath his calm. Cold wind caught stray strands of his dark hair, tossing them like dull flames against the charcoal sky. His eyes flicked briefly toward the horizon, where the sun's last breath stained the clouds blood-red.

Silence stretched between them. The distant murmur of cadets drifted from the barracks—faint, restless voices in the gathering dark. Twilight smelled of cooling tarmac and salt-tinged air, adding a wild edge to the stillness between them.

Finally, Blaze turned away. Gravel crunched beneath his boots as he moved toward the barracks with measured steps. The half-crushed paper cup dripped a thin line of cold water onto the ground, mirroring the remnants of the man's internal storm.

Calloway remained a moment longer, her gaze lingering on his retreating form. She had seen this before—soldiers carrying ghosts they thought were too heavy to name. She had lost one to silence once. Not him. Not if she could help it.

"Don't let the past own you, Jareck," she whispered.

He didn't look back.

The fading light deepened, swallowing the last hues of sunset as night claimed Astra Flight Command. Near the med office, the hum of evening activity grew subdued. Cadets began drifting back to their quarters, their tired feet shuffling softly, low conversations stitching the air with fragile life beats.

Calloway's eyes remained fixed on the path Blaze had taken, her face etched with quiet concern—the kind worn by those who tend not just to wounds on the skin, but also to those carved deep into the soul.

The wind stirred, carrying away both the remnants of the day and the fragile hope that even the darkest storms might someday pass.

Whispers creep along the barracks' narrow corridors like restless shadows, slipping under doors and curling around lockers. Voices dip to urgent murmurs, sharp with speculation yet wrapped in tight secrecy. Cadets cluster in broken circles, heads bent close, breath puffing clouds in the cold, recycled air.

"Did you hear how Lyra called out Blaze in front of everyone?" One cadet's eyes widen. "No one has ever dared that."

A hand gestures toward a shadowed door where Captain "Ace" Arden stands, guarded by silence as much as by authority.

"She's fire," another replies, fingers drumming against cold metal lockers. "But maybe too much."

"Blaze?" A third cadet leans back, studying the worn hallway tiles. "He's always been untouchable. Today, though? His armor cracked. Just a little."

"Maybe this one breaks through. Finally."

Some pace in tight circles, the faint scent of sweat and fuel lingering like ghosts of exertion. Others lean motionless against lockers, waiting. The murmur travels fast—a wildfire on dry grass. Did Lyra's bold defiance mark her as reckless or revolutionary? And Blaze, steely and controlled—was that flicker of doubt a crack in his iron mask or the first shudder of something reshaping beneath?

"Blaze isn't just some cold legend," one cadet mutters as the group tightens, their voices dropping lower. "There's history—loss stitched into every move."

"And Lyra's like a spark in a bunker. Dangerous."

"Maybe exactly what he needs," someone offers.

"Or a fuse that sets everything off."

"Doesn't matter." A shrug cuts through the tension. "Either way, the air's charged now. We're all waiting to see if they fall or fly."

The walls seem to close in and expand at once, the warmth of collective breath mingling with the sharp tang of anticipation. Outside, the distant drone of the airbase hums low—a steady reminder that the world beyond these barracks pulses on, indifferent to the fragile battles inside.

Deep inside the barracks, Lyra lies sprawled across her bunk, the thin gray mattress cold beneath her flight suit. The ceiling—the same sterile white she has stared at since her recruit days—offers no refuge from the relentless reel turning behind her closed eyelids.

Blaze's clipped reprimand cuts sharper than any cockpit warning siren. His eyes, usually volcanic, hold a fragile flicker that unsettles her just enough to crack open a fissure beneath her defiance. She traces the seam where anger folds into something like understanding, her breath catching as if the walls were closing in. The silence between unspoken words feels heavier than any helmet strap.

Jazz sits sentinel on the footlocker beside her—a quiet presence against the darkened room. Her gaze doesn't waver from Lyra, steady and unflinching, a shield and a challenge all at once. The evening quiet hums around them, punctuated only by the soft scrape of boots passing outside or the distant metallic clatter of lockers shutting down for the night.

Jazz's lips part as if to offer words, but none come. Tonight, silence speaks louder—a shared language between two souls tangled in unspoken storms.

Footsteps stir beyond their door. Bursts of laughter and low voices leak under the frame. Cadets linger outside their own rooms in hesitant knots, the hours stretching late into the night like a waiting game. Some voice their admiration for Lyra's boldness, while others murmur warnings about the invisible hierarchies that govern the program. A few speak of Blaze with something close to reverence, understanding his restraint as the mark of true authority. The tension between factions simmers beneath casual words—those who see change as necessary and those who fear it.

Debate coils in the chill air. Will this storm between ace and cadet end with the program shattered, or will it be forged anew beneath pressure?

Back on her bunk, Lyra cracks her eyes open just enough to catch Jazz's steady presence beside her. A raw edge softens in her chest. Not quite resilience. Not quite refuge. Something in between pulls her taut with every tick of the clock.

Her gaze drifts back to the ceiling, the sterile light now dimmed to a breath. A hush falls deep over the barracks. Sleep remains just out of reach. Her mind unravels and rewinds fractured moments like a broken loop—the taunt, the glare, the flash of pain behind Blaze's eyes that she wasn't meant to see.

A breath hitches. She lets it go, slow and deliberate, as the room fades into darkness and quiet. The rumors buzz just beyond the thin walls, but here, in this fragile stillness, Lyra closes her eyes without letting the night swallow her whole. The tension hums beneath her skin—alive, electric, waiting.

The barracks breathe around them, heavy with secrets and shrouded truths, while on Lyra's bunk, the silence gathers. The night deepens, and the whispered stories settle into shadows that won't soon fade.

The briefing room sat tight with recycled air, its walls lined with muted grey panels. Fluorescents hummed low overhead. Reports lay scattered across the scarred mahogany table, their edges curling under the weight of red ink and sticky notes. Lt. Marcus "Sarge" Sullivan leaned forward, fingers splayed, eyes scanning the charts. Major Elena Voss stood nearby, arms folded, the crease between her brows deepening with each passing moment.

"Day's incidents," Sarge started, his voice calm but edged with concern. "The simulator crash has been flagged again—plus that locker room blowup. Cadet morale is more fractured than usual." He glanced up sharply, catching the thin line forming at the corners of Voss's mouth.

Voss cut in, his voice clipped like a well-honed blade. "Discipline is slipping under Arden's watch. His responses have grown reactive—unpredictable, even. We can't afford cracks in this program—not now."

Sarge nodded slowly, rubbing a line on the report with his thumb. "Nah, he's doing more than just reacting," he muttered, low enough for only her to hear. "Something's off. The cadets—some follow, sure, but more of them flinch when he commands. There's hesitation where there shouldn't be."

Elena shifted her weight, her fingers drumming a restless rhythm against her temple. Her gaze sharpened as if the weight of the decision was a storm cloud threatening to break. "Pairing him with Hale was a gamble. Blaze—he's a veteran of classified ops, decorated but haunted by what he's seen. Lyra is all fire and defiance, the kind that either forges steel or shatters it." She paused, letting the silence settle. "I hoped this would sharpen him and bring the old fire back."

"Or," Sarge countered softly, "it could burn him out completely."

Their eyes met—steel and empathy locked in a subtle power play.

Between them, the lingering scent of stale coffee and electronics thickened the air.

Voss pivoted toward the window, her voice low but stern. "Lyra's spirit is raw and untamed. I see potential, but I wonder if it's a flame too wild. Arden isn't just an instructor; he's a relic of battles fought in blood and silence." Her gaze narrowed. "Is this partnership punishment or redemption?"

Sarge exhaled slowly, his shoulders loosening just a fraction. "Neither, if we handle it right. But right now?" He shook his head. "It's a volatile mix. Arden's haunted, and Hale's defiant. We tread a fine line between harnessing that energy and letting it combust."

Voss picked up a report labeled "Simulator Incident: Lyra Hale." Her fingers traced the margins where telemetry spikes and error codes clustered like warning flares. The paper crinkled under her touch.

"That simulated crash sent ripple effects through the entire cadet wing," she mused. "Instructor reprimands aired publicly—Blaze's sharp words, followed by her retort. The optics aren't good."

Sarge glanced toward the window, where the low sun cast pale light on the airstrip beyond. Engines rumbled in the distance, a restless sound. "He didn't just reprimand her; he challenged the system—his own process. That locker room confrontation?" He leaned back in his chair. "It wasn't just anger; it was personal. Now everyone knows."

"And rumors," Voss added, her voice barely above a whisper, "are circulating faster than we can contain. Distractions like these risk unraveling more than just discipline."

Sarge tapped his chin thoughtfully and then nodded. "We monitor them closely. Keep a tight leash, but not so tight that it snaps."

"Formal corrective measures?" Voss's fingers steepled, and her eyes sharpened with resolve.

"On standby. For now, we will focus on observation and data collection. No knee-jerk responses." Sarge's gaze drifted to the charts before him, his muscles tight under the weight of command. "This is a crucible. If either breaks, it won't just be careers on the line—not with their history and not with what's riding on this program."

Voss stepped back, the measured calculator masking flickers of unease beneath. "I'll pull a scheduled review, tighten oversight, and if either shows dangerous patterns—" She didn't finish; she didn't need to.

"Understood," Sarge replied, rising from his chair. His posture broadened, exuding quiet authority. "I'm keeping both under close watch during the upcoming drills. If something goes sideways, I'll be the first to spot it."

He strode toward the door, his boots clicking softly against the floor.

The faint echo lingered, mingling with the distant rumble of engines warming up on the runway outside.

Voss folded her arms again, her eyes lingering on the empty chair. The room felt momentarily hollow. The dread of what was to come settled like a crease beneath a polished uniform. Outside, the base hummed with the restless energy of cadets unaware that the storm was far from over.

Sarge paused by the threshold, glancing back over his shoulder. "We'll see if the 'Ace' can fly straight," he said quietly, "or if he crashes under the weight." His voice carried both promise and warning.

He stepped out, closing the door behind him.

Voss stood alone, surrounded by the faint scent of jet exhaust and a dossier full of volatile potential. The silence stretched, pregnant with unspoken fears and calculated hope.

###

A jolt pulls him from dreams darker than the night itself. Sweat soaks through the thin sheets, clinging to his skin like a second body he can't shed. Flames lick at his chest—not fire from the sky, but memories scorching his mind, burning paths he thought he had buried. He shoves back the tangled blanket and stumbles into the half-light, his bare feet cold on the barracks floor. The shock of it grounds him, barely.

His hands tremble. Blind, he reaches out until his fingers brush the cold steel of his roommate's locker. Metal. Real. Something to anchor to.

He slides down with a scrape, relief flooding through him as the upright pressure of the cot releases. The hum of the base is distant now—soft echoes through reinforced walls—but inside, the ghostly shadows crowd closer. His breath hitches as the nightmare replays, a broken reel of smoke and silence, lost radio chatter, and a patch fluttering in a breeze he can no longer feel. That patch. That *wingman*. Gone.

From the depths of the locker, he pulls out a small wooden box, rough-hewn but polished from years of handling. The lid opens with a faint creak, revealing the faded insignia of his late wingman—a falcon mid-dive, its wings caught in an eternal, frozen moment. His fingers brush the patch's threadbare edges, tracing the curves like a prayer he never dares to speak aloud. The fabric is rough against his skin, worn soft by too many nights just like this one.

The ache twists in his chest, sharp and familiar. Somewhere in the stillness, Lyra's voice cuts through—sharp as broken glass, unforgiving.

"Maybe if you felt something in the cockpit, you wouldn't fly like you're already dead."

His jaw tightens until the muscles hum. A bitter knot rises in his throat, and he swallows it down hard, tasting copper and shame. She doesn't understand. Or maybe she does—maybe that's what terrifies him. He pulls out his phone, his thumbs hovering over the screen. The draft of a message forms: an apology, a justification, something to bridge the widening silence between them.

Maybe she's right. But feeling means weakness here. I can't afford that. I can't afford to let her see it.

His fingers hesitate. Words catch in the chasm between pride and pain, between the man he needs to be and the man he's becoming in this dark room. The space stretches endlessly, unbridgeable.

Then, slowly, he closes the device. No message goes out into the void.

His palm rests on the patch again. The rough fabric presses against his skin, grounding him in a past he can't rewrite, in a loss that rewrites him every single night. Time stretches in the dim room, the only sound the soft buzz of the overhead light, casting long lines across the ceiling like prison bars. His eyes scan every crack, every shadow, trying to map the weight pressing down on his chest.

A memory flickers—Lyra's fire, her reckless hope battling his cold discipline. The raw edges of her defiance still cut deeper than he'd admit. She pushes him toward something he's not sure he can survive. He wants to protect that spark, but not if it burns him down first.

His throat tightens. The room feels too small, the air too thick, the walls pressing in with the weight of guilt and longing.

"You ever think maybe you're running faster to escape the mess you've made of yourself?" The voice cuts through the silence—a whisper from the past or from his own fractured mind. He doesn't know which is worse.

He shakes it off, blinking the shadows away. The bed calls him back with soft promises of rest, though his mind knows better. He slides the patch back into the box, sealing it away alongside the ghosts and everything he can't change. The wooden lid snaps shut, final and cold.

He slumps against the locker, his breath shallow, the cold metal pressing into his back like a weight he can't shrug off. Lying back under the thin blanket moments later, he stares up through the muted glow, his muscles tense beneath the fabric. The quiet hum of the bass wraps around him like a shroud, familiar and unforgiving. Somewhere in the dark, the chance to reach out flickers—brief and fragile—but the night swallows it whole.

He exhales slowly and shallowly, the breath barely stirring the still air. The decision lingers—silent and unresolved—between him and the ceiling, heavy as the weight on his chest, heavy as the weight of all the things he'll never say.

The Night Simulation

B laze steps into the simulation hangar first, his shoulders squared and jaw clenched—as if bracing against a winter wind. Around him, the low hum of machinery mixes with faint ozone, curling like a ghost around the rigid rows of simulator pods. His green eyes scan the dimness for Sarge on the raised operator platform, the man a steady silhouette bathed in cold blue LED light. Every muscle in his lean frame pulls taut. Even the faint scrape of metal underfoot sounds sharp in the charged silence.

Behind him, Lyra slips through the threshold. Her duffel bag digs into her shoulder, and she shifts it, her fingers tightening around the strap until her knuckles pale. She pastes on a smile—crooked and fragile—the kind that never quite reaches her eyes. Her gaze skims across the milling cadets and instructors beneath the flickering LED strips, catching fragments of whispered conversations and the electric spark of unspoken tension. The cool air prickles her skin. Sweat and electronics cling beneath the surface of her practiced calm, but she forces herself to move forward anyway.

Sarge's voice cuts through the murmurs: clear and unyielding. He steps from the platform's edge, the weight of command settling into his shoulders.

"Alright, listen up. Tonight's objective: a night mission over hostile terrain. Simulated," he adds with a half-smile that does not soften the edge in his voice. "Expect weather triggers. We're ramping up the difficulty. Systems will throw unexpected events your way—stay sharp." His gaze fastens on them both. The words fold into the stillness like stones sinking into still water.

Across the room, Harper's fingers tap rapid code into her console, her eyes flicking between the script and telemetry. Her voice crackles sharply over the comms.

"Sarge, I'm inputting rain and wind anomalies. Adjusting the turbulence vector."

"You're trying to drown us on this run, huh?" Sarge's dry chuckle carries a note of begrudging respect.

"Just making sure you don't get bored." Harper's smirk is nearly audible through the static.

The console lights dance as Sarge punches in the mission variables. The simulator pods respond with a low mechanical whirr. Eyes flicker open beneath the hangar's shadowed roof like waking predators.

Blaze clears his throat and gestures to the laminated checklist clipped to his board. His voice emerges steady and flat.

"Emergency protocols alpha through delta. Confirm comm redundancy. Oxygen systems on manual override. Memory drills locked."

Lyra's gaze catches his across the breadth of the hangar. Her smile firms, but something brittle lurks beneath the surface. She nods, forcing lightness into the gesture. Her pulse hammers faintly in her ears.

Her hands twitch—tremors wrapped in adrenaline that she buries deep beneath practiced bravado.

"You nailed the prep yesterday," Blaze's voice sharpens. "But today, we fly like it counts. No improvisations unless ordered."

Her lips tighten at the edges, a quiet challenge buried in the silence that follows.

Then—a flicker.

The overhead fluorescents hesitate. The blue-white glow stutters and warps for a heartbeat, sending ripples across the polished steel floor. Outside, a storm murmurs its gathering fury beyond the hangar walls. Invisible. Unmistakable. The shift tightens voices and stiffens stances. The academy holds its breath.

The approaching storm mirrors something coiled in Blaze's chest—that same unpredictability, that same pressure building toward inevitable release.

Sarge's fingers snap a final command into the console. He turns to face them, his eyes glinting with command and caution. His hand rises—tall, steady.

He nods sharply.

"Go."

Blaze moves first, each step deliberate and measured. His boots echo with cold authority across the concrete as he approaches the nearest simulator pod. Lyra follows, her stride less controlled, the weight of the moment pressing into her spine. Between them, tension hums—a taut wire ready to snap at the slightest misstep.

The simulators deepen their hum, swallowing the low crackle of their breathing and the rustle of uniform fabric. Neither dares to look away. Every unspoken word hangs between them—charged, electric.

"You think they'll throw a curveball tonight?" Lyra's voice is low and casual, but the flicker in her eyes reveals the spark of anticipation beneath.

Blaze glances sideways, his expression etched with shadows beneath the LED glow.

"If they don't, it's not a real mission."

"So, you've decided then? Color inside the lines tonight? Play by the bloody book?" Her grin flashes sharp as broken glass.

He meets her gaze. His voice clips with restrained irritation.

"I'm flying the mission. You're flying cover."

She laughs—short, rough. "Let's see how long that lasts."

Their breath mingles faintly in the cool air as Sarge calls from his platform: crisp and steady.

"Pods are prepped. All systems green. Comm's open. Everyone's locked in."

The tension coils tighter as they reach their pods. Cold metal brushes their palms. Each breath tastes of electric anticipation, storm clouds, and adrenaline poised on the edge of the night.

Blaze's jaw flexes. His eyes flick to Lyra's steady stare before he moves forward. The invisible line between them crackles like static.

Inside, the simulators await: barren cockpits wrapped in steel and screens, silent sentinels that will witness every command, every hesitation, every fault.

Sarge's final nod sends them home to their pods, the hungering silence before the dive, before they lose themselves in the storm.

###

Lyra slips into her simulator pod, the cold snap of the sealed cockpit door closing behind her. The faint hiss of pressurization fills the air as she settles in, her fingers already dancing over the array of buttons and screens before her.

She checks each gauge with practiced precision, her voice low but steady as she runs through her pre-flight checklist aloud. "Pressure stable. Flaps set to zero. Harness tight." She clasps the five-point strap, pulling it snug until it pins her shoulders in place without choking her. The ritual steadies her—a familiar anchor against the adrenaline buzzing beneath her ribs. Her eyes flick up to the domed screen as she taps the command to boot the visual interface, watching the instruments light up one by one like stars awakening in a dark sky.

In the next pod over, Blaze slides in with the smooth economy of a man born to this ritual. His movements are deliberate, muscles taut beneath his flight suit as he cinches down his harness and locks it with a crisp click. His jaw tightens as his hands fall into a familiar rhythm, reciting emergency protocols under his breath—commands ingrained by years of drills and hard-earned survival.

The simulation hums to life around them.

Above, the dome flickers—a vast night squadron unfolding. Thunderheads roll forward like spectral beasts, swallowing the stars in pools of shadow. A cold blue wash spills across the cockpits, a silky chill brushing the back of her neck even beneath the warmth of her flight suit.

Lyra's gaze shifted involuntarily toward Blaze's pod. Their eyes met—a flash of calculating cool exchanged in the dimness, with no words spoken. Neither cracked the fragile veneer of calm. Her fingers flexed around the stick, knuckles whitening, though her gaze remained steady. The projected runway numbers whirled past their line of sight, scrolling through the pre-takeoff sequence with mechanical precision.

From the operator platform, Sarge's voice cut crisply through the comms, steady and unflappable as always. "Formation set, vector zero-two-one. Maintain radio discipline. Watch for turbulence triggers." Lyra's shoulders relaxed just slightly at the familiar tone.

The drones of machines deepened, systems aligning. Keystrokes and clicks echoed faintly as telemetry streamed in, filling Sarge's console with lifeblood data. Beside him, Harper's fingers flickered across her keyboard—sharp, sure, and unfailingly precise—soldering the mission parameters into the simulator's core.

Lyra shifted, fingers curling tighter around the controls. The headset crackled: "Systems nominal." She nodded, swallowing a swell of anticipation.

A low vibration coursed beneath her—a pulse that mimicked the growl of engines rousing to life. The pod shuddered gently as simulated tires kissed the tarmac, the sensation of taxiing humming through every fiber of her body. She felt the coiled energy, the impending surge of takeoff.

Blaze slid his hands onto the yoke, matching the cadence of the machine's heartbeat. Muscles coiled. Breath steady. His green eyes narrowed, and his body was taut with anticipation. The simulator's quiet growl reverberated around them, melding with the electric charge of the storm beginning to rumble beyond the hangar's walls.

"Ready to dance with the dark, Captain?" Lyra's voice slipped through the comm, edged with challenge and eagerness.

Blaze's reply was clipped, almost reluctant, but dry humor flickered beneath the surface. "After yesterday, I'm just bracing for trouble."

"Don't get soft on me," she shot back, a wry smile tugging at the corner of her mouth. "Or maybe you just don't like flying blind."

He didn't retort immediately, his eyes fixed on the dimming runway ahead. His jaw clenched so tightly that the muscle twitched beneath his skin. The tension between them was a taut wire sparking in the dark—uneasy, charged, but undeniably alive.

Sarge's voice broke through again, the edge of command tempered with quiet assurance. "Wind calm. Altitude twelve hundred. Proceed to hold pattern Alpha. Remember, our simulators replicate real combat stress—weather and system failures come unpredictably. Stay sharp."

Lyra's fingers tapped rapidly over the controls, coaxing a response from instruments that felt suddenly too synthetic, too brittle under her touch. The world beyond the dome darkened further, heavy clouds swallowing the faint glow of distant stars and casting the cockpit in shadowed cobalt light.

Blaze let out a slow breath, the briefest easing of his rigid posture. His voice sliced through the static-filled air. "Maintain formation tight. No surprises."

Lyra swallowed the flare of rebellion tightening her chest. She nodded, though he couldn't see it, and fell into step behind his lead. Yet beneath the outward calm, a restless spark flickered—promising that the storm wouldn't just come from the sky.

Blaze cut through the dim blue haze of the simulation dome. "Maintain heading zero-seven-five. Mountain pass dead ahead." His voice fell like metal bolts. "Stay in tight formation. Watch your six."

Lyra's fingers tensed on her controls. She acknowledged, sharp and clipped: "Copy, lead." Beneath the calm words, her instincts clawed at her to veer off the scripted path, to trust something beyond the algorithm's narrow boundaries.

Outside the dome, digital lightning fractured the dark sky—sharp white cracks that flooded the cockpit with stark, icy light. The simulation tightened. Gusts rattled the pod like fists hammering steel, and turbulence escalated faster than any training run. The aircraft twisted with a ferocity that set her teeth on edge. The usual hum deepened into a growl, and adrenaline flooded her veins, electric and sharp.

She leaned into the mic, her voice low but alert. "The storm's kicking harder than the last run. Lightning strikes look off-pattern." The synthetic rain drummed against the pod's shell. Each thunderclap echoed through the cramped space like a second heartbeat, erratic and wrong.

Blaze's fingers curl tighter around the stick, the leather creaking under the strain. White-knuckled, he studies the instruments, reading the flicker of incoming data with suspicion. "Sarge is cranking this," he warns, his tone threaded with concern. "Stick to formation, Lyra. No improvising."

She nods, swallowing back the restlessness coiling in her chest. Her smile is quick and tight—a mask for the electric burn in her fingers as she shapes her flight to match his line.

Then the first hiccups ripple through the systems. Gauges hesitate. The HUD winks out for a sliver of a second, then blinks back to life, flickering like a faltering pulse. Static skitters through the comm line—an unwanted hiss beneath their voices. Harper's tone cuts through the crackles, shaky but controlled. "Patchwork on feedback loops. Hang tight. I'm rerouting systems now." Her fingers tap across distant keys, the rhythm sharp and urgent.

Lyra's breath catches as a searing lightning flash arcs across the dome walls, painting the surface in blinding white. Instrument readouts stutter and shutter. Screens phase into ghostly glitches. Both pilots press deeper into their harnesses, every muscle tightening in anticipation of what waits beyond the next flicker of light.

"How's it looking on your end, Hale?" Blaze's voice cuts through the static, calm but taut.

"Too real." Lyra's eyes skim the faltering displays. "The lightning's as if it's trying to rewrite the storm's script. It feels like the sky might break before we do."

Blaze's jaw flexes, his voice hardening. "Keep formation. Trust the flight plan, not the lightning's tantrums."

"Right." Lyra breathes it out, her fingers steadying on the controls. But underneath, every instinct claws at her to break free, to find the rhythm of the real sky instead of this carefully constructed lie.

The cockpit's artificial night deepens, with bluish shadows carved by intermittent glare. Each flash throws a fractured landscape onto the curved dome—peaks and valleys whispered into existence by light and shadow. The storm grows wild, a beast released. In the thickening air, the line between pilot and machine blurs further, eroded by failing instruments and crackled communications.

Blaze's voice lowers, clipped but edged with something fiercer. "Eyes ahead. Formation is life." His tone hardens assurance into command—a tether in the dark swell.

"Copy that, lead." Lyra's voice folds into radio static. "Locked in. Watching every shadow." The words rasp into the simulated storm, a fragile vow tossed between flickering screens.

Another blast of white light floods the dome—merciless and cold. The instruments quiver, and the screens flicker in final, stuttered flashes. The pod vibrates—a humming growl underscored by the distant roar of thunder vibrating through the metal ribs of the hangar.

In the sudden lull that follows, silence buzzes with electricity. The entire world pauses, holding its breath through the stillness before the next command.

The lightning flash sears across the dome overhead—a sudden slash of white-hot fury. Then, power surges through the hangar and snaps out.

Darkness swallows the cockpit.

Lyra's pulse hammers as her HUD flickers. Once. Twice. Then it goes opaque black. The silence that follows is worse than the surge—a dead, suffocating void where the electronic hum used to live. Cold backup indicators sputter to life around her, casting feeble halos across her gloved hands.

Beside her, Blaze's pod mirrors the blackout. His displays collapse into darkness. The electronics shutter into sudden silence.

Blaze exhales sharply, a flicker of muscle tightening in his jaw. His voice remains clipped, the razor edge steady even as adrenaline coils beneath his ribs. "Loss of instruments. Protocol Alpha. Switch to standby systems. Visual navigation only. Lyra, confirm."

His words cut through the static-laced comm, firm and controlled—the kind of control born from muscle memory and dozens of simulations before this one.

"Artificial horizon is dead," Lyra replies, fingers darting across tactile switches. The metal is ice-cold beneath her palms. "Nav readouts are offline."

She cycles through emergency recovery routines, her thumb pressing button after button. Each one responds with failure.

"Auxiliary power is failing. Backup radar is flickering. Stabilizers are off nominal."

Her voice held steady, but her knuckles whitened on the controls. The confined space of the cockpit suddenly felt smaller, and the air felt thinner. She bit down hard, refusing to let the tremor break through.

Across the hangar, Harper lunged toward the master control console. Her fingers flew over the keyboard, slamming knobs and toggles in a desperate rhythm. Sparks spattered and crackled in brief electrical bursts. The air reeked of ozone and burnt circuitry—acrid and choking.

Harper's voice boomed into the handset, but static gnawed at her commands. The words splintered and fractured across the comms, barely coherent. "...restoring power... standby grids are failing... repeat, standby grids... patching through... hold..."

The storm's severity pressed against the base's systems like a predator. Rain hammered the steel roof in a frantic pulse, and the interference it created for their electronics was relentless and unforgiving.

Blaze adjusted his headset, straining against the broken signal. Then, through the ragged static, Sarge's voice cut in—gruff but steady, the cadence of a man who had flown through worse. "Fallback vectors to zero-six-zero. Altitude—maintain two thousand feet. No visual markers. Use the edge of the cloud cover for orientation."

But Sarge's instructions drifted in and out, caught in the storm's merciless grip. Thunder shifted from distant growls to a near roar. The hangar's metal girders rattled, singing an anxious song. Backup floodlights snapped on in a pale, reluctant glow, stretching long, jittery shadows that crawled across concrete and steel like living things.

The chill inside the pod seeped through Lyra's flight suit. Her fingers, numb, danced over the switches as she called out each status check. The confined space pressed in—just her, the harness straps cutting into her shoulders, and the vast darkness beyond the canopy.

Inside both pods, panic bubbled beneath taut control.

Each breath sounded loud in the suffocating cockpit. The once-fluid mechanical heartbeat of the simulation stuttered. The pods shuddered violently, jolted by a false "impact" alert screaming through Blaze's console—an eerie mimicry of disaster. The warning howled, false but insistent, a phantom collision hanging in the charged air.

Both pilots froze, shoulders locked, gripping the harness straps as the memory of real crashes lingered sharp in their nerves—bone-deep and unforgiving.

Outside, the storm's growl pressed in, steady and menacing. Inside, the only sounds were racing heartbeats and shallow breaths.

"We're flying blind," Blaze muttered, his voice rough. His eyes were wide in the gloom, knuckles white on the stick, every muscle coiled to react. "Stay with me."

Lyra's gaze hunted the darkened dome, catching ghostly impressions of the simulated moonlight brushing faint silhouettes on the terrain below. No instruments. No HUD. Just shadow play on the canopy's curve—an ocean of darkness punctuated by the stench of fear and sweat clinging to her suit.

She bit back a surge of frustration, her muscles tensing as she ran through every mental checklist she knew. Her breath came quickly, tasting sharp in the cold air.

"Systems failed," Lyra said quietly, her voice steadying despite the tremor beneath it. "Backup comms are noisy, but I'm cycling manual overrides now. Stabilizers are cold... but thrusters are responding."

She glanced toward where Blaze's silhouette should be—barely visible in the darkness. "I'm still here."

Sarge's voice splintered again through static, the cadence fractured but urgent. "Vector zero-six-zero... altitude two thousand... contingency procedures active. Repeat, contingency procedures. Look for visual markers. It's your only guide now."

"Visual," Blaze echoed under his breath. He lifted his chin, the stark flicker of cockpit indicator lights a dim third eye blinking to life. "Eyes sharp. Trust your gut. It's all we've got."

The clamor of emergency flickered, blindsiding their senses. A spike of electricity whined, then dropped. Nervous energy sparked in the confined space. Outside, the storm wailed through the concrete ribs of Astra's hangar, water thrumming against steel and glass like a frantic pulse.

Lyra shifted, her palms cold and sticky as she gripped the controls. Her muscles coiled like springs beneath her flight suit, ready to snap.

"Harper—status?" Blaze called over the crackling comms, his voice a low anchor.

"Patching power grids... still flickering," Harper's reply burst through, grit threading through her tone. "Backup generators are struggling to hold. Almost stable—maybe a minute."

Blaze nodded, though no one saw it. The hum of the pods deepened, shifting beneath them. The tension inside the cockpit thickened—a living thing between them, taut and electrified.

Under the staccato boom of thunder, they sat in suspended silence.

Time distorted. Seconds stretched thin, filled with the soft shuffle of breathing and the storm's distant roar. Harnesses grated against collarbones. Sweat prickled at the skin beneath their helmets, cold and clammy.

Then, just as the first faint pulse of power winked through the electronic fog, the pods jerked sharply.

A phantom tremor resonated bone-deep.

False impact.

Blaze's throat tightened. His eyes flicked to all sides of the console, the ghost warning blazing with accusing insistence. His jaw clenched. Somewhere beneath the steady storm, instinct screamed—this was the moment when steel nerves met raw survival, where training bent or shattered.

For a long breath, the hangar hung in quiet suspension.

Pilots bound by protocol and peril, shrouded in heavy night and tangled in cold, electric thunder.

The distant rumble faded to a murmured heartbeat as the storm outside wrapped Astra Flight Command like a coil.

And in the dark, harnessed tight, they listened.

Only to the storm and breath.

Blaze's voice cut through the blackout like a blade—firm and low. "Keep my heading. Use visual cues. Remember this terrain. Eyes sharp." His fingers hovered over the stick, searching the dark cockpit for any flicker of life. Nothing. The screens stared back, dead and empty.

Lyra's breath caught in her throat. A cold twist curled deep in her belly as her eyes snapped to a shifting shadow beneath the moon's pale glow. Instinct prickled sharply against the silence of the dead instruments. The projected moonlight spilled over jagged peaks in the dome's faint glow, but there—a dark ribbon lurking just beyond the display's edge. Real. Deadly.

Her hands twitched. No hesitation. She pulled hard into a bank, carving through the virtual night without waiting for clearance. The pod tilted sharply. The mechanical hum surged in her ears as the simulated ground rushed beneath them, close enough to taste metal on her tongue. She twisted away from Blaze's line, forging a new path through the dark.

Blaze's jaw clenched. His mouth opened—ready to bark a sharp reprimand. Then the pod's external camera flickered on. There it was: Lyra's evasive move, clean and precise. Suddenly, his display screamed an impact warning—a false alarm triggered by their near miss. His breath caught. Muscles tensed. Recalibrate. Reroute. Survive.

The conflict twisted in his chest—trained instincts demanding strict formation warred against the undeniable fact that she had seen what his instruments had missed. Protocol crumbled under the weight of split-second judgment. Trust, fragile and electric, flickered between them.

Across the comm, Lyra's voice was tight but clear. "Shadow caught a slant of moonlight. Ridge line unlit in the dead zone. Had to break formation. Eyes on the ground, not screens."

Blaze's fingers tightened on the stick, his knuckles white. He swallowed the reprimand lodged deep in his throat. The stale tang of overheated circuits mingled with ozone from the distant storm. Lightning flickered across the cramped cockpit, casting sharp shadows on her tense features.

"You shouldn't deviate without comms," he said, his voice low but edged with tension.

"Didn't have time to ask." Her hands moved expertly over the controls, coaxing the pod away from unseen danger. "That shadow was a blind spot. Follow protocol? We'd be curling over a ridge." She glanced at him, her eyes sharp and scanning. "Controls are responding. Terrain's too close."

The low hum of failing electronics filled the space between them. Outside, the projected moon fractured through tempest clouds, shadows deepening in the dome's curvature. Wind from the storm whispered menace through the hangar's walls.

His voice tightened, steeling into something new. "Alright. Eyes sharp. Lead the way."

Lyra's nod was invisible, but the cadence of her breathing steadied, syncing with the rhythm of the pod's subtle tilts and hums.

The last vestiges of instrument light flickered and died. Blaze leaned forward, jaw clenched, watching as Lyra guided them through the unseen labyrinth carved by instinct and raw nerve. Lightning illuminated her face—flushed, focused, alive with adrenaline.

No words filled the static-burdened comms, just the unspoken acknowledgment that this flight now depended on more than protocol. It relied on second sight and the kind of courage that shattered the safety net of procedure, binding them together in fragile, urgent trust.

Lyra's voice cut sharply through the crackling comms—a lifeline. "Descending low over the eastern ridge. Shadowed valley below—knife's edge between those tree lines. Bank left three degrees."

Blaze's hands snapped to the controls. Match her rhythm. Follow.

For the first time, the pilot who usually carved the sky with clipped commands relinquished that steady grip. He had built his reputation on control, on precision, on being the one others trailed behind. Now he was the one trailing. The sting of it—pride clenched tight—hummed beneath his skin, but he pushed it down. Survival first.

"Banking three degrees, matching throttle," he confirmed, eyes flicking between the scant visuals and the subtle dance of her maneuvers on the shared radar. "Visual confirmation on shadow contours."

A click. Lyra trimmed her ailerons, the mechanical whisper almost swallowed by the storm raging outside their sealed pods. "Speed is holding at two hundred knots. Flaps up. We're skimming the ridge shadow now. Eyes sharp for spikes."

She paused. "I have visual on the moonlight bouncing off the treetops."

Lyra relied on instinct—built from years of adapting when systems failed, when instruments went dark, and only sight and feel remained. That is what made her dangerous. That is what made her dangerous *to him.*

Blaze slid his fingers across the panel, nudging the flaps. Metal responded with soft clicks. "Flaps set. Airspeed steady. Following your glide path." His gaze tightened on the ghostly shapes shifting beneath them: silvery moon against the ink-black valley floor. One wrong turn meant disaster.

Thunder boomed. It rattled the pods and shook their seats.

Alarms wailed sharply and persistently, slicing through the static of faltering instruments. Lyra's voice never wavered—a steady beacon cutting through chaos.

"Prepare for glide approach. Count with me. Three hundred feet, descending." Her words came clipped, each one precise. "Two hundred. Slow descent. Trim adjustments coming. Bank slight left. Adjust airspeed down by five knots."

Blaze exhaled slowly. His shoulders knotted tight, muscles coiling with tension. This was control inverted; his usual role folded into necessity.

"Watch the dim tree line ahead," Lyra continued. "It marks the edge of the landing strip. I see a faint glimmer of runway lights struggling through the storm."

"Reducing throttle," Blaze responded, his fingers trained and precise. "Matching a five-knot decrease. Banking left per your call. Adjusting trim."

The pod hummed around them. Servos whispered. Simulated wind shuddered through the fuselage.

"Altitude down to one hundred feet. Visual markers aligning." Lyra's call pulled taut like wire. "Fingers ready for flare."

Blaze locked his eyes onto the dim glow flickering across the dome, scrabbling to read the texture and contour. His focus sharpened. The instrument blackout fell away, replaced by tactile sensation—the pulse of the stick beneath his palms, the whispered hum of servos, and gravity's pull mimicked with cruel fidelity.

"Flare initiation at fifty feet," he said. "Controls steady. Hovering on your count."

Lyra's breath caught in the comm channel. Measured. Sure. "Thirty feet. Twenty. Prepare for flare."

Thunder rolled closer, a low rumble shaking their sealed world.

"Hold steady," she whispered.

"Ten feet. Five."

Blaze's hands responded in perfect harmony, muscles coiling, eyes narrowing against the sparse moonlit blur. "Jet steady. Throttle down. Flaring now."

"Touchdown imminent."

The pod lurched, pressing them into their harnesses with brutal intimacy. Impact. Momentum. The weight of physics made real.

"Landing sequence complete," the simulation intoned, cold and unyielding.

Silence swallowed the space between them. Outside, the distant thrum of thunder faded to a low growl—a reminder of the real tempest pounding against the academy's walls.

Their rapid breaths filled the dark cocoon of the pods. The electric hum receded, fading.

For a fleeting second, their eyes met through visors fogged with sweat. In the dim glow of emergency lights filtering through the pod doors, something passed between them. Not protocol. Not procedure. Understanding. A truce forged in survival and trust.

"Never thought I'd see the day you'd fly that close behind me," Blaze admitted. His voice was rough, but beneath it—something else. Reluctant respect, maybe. Or something closer to awe.

Lyra's mouth twitched upward into a smirk. "Maybe you just needed to learn how to follow for once."

"Don't push your luck." His warning softened at the edges, the words catching on something unspoken.

"No promises," she shot back. Her tone was lighter now, but her eyes remained steady, locked on his.

The shared silence between them filled with something electric. Fragile. Utterly alive.

The pods powered down around them. The storm outside swelled. The quiet between them swelled in tandem.

Lyra's hands dropped with gravity's pull, steady on the controls. She guided the pod low over the shadowed valley, her voice sharp against the dying hum of the systems. "Flare in two. Steady. Trim left—small correction." Her eyes darted between fractured moonlight and the faint glow of instruments long dead, tracking shifting patches of shadow beneath them. The runway on the dome above was barely a sketch in bleach-white, an afterthought swallowed by darkness. Every movement leaned on raw instinct. Every breath she forced through gritted teeth was a prayer.

Beside her, Blaze mirrored her inputs with grim precision. His fingers tightened around the throttle and stick as if they were tethering him to survival itself. The pod shuddered violently, simulating the jolt of touchdown. His spine pressed hard into the molded seat, and his jaw clenched as the system registered their heavy but controlled landing; the nerve endings in his hands buzzed from the feedback.

A dull clang echoed through the cabin.

Then—nothing. The systems quieted, and alarms cut out in an abrupt, hollow silence.

For a long moment, all that remained was their ragged breathing, limbs slick with sweat, and helmets abandoned like discarded armor. The faint smell of recycled air mixed with the sharp tang of overheated electronics lingered in the tight space, wrapping around them like an invisible shroud.

Lyra's shirt clung to her back, soaked at the collar. Her hair matted against her forehead, strands slick with exertion. Relief flooded through her—raw, physical, and almost painful in its intensity. She had made the right call. The pod's instruments had failed, but her instincts had not.

Blaze sat motionless for a beat, his damp hair tousled against his scalp, eyes narrowed beneath creased brows. His chest still heaved. Something shifted in his expression—not quite a smile, but a loosening of the tension that usually defined him.

The simulation doors hissed open with mechanical precision, flooding the hangar floor with harsh, pale emergency lighting. Outside the pods, the storm raged on beyond the hangar walls—thunder muttering like a steady drum beneath their rattled heartbeats, and wind patterning against metal in a relentless rhythm.

Sarge's broad frame appeared first. His face was hard, etched with years of command, but the edges softened as he took in the sight of both pilots intact. Relief flickered across his features before discipline reasserted itself. He had seen the telemetry spike; they had broken protocol. And yet—they had lived.

Harper followed closely behind, her hair wildly tousled from frantic console dashes, and her eyes bright with urgency. She barely paused before diving into the rapid-fire debrief at her console, her fingers dancing across the touchscreen as she pulled up telemetry and play-back clips. The cadence of tapping was relentless—staccato and alive.

"Instinctual sight flying and real-time teamwork saved you both," Harper said, her voice clipped yet tinged with unguarded respect. She tapped a series of frames, highlighting the tight arc of Lyra's evasive banking maneuver. "Had you adhered strictly to protocol, the system's failure would have meant a catastrophic crash."

Lyra didn't flinch. Her gaze remained steady on the flickering images. "I trusted what I saw, not what the instruments said." Her voice was rough around the edges but firm. The weight of hours spent battling twitchy displays and fragmented comms hung heavy between her words.

Blaze's shoulders slackened for the first time in hours. He ran a hand through his damp hair, his voice rough but low: "You made the right call. It took guts to break formation."

There was no flourish, no praise exactly, but something raw and new threaded through his tone—something heavier than grudging respect. For the first time since the blackout, the crackling tension between them eased. The usual spark of challenge softened, giving way to fragile relief and something akin to understanding.

Sarge exchanged a glance with Harper, a silent conversation passing between them. The shift was palpable. Lyra had moved from liability to asset in a single, hard-fought moment. Sarge's mind already ran through scenarios—training reroutes that included sight-based navigation and contingency drills building on instinct rather than a checklist.

Lyra exhaled, her fingers curling around the edge of the pod's console as she met Blaze's eyes. "Why didn't you call it?"

He shrugged, his voice tightening with the weight of years. "Because sometimes, the rules don't save you."

Her grin was ghosted but real, a flicker across her sweat-stung skin. "I'm glad you found that out before I crashed us both."

"Don't make me regret it." His words came out clipped, but the edge softened beneath the weight of the moment.

They unstrapped with slow deliberation, their muscles humming with exhaustion and the fading burn of adrenaline. Legs swung over the edge of their pods, and their feet found the cold steel floor, grounding them once again in the harshly lit hangar.

The storm raged on beyond, its patter against the walls a relentless reminder—out here, in the dark spaces between lightning and thunder, survival was never guaranteed. But for now, inside the brittle calm of the simulator, they had lived to meet each other's eyes once more.

Sarge stood waiting beside the pod exits, emergency lights casting his weathered face in sharp relief. His gaze swept over Blaze and Lyra with the deliberation of a man accustomed to reading what people wouldn't say. The hangar still thrummed with residual tension—the kind that clung to the skin like a static charge.

"Who made the call to break formation?" His voice dropped low, calibrated but edged with something that might have been concern. "I need to know you were clear-headed. This wasn't reckless."

Blaze's shoulders stiffened; his green eyes narrowed to slits. Lyra's gaze slid to the floor, her lips thinning like a wire ready to snap. Neither spoke. Sarge's fingers drummed against the clipboard at his side as he cataloged the fatigue etched into their faces, the tightness bracketing their eyes—the weight of choices made in fractured seconds.

The weight bore down on him too. He had trained them to trust instruments, to follow protocol. But out there, protocol had become their cage.

Harper approached then, her strides swift and purposeful, a slim tablet glowing in her grip. The faint bite of ozone trailed behind her as she connected at their side, her voice crisp but threaded with rare respect.

"Telemetry confirms that those instrument failures weren't a simulation glitch." She swiped through the footage—frozen frames flickering with darkness, HUD screens going black, and lightning fracturing across the dome projections like ruptured capillaries. "External electrical interference from the storm compounded everything. Your instruments failed you both."

She paused, allowing that to sink in.

"Your sight-based piloting prevented a crash. It was instinct where instruments couldn't reach." Her eyes moved between them, frank and measured. "Lyra's evasive banking maneuver pulled you clear of that hazard."

The academy trained pilots to trust dials and readouts, but it had never accounted for storms that rewrote the rules.

"I trusted my gut," Lyra said quietly, her eyes fixed on the screen where moonlight caught the edge of a shadowed ridge. Her voice came bare as bone. "I saw it and banked out."

Blaze shifted his weight; his jaw clenched tight. Silence dragged on, thick as the room seemed to shrink around them, every heartbeat pounding loud enough to hear.

When he finally spoke, the words came slow and deliberate, stripped of their usual edge. "You made the right call."

The admission hung between them, stark in its rarity. Not praise—not from Blaze. Something harder won. Something that mattered.

Sarge exchanged a brief glance with Harper. The shift was unmistakable. Lyra was no longer the wildcard threatening protocol; she had become an indispensable asset, her instincts a lifeline when everything else failed. Both of them made their notes—new lines warming their assessments, trajectories already recalculating.

Sarge's mind was already turning, plotting how to fold sight-based contingencies into the training matrix and how to adapt without abandoning discipline. The day's lessons had cracked something open in the program—something that needed to change.

Lyra lifted her eyes, locking gazes with Blaze. The hard edge softened from her expression, folding into something fragile and raw. Relief moved through her posture—a quiet surrender to recognition earned not from following rules, but from both of them walking out alive.

"I thought you were going to tear me apart," she murmured, half a breath.

Blaze's mouth flickered, the ghost of a reluctant smile playing at the corner. "Not this time."

Undeniable Gravity

The first shards of sunrise sliced through the haze, casting a pale gold flare over Astra Flight Command's sprawling tarmac.

Cadets clustered like steady knots of determination, their flight suits stiff and dusty from the night simulation. The sharp tang of jet fuel laced the cold air, mixing with the crisp bite of morning frost still clinging to the concrete. Each cadet carried the familiar weight of a standard-issue emergency pack slung tight against their backs, with two ration bars tucked into vest pockets that glinted like promises of meager sustenance.

Above them, Lt. Marcus "Sarge" Sullivan stood firm on the raised platform—a steady silhouette against the awakening sky. His eyes, weathered and watchful, swept over the stiff ranks beneath him. Beside him, Major Elena Voss exuded command. Her posture was precise, and her gaze was unyielding as the final light caught the edge of her sharply pressed uniform.

Sarge's voice cut through the morning chill, deliberate and authoritative. "Cadets, listen up." His words hung in the quiet, every syllable ringing with ironclad clarity. "This drill is mandatory. You'll be airlifted in pairs to separate wilderness coordinates. No contact with base until morning. Navigation relies solely on the supplied maps and compasses. Supplies are fixed. Ration strictly. No exceptions. Every deviation counts against your team's evaluations."

He paused. The weight of the rules settled like frost on bare skin.

Major Voss stepped forward, her voice sharp and carrying. "We expect absolute adherence," she said, her eyes sweeping over the cadet line. "Survival is about discipline under pressure. Breaking protocol isn't just a mark against you—it endangers the entire unit." Her words were a chill breeze that slipped beneath the ranks and into the marrow.

Amid the steady shuffle of boots, Blaze and Lyra lingered at the back of the formation, the last pair called. The tension between them hummed beneath layers of fabric and gear. When their names finally pierced the morning calm, their eyes met—a hard, electric current sparking in that swift exchange. Neither broke the gaze. Neither spoke. The silence thickened with unspoken remnants from the night before.

Other cadets moved forward, their steps purposeful as they climbed the metal steps onto the waiting helicopter. The rotors thrummed low and menacing, a beast awakening. Dust and fragmented gravel leaped into the air, stinging their eyes and coating their skin with a gritty film.

Blaze's boots struck the aluminum floor first, his body taut under the gear, shoulders squared against the relentless roar. Lyra followed, her breath steady despite the surge of adrenaline coiling in her chest. The cabin vibrated beneath them—a steel cage lifting from the earth. The ridge and runway shrank beneath a veil of swirling haze and spilled light.

Outside, the land unfurled, with rock-strewn clearings guarded by dense knots of evergreens, their shadows deep and tangled. Jagged mountain silhouettes hovered on the horizon, etched sharply against the growing light. The helicopter banked and then slammed its skids onto the gravel beside a rocky plateau, where the air tasted colder and sharper, as if the earth exhaled a warning.

A gust whipped through the clearing like a ghost's breath, tangling in Blaze's dark hair and tugging at Lyra's jacket. The wind hissed low, threading a chill through the rising sun's warmth. The helicopter's blades sliced through the air again, causing loose stones to spatter. Frost dust swirled, vanishing into the cold.

The pilot's voice crackled once, then twice, before the thump of ascent filled the empty space where solid ground slipped away. The aircraft rose, swallowing the landscape into a shrinking mosaic of moss, stone, and the distant shimmer of a forest edge.

Blaze and Lyra stood apart on the rocky clearing, each rooted and silent. Between them, only the rush of cold wind and the vast expanse of wilderness stretched in taut quiet. The helicopter's shadow blurred behind them, then receded—a reluctant farewell, leaving two figures watching, isolated amid the breathless vastness.

The wilderness area had earned its reputation among cadets: an unforgiving terrain that demanded everything and gave nothing. Rocky plateaus gave way to dense forests, and beyond, the jagged peaks promised altitude, exposure, and cold that cut like broken glass. Few survival drills ended here without consequence.

Lyra's gaze drifted over the jagged skyline before flicking back to Blaze. His jaw was set, and his eyes scanned the horizon like a man already plotting their next move. Something unreadable hid there—a flicker in the forest shadows, a shadow barely captured by the first light.

Blaze's stance was unyielding, grounded like the stones beneath their boots. His glance, sharp and piercing, lingered just long enough to catch the silent admission flashing in Lyra's eyes: a shared history, last night's trial, and survival stitched in sweat and whispered commands. It hung heavy in the air—unspoken but electric.

Another gust tore through, carrying loose, hardened leaves and the scent of damp pine and distant snow down from the peaks. The air was cold enough to prick fingers and noses with a chilly alertness, sharp enough to awaken tight senses.

Blaze gritted his teeth against the sharpness and shoved his hands into his jacket pockets, turning slightly away.

Lyra's fingers drummed lightly against her pack strap, hesitation tightening her jaw. She glanced sideways, catching the corner of Blaze's stiffened stance before dropping her gaze.

"Last night felt like a lifetime ago," Lyra said quietly, her voice low enough to be swallowed by the breeze but clear.

Blaze didn't answer. His eyes remained locked on the distant treeline, where shadows deepened.

"You're flying with your heart again, huh?" Lyra's voice teetered on a tease.

Blaze's lips twitched—a smirk trying to squeeze past the line of grit. "The heart won't keep you alive."

Lyra stepped closer, her eyes flickering with fire. "Maybe it's all you've got when the rest falls apart."

His eyes flicked to hers, then away. The widening gap between them filled with things too dangerous to speak.

No words came as the helicopter's faint roar faded, and the wilderness stretched unyielding before them—two solitary figures framed within the dawn's fragile glow, silent witnesses in the cold.

Blaze dropped onto a flat slab of stone. Cold bit through the soles of his boots. He snapped open their emergency packs without hesitation, his fingers working the clasps with practiced efficiency.

The scent hit him first—aged canvas and faint antiseptic drifting upward as he peeled back the canvas lids. He pulled out the contents with deliberate precision, laying each item in a neat row along the rock's edge: two ration bars, their matte silver mylar glinting faintly in the gray light—dense, compact energy pockets; a folded thermal blanket that shimmered with synthetic sheen; and a heavy compass, spun brass catching what little light filtered through the clouds, followed by two matte steel canteens.

"Two ration bars each," Blaze mutters, his voice low but sharp as he counts aloud. "Thermal blanket. Compass. Canteens filled to capacity." He flicks his eyes toward Lyra and then back to their cache. "Strict rationing. No exceptions."

Lyra's gaze sharpens. She folds her arms tightly across her chest, each strand of her short hair snapping like brittle wire in the restless wind. Her stance dares him, though something flickers behind her eyes—challenge, perhaps respect. She taps a finger on his inventory.

"You're way too rigid," she fires back, her voice quick. Breath puffs small clouds into the chilly air. "Eating everything tonight won't leave us fresh for tomorrow. We need a morale boost, especially in the morning." She gestures toward the tree line, where the dark thicket waits, shadows pooling like ink. "Besides, those low pines there look prime for shelter. Less wind exposure."

Blaze's jaw tightens. His green eyes flicker like flint—that familiar tension coiling beneath his control, the weight of past miscalculations pressing down. He needs order. He needs certainty. Out here, unpredictability is a liability he can't afford.

"We prioritize survival over comfort," he says flatly.

Lyra steps closer, her voice lowering in a challenging cadence. "Survival needs wit, too. And flexibility. You fight the rules like they're add-ons, Blaze, but out here, every rule has a reason—except when you make no room for instinct."

He snorts, then snaps his gaze to the rough scatter of dead branches and twigs strewn across the outcrop.

"Assignments."

Lyra coughs but doesn't interrupt.

"Firewood. You collect." His tone leaves no room for debate. "Shelter site—I secure it. Water recon. You scout." He pauses, meeting her eyes. "Move."

Without waiting for a reply, Blaze strides toward the ragged pile of dry wood. His hands brush the brittle twigs, gathering them with methodical purpose. Lyra watches the rigid set of his shoulders and the restless energy coiled beneath his control before her fingers begin working their own solution.

With swift efficiency, she tears the edge of her sleeve. The fabric rips with a sharp snap that briefly cuts through the wind's moan. The strip becomes a binding—fraying but sturdy. Her hands dart between branches, knotting the makeshift twine around a thin sapling and securing an array of twigs and dead leaves into a crude windbreak. The ragged edge flutters against the chill, transforming the shallow rocky outcrop from an exposed battleground into a refuge.

She steps back, her hands lifting to hold the stretching fabric taut. Her eyes flick toward Blaze.

He stands silent, a tight bundle of branches resting near his feet. He watches her handiwork. The shadows of wood and stone knit together on the uneven ground beneath them. A brief nod brushes his features—almost imperceptible, almost approving.

Neither speaks.

The thread of mutual respect tightens in the space between them.

Wind whips debris across the clearing. Leaves scrape like whispers. Blaze drags his collected wood to the rock, stacking the brittle limbs with methodical care. Lyra tightens the last knot. Silence stretches between them—heavy and thick. Their measured breaths are the only sounds, save for a lone hawk spiraling in the distance.

Time thins.

Blaze's eyes sweep the landscape: a rugged rim of mountain silhouettes hazed by soft golden light. The forest's edge forms a jagged line, beckoning with unknown shelter.

"Flexible is one thing," Blaze finally says, his voice low but firm. "Waste isn't."

Lyra smirks. The faintest curve of a grin dares to emerge beneath her cool exterior.

"Neither is letting pride starve us." Her fingertips brush the fluttering fabric once more. "Let's prove we can do both."

Blaze kneels on the earth. His fingers curl around a sturdy branch he has pried from a fallen tree. The soil beneath him is soft—loam crumbled by morning dew and restless winds, giving way beneath his careful grip.

He thrusts the branch into the dirt, scraping and levering until a shallow pit takes shape. Around it, he drags stones—rough-edged, weathered gray—and arranges them in a rough circle. No gaps. His movements are precise and deliberate, tracing an invisible architecture of survival learned in past drills where structure was the only thing that kept chaos at bay.

He sweeps leaves and dry twigs aside with his palm, gathering tinder into a neat pile inside the stone ring. Silence settles between them like armor.

Lyra watches him, her breath rising in faint puffs that dissolve into the sharp air. Her shoulders square. She breaks the quiet with a crooked grin—one that masks the day's exhaustion and the deeper frustration simmering beneath her steady exterior.

"Seriously, Blaze?" She tilts her head. "That glare of yours could probably take down a drone at fifty yards."

He doesn't look up. His jaw stiffens as he levels the ground with the flat side of the branch. The dry brush scratches under his fingers—a rasp cutting through the cold stillness. He clamps his mouth shut, but her words hang there, half tease and half challenge.

Then he replies, "Yeah, well. It might actually keep the cold off."

Not quite approval, but close enough.

Lyra steps to the edge of their campsite. She pulls at the rough fabric of her sleeve—a jagged tear from earlier—and unravels a strip just long enough. Between two low saplings thick with moss, she strings the makeshift cord tight, weaving over and under with practiced ease. The faded fabric snaps softly, a whispered rustle in the crisp breeze, shielding them from the biting cold that creeps down from the shadowed trees. Fraying edges catch on the bark.

Blaze glances over his shoulder. The crease between his brows deepens for a moment before he shifts closer.

He gestures to the lean-to, his voice gruff but laced with reluctant approval. "Clever."

She nods, her eyes bright under the rush of energy and cold, then watches as he lifts the crumpled emergency blanket. Its silver sheen catches the dappled sunlight filtering through the canopy. Together, they tuck it beneath the shelter's lip, smoothing the edges down against the earth.

Their hands brush—brief, electric.

They pull away, but their fingers linger for an extra second despite themselves, the moment dissolving into the hum of the forest, leaves whispering secrets overhead.

Blaze pulls a worn map and compass from their pack, laying them on a flat rock nearby.

Clear-headed now, he traces strict lines in the dirt with a blunt stick. Each mark delineates rations and water reserves. The dry earth curls at the edges where he sketches their consumption schedule—how much water to sip, when to eat the ration bars, and timing the calorie burns against their survival timeline. The stick taps sharply against stone with each command of economy.

Lyra crouches beside him, her brow furrowed. She tugs at her gloves as she counters, her voice low but insistent.

"We can't treat this like some prison sentence." She dares to meet his eyes, steady and unblinking. "If we don't save a little bite for the morning—a morale boost—we'll freeze with nothing but hunger and cold in our bones." Her gaze flicks toward the shelter wall, where shadows pool in the waning light. "Just a handful of crumbs. You need something to look forward to, Blaze."

He stares down at her. The faintest shadow of a smile tugs at his lips before vanishing under the weight he carries. His fingers grip the stick tighter.

Then, with a slow nod, he adjusts the schedule.

"You're playing with fire," he says.

"Maybe I am." She holds his gaze steady. "But that fire... it's what keeps us human. Not just surviving."

He exhales hard, his breath misting in the cold air as he gestures to the lean-to and fire pit. The two pieces of their refuge form an unspoken treaty between order and improvisation. They settle back on their heels, the sun warming their backs, faces drawn but eyes sharp with quiet respect.

Around them, the wilderness holds its breath. Trees stiffen in the wind. Pine resin and damp earth thicken the air. The lean-to stands firm—a patchwork sentinel against the open sky—while the fire pit, circled with gathered kindling, waits patiently for its spark.

Two halves of the same coin: method and instinct, rule and rebellion, woven together by the fragile thread of necessity.

Blaze crouches low, his hands brushing loose dirt aside as his eyes scan the expanse of terrain beyond their lean-to. His fingers trace the faint ridges of a topographic map he has drawn in the soil—a rough blueprint of rocky outcrops, dips, and treelines. Deliberate stone markers appear in the dirt, small and heavy, outlining probable drainage hollows. Natural funnels. Lifelines where water might gather unseen in this parched stretch of wilderness, where dehydration could claim them before cold or hunger ever does.

The air tastes dry but carries a subtle, cold edge, whispering of the approaching evening chill. His breath fogs briefly, then fades.

Without a word, Lyra steps forward. The crunch of ferns under her boots cuts sharply and suddenly through the stillness. "I'll check the mossy ravine near those saplings," she says, nodding toward a dense patch of greenery squeezed between boulders. Her voice carries impatience—a restless edge that matches the quickness in her stride as she ducks beneath swaying fronds.

Blaze remains crouched by the dirt map. Minutes stretch. His eyes flick to the horizon, catching every shift in shadow and leaf. He has learned through past survival courses that discipline matters, that control is the difference between calculated risk and panic. His jaw tightens as the wind rustles through the pines, a reminder of how quickly the temperature drops once the sun dips behind the peaks.

Then she returns. Her breath is shallow but steady as Lyra kneels beside him, a small clump of moss tightly palmed in her gloved hand. The damp green spills faintly between her fingers, juicy and heavy with moisture.

"Found this," she offers. Triumph flashes across her face before fatigue settles back in. Her cheeks burn from the cold, and her fingers are tinged pink where the fabric of her gloves thins.

She reaches into their shared emergency pack and pulls out a slender survival straw. Matte. Utilitarian. Precise.

Blaze watches as Lyra presses the straw against the moss, tilting the canteen beneath it. She demonstrates the method with precision, inhaling just enough to draw out a thread of muddy water. The trickle is thin, like earth-starved tears squeezing from stone. But it's enough. Her hands tremble slightly—the bite of cold persists despite layers of gear—and she steadies herself before continuing.

"They don't make this stuff easy on purpose," Lyra murmurs, tracing the path of the water into the canteen. "They say you have to keep it slow and steady. It keeps dirt out, somehow."

Blaze nods, his lips pressed tight. They both lean in, the canteen resting between them on the dry ground, its rattle faint beneath the rustling pines. Lyra raises it to her lips first, her eyes lowered, careful not to spill a precious drop. The sharp tang of earth and metal lingers on her tongue.

When she passes the canteen sideways, her fingertips brush against his—electric, brief. Her fingers linger a heartbeat too long before releasing him.

Blaze catches the canteen with steady hands, despite the sudden surge in his chest. Their faces draw close, nostrils flaring. Breath mingles in the thin air as he drinks. The scant water slips down his rough throat—a quiet lifeline. He swallows hard, his eyes flickering to her lips before settling on her steady gaze.

A hush settles under the lean-to, broken only by the distant creak of branches and the faint sigh of the wind. The canteen lies between them like a shared secret, reserved only for survival's bare necessities.

Both sit back on their heels, the space between them measured by unspoken acknowledgments rather than words.

Lyra's eyes flicker upward, catching the last golden rays slipping behind the mountains. Blaze follows her gaze. The tension eases into something less guarded, more fragile. The chill creeps closer, but here—in the shared hush beneath green shadows and rustling boughs—the cold feels softer, tempered by their quiet proximity.

"I'm thinking water," Blaze says softly, his voice low and steady. "Not food. That should be our first priority. Rationing the bars makes sense, but dehydration kills faster."

Lyra bites her lip, nodding slowly. "Yeah. But a small boost might keep spirits alive when the night really sinks in." She bumps her shoulder lightly against his. "Don't tell me you don't think about morale."

He scowls, but the edge softens. "Morale is a luxury we're buying on credit."

She smirks, her eyes glinting. "Guess I'm the one betting on a payoff, then."

"Just don't spend the whole stash before we get back." He pulls a thin, cracked knife from his pocket and taps it against the stone edge near the canteen. "We've got a rough night ahead."

Lyra laughs—brief and bright. The sound slips out like a flash of warmth in the gathering dusk.

"Always so serious, Captain," she says.

"We're not here for fun, Hale." His voice shifts from the clipped command of the instructor to something softer, more human. "We're here to survive."

The wind picks up, threading through their tangled quiet. The scent of moss mellows into the sharper tang of pine resin and cold stone. Loose dirt swirls around their boots.

Lyra slides her hand toward the emergency blanket tucked beneath their lean-to, pulling it tighter around her shoulders. Blaze follows, resting his arm briefly against hers—an unspoken truce in their shared fight against the wilderness.

Their eyes meet. A spark grazes through the silent moments between breaths. The canteen lies empty. The loneliness of the wild settles deep around them. But here, in the space between, there is the fragile promise of trust, carved out beneath the endless sky.

The chill of twilight seeps into the clearing, pressing against skin already memory-slimmed by the day's demands. Blaze kneels by the shallow fire pit, a rough circle of stones framing a bed of dry tinder. His fingers close around the flint and steel tucked in the emergency kit. A sharp snap sounds, and a shower of sparks cascades into the brittle leaves. He shields the fledgling flame with the upturned hem of his jacket, his breath quiet and slow in the cooling air.

The fragile glow grows stubborn. Orange tongues lick upward as Lyra crouches close beside him. She fans the embers gently with a cupped palm, her breath puffing soft mist into the gathering dark. The scent of dry pine needles and earth rises from the forest's edge, mingling with the faint metallic tang of the evening air. Her fingers arrange kindling—thin sticks, brittle and pliant—layered with careful precision. Her cheeks shine with a thin film of perspiration, the chill wrestled back by the quiet heat.

In this wilderness, fire isn't just comfort; it's survival. Every spark matters, and they both know it. When a hungry spark finally catches flame, the small fire churns to life, scattering bright fragments into the darkening sky.

Lyra folds into herself on the log, drawing her knees tight and trembling as the chill nips through her layers. Her side brushes against Blaze's, the warmth a faint promise against the creeping cold. Blaze's jacket still hangs off one shoulder, flapping irregularly as the breeze picks up. Silence settles, measured and stiff, woven with the crackle of wood and the occasional pop of sap exploding in the heat.

A sharp snap echoes nearby—a startled squirrel fleeing into the shadows. Both their faces turn toward the darkened forest, that instinctive shared flinch binding them for just a moment.

Breaking the tension, Lyra nudges him with her elbow, her voice teasingly light against the low roar of the flames. "There's probably a drone out there shaking in its rotors just because you're eyeing it like a predator." Her eyes glitter with mischief under the flickering firelight.

Blaze's jaw tightens, but the corner of his mouth twitches upward—a reluctant, brief smile that doesn't reach the guarded depths of his green gaze. His usual brick-like expression softens, however slightly. "If the drone knew what was good for it, it would be running."

Lyra grins, the sparkle in her eyes unyielding. "Good to know you've got the intimidation down. It makes the 'silent and brooding' act more believable."

He shifts, the firelight casting sharp shadows across the planes of his face. "You're lucky I'm tired."

They lapse back into silence, the ember glow crisp against the growing dark. The conversation drifts toward the day's logistics—ration calculations etched in dirt and the moss-lined ravine where Lyra found their precious water. Their voices lower, becoming hushed confessions in the wilderness, softened by the crackling hearth.

"So," Lyra begins, her voice gentle, her eyes flicking to the uneven circle of flames, "your rationing plan—you really don't want to give an inch on that?"

Blaze's eyes narrow, the lines of command etched deep into his features. "Every calorie counts. Waste or excess means failure. Besides, morale can't replace hydration."

She laughs—a dry, sharp sound. "You're such a hard-ass; it's impressive. I might have to nick one of your rations for a midnight morale boost, just to keep the fire alive."

"Morale doesn't burn calories." He shifts again, then glances sidelong at her. "But I'll let you make just that call—for now."

The silence stretches out like smoke curling into the star-spattered darkness. Neither rushes to fill it, both tethered by the same unspoken gravity, the weight of expectation and a day's shared strain.

"Funny," Lyra murmurs after a long pause, "how rules that sound so sharp in the briefing room just... melt away out here. Like they don't matter when it's just you and me against the cold."

Blaze's gaze flicks up from the fire, meeting hers with an intensity softened by the night's reprieve. "Rules don't stop being rules; they're just harder to enforce when it's personal."

In his chest, something wars with itself—duty against the thread of connection forming between them. He knows the cost of bending protocol and understands it shouldn't matter that her shoulder presses against his, that her voice carries weight beyond the words themselves.

Lyra leans closer, the heat of the fire casting her face in warm relief. "Maybe some rules are meant to bend. Just a little." Her voice trails off, a whisper swallowed by rustling leaves.

He doesn't reply immediately; his eyes trace the shifting shadows cast by the dancing flames. The crackle of burning wood fills the pause, raw and alive.

"Guess we're both breaking protocol in our own ways," Blaze says finally, his voice low and rough with something like vulnerability. "Tonight, anyway."

Lyra's smile is subtle but sure, a quiet support threading through the night air. They settle further into the worn log, their bodies angled toward the fire but leaning gently toward the fragile understanding growing between them.

The distant forest hums with unseen life—chirps, rustles, and the soft thrum of a nocturnal pulse. Above, stars gleam, indifferent yet intimate, their ancient light threading secrets into the smoke curling skyward.

In that moment, the academy's iron grip seems a world away—forgotten beneath the vast, unanswerable sky, where firelight and shadow conjure a fragile truce that might just last until dawn.

The flames cast long, flickering shadows on their faces, painting the lean-to shelter with a restless glow. It dances to the rhythm of the crackling wood.

Lyra's voice softens. The sharp edge she wears during daylight hours folds into reverence. "My grandfather's old flight jacket still hangs in the back of his garage. It is faded olive green, heavy and worn beyond repair, but he kept it there like a relic." She pauses, as if feeling the weight of it across her shoulders. "He said it smelled like 'freedom and failure,' though I'm not sure which scent was stronger."

Blaze's eyes remain fixed on the fire, the amber lights reflecting off the dusky planes of his face. The world beyond the flames feels distant, held at bay by the crisp night air and the faint scent of pine creeping into the clearing. Lyra's words thread through the silence, pulling a fragile warmth between them.

"My mother... she used to hum before every takeoff," Lyra says, tilting her head as if hearing the melody lull in her memory. "Not just any tune—something quiet and steady, like a mantra. It settled her nerves." She traces the distant treeline with her gaze, where moonlight smooths the jagged outlines of the sleeping forest. "It made the skies feel a little less endless."

Her fingers flex against her knees, like wings. "Flying is where I've always felt... right. Like I belonged somewhere, even when everything else felt broken. I watched my godfather's plane go down when I was nine. I saw the smoke rise from the valley below our house." She speaks plainly, without performance. "After that, I needed to understand the sky instead of fear it. I needed to master what had taken him."

She shifts closer to the fire, her elbows resting on her knees, her hands beginning to move. "I remember my first solo flight as if it were yesterday. The plane throbbed beneath me on takeoff, engines roaring. My heart slammed against my ribs while the runway vanished beneath the wheels."

Her fingers arc through the air, sketching invisible climbs and dives. "Coming in for landing, the sky suddenly felt impossibly wide. The controls were stiff. The whole world leaned too far to one side, and terror settled deep and icy in my gut." She pauses, her breath steadying. "But then—touchdown. Nothing compared to the hollow ache of knowing I'd flown alone and still landed safely. It was like carrying all the voices of those who came before me. I was their echo."

Blaze's chest rises and falls—slow, steady. His usual guard slips, if only for a moment. The firelight glints off a subtle scar along his left jawline, a quiet testament to battles waged inside and out. After a long pause, his voice surfaces—low, raw.

"Flying... it was the only time I felt nothing at all," he admits, the words heavy, almost swallowed by the crackle of burning wood.

Lyra turns her full gaze toward him—curious, careful not to pry too soon. "What changed?" she asks softly. "If you want to share."

He looks away, his eyes tracing the swirling smoke above the fire, his fingertips tapping the charred log. The seconds stretch between them. "You don't come back the same," he finally says, his voice tight with memory. "Not after you've been up there—in the fight, where every second drags the weight of the lives depending on you." He draws a breath, his jaw working. "That silence? It haunts the loudest when you're on the ground."

The space between their words swells with unspoken grief. Lyra's hand twitches, betraying a nervous hope, before tracing a tentative path toward his palm. She stops, her breath catching, as if daring to bridge the distance.

He doesn't pull away.

Blaze's gaze flickers up, meeting hers. There—a flicker of vulnerability that the firelight barely reveals. He's terrified of exposure, of letting his walls down completely. But in this moment, in the dark, the burden of his armor feels heavier than the risk. His jaw tightens as he glances back down, drawing a slow breath. His fingers don't move away from hers.

"You ever feel like you're holding onto something invisible?" Lyra whispers. Her voice threads tenderly through the quiet. "Something you don't want to lose but can't quite keep?"

He doesn't answer. But the brief lock of their eyes says more than words could. Beneath the lean-to's shadowed canopy, the walls they've both built—the strict discipline, the emotional armor—lower, if only a little.

Smoke curls upward against a firmament littered with stars—indifferent, eternal.

They sit close now. The heat of the fire mingles with the fragile trace of connection. A silent promise hovers in the cool night air between them.

The fire crackles softly, casting warm amber flickers across the rough-hewn logs where they sit. The night wraps around them like a velvet cloak, with thick silhouettes of pine stabbing at the sky, stars distant and cold.

Lyra's hand trembles slightly as it edges toward Blaze's resting palm, fingers brushing the edge of her glove as if fearful of the cold air between them. His fingers twitch. He hesitates for a breath, then closes over hers with quiet deliberation—rough and sure. The warmth of his skin hums through her glove.

Eyes lock. The world narrows. Lyra's breath falters—a caught melody in the chilled air. Blaze's gaze drifts like a compass, flicking to her lips, lingering for a fraction too long, then snapping back to the steel green of her eyes. Their bodies lean in, subtle yet charged, drawn by an unseen gravity as ancient as the mountains watching over them. The forest holds its breath; even the fire seems to hush its crackle.

A sudden crack. A sharp snap of a twig and a brittle branch shatters the fragile spell. Boots crunch against gravel and fallen leaves, a deliberate tread pressing close. Flashlights blaze through the darkness, rivers of stark white slashing across their faces and the makeshift shelter. The welcoming warmth of firelight is replaced by a cold, clinical glare.

"Looks like you two got yourselves pretty cozy out here..." A voice breaks the silence, light but betraying a quick flush of caught-off-guard embarrassment. A rescue cadet steps forward, broad-shouldered, his military-pressed uniform catching the sporadic light. Two more figures trail behind him, their eyes flickering between the fire's glow and the heavy tension in the air.

The academy's rescue protocol was unforgiving—protocol that demanded immediate extraction, clinical efficiency, and no room for anything resembling personal moments. That was the academy way. That was the cost of their training.

Blaze's muscles tense. Every nerve in his body screams against the intrusion, against the necessity of it. He needs control. He always needs control. But Lyra springs upright with a swift motion, and they trade a sharp glance—an unspoken understanding knitting them into a seamless unit again. Grace under pressure. Silent and seamless, they gather their gear. The damp lean-to blanket folds taut. The last embers of the fire swallow smoke curls that rise and drift.

Blaze's jaw tightens as the rescue team sweeps the shelter's perimeter, their voices low but thorough as a roll is called. Lyra's eyes flick to his, a shared acknowledgment flickering like dying flames—a moment stolen, now irrevocably public.

Shoulder straps tighten, and packs settle into place. The fire's amber light dims behind them as they fall into step, a quiet column moving away from the campsite. Flashlight beams carve a path through the underbrush, slicing shadows between twisted roots and granite outcrops. The night hums with whispered rustles and the distant calls of nocturnal life. Yet nothing breaks the heavy silence between Blaze and Lyra as they trail behind their rescuers.

"So, are you guys taking this big, scary wilderness thing seriously, or are you just here for the sightseeing?" the first cadet quips, breaking the taut quiet.

Lyra shoots a glance back, her tight smile barely concealing a flicker of annoyance. Blaze's lips press into a thin line, his pace steady, his eyes scanning the darkness beyond the flashlit perimeter.

"We're not here for fun," Blaze says, his voice low and edged.

The cadet snorts, shaking his head as the group quickens its pace.

Lyra catches Blaze's sidelong glance—the flicker of something unsaid—and lets her gaze fall ahead. The helicopter's distant hum sounds like a promise, waiting beyond the tangled night.

Together, they march forward beneath the canopy, the extinguished fire a quiet witness to the closeness that was stolen and lost.

The narrow path snakes through the dark forest. Jagged rocks bite at their boots. Roots snag careless ankles. Blaze moves ahead, his broad shoulders tense beneath his flight jacket, eyes flicking to the shadows where trees crowd close. Whispers of silence stretch tight. His pulse hums quick and controlled—alert, scanning the black canopy for threats or signals. Behind him, Lyra strides with steady steps, her breath fogging the cold night air. The scrape of her boots echoes softly, a shadow following a shadow. The space between them hangs heavy, words swallowed by the hush. The forest swallows sound whole.

A rescue cadet breaks the fragile quiet with a half-joke, his voice laced with forced lightness. "Who knew survival training came with a side of midnight bonding?" He grins, waving a flashlight like a clumsy sword.

The others chuckle—more from relief than humor. Lyra's lips twitch into a smile that doesn't reach her eyes. Her jaw tightens for a moment. She glances sideways at Blaze, her fingers curling into a loose fist at her side, but he stares straight ahead, jaw clenched, eyes sharp.

"I prefer bonding over grub, not grudges," Lyra murmurs, her voice low but edged with dry wit.

Sarge, just behind, snorts softly. "I've seen you demolish rations before the embers die."

"Only if you promise decent java." She arches an eyebrow, but her words trail off as the group presses on.

The forest thins, and a clearing opens before them, bathed in swirling rotor wash. The helicopter looms, its blades carving arcs of cold wind that snatch at loose leaves and stray hairs. The metal beast purrs with idle power, ready to launch. Damp lean-to blankets and a spiraling wisp of smoke from the dying fire pile are tucked away under watchful eyes.

Blaze and Lyra move without hesitation, guided by muscle memory—steps practiced a hundred times before. They fold the soggy shelter with quiet efficiency, the coarse fabric whispering through fingers chilled by contact. Blaze's hands linger a moment too long over the warped edges of the blanket, his knuckles whitening. He tucks it away. Lyra watches, her mouth a thin line.

Inside the helicopter's cramped cabin, the scent of heated metal and faint gun oil mingles with a sharp tang—sweat and pine. The seats are cold leather against their skin. Blaze slips into his chair, his frame rigid, eyes scanning as Lyra takes the one separated from him by a stubborn empty seat. Between them lies an unbridgeable gap—not just space, but unspoken tension that settles like weight.

Neither speaks. The hum of the rotors is a low pulse beneath a pressurized silence. Fabric creases. A breath is drawn a little too sharply. Their glances flicker, hesitant and guarded—shadows skimming the edges, afraid to settle but unable to look away.

Outside, the world tilts beneath them. The lights of the base shimmer through a haze—small constellations anchored to the earth. The familiar geometry of runways and hangars grows sharper, a bright necklace tightening around the airfield's throat.

Blaze's jaw clenches. The weight of returning to the academy settles deep, knotting muscles beneath his skin. Lyra's fingers tap a silent rhythm against her thigh—an anxious metronome.

"You think they'll buy the whole 'stuck in the wilderness' story?" Lyra's voice cuts through the quiet, low but steady, laced with irony.

"They better," Blaze replies without turning. "There's no room for 'almost-kisses' in the official reports."

Lyra snorts softly, bitterness threading through the sound. "Yeah. More like 'almost fired.'"

The helicopter banks. Runway lights wash over the ghost of their lean-to and the wilderness they left behind. A strange weight settles between them—something fragile, unspoken, caught beneath fading stars and humming blades.

For a moment, neither looks away. Lyra's throat tightens as she recalls the raw vulnerability of those hours in the wild—how real it felt, how terrifying. Blaze's shoulders remain rigid, but something in his eyes betrays the same memory, the same reckoning.

The moment remains suspended as Astra Flight Command draws near, a waking beast stretching its concrete limbs and steel spines to welcome—or condemn—their return.

Gossip and Guilt

The transport hatch groaned open, the metal frame hitching against the biting wind that sliced across Astra's ridge. Blaze stepped off first, his boots thudding against the weathered tarmac, shoulders squared and steady. Behind him, the cadets filed out in clusters—some moving with purpose, others dragging. The way they watched Blaze, the slight straightening of their spines when he turned to scan the group, told Lyra everything about how much his presence mattered.

The sky above was harsh and pale blue, but the cold descending from the dunes beyond wrapped around them like an unwelcome shroud. Each footstep on the tarmac sounded brittle, like frost underfoot.

Lyra lagged a step behind Blaze, her shoulders drawn tight against the chill that gnawed at her. After nights spent under stars and relentless wind, her body ached in ways she hadn't known possible. Her cheeks burned—skin cracked and tight, stinging like frostbite's cruel kiss after endless sleepless nights. She inhaled, and her breaths came shallow and ragged, mist curling in quicksilver bursts before vanishing into the thin air.

The weariness in her gait was heavy, her limbs dragging with the hollow ache that wilderness survival carves into the soul. Her eyes stayed downcast, tracking the cracked concrete beneath her worn boots as the group moved toward the barracks.

The row of angular buildings of Astra Flight Command rose ahead, their bone-white walls gleaming faintly under the wan sunlight. A brittle scent of jet fuel lingered in the air alongside the sharp tang of frost. Voices buzzed in fragments up ahead—cadets gathering and reuniting after the rigorous drill, their tones bright with relief and exhaustion.

Inside, the barracks felt closed off. The narrow corridors pressed tighter after the open wild, and the fluorescent lights hummed overhead, casting a sterile glow that did little to warm the chill settled in her bones. Lyra's footsteps fell lighter on the polished floor, yet every muscle still carried the weight of the desert's silent nights.

Passing cadets glanced sideways, whispers trailing in the air like smoke. Some of the looks held the sharp edge of suspicion, while others lingered a beat too long, searching her face for something—a crack, a tell, proof that she didn't belong among them. Lyra felt each glance like a small weight pressing against her ribs. Her eyes flickered up briefly but quickly dipped again, pulling her gaze to the gray linoleum floor. The sharp sting of exhaustion etched lines beneath her eyes, and her cheeks bore the ruddy imprint of frostbite, a map of nights spent exposed to the wilderness—a map everyone seemed determined to read.

Her palms itched to find warmth in her sleeves. Her hands remained clenched at her sides, fingers tightening quietly as the whispers coiled around her, each one heavier than the last.

A soft breath steeled past her ear as Jazz stepped up close, her warmth a sudden barrier against the cold and the murmurs. Without hesitation, Jazz slipped an arm around Lyra's shoulder, her fingers pressing steadily. The movement was small but fierce—a shield against the mocking glances dotting the corridor. Jazz's eyes flashed with protective fire, her gaze sharpening as she scanned the passing cadets. That look dared any smirks or sideways glances to stay in their place.

"Come on," Jazz murmured, her voice low and steady but carrying an edge that sliced through the atmosphere thick with speculation. She nudged Lyra forward gently but firmly, steering her toward the mess hall. Their footsteps echoed in rhythm down the corridor.

The passage widened as they approached the canteen. Voices melded into a low, persistent hum that felt both distant and immediate. The smell of reheated food and stale coffee drifted outward, mixed with the faint metallic tang beneath it. Through the open door, clusters of cadets gathered—some in tight knots, others sprawled across tables, all carrying the tiredness of training etched into their faces.

Jazz and Lyra stepped inside together. The murmur folded around them like distant wind rustling through dry leaves. Their shadows stretched long across the scuffed tile floor, moving fluidly with the ebb and flow of scattered conversations.

Lyra's lungs felt heavy, like thick smoke curling after a fire. The heat of the crowded room pressed against her skin—a stark contrast to the cold canvas of the wilderness. She inhaled the mix of sweat, cheap instant coffee, and traces of burnt toast. Her shoulders relaxed fractionally as she caught Jazz's gaze: steady and unwavering. There was strength there, along with an unspoken promise to stand firm in a place suddenly crowded with whispered suspicions.

Jazz leaned in, her voice barely above the low din. "Shred the noise. You flew circles around those drills. Don't let them make you doubt that."

Lyra's lips pressed into a thin line. Exhaustion flickered with a faint blaze of stubborn defiance.

"It's like they're waiting for me to screw up," Lyra whispered back, the weight of cold and sleepless nights folding into her tone. "But I didn't. I couldn't."

Jazz slung her arm tighter around Lyra's shoulder, her grip firm. "Then don't give them the satisfaction. Let them talk. We know the truth."

A hollow silence fell between them for a heartbeat, swallowed by the steady cadence of voices around the room. Lyra's gaze dropped to her hands—calloused and rough from gripping gear, trembling faintly not from the cold but from the surge of emotions tangled with exhaustion and relief.

The stalls at the far end bustled with familiar faces. The clatter of trays and the clink of cutlery sounded ordinary yet grounding. Voices rippled—a blend of laughter and low complaints, weaving a tapestry of camaraderie and quiet tension.

Jazz broke the silence, a teasing curl at the edge of her mouth. "Besides, if half of what they say were true, I'd be first in line to call you out."

Lyra let out a quiet chuckle—ragged but real. Her shoulders relaxed just enough to breathe easier. The murmur of the canteen folded around them, a familiar soundtrack to the fraught moments after the wild.

And behind them, the fire of whispered rumors waited to spark.

Clusters of cadets huddled at the far end of the canteen, their voices a low hum punctuated by sharp nudges and stifled snickers. One tall cadet leaned toward another, a conspiratorial grin spreading across his face.

"So, what do you think really went down between Arden and Hale out there?" His eyes flicked around the group, gathering witnesses like trophies. "They say Lyra was all over him—reckless flying or some kind of stunt. And Blaze?" He paused for effect. "The way he snapped at her? It's like there's more beneath the surface."

Whispers rippled through the room, wild and spreading quickly. Voices wove together, building into a crescendo of speculation—like distant engines revving, ready for takeoff.

Lyra perched in her usual spot, the cold metal edge biting into her palms as she clenched a chipped ceramic cup. The taste of stale coffee coated her tongue, mixing with the faint metallic tang of jet fuel that never quite left the canteen air. Her jaw tightened, a sharp line carving her cheek as she stared into the cup, tracking the conversations that scraped against her skin like sandpaper.

Jazz slid in beside her, the warmth of her presence a fragile shield. But it didn't matter; snide remarks looped through the room, loud enough to sting.

"Crazy, right? How does someone survive a night out in the wild and still act like she owns the sky?" one voice carried sharply.

Another scoffed, "Probably using Blaze to cover her mistakes."

Lyra's spine snapped rigid—as if she were bracing for impact. Her senses narrowed, zeroing in on each cruel word as if targeting a distant aircraft. Dark eyes flicked toward the murmuring crowd, hard and unblinking.

Jazz's hand tightened on her arm, the only anchor keeping her grounded.

Jazz pushed back without hesitation. She rose from the table in one fluid motion, pointing directly at a smirking cadet lounging near the food service line. "Enough." Her voice cut through the chatter, clear and unwavering. "You think running your mouth makes you tough? Please. It's childish. Hell, it's downright dangerous." She jabbed a finger for emphasis. "We fly by skill, not by slander. If you want to prove something, prove it in the cockpit—not by tearing someone apart while they're bleeding."

Her glare pinned the group like an unyielding spotlight. A few cadets shuffled back, their bravado deflating under the weight of the truth.

Jazz plopped back into her seat, breathing harder now, but her resolve didn't waver. Lyra's shoulders relaxed a fraction, though the atmosphere remained thick, pressing down like the hull of a jet under strain.

In the canteen's narrow corridor, Sarge stepped through the steady flow of cadets. He slid alongside Blaze with practiced ease, his voice barely more than a shadow between them.

"Anything I should know?"

Sarge's concern flickered in his eyes—he had known Blaze long enough to read the tension knotted in his shoulders, the way he carried himself like a man holding back. Blaze brushed his fingers along the rim of his coffee cup, the contact brief and deliberate, grounding. His jaw twitched, a hard line cutting into his pale skin.

He shook his head. Sharp. Final.

"Nothing. Just noise."

Sarge watched him a moment longer before nodding and disappearing back into the crowd.

Blaze turned away, shoulders squared, expression shuttered—a fortress locked tight. The slow crunch of his boots echoed down the corridor. Behind him, whispers trailed in his wake, faint as the disturbance left by a departing plane.

Lyra's gaze lingered after him, her stomach twisting. A low, familiar knot tightened with each whispered syllable hanging in the air behind him.

The conference room's hum pressed against Elena Voss's ears—a low, constant drone beneath the weight of unspoken accusations. Dim light from a single overhead panel carved angular shadows across the polished table. Two junior instructors sat rigidly in their chairs. Three cadets fidgeted, their eyes darting between defiance and something closer to fear.

The tang of stale coffee lingered beneath the ventilation's whisper.

Lyra's name hadn't been spoken aloud. It didn't need to be. It hung in the room like smoke—visible only in how people's shoulders tensed and how glances skittered away from the center of the table where Voss now sat.

She leaned forward. Her fingertips tapped the table in a slow, deliberate rhythm. Once. Twice. Three times.

"I want to know exactly where this so-called 'special treatment' started," she said, her voice low and clipped. "The protocols are clear. Everyone earns their place. No exceptions."

Her gaze settled on the youngest cadet—the one whose jaw had tightened the moment she entered the room.

The silence pressed down like a physical weight. The cadet's shoulders jerked. He swallowed hard, his throat working before his whisper escaped. "Sir, it's just... people say things. That Lyra had Captain Arden watching her more closely than anyone else."

The words hung in the air—an accusation without teeth, without proof.

Voss's mouth curved at one corner. "Unusual, perhaps. One might call it diligent oversight, or one might call it something else entirely." She shifted her attention to the junior instructors, her eyes cutting across the table. "Your observations? Have either of you witnessed anything that might concern us? Anything beyond professional conduct?"

Neither instructor met her gaze directly. Their glances darted sideways, unwilling to commit to words that couldn't be taken back. The cadets exchanged looks—wary now, uncertain. Seeds of doubt had already begun to take root, spreading through the room like cracks in ice.

Voss waited, letting the silence extend, allowing them to marinate in it.

Hours later, the faculty meeting room bristled with the energy of the gathered senior staff. Elena Voss stood at the head of the conference table, regarding Commander Reynolds with the practiced respect of a subordinate who knew exactly how to wield it.

"Commander," she began, her tone measured but carrying a sharpened edge, "your instinct to trust Captain Arden's judgment is commendable. However, I must question whether pairing a seasoned combat pilot with such a... volatile cadet truly serves the High-G program's reputation."

Reynolds's lips pressed into a thin line. His fingers drummed once against the armrest of his chair before stilling.

"The academy's profile depends on careful stewardship," Voss continued, her eyes sweeping the room and catching each face in turn. "We all bear that responsibility. Even the appearance of impropriety can damage what we've built here. I trust you understand the gravity of that."

The implication settled over the room like ash. No one spoke. No one needed to.

Reynolds met her gaze but said nothing.

The officers' lounge hummed with its usual fluorescent buzz. Voss found Blaze near the coffee station, his back to her as he poured. She approached with her hands folded neatly at her waist, her posture uncompromising.

"Captain Arden."

He turned. His expression remained unreadable, but the muscles along his jaw tightened.

"I hope you understand your position here," she said, her voice smooth—a drawl sharpened by warning. "The academy holds you to the highest standards, even outside the cockpit. Any deviation from those standards could jeopardize not only your cadet's progress but also your own career trajectory."

His jaw clenched tighter. He said nothing.

"No exceptions," she added softly and turned away.

The clink of her spoon against the ceramic echoed as she left him there. Blaze remained motionless, the weight of her words settling into his chest like lead—heavier than any G-force could ever be. His fingers tightened around the coffee mug until his knuckles blanched white.

Around him, the academy hummed on, but that hum seemed distant now, muffled. All he could hear was the warning etched into the margins of his day—the cage she'd forged from whispered allegiances and shadowed doubts.

A cage with very clear walls.

Flight Officer Harper stood just beyond the tarmac's edge. The salt-tinged breeze tugged strands of her short dark hair against her jacket's contoured collar. Her eyes tracked the parade of pilots and cadets—sharp, unblinking.

There, near the center of the swarm, Blaze and Lyra moved with tension barely masked by routine. A subtle lean toward each other, a glance that lingered too long. Shoulders stiffened as they parted ways.

Harper's gaze narrows as she catalogs every flicker of expression, timing their separate exits with clinical precision. What story do their bodies tell? Are they careful enough, or do their instincts betray them? The questions fold into her observations like creases in paper.

Blaze strides away, his jaw tight and nostrils flaring faintly. Lyra's shoulders hunch beneath her flight jacket, her fingers flexing restlessly at her sides. In the crunch of gravel beneath their boots, Harper hears unspoken words—pauses that stretch just a heartbeat too long. A distant jet engine hums steadily as she reaches for her tablet, her fingers tapping out a series of notes.

Later, in the quiet hum of the administration block, Harper composes a summons. The message is tight and formal—no hint of accusation, only bland phrasing about "routine clarification concerning instructor-cadet boundaries." But she knows the subtext will ripple far beyond the words.

The academy is under pressure. Recent fraternization scandals have made the brass hypersensitive, and Harper's own scrutiny has intensified accordingly. What passes for routine now carries teeth; a simple summons becomes a warning shot.

Blaze reads the message beside the flight line. The printed page stiffens between his fingers as activity blurs around him. His gaze sharpens, his eyes glinting with suppressed irritation. His posture straightens—the old military habit kicking in the moment discipline tastes bitter. Without a word, he tucks the paper beneath his arm and heads toward the instructors' office.

Inside the interview room, fluorescent lights cast a sterile glow over the compact space. Harper sits with a tablet balanced on her knees, her wristwatch gleaming. She meets Blaze's eyes as he enters, and her jaw tightens, barely perceptibly. Her gaze narrows—a silent calculation unfolds behind her calm mask.

Blaze settles opposite her, his expression unreadable, a fortress. The hum of filtered air fills the silence before she begins.

"We're here to review the parameters of your role as an instructor," Harper says evenly. Her voice is smooth but edged. "Specifically, your interactions with Cadet Hale."

Blaze leans back, his fingers tented before him. "I adhere to protocol. No deviations."

Harper's pen scribbles across the page. "Noted. Yet reports suggest something less formal."

"Rumors follow exceptional cadets." He meets her gaze coolly. "I train pilots. Nothing more."

She taps the tablet screen. "One must consider the example set for the program. Appearances matter."

Blaze exhales, and the corner of his mouth twitches briefly. "I doubt I need lessons on maintaining professionalism."

"Of course not, Captain Arden." Harper's tone softens just enough to press like a scalpel. "This is about ensuring clarity. All instructors must be beyond reproach. Wouldn't you agree?"

"That's understood." His voice is low and guarded.

Their exchange hangs suspended—an invisible web of restrained accusation and measured defense. Harper closes her notebook with a snap that echoes sharply and finally.

"For transparency," she says, meeting his eyes directly, "this interview is being recorded. The record goes up the chain."

Blaze nods, tight-lipped. The flicker of emotion in his eyes vanishes as quickly as it appeared. He rises, straightening his jacket with practiced precision. The weight of another unseen burden settles heavily on his shoulders.

Harper watches him go. The door closes behind him with a muted click. His retreating figure tightens, shoulders squared against mounting pressure—pressure that no amount of training can soften.

Outside, the late afternoon sun filters through the high windows. Dust motes dance lazily in shafts of light. The distant roar of jets taking off punctuates the charged silence left behind.

The door slides closed with a sharp click behind Lyra. The faint hum of the command center fades until all that remains is the cold, unyielding space of Commander Reynolds' office. The air tastes dry and metallic, as if even the atmosphere resists softening the weight pressing down on the room.

Commander Reynolds sits rigidly behind her mahogany desk. Her fingers lace together, exuding quiet authority in every gesture. Her eyes fix on Lyra like a hawk sizing up its prey—hard and unblinking. A thick folder slides across the desk, its surface edged with official seals and stamped with harsh words. The paper catches the light, casting a brief glint before settling flat.

"You're suspended from the High-G program," Reynolds states, her voice taut and precise, each word falling like a command carved in stone. "Pending a full conduct review."

Reynolds's jaw tightens almost imperceptibly. Lyra doesn't catch it, but it's there—the weight of orders handed down from higher command, the necessity of enforcement, the cold machinery of duty grinding on without mercy. Reynolds has no choice. She never does.

Lyra's throat tightens. Her mouth presses into a thin line. Her fingers twitch against the edge of the desk like an anchor against the storm inside her. She forces herself to look up, but the commander's gaze is steel, unyielding.

"I followed the protocol," Lyra says, her voice brittle but steady. "Every step of the drill. The verification sequence, the secondary systems check, the safety parameters—all of it. I followed it. The rules aren't different just because of who you're paired with."

The specificity of those steps feels solid in her mouth, a shield of procedure and competence against the accusation hanging unspoken between them.

Reynolds leans forward just enough. The scent of her peppermint lozenge cuts through the sterile air, sharp and cloying.

"Is that so?" she replies crisply. "There are reports suggestive of inappropriate conduct, Lyra—actions that compromise not only you but the integrity of the program. We cannot ignore them."

Lyra's voice falters, dangerously fragile. She swallows hard, her Adam's apple bobbing like a captive bird. Her fingers curl into trembling fists at her sides.

"It's not fair," she whispers. The words are almost too small, swallowed by the oppressive quiet. "I didn't do anything wrong."

Her knuckles whiten as her hands clench. Her eyes remain fixed on the dark wood grain beneath the folder, unable to meet Reynolds's gaze.

Outside, Jazz shifts uneasily against the cold steel of the command center's tile floor. She curls her arms tightly around herself, the buzz of distant monitors fading as she focuses on the door. Her gaze sharpens at every creak and every muted shuffle, waiting for the moment it will open.

When it finally does, Lyra steps out. Her skin is pale, and her eyes are glossy like the aftermath of a storm. Her breath catches as she moves forward, trembling just enough for Jazz to notice.

Wordlessly, Jazz slips an arm around her shoulder. The warmth of her body is a stark contrast to the chill of the corridor. Without speaking, she becomes a shield against the invisible arrows of accusation and judgment that trail behind them.

They move through the dim corridor, footsteps muffled. Every step feels hellish in intensity.

The building seems colder now. Shadows stretch longer and darker with every step away from that suffocating room.

Lyra's fingers clutch the suspension notice so tightly that the edges press into her skin, biting reminders of a verdict that wasn't hers to deliver. The paper flaps faintly in the stale air, a flag marking the territory from which she has been exiled.

"I didn't break the rules," Lyra says at last, her voice rough and raw—a thread unraveling from the knots of anguish. "I did what I was supposed to do. You all just see what you want."

Jazz's eyes flicker with fierce loyalty. Her lips twist into a resolute snarl. She tightens her hold, physically grounding Lyra in a world that keeps tilting beneath her feet.

"You're better than their whispers, Ly," Jazz says low, fierce enough to burn through the cold. "They haven't earned you. They don't get to take you down."

Lyra's breath catches again, sharper this time. The crush of humiliation bends her spine but doesn't break it. Her gaze sweeps past the corridor's harsh lines, falling on the distant tangle of barracks where safety feels both close and impossibly far away.

She folds the suspension notice flat against her palm, her knuckles flushed.

The silence swells between them—thick, suffocating. A heavy curtain is drawn over all the unsaid words and the innocence lost before any defense could rise.

The corridor lights flicker, casting a weak, cold glow against the unyielding steel walls. Lyra's steps slow near the barracks entrance, and hesitation catches in the stiff curve of her shoulders.

Her eyes lock with Jazz's steady stare. A quiet promise passes between them that neither official decree nor whispered rumor will redefine who she is.

Not yet.

Lyra pulls her shoulders back, masking the raw edges beneath with a brittle composure. The suspension paper flutters once more before settling still, a stark emblem of a life interrupted.

She steps forward, and the thin crackling sound of whispered judgments trails behind her like ghosts she can't yet shake.

But her eyes burn—fierce, refusing to be broken, even under the coldest, hardest stare.

The command center door clicks closed again, leaving behind the echo of a sentence passed long before the truth had room to breathe.

The office air bites cold and sterile. The ventilation system hums low, providing a backdrop to hard edges and harder silences. Commander Reynolds sits behind her polished mahogany desk, her gray eyes tracking Blaze with the unflinching steel of command. Behind him, the door clicks shut—firm, final.

The faint scent of furniture polish lingered, mingling with the crisp chill from the vents overhead.

Without preamble, Reynolds pushed a crisp sheet of paper across the desk. The textured weight of it seemed to press into the air itself as her voice cut through the stillness—blunt and unyielding.

"This is a formal reprimand, Captain Arden. Any further breach of protocol, any spark of impropriety, and your career at Astra ends. Understand?"

Blaze's lips thinned. His jaw clenched, muscles tightening like knotted wire beneath his skin. History and expectation lingered in his gaze, but he said nothing. He reached forward. The pen was cold in his grip—unyielding. One clean stroke signed the paper. No flourish. No hesitation.

Silence settled like dust. The scrape of the pen's final breath echoed as he pushed the document back toward her. It landed with a soft thud—an unspoken acknowledgment. No words. No protest.

Beyond the office door, Lieutenant Marcus "Sarge" Sullivan waited, arms crossed and brow furrowed. The steel in his gaze softened fractionally as Blaze rose to leave, the door hissing open with a low sigh.

The corridor was filled with fluorescent glare and long shadows. Sarge closed the distance with measured steps, his voice a low murmur laden with caution.

"Voss is circling like a hawk, buddy. She's digging through every little thing—building a case. You can't slip up. Not for a second."

Blaze's eyes shifted toward him—dark, unreadable pools beneath heavy lids. For a moment, the green sharpness dimmed, weighed down by something heavier, something invisible but palpable.

He let Sarge's words hang in the spaces between them, unspoken truths buried deep. Then, almost reflexively, his hand brushed away the tentative touch on his arm—cool rejection, a wall rising, silent and unyielding.

"No," Blaze said under his breath—low, firm, more to himself than to anyone else.

Sarge's mouth opened and closed. Concern bit sharply on his tongue.

Blaze turned away. His heavy boots struck the polished floor, each impact punctuating the distance growing between them.

The reprimand weighed on his shoulders—thick, suffocating. Each breath chafed against the confines of expectation and regret. His stride was steady, but the stiffness in his stance betrayed the burden settling deep into his bones, coiling tighter with every footfall.

"Just keep your head in the game," Sarge called softly after him.

The words fell flat. Blaze didn't look back.

Behind him, the corridor stretched cold and empty. The echo of his boots served as a reminder that some battles are waged in silence. The warning nested itself in the hollow between his ribs—a new enemy, relentless as the skies he flew.

Lyra shoved open the barracks door. The sharp clang echoed off the cold concrete walls.

The usual hum of chatter and clattering boots dissolved into thick silence. It pressed around her like fog. She was drained—the scrape of wind and sleepless hours in the wilderness had hollowed her out—but it was what she saw that stopped her dead.

The flight roster. The whiteboard near the entrance. Names lined up under fluorescent lights like drill sergeants' orders.

Hers was gone. Erased. As if she had never belonged here.

She stood frozen. A slow ache curled through her chest. Eyes slid past her as if she were a ghost.

Cadets shuffled by, shoulders rigid. Some turned away. Others offered cold glances. A few lips twitched into suppressed smirks. Somewhere, a cough. The air tasted metallic and stale—thick with unsaid accusations, sharp with the kind of distance that stings worse than any medicine. Her throat tightened. Wire-taut. As if the barracks itself were silencing her.

Not far off, two cadets lean close. Their whispered voices cut sharp lines into the room's quiet.

"Did you see? Lyra used Blaze to get ahead. Classic move—slick and reckless all at once."

"Yeah, and those fancy stunts she pulled out there? A flying wreck waiting to happen. She's not cut out for this."

The words sting. Lyra flinches. Her fists clench so tightly that her knuckles blanch white. Her breath hitches—frantic, matching her racing heart. Each accusation lands like hail on bare skin: brutal and numbing. She steps back, wishing to disappear beneath the dull gray linoleum.

Jazz slides beside her with familiar ease, elbow nudging Lyra's ribs. Her quiet loyalty cuts through the harsh atmosphere like a sudden breeze breaking a storm.

At lunch, Jazz stakes their claim—seating Lyra where the vultures' gaze can't reach and standing guard with a pointed glare when a passing cadet's joke curls poisonous in the air.

"Hey, maybe you should try flying blind sometime," a smirking cadet tosses over a greedy grin. Half-joking. Fully threatening.

Jazz doesn't miss a beat. "And maybe you should learn what respect means before mouthing off. Try that sometime." Her voice is low, sharp, and final.

She plants Lyra's tray steadily in front of her—a silent anchor against the swirling chill that refuses to thaw. But the snickers, the sidelong glances, and the rumors spinning webs just out of sight wrap around Lyra like barbed wire, no matter how fiercely Jazz defends her.

That evening, the barracks dim to muted blues and shadows. The only light comes from a dim overhead fixture and the restless flicker of a screen. Lyra's bunk becomes a solitary island. She sinks onto the thin mattress and traces the cold, stiff seam of her unused flight suit folded beside her. The fabric feels foreign yet intimate—a reminder of battles not yet fought.

Her mind drifts back to the campfire. The acrid sting of smoke clings to her clothes. Flickering flames throw jittery shadows across Blaze's face, his jaw set tight in the night's cold silence. She recalls the hollowness in his eyes, the way tension stretched between them when neither spoke. The near-kiss—electric and tentative—burns hotter than the fire itself. She touches her own lips, haunted by what almost was and what could never be.

Guilt coils in her stomach, folding in with each memory. How did it all unravel so fast? Was she foolish to let her walls crumble, only to be shattered by the cold reality surrounding them now? Her breath hitches. The room contracts under the weight of silence.

Phone in hand, she scrolls through messages and hesitates over the screen. Her fingers tremble against the glass, unable to dial the number she longs to hear. The distant drone of the base's engines hums through the night—a steady heartbeat in the darkness. Neither comforting nor cruel. She closes her eyes. The buzzing fills the spaces where words fail, where loneliness gathers and settles heavily.

"Could be worse," Jazz's voice breaks through the quiet the next day, softer but steady, with words hanging in the space between them.

"Worse how? It looks like I'm done here," Lyra breathes out, her voice cracked and brittle as dry leaves.

"Nah, you're not done. They're just scared of what you bring. I've seen it. They'll come around." Jazz's fingers tighten around Lyra's wrist—a tether anchoring her in the storm.

"I'm tired of fighting shadows."

"Then you fight the damn dawn."

The classroom-turned-conference room was stark, with white walls and humming fluorescents casting an antiseptic glow over the long table where the instructors sat, stiff and silent. Blaze perched near one end, the leather chair scraping faintly against the polished floor. Major Voss sat opposite him, her eyes like ice shards, cutting into everyone present with unwavering focus. Alongside her, senior staff wore unreadable expressions, their pens poised over sheets peppered with technical jargon.

A junior officer clicked a pen. Keys tapped. The tablet flickered names and answers in rhythm with the clicks.

Blaze's jaw tightened, fingers curling into fists beneath the table as he gave measured replies—each word a deliberate barrier against the scrutiny pressing in. Procedure. Protocol. No hesitation. When questioned about his interactions with Cadet Hale, his gaze didn't waver, but a tightness curled behind his green eyes, like a hawk eyeing distant prey just out of reach.

"You understand the gravity of following Academy protocol regarding instructor-cadet relationships?" Voss's voice was calm, but it carried an edge sharper than any blade.

"I do." The word was tight and clipped, as if he were swallowing his irritation whole.

Her stare didn't soften. The silence stretched between them, heavy with unspoken knowledge. Blaze felt it then—the awareness of what he couldn't say, the pull toward Lyra that no protocol could fully suppress, and the consequences waiting if he stumbled. Voss was watching for that stumble.

"And yet, your proximity to Cadet Hale during the wilderness drill raised concerns."

He allowed himself a fraction of a sigh. "Training required close coordination."

The note-taker's stylus hesitated, then resumed its scratching. Blaze's fingers flexed against the table's cold veneer. The sterile scent of disinfectant hung thick in the air, mixing faintly with the underlying tang of jet fuel seeping through the vents. The room seemed to shrink, pressing in with expectation.

The meeting adjourned with a firm nod from Voss. The gathered instructors dispersed in quiet murmurs.

Outside, the cold bite of morning air hit Blaze's face as he stepped into the hangar corridor. Huge jet shadows loomed overhead, suspended like sleeping beasts. The concrete floor was slick in patches where mechanics had spilled hydraulic fluid, catching the pale light like dark mirrors.

A solid hand landed on Blaze's shoulder. Sarge's voice was low but tense, a rough edge slicing through the hum of distant machinery.

"She's building a file, Jareck." Sarge leaned in, his eyes flicking toward the busy hangar. "Voss isn't just watching—she's collecting. Every slip, every whispered comment. That woman has been climbing the hierarchy for years, and she uses protocol violations like rungs on a ladder. She doesn't let them go."

Blaze didn't move, his gaze fixed on the hangar doors rattling in the morning breeze. "I know."

Sarge's fingers tightened briefly. "Look, I get it. But you've got to keep it tight. No more private talks. No unnecessary risks. We're all under a microscope."

"Thanks for the heads-up." Blaze's lips pressed into a thin line. "That doesn't mean I like it."

"None of us do. But it's the game now." Sarge's voice dropped almost to a whisper as he tapped Blaze's chest lightly. "Don't lose your head."

The warning lingered between them as Sarge stepped back, fading into the wake of busy mechanics and shift changes.

For the rest of the day, Blaze became a man on autopilot. He delivered briefings in the stuffy instructor room, his voice steady as he drilled standard flight safety protocols and simulated combat strategies. He checked flight logs, cross-referenced cadet performance data, and signed off on reports with clinical detachment. Every movement was calculated. Every interaction was measured.

When Lyra appeared briefly in the hallways, her tired eyes met his for a flicker of a moment. He turned away, masking the churn of conflicting thoughts. The unspoken tension coiled beneath layers of discipline like a dormant storm.

In the sterile office spaces, whispers followed him—a chorus of doubts and accusations masked behind polite nods. The hypocrisy clawed at him, sharp as the bitter wind whipping off the tarmac outside.

As dusk draped the base in smoky twilight, Blaze found himself alone at the edge of the flight line. The roar and rumble of jets taking off and landing echoed in syncopated bursts. Blue-gray engines sliced through the thickening cold, their metal skins catching the last golden strands of sunlight like silver birds gliding through an ash-lit sky.

He stood rigid, hands shoved deep into his flight jacket pockets as shadows stretched long across the concrete. He didn't flinch. He didn't waver. His gaze hardened—cool and controlled—as if steeling himself against everything closing in.

"The academy's gone blind. They watch for cracks but miss what's inside." His voice was rough, barely audible beneath the distant roar of engines.

A faint rustling broke the silence. Distant voices came from the hangar. Blaze took one last steady breath, the tang of jet fuel and cold air mingling on his tongue.

No cracks are visible.

Not yet.

The night air bites at Lyra's skin. A cold line traces her exposed neck where her jacket collar gapes open. The rooftop patio stretches before her—an open platform overlooking the tarmac below, its cracked concrete glazed in the sickly glow of floodlights. The base had thrummed with activity hours ago; now it is a graveyard of waiting. The buzz of distant machinery hums low, mingling with the occasional scrape of wind through metal railings. She leans against the cold steel barrier, her shoulders tight, and her gaze fixed on the sprawling silence beneath the stars.

Jazz's footsteps crunch softly on the gravel. Deliberate. She slides onto the narrow bench beside Lyra, their shoulders nearly touching. The warmth radiating from her is a stark contrast to the chill that laces through the night—a contrast Lyra feels like a physical accusation. Jazz's dark eyes assess her for a moment, reading the exhaustion etched into her face and the way shame sits heavy in her jaw. Anger flickers across Jazz's expression—anger not at Lyra, but at the unfairness of it all. At the way the academy devours its own when they stumble.

"You aren't letting them pin you down," Jazz says, her voice blunt and sharp as a blade. "It doesn't matter what crap they scribble on those boards. You fought tooth and claw to get here. You fight for your place, not for their approval."

Lyra's throat tightens. Her hands curl into fists, knuckles paling before she exhales, her voice barely above a rasp as the words claw free. "I don't know if I'm strong enough. I didn't just mess up my future—maybe I wrecked his too." Her eyes catch the stars above, shimmering cold and indifferent. "Blaze is already carrying so much, and I just added to it. Maybe it's better if I'm alone."

Jazz's jaw clenches, frustration mingling with something fierce and protective beneath. She reaches out, her fingers pressing steadily onto Lyra's shoulder, grounding her. "Listen. No one's asking you to be perfect. Hell, no one is." She taps a fingertip against Lyra's sternum, feeling the rapid thud of her heartbeat. "But you—you're not some reckless kid. You fly with guts and brains. Blaze sees it, whether he shows it or not."

Her voice softens, but the certainty in it doesn't waver. "I'll stand with you. Every damn step. You're not carrying this alone."

Lyra's breath catches. A flicker of something hopeful stirs in the hollow left by doubt.

Her hands inch out, fingers brushing over Jazz's in return. The touch is tentative but electric—a promise amidst the shadows.

The two friends sit in silence, the night wrapping around them like a flight jacket. The base carries a faint tang of jet fuel and damp concrete, sharp beneath the cold that radiates from the metal beneath them. Out over the tarmac, the harsh floodlights cast long, skeletal shadows from the grounded jets—cold steel beasts waiting for commands that never come tonight. Lyra's eyes trace the sharp edges and smooth curves, a mix of danger and beauty that mirrors her own conflicted heart. The sting of guilt coils tightly in her belly, a tether pulling her down like gravity.

Jazz's grip tightens, a silent vow against the creeping shame. "You're tougher than they think, stronger than you believe."

The words float between them like lanterns in the dark. Lyra closes her eyes, the cool night air filling her lungs and the distant hum of the bass a steady thrum beneath the stars. She lets the silence settle over her like a shield and a weight at once, while Jazz's hand remains firm on her shoulder, a steady anchor in a sea of uncertainty.

The Crash Report

A cold gray light seeps through the mess hall's broad window, staining the room in pale, early morning hues. Lyra Hale leans against the frame, her eyes locked on the runway beyond. Concrete stretches smooth and vast, a runway scarred by tire marks and faintly soaked with the smell of jet fuel and burnt ozone. Emergency vehicles converge like ants, their red and blue lights painting frantic flashes against the steel-gray tarmac.

Cadets cluster near the perimeter, their faces taut, murmuring in tight groups like storm warnings whispered under breath. Ground crew cut sharp silhouettes as they dart with purpose: a stretcher here, heavy cases of medical gear there, gears in motion. Lyra watches the silent choreography—the precise tension in their shoulders, the crisp exchanges, the way they haul hoses and oxygen tanks toward a downed training jet parked askew near the hangar. The aircraft's blackened wing scrapes the concrete, its nose tilted in a jagged frown against the cold dawn.

"Looks bad," murmurs Jazz from behind her, the quiet crackle of her voice mixing with distant shouts and revving engines. Jazz's eyes scan the scene, trying to read any hint of relief.

Lyra says nothing, but the knot tightening in her chest speaks for both of them. Something smells off—beyond the acrid mix of burnt rubber and hydraulic fluid.

A low drone hums behind them, growing into crisp, commanding footsteps. Blaze appears at the perimeter, shoulders squared against the chill. His boots hit the tarmac with the surety of a man accustomed to cold ground beneath him. Beside him, Sarge's steady presence serves as a muted anchor.

Blaze's gaze sweeps the chaos with clinical precision. His voice cuts through the hum of activity—quiet, clipped orders aimed at triage teams, runners, and the tech squad lofting stretchers with care. The composure he wears now is armor, forged in the wreckage of previous losses. Years ago, a pilot under his watch hadn't made it home—engine failure, they had said, though the true culprit was maintenance negligence buried in paperwork and silence. The memory lives in his joints, in the tight set of his jaw. It sharpens his attention now, making him read every movement on the tarmac for signs of the same carelessness.

"Clear runway four-zero," Blaze calls, his voice flat but edged with urgency. "Med evac inbound. Sarge, coordinate with the tower for immediate clearance."

Sarge acknowledges with a tight nod, stepping into the radio chatter as Blaze's eyes flash briefly toward the mangled jet. Fingers clenched on his belt, Blaze's jaw tightens against the weight of unseen ghosts. Around him, urgency swells, but his demeanor remains ice-calm—the calm before the storm, brittle and sharp.

The rumble of a command vehicle interrupts the rhythm. Commander Reynolds steps out first, her heels echoing crisply and unforgivingly on the cracked concrete. Major Elena Voss follows, her stride long and purposeful, her eyes sharp beneath the brim of her cap. Flight Officer Harper glides closely behind, surveying the unfolding scene with hawk-like focus.

Their approach is a studied storm—silent and efficient. Words pass quickly between their set jaws, terse and edged with the weight of consequence. The three sweep the site like judges at a grim tribunal—cold glances cast over bent figures hauling gear, over scarred fuselage, and scattered debris.

Blaze straightens, watching as the officers fan out, tension rippling through the air like static. Reynolds's steely eyes meet Blaze's for a moment—the unspoken calculus of blame and responsibility blossoming between them like winter frost.

Sarge murmurs beside Blaze, his voice low under the roar of activity: "Reynolds is not here to offer sympathy."

Blaze tightens his grip on his radio, his throat dry. "She's here to find fault."

Harper's voice crackles through the comms, precise and clipped: "Pilot stable. Minor injuries. Cause preliminary: engine anomaly."

Lyra's gaze sharpens; that phrase hangs heavy in the thick morning air—slick and too tidy. Her eyes catch a shift—a whispered glance between crew members, a frown hidden behind a mask, the quick exchange of glances heavy with unspoken questions. The incongruity needles at her. Engine anomaly. The words sit wrong, smooth as a lie polished in a corridor before the truth could breathe. Her instinct, honed by years of watching authority move through rooms like smoke, tells her something else lurks beneath the official account. The base has its narrative now, neat and closed. But Lyra reads bodies better than briefings—she sees the hesitation in how they move, the weight they are all carrying. Her suspicion blooms quickly and bitterly. If the cause was truly mechanical, why do their faces say otherwise? Why the careful distance between their words and their eyes?

Near the mess hall window, cadets shuffle on restless feet, murmurs turning into anxious conversations. Lyra turns slowly, her chest tightening as the weight of the base's silence presses in, thick and expectant. She can almost taste the undercurrent of fear and suspicion—tangy and metallic on her tongue, hot and bitter in her gut.

Her fingers drift across the cold glass, fogging faintly under the quiet heat of her palm. The haze distorts the frantic scene outside, blurring sharp edges into shadows.

A voice from somewhere nearby—a cadet, perhaps—murmurs, "Feels like something's being covered up."

Lyra swallows, the bitter aftertaste of doubt rising alongside the dawn.

Outside, the wind picks up suddenly, whipping around the edge of the hangar with a sharp whistle, tugging at stray papers and loose gear. The tension hanging in the air tightens as if the entire base braces for a storm yet to break.

She steps back from the window, her shoulders stiffening against the chill that settles deep inside her. The air tastes of burnt fuel and secrets. Lyra's stomach twists; she reads the base's tension like a new weather front—looming, restless, threatening. Something buried beneath the surface waits to erupt.

Her gaze lingers on the chaos below; then she turns away, resolve hardening like steel forged in winter fire.

The room smells of recycled air and freshly brewed coffee, with harsh overhead fluorescents slicing through the morning haze. Flight Officer Harper steps onto the narrow platform. Her boots click softly against the metal grate. Her dark eyes scan the packed briefing room, resting briefly on the rows of folding chairs where cadets and instructors crowd closely, shoulders tense beneath their uniforms.

Her voice cuts through the low murmur—calm but edged with authority. "The pilot sustained minor injuries and is expected to make a full recovery. The cause of the incident has been preliminarily identified as an engine anomaly. Further investigation is underway."

A flicker of restless glances ripples through the room—whispers smothered beneath nodding heads. Hands tug at sleeves, and eyes flicker to one another, some searching for answers deeper than the clipped statement offers. Lyra knows the academy's history well enough. "Engine anomaly" is the convenient answer, the official lie that masks deeper failures. It is always "engine anomaly."

Lt. Marcus "Sarge" Sullivan rises from his seat, his height imposing yet his voice steady, tempered with seasoned patience. "Everyone, hold tight and let the investigation run its course. Speculation won't help; it will only muddy the waters. Maintain your focus and discipline." His gaze sweeps across the crowded space, landing on each face with the weight of experience.

The cadets folded back into their chairs, some settling their shoulders, while others bristled with quiet frustration. Sarge's words seemed to smooth tensions, like a cautious pilot steering a turbulent descent, but the undercurrent of doubt remained, stubborn and alive.

From the back, Major Elena Voss stepped forward, her sharp gaze locking onto the High-G team with surgical precision. "Effective immediately, all protocols regarding maintenance and operational checks will be tightened. No exceptions. Discipline is not negotiable." Her tone left no room for argument. Eyes flickered uneasily, especially among the High-G cadets, who exchanged tight-lipped glances under the weight of her scrutiny.

She paused, letting the silence stretch. The hum of the air conditioning filled the space. Then, crisply: "We owe it to the safety of every pilot and crew member here to uphold the highest standards. Complacency will not be tolerated."

The room's atmosphere thickened, a blend of restraint and simmering unease. Lyra remained rooted near the back, her jaw tight, fingers curled against the edge of her seat.

Harper's eyes caught hers—almost a fraction too long.

A shadow danced behind those professional lenses—something that didn't quite vanish. Lyra's breath hitched. She and Harper had history, the kind that lived in careful silences and averted glances. There was something unresolved there, a tension that buzzed beneath every official interaction. The look now felt loaded: a warning or an admission of complicity.

Lyra's fingers dug into the seat's worn fabric as the air thickened, heavy with unspoken questions. The official story didn't fit. She could feel it in the way the words hung, the overly controlled expressions, and the tight circles exchanged among instructors. Something else had happened—something worse.

She forced herself to stand slowly, her muscles taut. The low murmur of the room rose behind her as cadets began to follow. Outside, the scent of jet fuel and warm metal seeped through the open hangar doors, mingling with the distant roar of an engine spooling. But inside, there was a cold edge—questions unasked, shadows never acknowledged.

Lyra walked out into the chill air just beyond the briefing room, swallowed by the sprawling shadows of the hangar. A whisper brushed past her ear as she moved: "Keep your head low. This isn't over."

She didn't answer. Her resolve hardened, but the knot in her gut tightened further. The explanation felt thin, and the glance from Harper was sharp and loaded with meaning just beyond reach.

Already plotting the next move.

The hum of milling cadets and the clatter of trays filled the mess hall, but Lyra's gaze sliced through the noise, hunting for the familiar figure she needed: Jasmine "Jazz" Turner. There she was, near the window, laughing easily with a group of friends. However, when Lyra caught her eye, the light in Jazz's expression flickered before she slid out of the cluster. Lyra grabbed Jazz's arm gently, pulling her into the shadowed corner by the beverage station, far from prying ears.

"Jazz, what do you know about that pilot?" Lyra's voice dropped, urgent but steady. "Who signed off on the jet last? I need facts, not the usual spin."

Jazz arched a brow, scanning the room before weighing her words. "You mean the one that went down?" Her tone was skeptical, treasuring caution like armor. "I heard the ground crew muttering about Quinn—dude's been steamed all week over rushed turnarounds. He's been real short with the supervisors, like he was ready to snap or something."

The sharp bite of burnt coffee lingered in the air, mingling with the greasy tang of fried eggs—comforting yet oddly oppressive given the morning's news. Lyra's eyes narrowed, tracing the spitting steam from a nearby cup. Her instinct pulled taut. How many times had she seen small negligence spiral into catastrophe? How many times had she ignored that whisper in her gut, only to regret it later?

"Sabotage?"

The word slipped out, unguarded, slicing through the din like a warning flare.

Jazz frowned, her lips tightening, her usual warmth cooling into somber pragmatism. Her fingers drummed lightly on the edge of the beverage station, betraying a flicker of anxiety beneath her calm exterior. She had always been the careful one, the one who weighed loyalty to the cadet corps against the weight of knowing something was wrong. It was why Lyra trusted her—Jazz didn't jump to conclusions, but once she committed to something, she didn't back down.

"Lyra, you're treading on thin ice. We can't just throw accusations without proof—people's careers, and possibly their lives, could be wrecked if we're wrong." Her voice softened, thick with concern but edged with resolve. "Still... I'm with you on quietly digging deeper. We just have to watch our backs."

Lyra's chest stiffened under the weight of unspoken dangers, but beneath it, a stubborn fire kindled brighter. "I can't sit on this. Not with the way things are. If Quinn's blowups were more than just stress..."

Jazz's eyes locked onto hers, steady. "Neither can I. Let's hit the maintenance bay, low-key. See if we can find anything that sticks."

The mess hall buzzed around them. Lyra pulled free, with Jazz close at her shoulder—a silent shadow. The knot in her gut tightened—a blend of suspicion and determination sharpening her focus. Around the tables, laughter and chatter seemed like a cruel mask over the tense air spiraling out from the runway and the crashed jet.

With each step away from the window, Lyra's resolve seized the moment, steady and unyielding. It was time to unravel the secrets hiding in the shadows of engines and circuit boards.

###

The steel door creaked open just wide enough for Lyra to slip through, an armful of flight gloves and helmets pressed against her chest. She and Jazz had "borrowed" them hours earlier—a small theft among larger ones.

Jazz hummed, deliberately off-key. The wavering note was shaky and unreliable, barely enough to mask their footsteps on the cold concrete. Oil stains bloomed like dark flowers across the floor, while scattered wrenches caught the fluorescent light. The clangs echoed faintly, swallowed by the hangar's vast throat.

A few mechanics glanced up from their work—quick bursts of chatter and shuffling boots—then looked away, absorbed in their own tasks.

"We're clear," Lyra whispered, her brow furrowing with sharp focus. "For now. Just keep the noise up."

Jazz grinned, her humming sliding into something that felt less like a lullaby and more like a dare. "If anyone asks, I'll tell them it's a new engine test. Off-key sabotage, maybe?"

Lyra's smile tugged at the corner of her mouth, but she didn't relax. She moved toward the maintenance terminal—a monolithic slab of scratched metal and wires, its screens flickering with lines of technical jargon that hummed like an incantation. Her fingers danced across the touchscreen, scrolling through logs shimmering in blues and whites, with timestamps bleeding together in suspicious patterns.

There. Her jaw tightened.

Maintenance checks were recorded hours *after* flights had lifted off. Edits were made moments before signatures that didn't match the rotation schedules posted weeks prior. The inconsistencies had a rhythm to them—deliberate and choreographed. Someone had scrubbed the logs clean and then dirtied them again.

Jazz stood sentinel beside a row of tool carts, her eyes sharp and unblinking. The tang of grease and metal hung thick in the air, sharp enough to cut. Her hand hovered near a hefty wrench, her fingers twitching with restless energy.

Footsteps. Slow. Measured. Crunching on gravel and concrete.

"Not now," Jazz muttered, her voice as thin as a cobweb.

The wrench slipped from her fingers.

It hit the floor with a sharp clang that shattered the silence like a gunshot. Jazz's breath hitched—a cold spike twisting in her gut. Just yards away, a mechanic paused mid-step, his head tilting slightly as if sensing a disturbance. His breath hissed through a mouth smeared with grease. For one stretched second, the world held its breath.

Then he turned back to his work.

Jazz picked up the wrench, her grin mischievous but her eyes blazing with tension. She exhaled slowly.

Lyra's fingers flew back to the terminal, more determined now. Lines of digital text flickered, codes and annotations threading through each other. Her eyes caught a flicker—a warning code, dark and blinking, once deleted, now scrubbed back in like a ghost. The timing was wrong. Everything about it was wrong.

Deliberate tampering. A silent scream ignored by everyone who should have heard it.

She angled her phone toward the monitor, the screen's soft glow cupped in her palm. Soft clicks marked each capture—secret signatures burning into her encrypted drive. The weight in her chest lightened with every frame saved, but mystery clawed at her mind. *Why?* Who would risk this?

"Got it," she whispered.

Out of the corner of her eye, Jazz stiffened. A shadow slid across the bay's threshold. Boots on concrete grew louder.

Lyra's breath caught. She ducked instinctively, her heartbeat shuddering against her ribs as if trying to escape. Jazz flattened herself against a massive engine cowling, the cool metal biting into her cheek, her breath fogging the shadowy curve.

Two figures stepped through. Harper moved first, her cold, appraising gaze sweeping the room with surgical precision. An officer trailed behind her, a clipboard clutched like a shield. The hum of electronics and the scent of oil mingled under the harsh glare of overhead fluorescents, casting sharp-edged shadows that crawled across every surface.

Jazz's fingers curled into a fist around the wrench. Her knuckles whitened. Her breath was steady but shallow—a tightrope walk between calm and panic.

Lyra's pulse drummed wildly in her ears. Every nerve sharpened like the whine of a jet engine seconds before takeoff. She held her phone tight, the faint glow a heartbeat away from discovery.

Harper's eyes lingered on the maintenance terminal—the ghost in the machine they had left behind.

But she did not see it. Not yet.

Boots echoed sharply against concrete, slicing through the clatter of tools and the low hum of machinery. Harper strode in, clipboard clutched tightly, her brows furrowed in suspicion. An officer followed closely behind, quieter but alert.

Her voice cut through the bay's murmur—calm, clipped, each word measured, "Engine inspection delayed. Timeline irregularities noted."

Harper's gaze swept across the room, ticking invisible boxes as she moved with practiced authority toward the terminals. The metallic tang of oil mixed faintly with burnt fuel, heavy and suffocating. Her steps were measured, cautious—deliberate.

She had seen too much. Six months ago, a pilot walked away from a faulty ejection mechanism by pure luck. This time, she wouldn't let sloppy maintenance hide in the shadows.

Behind the cavernous bulk of a jet's engine cowling, Lyra's back pressed hard against cool steel, the cold biting into her skin. Her fingers curled around the smooth glass of her phone, knuckles whitening. Jazz barely dared to breathe beside her, his chest tight, eyes darting toward the door.

The soft hum of ventilation mingled with the subtle hiss of hydraulic lifts. Lyra's eyes flicked to Harper, caught in that measured dance near the terminals—a heartbeat away from discovery.

Harper leaned toward the cluttered workbench, her lips barely moving as she muttered, "Signatures don't align. Timelines contradict reports."

She tapped a finger against a logbook, skimming the pages with the precision of a surgeon. The crisp rustle of paper punctuated her inspection. Then, with deliberate steps, she shifted toward a technician's clipboard against the wall, her eyes narrowing as she flipped through it.

Jazz stole a glance at Lyra. Their eyes met—a silent agreement passing between them. The moment they had been waiting for edged closer.

"They're playing fast and loose with the logs," Jazz whispered, her voice barely more than a breath. "Either they forged the timestamps... or someone just didn't care. And being that sloppy? That'll get people killed."

The High-G program was already under scrutiny after last week's near miss. One more accident, one more death, and the whole thing would crater. Lyra knew it. They all did.

Lyra's phone vibrated softly in her palm. The images flickered in the harsh overhead light—deleted warnings, altered logs. Pieces of a puzzle that felt as cold as steel.

"I can't let this slide," Lyra said, her breath hitching with the weight of the risk. "If those records are off, somebody covered their tracks."

Jazz's eyes snapped toward the footsteps moving closer. "Not a word," she mouthed, her voice barely more than a breath. Her hand clenched around the wrench in her grip, ready to drop it if needed.

Harper moved away from the clipboard, her back momentarily turned. A scrape of rubber wheels on concrete echoed through the bay, followed by a slight pause.

Lyra and Jazz exchanged a sharp glance.

The moment had come.

Slowly, they slid from behind the cowling. The cool metal numbed the backs of their hands as they stepped lightly over scattered tools, careful to avoid shadows. Jazz's steps fell in a muted cadence, her nervous energy barely contained. The scent of grease and cold steel pressed close around them, grounding them as they edged toward the side door.

They took a steady breath in; the air tasted faintly metallic. The door's worn handle gleamed under the flickering lights. Lyra's fingers touched the surface—tremulous but steady.

Behind them, Harper's voice rose in quiet inquiry. "We'll be cross-referencing these signatures and times with pilot reports first thing. Anything out of place will be flagged for immediate review."

The scrape of her boots stilled. A breath held in time.

Lyra caught the edge of the sound and swallowed hard. Jazz's eyes flickered toward the entrance.

Harper started moving again, her voice lowered but firm. "We'll proceed methodically. There's no room for error—not after last week."

Two sets of shadows slipped through the narrow door, swallowed by the muted hum beyond the bay. Hearts hammered in unison.

Outside, distant jets hissed as their engines spooled for flight—a harsh counterpoint to their quiet escape. Dust and diesel oil lingered in the air, sharp and acrid.

Jazz leaned in as they reached a modest clearing, her voice urgent. "Next step: find Quinn. If anyone's hiding fingerprints, it's him."

Lyra nodded, her eyes bright with contained fire. "And we'll prove it. No one plays games that end with dying pilots."

Jazz cracked a rare smile, tension easing briefly. But the weight returned, heavy, as the hangar door swung shut behind them.

Harper's footsteps faded in the distance, but her shadow lingered—a threat they couldn't shake.

Their breaths came ragged but victorious. Phones were safe. Secrets captured.

For now.

The hangar's cavernous interior hummed with the low drone of distant jet engines, shadows pooling beneath towering fighter frames. Captain Jareck "Blaze" Arden stepped from the dim edge, his boots thudding against the concrete. His eyes—sharp beneath heavy brows—swept the space with the practiced assessment of a man accustomed to reading rooms the way others read maps.

Flight Officer Harper stood nearby, scanning clipboards and murmuring into her radio. Her posture was taut, and professional focus was carved into every line of her shoulders.

Blaze had worked with Harper long enough to know when she was thinking three moves ahead. That made her dangerous and valuable. It also made conversations like this one necessary—and carefully choreographed.

"Harper." His voice cut through the ambient clatter, even but sharper than usual. "About the new safety protocols: how thoroughly are they being enforced? Specifically, what are the post-debrief procedures following the incident?"

She pivoted toward him, a faint crease deepening between her brows. "Protocols are being stepped up base-wide. All post-flight checks are mandatory, and flagged faults receive immediate attention." Her gaze narrowed as it flicked toward the maintenance bay. The harsh light caught the faint scar above her eyebrow. "The pilot's medical evaluation reported minor concussion symptoms. Additional tests are being conducted as a precaution."

Blaze shifted his weight and nodded slowly, but pressed on, lowering his voice to a clipped, tactical cadence. "Psychological status checks. Is there a formal checklist post-mission that includes cognitive screening? Because without that—" He paused, letting the implication hang. "Underlying issues can slip through."

"Yes." Harper folded her arms. "Cognitive screenings are standard for all High-G program personnel after in-mission anomalies. No irregularities have been flagged so far."

The conversation flowed with the precision of cogs fitting into machinery—clinical, professional, safe.

But Blaze's eyes flickered toward the far side of the hangar—a subtle gesture barely perceptible. His fingers curled briefly, then released. The exit door lay beyond the jet frames, just beyond.

Lyra stood near the maintenance bay's side door, with Jazz beside her. Their lean frames radiated quiet anticipation, backs turned, eyes darting like birds measuring the distance to open sky. Lyra's chest tightened—the familiar clench of doubt mixed with purpose. Her fingers flexed against her thighs. This was the moment: the slip between careful planning and real risk. There would be no turning back after this.

Blaze's nod came almost imperceptibly, a faint tightening of his jaw and a slight tilt of his head.

Lyra caught it.

Without hesitation, she slipped through the open space, and Jazz followed like a shadow. The weight of the moment pressed against their ribs. Their breaths slowed, stilled. They moved through the gap and vanished beyond the side door—gone before the air they had displaced had time to settle.

Harper's dark eyes tightened. The crease between her brows drew like a shutter closing. She leaned forward slightly, and the click of her boots echoed sharply against the steel as suspicion lingered like static in the air.

But duty was louder than suspicion.

"I need to get back to the debrief." Her voice was crisp and controlled. "Every minute counts."

Blaze's tone remained low and probing, yet measured enough to avoid friction. "Understood. But if you receive updates on protocol changes or pilot performance metrics, I expect a full briefing."

Her nod was curt, professional respect tempered by the weight of command. Yet her gaze lingered a moment too long in the direction

Lyra and Jazz had disappeared—an unspoken question hanging between them like static before a storm breaks.

Harper turned and retreated down the hangar's gleaming expanse, her rigid posture reinforcing every protocol she upheld and every rule she'd never break.

Blaze watched her go.

"She won't let this go," he murmured.

A charged silence filled the space. Unspoken urgency threaded through it like wire pulled taut.

The scent of jet fuel and metal grease mingled with faint ozone, tangling in the stagnant stillness. Blaze's gaze drifted beyond the rows of steel birds, settling on nothing in particular and everything in general. His hand rose to his jawline, thumb brushing the faint scar there, as if checking that he was still whole, still present, still ready for whatever came next.

"Setting traps with words," he said quietly. His voice held a dry edge. "We buy time. That's all we need."

His fingers curled tightly around the edge of a ledger resting nearby, balancing invisible scales, guarding secrets beneath calm eyes.

The distraction was set.

The next move was theirs to play.

Blaze's boots thud against the cracked concrete of the flight line, each step carrying the weight of controlled fury. Lyra doesn't move.

She stands alone ahead, shoulders squared against the fading afternoon heat, eyes fixed on a tangle of jet engines parked like sleeping beasts. His voice cuts through the quiet hum of idling planes—sharp, controlled, just below the threshold of drawing witnesses.

"What were you doing in the maintenance bay, Lyra?"

His green eyes lock onto hers—piercing, demanding.

She doesn't flinch. Her breath stays steady despite the sudden pressure pressing down. "Looking," she replies evenly, each word edged with stubborn defiance. "Checking the logs. Something isn't right."

Before he can press further, a shadow falls over them both.

Sarge steps into view, his broad frame blocking the golden light slipping past the hangar. The metallic scent of jet fuel clings thickly to the air now, mingling with the sharper tang of sweat and something burned out, exhausted. His rough baritone lowers, laced with warning.

"Blaze, I heard you were stirring things up again." He shifts his weight, eyes moving between them. "Lyra, listen to me. This isn't a game."

Lyra's teeth press into her cheek. Her eyes dart from Blaze's steady gaze to Sarge's wary stance, caught between two forces, neither willing to bend.

"Voss and Reynolds are already hunting," Sarge continues, his voice hardening. "They're looking for someone to pin this on. If you dig too deep, they'll bury whatever answers you find—and your careers along with it."

The distant thrum of an engine revving cuts through the tension, a reminder of stakes far higher than protocol.

Blaze hunches forward slightly, his jaw tight. "We can't just ignore it," he says quietly, each word measured. "But we have to be smart. Reckless moves won't save anyone."

They won't do anything but bury us deeper.

Lyra's fingers curl into fists at her sides. "The timestamps were doctored. Multiple edits, signatures that don't add up." Her voice drops, fierce and quiet. "If we don't act, someone else could die."

Sarge steps between them, palms open in a calming gesture that contrasts sharply with the hard lines of his face. "You both have fire—fine." He pauses, letting the weight settle. "But this isn't just about you."

He looks at each of them in turn.

"It's about the whole program. One wrong step, and they shut us down." His voice hardens further. "You won't like how clean the sweep is when that happens."

Lyra meets his eyes, raw determination flashing there like a flare in the dimming light. The knot in her throat tightens, but she forces the words out anyway. "I get it. I do. But letting this go..." She shakes her head. "I can't. Not without a fight."

The moment stretches thin, tension humming like a live wire between all three of them.

Sarge exhales sharply, his voice dropping into a quieter, almost weary timbre. "I'm serious. Watch yourselves—and each other." His gaze lingers on Lyra, reluctant respect softening the corners of his hardened expression. "This isn't just about being right. It's about surviving with your skin intact. You've got a lot to prove, Cadet."

He lets that hang in the air.

"Don't waste it recklessly."

Lyra swallows hard, the weight of his caution settling over her like a thin, cold cloak. She nods once—tight, deliberate. The fight isn't extinguished. Not yet. But it's tempered now by the hard edges of reality pressing in from all sides.

Blaze steps back, releasing a breath that feels like it has been held too long. His green eyes flicker with unspoken warnings beneath the fire—warnings not just for her, but for himself as well. He knows what happens to people who push too hard in places like this.

Around them, the low drone of the flight line resumed its steady chorus, indifferent to the fragile alliance now forged in quiet urgency. The sun continued its descent behind the hangars, and somewhere in that fading light, three people stood closer to the truth than they realized—and much closer to the edge.

The sun sliced low across the flight line, casting long shadows beneath the stationary jets. Lyra pulled Blaze toward a patch of tarmac, darkness swallowing the fading light. The hum of distant engines retreated, leaving only the echo of their footsteps.

She flipped open her phone. Her fingers trembled—just enough to betray the urgency coiled beneath her calm exterior. The screen glowed with maintenance logs, timestamps misaligned like crooked weather vanes. Minute edits lay hidden beneath routine updates. Blaze leaned in, his green eyes narrowing on the deleted warning code now resurrected on the display.

"Someone erased this before the engine check was signed off," Lyra whispered, her fingers tightening on the phone as if bracing for a strike. "It doesn't sit right, Blaze."

He swallowed hard. The air tasted metallic—jet fuel mixed with tension, stinging faintly against the back of his throat. "If that's true..." His thumb traced the numbers. "This goes beyond a tech error." His gaze flicked up, sharp and guarded. "But poking around? We're playing with fire. You know what the academy does if they catch us."

Lyra's shoulder shifted, and her eyes hardened with stubborn resolve. "We're supposed to keep flying. Trust the logs. Trust the procedures." She paused. "But if we don't dig deeper, someone else could crack up—maybe worse." Her voice dropped even lower, barely audible above the wind. "I'm not risking my life to cover someone else's sabotage."

She knew the price if she crossed the line, but staying silent felt like signing a death warrant.

Blaze's fists clenched at his sides, his knuckles white beneath calloused skin hardened by years in the cockpit. "You've got guts. I hate it, but I respect it." The old protective fire flickered behind his eyes. "I'm backing you. If things go sideways, I'll take the fall. But keep your head—no reckless dives."

"No promises on that," Lyra said, a half-smile ghosting her lips despite the tension curling between them.

Before Blaze could answer, Jazz's voice cut through—breathless but steady. "The report's closing tomorrow. They're scrubbing the logs. If we don't get hard copies tonight, it's done."

Lyra's pulse jumped. The warning struck like a siren.

Blaze exchanged a quick, loaded look with her—the silent language of two fighters allied beneath the same dangerous sky.

Jazz moved between them, weaving closer. "Quinn, the ground tech—he was storming around the hangar last week. He said they were rushing the turnaround too much. There was shouting with the supervisors." She hesitated, shadows flickering across her face. "If anyone's been messing with those logs, it's him."

A sharp gust carried the acrid bite of jet fuel, with bits of dust swirling around their boots. Blaze gestured toward a dim alcove against the chain-link fence where the setting sun struggled to reach. The three crouched together, close enough that the soft scrape of fabric and shared breath filled the tiny bubble of shadow.

"We split up," Blaze whispered, glancing at Lyra and then Jazz. "Lyra, you dig deeper into the maintenance records. Jazz, you shadow Quinn. Find out what buttons to press." His fingers brushed against Lyra's hand—a fleeting touch heavy with unspoken promises. The space between them tightened, charged. Neither pulled away.

Lyra's reply was a firm squeeze, fire kindling behind her eyes. "Got it."

Jazz nodded, his voice sharp with determination. "We're not letting this slide. Not on our watch."

Blaze's jaw relaxed slightly. The sharp edge of worry dulled in their shared resolve. "We stay tight. Head down. Stories straight if we get caught. The academy's not forgiving, especially with Voss breathing down our necks."

His words hung in the cooling air—brittle tension wrapped in unyielding loyalty. Lyra looked up at the rising stars pricking the twilight sky. Cold, distant, and unblinking witnesses to their secret pact.

"We'll expose whoever's behind this," she promised, her voice steady as the surf pounding distant shores.

Jazz slung an arm lightly around Lyra's shoulders, her grin quick and fierce. "When we do, nobody is going to forget who stood up."

They broke apart slowly, each stepping back into the dim embrace of the flight line's shadows. The buzz of the base settled around them like a living pulse—sharp and relentless. Lyra's resolve hardened, forging itself anew in the glow of Blaze's support and Jazz's unwavering loyalty.

Tonight, the hunt began.

Impossible Choices

Blaze's boots thud against the rough edge of the main runway, each step crunching on scattered gravel with a brittle sharpness that echoes the stillness around him. The night air bites deep into his jacket, cold enough to pull the sting from his skin and steady the tight coil in his chest. He stares past the glowing campus lights, their halo soft against the silhouette of distant hangars—metallic monoliths folded into shadows and distant haze. Somewhere beyond, the breakers pound the rocky shore, a dark rhythm pressing against the back of his mind—restless like his thoughts.

The crash investigation won't let him sleep. Pages of reports swirl in his mind, heavy with dead weight and questions that loop without answers. He runs a hand through his dark hair, feeling the faint grit of dust and sweat still clinging after hours spent poring over flight logs and testimonies. Faces blur behind his eyes—pilots he trained, mistakes he should have caught. The guilt sits low in his gut, a stone that grows heavier each time he replays those final seconds, searching for the moment everything fractured.

His eyes narrow, searching the horizon as if it might yield peace tonight. But all that stretches out is an empty sky—open, cold, and merciless.

The quiet crunch of boots over gravel punctuates the night. Lyra emerges from the cadet barracks, restless and sharp-eyed. The runway lights soften her silhouette, contrasting with the stark stillness surrounding them both. Her worn leather boots scuff rhythmically, scattering small stones that skim the cracked pavement. Her breath condenses faintly in the sharp air as she moves with a purpose born of frustration and unspoken questions. The academy's decision to suspend her still burns—a bitter injustice that coils beneath her ribs. Yet doubt whispers too, threading through her resolve like a shadow. She has made choices, some of them costly. The night offers no answers, only the cool air and the weight of things left unsaid.

She spots Blaze, a shadow carved against the dim glow of a tarmac light. His figure is rigid—shoulders squared but burdened, standing like a sentinel watching over a battlefield no one else can see. For a moment, Lyra hesitates. Then she forges her own path across the cracked asphalt, crossing the divide that separates them, drawn by a quiet gravity.

Blaze turns slowly. The night flattens his features into something unreadable. He lifts a single hand, fingers curling in a muted gesture—half invitation, half acknowledgment. He says nothing; words feel unnecessary in the quiet pull between them. The air hums softly, filled with the chill scent of jet fuel and ozone, the last traces of a day's relentless noise giving way to a heavier silence.

Lyra steps forward without a word. The cracked asphalt shivers beneath her feet. The distance closes until she falls into step beside him. She maintains a careful space between them—not quite close, but close enough to feel the unspoken tension threaded through the night. Her eyes do not meet his. Instead, she scans the horizon, letting the silence stretch long and thick like the shadows pooling at their feet.

The runway unfolds before them—a wide, empty ribbon of cracked asphalt and fading light, stretching past the edge of the academy's reach, bound by nothing but night and memory. The campus behind them flickers faintly: distant engines hum like a far-off pulse, the low murmur of a night shift never fully resting. To their left, a flag snaps sharply in the breeze, the sound cutting clean through the quiet.

Blaze shifts his weight. His jacket whispers softly as it rubs against the cool air. The breeze lifts loose strands of Lyra's hair, tangling them gently against her cheek. Neither speaks. Their footsteps fall in sync now, steady and deliberate—a fragile harmony forged in shared unrest.

She glances sideways. Moonlight traces the line of his jaw, catches the faint gleam of a scar, and softens the sharp outline in silver and shadow. His green eyes flicker toward her, unreadable but no longer guarded—the flint of a man weighed down yet unwilling to collapse. The faint tang of ozone prickles her nostrils, mingling with the distant, rhythmic pounding of surf beyond the base. The chill seeps past her jacket, threading through her nerves like an electric current.

Lyra's voice breaks the stillness—low, tentative, cutting through the night with fragile warmth.

"Funny how stars seem sharper at night—like they're watching us, not just shining past."

Blaze nods slowly. His voice comes out rough, quieter than usual.

"The wind's picking up. Runway lights slash through the dark."

A sudden roar fills the air. Metal splits the silence as a training jet thunders down the strip, engines blazing as it claws into the ink-black sky. Blaze flinches sharply; his shoulders jerk beneath his jacket, and his hands clench at his sides, knuckles whitening in the dim glow.

The sound echoes in his chest, pulling him back to the crash logs, to that moment, to failure.

Lyra halts their pace. Her hand drifts toward him, stopping short of contact. Concern softens her voice.

"You okay?"

His eyes flick to hers briefly—sharp, searching—then drift away, as if afraid to find the answer staring back. The cool air thickens with something unspoken, fragile enough to break with a whisper.

For a long moment, Blaze stands at the tarmac's edge, watching the jet diminish to a ribbon of light—a fleeting blaze against a canvas of black. The distant hum folds into silence, and the night swells around them, full of ghosts, full of unvoiced burdens.

He exhales slowly. The weight of unsaid words presses down. Yet in the quiet gesture—her hand almost touching his, the space between them charged with possibility—there's a fragile promise, one that gently pulls her close.

Stars flicker, sparse and cold, above the endless stretch of runway, their crisp pinpricks glaring against the spilled amber of the distant hangar lights. Lyra's finger rises hesitantly, tracing a path between scattered clusters.

"Kinda strange, you know?" Her voice drifts across the asphalt. "Up there, it's all dials and glass, tight and closed in. But here? It's... open. It feels like it's breathing."

Blaze's jaw tightens. The corners of his mouth pull into a line—less sharp tonight, more wearied than wary. He shifts his weight where cracked asphalt meets damp gravel, exhaling slowly. "The wind's picked up. It blows the runway lights slick like oil."

His voice is low and clipped, the usual harsh edge softened by exhaustion.

The night tears apart.

A training jet blasts off with jagged thunder, and Blaze flinches. His shoulders jerk, muscles tightening. Fingers curl into tight fists at his sides, nails digging into rough palms. The roar scrapes something raw inside him—a memory he's spent months trying to bury. His breath shallows, and his body goes rigid, bracing against the sound the way he once braced against ejection seats, spinning fuselages, and the smell of burning hydraulics.

Lyra slows beside him, her boots crunching softly on the gravel. She catches the flicker of pain—or memory—in his posture and voice. Her gaze drifts down to the path.

"You alright?"

The question slips out quietly, carefully. Not probing. Just holding the silence. She waits. Patient. Not pushing.

Blaze's eyes remain fixed on the fading pulse of the departing jet, a thin thread of white carving through the black beyond the far end of the runway. The hum of its engines dwindles to a fragile whisper, a ribbon of light dissolving into shadows. He hesitates, caught between the weight of silence and the words itching on his tongue.

"Funny," Lyra says after a beat, her voice barely above the night breeze. "How different the stars look when you're actually under them. Up there, you barely notice them through the glass and instruments. Down here..." She trails off. "They're loud."

Blaze shifts. Gravel crunches under his boots, breaking the steady rhythm of the wind. "Runway lights don't help either," he mutters, his gaze tracing the harsh halos leaking from each tall mast, searching the dark stretches in between. "They scatter everything. Make it harder to see what's real."

A thin thread of tension coils tight, then loosens.

His shoulders drop, almost imperceptibly. The veneer of rigid control slides just enough to let something through.

A fresh gust sweeps cold air across the runway, carrying the distant smell of burnt fuel and cold metal. Lyra draws her jacket tighter. "Sometimes I wonder if that's why I mess up—because I'm trying to catch the world all at once, not just the instrument panel."

Blaze's jaw slackens just a fraction. He nods, and his eyes soften—the sharp green shade dimming like the last light before dusk. The night settles between them, charged and heavy, but not uncomfortable.

Another jet slices through the quiet, far off now. Engines drone, fading into the distance. Blaze's hands unclench, flexing lightly, but the sting of tension lingers in his knuckles. Lyra steps closer, just enough to close the space without breaking the fragile rhythm they've found.

"You don't have to carry it alone."

The words slip out soft and deliberate, offering more than comfort—a quiet acknowledgment of the weight he bears.

Blaze doesn't answer immediately. He takes a breath that ruffles the edges of his usual reserve and looks out past the tarmac, where the glow of the base flickers like a distant heartbeat. For a fleeting second, his eyes lift to meet hers. Cracks of vulnerability thread through the usual stormy green.

The cold air tastes sharp—metallic, real.

The night hums with possibility and the unspoken, the cold air crisp against their skin, carrying faint echoes of distant jets and the sharp tang of burnt fuel. They stand side by side, shadows long and mingling, tethered by a moment that refuses to be quieted. The silence between them resonates, thick with what's left hanging, waiting just beneath the next breath.

Blaze pulls a slow, deliberate breath, the cold air biting at his lungs. His boots scuff against the cracked asphalt as he shifts his weight toward the halo of runway lights, fingers twitching at his side. Beneath the harsh glare, his eyes narrow, dredging a memory from years past—the night when everything spiraled out of control.

"It was quiet," he exhales, his voice low and steady. "At first."

Words wrestle out of some deep hollow. "Routine sortie. This pattern was old hat by then. We'd run the grid a dozen times without incident. Radio chatter buzzed with static—the kind that makes you lean in, straining to catch a signal through the noise."

His gaze drills into the shadows beyond the runway, the hum of distant engines like ghosts threading through the night. "Then the fire came. Not the slow burn of an approaching storm." He swallows. "The sudden crack of enemy tracers—whipping past us, shattering the silence."

He inhales again, his voice catching on the unspoken weight. "The world shifted in a blur of flashes and alarms."

Lyra stands just a few steps away, her jaw tight, her eyes tracing his silhouette as if trying to decode a language written in scars. She doesn't interrupt; she only listens.

Blaze's hands clench, his knuckles paling beneath his gloves. "I gave the order to Callen." He pauses, the air thick with memory. "Break formation."

Another pause—longer this time.

"I hesitated—long enough for it to feel like a lifetime—and he pulled away, just like I said. Then..." He bites the edge of the memory, his tongue pressed like an old wound. "Then he was hit, right after turning left."

The metallic shriek rings in his ears even now—a high-pitched scream of twisting steel and tearing metal. In that fraction of a second before impact, he had seen the flash bloom bright against the dark sky, Callen's jet swallowed whole by orange and flame.

"I watched that jet—my wingman's jet—rip apart in midair." His throat tightens, the pain raw beneath the cold runway lights.

"He didn't stand a chance."

The night presses in around them, thick with the smell of ozone and distant gasoline. His shoulders snap taut; his hands curl into fists as a cold heaviness presses down from deep inside him, settling like lead.

"Every flight since—I replay that moment: the hesitation, the order, the silence after the crash." His voice drops, barely a whisper now. "It never leaves me. I don't deserve to lead, not after what I let happen."

Lyra's breath was shallow, held tight as if afraid to disturb the fragile space he had carved out in the darkness. Her gaze didn't waver, fixed on the hard line of his jaw and the set of his shoulders. But her fingers twitched at her side, betraying the storm beneath her calm.

No soft words came from her—no hurried assurances—but that quiet stillness carried its own gravity. She stood with him on the cracked edge of the runway, where light and shadow blurred, absorbing the raw edges of his confession in silence.

Blaze exhaled slowly, the last syllables hanging heavy between them. Then the quiet swallowed his words, leaving only the subtle hum of distant base activity and the muffled throb of engines far away.

He didn't ask for pity. He didn't seek absolution—only the momentary relief of having finally said it aloud.

The cold wrapped around them, and Blaze's shoulders remained rigid beneath the pale floodlights, as if bracing against the night itself. Behind his tired eyes, something shifted—a fragment of guilt finally set loose, fading into the darkness.

Lyra exhales. The sound is soft and slow—like she's finally releasing weeks of restless energy into the night air. She glances down at the cracked asphalt beneath their boots. Dim pools of light from the runway lamps cast long, brittle shadows across the tarmac.

The tension in her jaw eases just enough for her voice to break the hush.

"There was this flight exam. My first real one. The kind that decides if you make it or break it." She swallows hard. "A storm rolled in suddenly, out of nowhere. Rain hit the canopy like a thousand needles—cold, sharp, and blinding. My instruments started going haywire, flickering as if they were alive and angry. That white noise on the radio swallowed everything."

She pauses, her fingers tightening against her flight jacket.

"My instructor spoke in a calm, steady voice. But I couldn't hear him. Not really." Her breath catches, the memory biting in the silence. "I froze. I just sat there. My head thrashed, and my hands gripped the controls so hard that my knuckles turned white. My heart pounded so loudly that I thought it would drown me out. I thought about quitting. Right there, in the sky. Giving up."

Her words fall between them like stones into still water.

Blaze doesn't move. He watches as her fingers tap against the fabric of her jacket in a restless rhythm. There is no judgment in his gaze—just watchful attention, as if he's seeing a different side of her—something raw and vulnerable beneath the fire.

Lyra's voice drops lower, steadying like the calm before a dive. "After that, shame wrapped around me like a second skin. I swore I would never be that helpless again. So, I learned to fly with my guts, not just from the book. Every risky twist, every wild maneuver you see? It's not rebellion—I swear—it's compensation. A way to prove to myself that I'm not the girl who froze in the storm."

Blaze's shoulders loosen slowly, the rigid line of his back softening as if the night air itself had eased the weight from his bones. The hard edge in his green eyes dims just a fraction. He shifts his weight, his voice gravelly but quiet when he speaks.

"I appreciate that. You telling me." His words cut through the stillness, small but genuine.

Lyra bites her lip, then meets his eyes with something unguarded flickering there. "It's funny, really. I thought you were untouchable. Like some legend who never bent, never broke." She shakes her head slowly. "But tonight, I see you're just a man. Human." Her gaze lingers on his scarred jaw, the tight line around his mouth. "And that changes everything."

The distance between them shifts—not physically, but in some deeper way. Their silhouettes stand side by side beneath the harsh runway glow, the battlefield of their rivalry softening into something fragile and shared.

The night air carries the faint scent of jet fuel mingled with saltgrass drifting off the tarmac. Their breaths mingle in the cold, each exhale a visible ghost in the beam of the runway light. The past and its fears, along with the raw trust forming between them—it all feels as tangible as the cracked concrete beneath their boots.

Lyra's gaze falters as she takes a step back.

Blaze holds her with a steady, unspoken invitation to stay.

"You make it sound like a victory," he says, his voice rough. "Flying on instinct instead of training. Like you learned something worth more than survival."

Lyra shrugs, the faintest wry curve touching her lips. "Maybe. Or maybe it's just me refusing to be afraid again. I don't want to be that girl who freezes in the storm ever again."

He lets out a dry chuckle—the sound like gravel sliding down metal. "Funny. You fight so hard to prove you're fearless, but it's clear you're just as scared as the rest of us."

Her eyes narrow, playful now. "Scared? Yeah. But what else is left when the sky's the only thing that keeps you breathing?"

"Being fearless doesn't mean you don't feel it." He shifts, scanning the dark horizon where airport lights wink through the night. "It means you push through anyway."

The silence that follows isn't empty; it's heavy with truth and tentative trust—the kind that settles between two people who have finally lowered their shields.

"You were my standard," Lyra says softly, breaking the quiet. "The guy who never lost a fight and never seemed to crack."

Blaze's jaw tightens. He doesn't deny it.

"And now?" She steps closer. "Tonight, you're just a man." Her words are tender and fragile—a confession that places a thread of connection between them.

He meets her gaze squarely, shadows dancing across his scarred face. "And you're not just a reckless cadet. You're someone who has been terrified and kept flying anyway."

Their eyes lock—two warriors stripped of shields, standing on that empty runway under harsh white lights and the indifferent stars above. The chains of past failures, admissions of fear, and survival shift and loosen with each breath.

They don't move closer. The silence between them buzzes with a different energy now, the kind that speaks louder than words: two people facing down their truths together. No masks. No bravado.

Distant jets roar like echoes of battles fought both in the sky and within themselves.

Runway lights flicker overhead, painting their long shadows side by side on the cracked asphalt. No longer opponents, but something cautiously new.

The night hums low beneath the vast dome of stars. Blaze's voice cuts through the quiet, grounded and measured, carrying the weight of unspoken threats.

"We're not just dealing with a rogue pilot's mistake or a cracked engine. This is academy politics." He pauses, letting the words settle. "The kind that seeps into every report, every file. Sirens echo because there's an investigation—one that will tie up loose ends without care for the truth."

He shifts his gaze toward the dim glow of the distant command center, where blinking monitors and sharp silhouettes hint at an army of eyes and ears. The chill night air pinches at their skin, carrying a faint scent of jet fuel and ozone.

"They'll look for anyone poking around where they shouldn't be. Alter logs. Erase data. Hide whatever suits their purpose to keep the academy clean on paper."

Lyra's jaw tightens. The dry scrape of her boots on gravel cuts through the stillness. Her breath is steady but resolute, though something sharper than anger flickers behind her eyes—fear, perhaps, that the truth would vanish before she could grab hold of it.

"I know." Her voice doesn't waver. "But I can't ignore those tampered logs. Jazz and I found them—changes that can't be chalked up to error or coincidence. Somebody wants this covered up." She turns to face him fully, her eyes flashing with quiet defiance. "I'll keep pushing. Rules or no rules, consequences or no consequences."

Blaze snorts, a short sound lost amid the wind sweeping across the tarmac. Then his voice lowers, softer but no less firm.

"You're not pushing alone. It's 'we' now."

The words land between them, stronger than any shouted command. A shift takes hold in the space where their shadows stretch thin against the cracked asphalt.

Without thinking, Lyra's hand brushes against his. His fingers curl slightly, as if anchoring himself in the quiet between them. The air pulses, charged and fragile. Neither pulls away. They stand suspended for a heartbeat—maybe two—before turning toward the horizon, where a lone jet carves a silver arc, its landing lights blinking a slow Morse code into the dark.

"It's a risk," Blaze says, his voice rough like gravel. His eyes track the fading glow, but when they return to her, something has shifted. An unspoken promise. A shared reckoning. "A damn good one."

Lyra swallows, the taste of cold air sharp on her tongue. "Then we fight. Side by side."

Sirens wail, distant yet piercing. A sudden reminder that the night won't shield them forever. The sound slices between their brief touch, snapping them back to reality.

They step apart. The unvoiced alliance folds tightly between them like a flight plan, compact and precise. The weight of what comes next presses against their chests as they move away from the runway, toward the glowing cluster of buildings that house rules, secrets, and everything they're about to defy.

Each footstep fades into the quiet roar of the bass, carrying a promise that neither can yet speak aloud—but both understand.

Embers in the Dark

B laze smooths the last sheet of flight reports. The crisp edges catch the faint amber glow from the desk lamp. The mahogany beneath his hands feels worn but solid—a grounding presence amid the piles of paperwork thickening like clouds. He stacks the papers carefully, aligning the corners with precision born from years of routine, then snaps the folder shut. The quiet click echoes in the near-empty hangar office, swallowed quickly by the vastness beyond.

For a moment, only the low hum of ventilation fills the silence, accompanied by the faint scrape of his fingers against the paper. Then laughter slices through—sharp, clear, tumbling, and bouncing off the steel girders overhead. It is a sound almost too lively for this sterile domain of concrete and metal.

Blaze straightens. His shoulders stiffen, a slow ache spreading through his limbs, the weight of the night refusing to ease. That laugh—bright, reckless, undeniably hers—threads through the cavernous space between grounded jets like a spark daring to ignite the cold dark. Even now, it stirs something he'd rather leave buried: recognition, longing, the dangerous pull of what he can't have.

His gaze sharpens as he swivels in his chair, catching the laugh again—a sound that teases the edges of his restraint, threading warmth into the chill of the office. For a breath, it serves as a tether to something beyond reports and rules, far from the ghosts gnawing at the corners of his mind.

He pushes back from the desk and stands. His boots thud softly on the floor. The hangar office door creaks open on brittle hinges as he steps out, his fingers brushing the cool steel frame. Darkness smothers the vast space, interrupted only by the dim glow of distant exterior lights that shimmer on the wet tarmac outside.

The fighter jets loom like shadows—silent sentinels, their outlines blurred by mist and rain-slick surfaces. This base and these planes are more than duty to him; they are the last anchor to a life of purpose before everything fractured. Reflections ripple across the oil-streaked concrete, each pool catching and distorting the dim glow.

The night air bites cold and sharp. Jet fuel tangles with damp earth and ozone, while storm moisture curls thin tendrils through the hangar's open bays. Blaze's eyes trace the path of that laugh—farther down the rows of planes, lost and found in the play of shadow and light. It carries the reckless certainty of youth, the kind he sometimes envies and often fears.

He lingers at the threshold, the sharp scent of rain and fuel enveloping his senses, the sound of laughter folding softly into the draft. Slowly, he closes the door but leaves it ajar, allowing that fragile echo to seep back into the room, threading itself through the quiet air.

The steady weight of the folder in his palm reminds him—time marches on. Rules to enforce. Reports to file. Lives to protect. Yet Lyra's laughter holds him a moment longer, a fragile promise of warmth in the cold, disciplined night. It is a reminder that some things can't be filed away so easily.

The desk lamp flickered—once, twice—then died. Darkness swallowed the cramped hangar office as the overhead lights finally gave out. The faint hum of electronics sputtered into silence, leaving only a thick quiet that pressed sharply against Blaze's ears. He slumped back in his chair for a heartbeat, the edges of the slip of paper caught in the last trace of lamp glow before shadow swallowed them whole. The mahogany surface where reports once lay gleamed dully in the black.

Fingers tapping against the armrest, Blaze instinctively reached for his comm unit. The handset felt cold and inert in his grip. He lifted it to his ear and waited for the crackle of static—nothing but hollow silence. He swiped at the touchscreen cautiously; there was no response. The entire internal system was dark, locked down like the rest of the base. His jaw tightened.

A sudden, mechanical thrum hummed low against the silence. After five years at Astra Flight Command, Blaze knew that sound in his bones—the backup generator awakening, a routine he had drilled through a dozen times. Relief and dread coiled through his chest in equal measure. He rose, muscles taut, and crossed to the office door.

Past the threshold, a faint amber flicker spilled from emergency floodlights that kicked to life under the cavernous roof. The hum deepened, steady and sure, as the backup generator breathed into motion. Steel beams above caught the dim light, glinting with the sheen of lingering raindrops.

Blaze stepped forward, his boots echoing against the cool concrete. The sharp bite of jet fuel sliced through the damp air, bitter and electric against his nostrils. He inhaled the scent deeply, steadying his racing thoughts—the familiar sting serving as a cold anchor in the chaos, a reminder that this cramped hangar was where he belonged, where he fought to maintain control.

The storm beyond raged unseen, a distant drum of wind and rain muffled beneath the hangar's steel ribs. Somewhere beyond the coastal airstrip, lightning would be splitting the sky, the kind of weather that tangled operations and kept training missions grounded. Water tapped relentlessly on metal surfaces, keeping time with the pulse hammering through his chest.

Fingers brushing against the cold fuselage of a parked fighter jet, Blaze let out a curt laugh—dry, rough, cutting through the heavy quiet.

"Lyra Hale," he called, his voice low and gravelly, "out here burning the midnight oil again, huh? The night owl's got to get her wings sooner or later."

The words hung against the half-light, teasing and tentative—a solitary chord in the darkness.

Lyra hisses under her breath, the word sharp in the cavernous dark. Her flashlight beam slices through the shadows, darting over the cold metal of the open flight panel. Instruments glow faintly—a ghostly maze of dials and switches catching the weak light in fragmented reflections. She kneels on the concrete, her knees scraping as she pries at a stubborn connector. Her fingers work with practiced urgency despite the creeping chill seeping through the hangar.

A muted chuckle ripples across the vast space, bouncing softly between steel beams and the silent hulks of grounded jets. Blaze's voice cuts through—gravelly and amused.

"Still wrestling with that connector?"

She doesn't look up, but her voice travels back, sharp and sardonic. "If that connector could bleed, you'd be a goner by now, Arden."

Her laugh follows—quick and bright despite the blackout. The iron scent of jet fuel hangs heavy beneath the damp air, mingling with the faint tang of ozone from the instruments. That familiar smell centers her somehow, anchoring her focus amid the quiet and the dark. The hum of adrenaline still pulses under her skin—leftover edge from hours earlier, now softened into tense waiting.

Minutes later, she perches atop a battered supply crate, rough wood pressing into her thighs beneath the thin flight suit. A portable work lamp struggles between them, its flickering glow painting wavering patterns across her face. Her gaze darts over the shadows, fingers tapping a rapid rhythm against the wood as Blaze emerges from the murk. His silhouette solidifies in the lamp's glow—a formidable shape softened by the unsteady light.

She swings her boots lazily, soles scraping against the concrete. "Since we're stuck here in the dark, how about we trade stories? Past glories, near misses—the kind of things that keep us awake at night?"

Blaze settles beside her with a heavy exhale, his jacket releasing the faint scent of leather and engine oil. His usual distance from her—that careful space they maintained—seems to ease slightly as he sits. She notices it in the way his shoulders drop, the way he doesn't position himself quite as far away as he normally would.

She props her elbows on her knees, tilting her head. "You go first. I want to know what 'Blaze' Arden was like before the nickname stuck."

Their eyes meet in the uncertain light. She holds his gaze—a silent dare wrapped in a crooked smile. For once, the usual edge between them softens into something raw and unguarded.

"Alright," he says quietly, his voice lowered against the night. "The first solo felt like the sky itself was holding its breath. Silent. Waiting.

Nothing but the hum of the throttle and the horizon's stare. The sun burned hot against the windshield. The wind sang inside the cockpit—like some secret song only the sky knows."

Her breath catches. The vividness in his voice pulls her deeper into a shared space beyond the blackout, beyond the cold concrete.

"That sounds... alive," she says softly.

He nods, his eyes distant. "It was. Before everything else."

Without breaking his gaze, Lyra leans back slightly. The light catches the curve of her jaw, revealing the hope that simmers beneath her fierce edges. "I was just a kid when I first saw an air show. My heartbeat rang in my ears like thunder. Watching the jets knife through the sky, I wanted in. I wanted to rise above all the noise, the rules, and the weight of everyone's expectations."

She lets her voice trail away, her breath warm in the stillness.

Blaze watches the shadows trace the lines of her face. That spark beneath her defiance flickers into something fragile—something he hadn't seen before. "You've got guts," he says, his voice low. "More than most."

Silence folds between them. Then Blaze shifts, resting his hand on the crate near hers. The air tightens. Charged.

His fingers hover too close. They brush against hers—a whisper of warmth beneath the chill.

Her fingers meet his. Tentative at first, then pressing firmer, sliding together in slow, deliberate motion. The backup generator hums around them, a steady pulse against the rain drumming rhythmically on the hangar roof.

Blaze curls his fingers until they entwine fully. Both inhale sharply. The shared heat becomes a tether in the dark.

The lamp flickers steadily. Shadows stretch across the floor, enclosing them in a fragile moment—one that lingers, untouched by duty's noise.

She smiles. Not fully, but crookedly enough to send a spark through the quiet.

"Are you always this soft when no one's watching, Captain?"

He doesn't answer. He only holds her hand a little tighter. The light wavers. The storm murmurs above. In the shadows of the hangar, two shapes lean into an unspoken promise.

The emergency lights hum quietly. The cavernous hangar transforms into a strange sanctuary—shadows stretching long in a soft amber glow, each corner softened into something almost reverent.

Blaze leans back against the cold steel crate, his voice dropping lower than usual as he meets Lyra's expectant gaze. Something more vulnerable than his usual clipped commands flickers across his features.

"My first solo?" He paused, his jaw working slightly. "It was as if the throttle hissed under my fingers—alive and insistent. The horizon stretched, endless and sharp, slicing the sky in two. For a heartbeat, I thought I might just float there forever—alone but free." He exhaled slowly, the memory painting the still air between them with the raw pulse of flight.

Lyra shifted, the light catching the curve of her jaw, the slight furrow of concentration softened by something quieter beneath her fire. "I remember a fair once. I was maybe seven." Her voice roughened with longing. "Planes buzzed over the beach, spinning like they owned the sky. I wanted to be one of those birds, breaking free from the noise." She swallowed. "It wasn't just about flying. It was about escaping, I think—about becoming something more than what I was."

Blaze watched the flicker of something fragile settle over her features—a sparkle dulled but not snuffed out. The warmth in her words found a crack in his own armor. His jaw tensed for a moment, his eyes flickering away before settling back on the crate beside them.

"After the mission that changed everything," he said quietly, "I wasn't sure if I'd ever feel that alive again. Not the rush or the edge." His fingers brushed the rough metal. "Just numb. It was as if my own skin had hardened, and I was flying blind inside. Every day since, I've been checking the instruments, but there's nobody really steering anymore."

He shifted his hand, settling it near hers, not quite touching at first. The intimate silence stretched—a breath held in the hush of the hangar. He sensed, then felt it: the delicate brush of Lyra's fingertips grazing his knuckles, tentative but deliberate. He didn't pull away.

Their fingers found each other, weaving slowly like tentative wings testing the air before flight. Blaze curled his hand around hers, the contact grounding them both in this fragile moment. Outside, rain began to drum on the hangar roof—sharp and steady, a dull echo of the steady thrum in his chest.

They breathed in sync, suspended in the dark with nothing but the quiet ceremony of shared space—the unspoken truth flickering like a beacon between their clasped hands.

"You ever think about what keeps us flying after everything?" Lyra's voice broke the silence, gentle but charged.

"Maybe it's the hope that something's still waiting on the other side," Blaze replied, his voice rough but steady, his eyes never leaving their entwined hands.

"You sound like a philosopher—kind of obnoxious for a night like this." A hint of a smile tugged at her mouth, playful and cheeky.

Blaze's lips twitched into the ghost of a smile. "Only when the lights go out."

Lyra laughed softly, the sound warm in the shadowed hangar.

"Do you ever think about that first flight?" she asked, shifting so her elbow brushed against his side. "How it changes you?"

Blaze nodded. "It's the moment you realize you're nothing but a speck against the sky, yet somehow everything at once. And the weight of that—suddenly, living feels heavier. But maybe that's what makes it worth it."

Lyra's smile turned wistful. "I've chased that weight all my life, trying to carry it without breaking."

"Sometimes carrying it is the breaking." His gaze flicked to hers, earnest and raw beneath the dim glow.

For a heartbeat, the world narrowed to the space between them—the faint scent of jet fuel mingling with rain, the chill of the night pressing in beyond the hangar's walls. Their fingers tightened, and neither pulled back. This—her hand in his, the trust unspoken—was rare territory for both of them. Blaze's usual armor lay scattered at their feet.

A distant chirp sliced through the quiet: an alarm from the emergency generator faltering, reminding them that the night wouldn't wait.

Blaze's hand twitched but stayed firm, holding onto the fragile tether between them—a silent promise hanging in the suspended darkness.

A shrill beep cuts through the quiet. The generator falters—a mechanical chirp, sharp and sudden. The dark cocoon they have shared shudders, dissolving like smoke in their ears. Lyra's hand slips from Blaze's, her fingers retreating like startled birds. Both freeze.

The spell breaks.

"I didn't mean to—" Blaze's voice rasps in the stillness, his eyes fixed on the floor.

Heat flares beneath Lyra's skin. She glances away, her fingers finding the loose strand of hair at her temple, tucking it with deliberate precision—as if rediscovering herself after an unexpected moment undone. "Yeah... I guess I'm the one who got caught off guard."

They stand there, the air between them folded tight with half-apology and half-acknowledgment. Neither wants to shatter the fragile thread tethering them to this secret space, but reality tugs insistently at its edges.

Blaze shifts, his chest rising with a steadying breath. His gaze drops to the crate beneath Lyra's feet. With slow, deliberate movement, he extends his hand upward. The gesture is simple and professional—but the length of his pause stretches it taut with unspoken meaning.

Lyra hesitates. Just a fraction. Then her fingers curl into his palm.

Their hands meet. Electric. Warmth bleeds through calloused skin, fingertips tracing the geography of a promise neither dares to voice. The hum of emergency lights casts their long shadows across polished concrete—an intimate flicker in the cavernous hangar.

"Let me help you down," Blaze said quietly, his voice low but steady.

She nodded. Weight shifted as he steadied her, his fingers holding the contact a moment longer—too long. Duty and desire pulled taut between them.

Then the generator sputtered. A mechanical roar shattered the moment.

Floodlights blazed overhead, piercing the dim corners with harsh white light. Both flinched, shielding their eyes against the glare. The hangar exploded from shadows into a clinical stage: gleaming jets, scattered equipment, polished steel beams—all thrown into sharp relief, exposing every line and edge.

Underneath the harsh glow, their closeness fractured. The spotlight demanded that they become colleagues once more. Blaze's jaw tightened. Lyra's breath caught; she tugged her jacket closer, stepping back an inch.

Jazz's voice echoed down the corridor—a clear, concerned question cutting across the sterile brightness. "You guys okay?"

They exchanged a quick glance. The weight of what passed between them compressed inside that look: soft confessions, fingers brushing, a brief escape from the rules that governed them.

Blaze's tone shifted instantly. "Everything's fine."

Lyra's nod was sharp, her eyes bright but cautious. "No problems here."

The corridor hummed with distant echoes of footsteps and the faint buzz of returning power. The moment had passed, sealed away beneath layers of protocol and necessity.

Side by side, they stepped from the pool of light into the corridor's cooler shadow. Fluorescent tubes flickered overhead, their long shadows mingling on the floor. Neither spoke. The silence was thick with unspoken truths; the closeness between them was undeniable yet carefully veiled.

In the harsh light of day—or night—they were pilot and cadet, instructor and student. But in the flickering shadows and suspended moments between alarms and lights, something fragile and fierce had taken root. The rules pressed down like steel girders around their shoulders, but the memory of that touch lingered—quiet, stubborn, and impossible to erase.

Punished for the Truth

Lyra slipped through the double doors into the base mess. The stale scent of burnt toast and reheated coffee coated the air. Her eyes darted across the room, hunting for Jazz's familiar shape amid the early shift cadets nursing trays of eggs and protein shakes.

Rumors rippled around the tables like low thunder, whispers taut with tension: the hangar blackout, the crash, secrets buried beneath flickering fluorescents last night—all humming underneath the clatter of cutlery and hollow conversations.

Her fingers tightened around the tray's edge, her knuckles paling, a faint tremor betraying the calm she tried to wear like armor.

Jazz waved her over from a shadowed corner near the back, a grin curving like a challenge, her eyes dancing with mischief. Lyra eased into the booth, and Jazz tugged her closer.

"You look like you spent the night hugging a live wire," Jazz said, her voice low and playful. "The cadet stress meter has never been this close to red. Commander Reynolds' voice was basically a restraining order by breakfast."

Lyra exhaled, nodding, but her gaze kept flicking toward the doorway. Every footstep sharpened, the scrape of chair legs, the metallic clink of trays—all heightened, as if danger pooled in the steam rising from the food stations.

Jazz leaned in, her voice dropping into a teasing whisper. "They're eyeing your pilot schedule like hawks. Word is, you're pushing limits again, flying circles around the rules. Heard anything juicy from the grapevine?"

Lyra's smile was tight, her answers clipped.

"Not much. Just noise."

Jazz's brow quirked, sensing the walls rising between them.

"You sure? Because you're MIA. And those eyes—they're volunteering for trouble."

If Lyra heard her, she didn't respond. The weight settling on her shoulders felt like frost.

From the far end of the mess, heavy boots drew her attention. Blaze strode past the tables, his head low and jaw rigid as stone. His eyes skipped over hers, refusing to meet, like ashes smoldering after a fire. He stopped at the serving line, his back to the windows, muscles taut as he surveyed the room. A tight knot of impatience and something colder settled behind his gaze. Unsaid things hummed in his silence.

Jazz shifted and nodded toward the other side, her voice soft.

"Guess he's avoiding you. Figures."

Before Lyra could respond, Sarge slipped up beside the table. His usually composed face was drawn taut. The warm sage hue of his eyes flickered with unease. He lowered his voice to barely above a whisper.

"Things have gotten heavier since last night," he said, rubbing the stubble along his jaw. "They're digging deep. You've been flagged—late-night access to the maintenance logs. Security is watching. This isn't small."

Lyra's chest tightened. Her fingers curled and uncurled on the tray as she processed the words.

The acidic scent of burnt coffee turned bitter on her tongue.

She pressed her thumb against the rim of her chipped mug, seeking purchase.

"Who's talking?" Her voice dropped, sharp and low. "Who turned me in?"

The question hung between them. Sarge's face deepened with the weight of what was to come.

"Hard to say for sure," he said. "Someone official, though. They're probably trying to cover their own tracks. They're playing it tight. If you're caught digging without clearance, it's not just a slap on the wrist."

Lyra's eyes sharpened. Her gaze flicked between the half-masked faces at the surrounding tables. Voices dimmed around her. Eyes flicked like whispers in the mist. Suspicion settled, thick as fog.

The clink of silverware sounded distant now, dampened by an undercurrent of anxiety that cracked the usual easy camaraderie.

Jazz squeezed Lyra's arm, her voice steady but fierce.

"We've got your back, Lyra. This isn't over."

Lyra exhaled a breath she hadn't realized she had been holding. Her spine straightened, resolve shaping every line of her body. She stood. The chair scraped sharply against the floor. Her eyes flickered past the window where dawn wrestled with the clouds.

Sarge cleared his throat, his voice steady but low.

"Be careful. This investigation has teeth now. The odds are that the stakes have just climbed."

The three of them moved through the mess, their steps muted yet purposeful, shadows trailing them as whispers chased their heels. The din of breakfast faded against the heavy hush hanging like fog—a fog threaded with distrust and unanswered questions that clung to every word left unspoken.

The courier's boots echoed sharply on the polished corridor floor before Lyra could catch the metallic thud of the sealed envelope landing on the edge of her bunk. She snatched it up, the official insignia of Astra Command emblazoned in cold blue ink across its crisp white surface. The typed summons inside was precise and unyielding: report to the Command Center immediately. Her breath hitched as her eyes scanned the words. A lead weight settled in her stomach, tightening as the edges of the paper seemed to burn through her fingers. What had they found? The question coiled through her chest like smoke—had someone talked, or had her tracks been sloppier than she thought? She clenched the letter, forcing herself to inhale slowly and steady her racing heart. Squaring her shoulders, she tucked the summons into her flight jacket and headed for the exit, each step measured yet filled with unspoken dread.

Blaze stood just beyond the corner of the hall, masked in shadow, his green eyes narrowing as they traced Lyra's retreating form. The tightness in his jaw deepened, and his fists clenched behind his back, knuckles whitening beneath the coarse fabric of his sleeves. Every fiber of his being screamed to follow—warn, protect, intervene—but the cold voice of command throbbed in his head: no contact, no interference. He swallowed the choke of helplessness, forcing his gaze away as she disappeared around the distant bend, swallowed by cold steel and sterile light.

Flight Officer Harper awaited at the threshold of the Command Center's austere conference room, arms crossed, eyes sharp and unblinking beneath a set of dark brows. Without a word, she gestured for Lyra to follow, her steps brisk on the gleaming tile. The doors slid shut with a pneumatic hiss behind them, sealing off the outside world. Inside, the long table gleamed under the artificial light, flanked by four figures—Commander Reynolds, her gray eyes like shards of ice; Major Voss, with a patient, calculating smile; and two other officials whose silent watchfulness filled the air with tension. The faint hum of ventilation blended with the sharp scratch of Reynolds clearing her throat.

Reynolds's voice sliced through the quiet like a whip. "Cadet Hale, you stand accused of unauthorized investigation, tampering with confidential files, and gross disregard for academy protocol." She gestured crisply to Harper, who set a sleek laptop onto the table, its screen flickering to life with an array of digital logs and time-stamped entries.

"Your repeated access to maintenance records without clearance is documented here," Harper explained, fingers tapping the keyboard with clinical precision. "We have security footage corroborating your presence in restricted hangar bays during unauthorized hours." The screen flashed images—grainy but unmistakable—that pinned Lyra to the charges like a moth in a glass case.

Lyra's stance bore the tension of steel tempered in fire, her hands clenched tight enough to whiten the folder she gripped at her side. She squared against the invisible weight pressing down on her chest, her voice steady and clear despite the racing pulse thrumming in her ears. "I didn't breach protocol out of defiance," she said, her eyes fixed on the panel. "I sought answers—not sabotage. The blackout wasn't an accident. I accessed those logs because I was fighting to keep us safe." Her words hung in the air, charged as static, raw and unapologetic.

Major Voss tilted her head slightly, a thin, enigmatic smile curling her lips. Lyra had seen that expression before in briefings and training sessions—the calculated warmth that masked something far colder beneath. Voss was the kind of officer who wielded power through subtlety, the sort who built loyalty and compliance through carefully measured approval, then destroyed those who stepped outside invisible lines. The cadets whispered about her political maneuvers within Command, the way she seemed to champion select pilots while quietly erasing others from advancement lists. That smile never reached her eyes.

"Your instinctive flying style is well-known, Cadet Hale," Voss mused, her voice silk over steel. "Impulsive, yes—but effective. However, that same temperament seems to extend beyond the cockpit." Her gaze flicked to each official before returning to Lyra, the question unspoken but unmistakable. "Your repeated rule-bending... it sets a precedent. An example for others that disregards discipline."

Lyra's jaw tightened. "I don't fly by instinct because I want to break rules. I fly because it keeps me alive—and the team. Sometimes that means trusting my gut over regulations." Her fingers curled more tightly around the folder, her nails digging into the thin cardboard. "But I never put anyone in danger intentionally."

The room fell into a brittle silence. Reynolds's sharp gaze remained fixed and unyielding. Harper's fingers flew over the keyboard, bringing up new streams of data—logs interlaced with security camera footage, each frame a piece of the narrative still unfolding. The cold glow of the monitors bathed the officials' faces, highlighting furrowed brows and pressed lips. The air thickened with the hum of restrained judgment, the kind that waits to see which way the scales will tip before striking.

Lyra shifted her weight slightly but remained poised, the flicker of doubt hidden beneath her composed exterior like a shadow at the edge of light.

"We'll review the evidence carefully," Reynolds finally said, her fingers steepled beneath her chin, her voice low but resonant, an unspoken verdict looming between the sterile walls. The others murmured their assent, and the room settled into a tense vigil, the moments stretching as Lyra stood alone beneath the harsh fluorescent glow, every heartbeat magnified in the silent watch of command.

The pale glow of the conference room's cold LEDs cast sharp shadows over the long mahogany table. Commander Reynolds sat at the head, her spine rigid, hands folded neatly atop the polished surface. Her gray eyes cut through the stale air as she leaned forward, her voice clipped and unyielding like the academy itself.

"Cadet Hale," she began, her words cool and authoritative, "your actions undermine not only our protocols but the very integrity of Astra Flight Command. The academy cannot tolerate such breaches without consequence. Allowing this behavior to go unpunished sets a dangerous precedent."

Her gaze narrowed, every syllable measured and precise. The weight in the room thickened—the silent pressure of tradition pressing down on Lyra's shoulders. Years of drilled obedience warred against her instinct to rebel, to demand answers. The cost of breaking protocol was measured not just in expulsion but in everything she had sacrificed to get here.

From the corner, Flight Officer Harper flicks a switch. Flickering images bloom on the screen: digital timestamps, access logs, and grainy security footage played on a sterile loop. Her finger traces the times—just past midnight, three a.m., over and over—each a mark against Lyra's name.

"These records show repeated unauthorized access to hangar maintenance systems," Harper reports steadily, her voice as sharp as the data she wields. "Correlation patterns indicate activity linked to the ongoing investigation, positioning Cadet Hale centrally—despite her denied involvement. The logs corroborate that these incidents were neither random nor accidental."

The dry mechanical hum of the projector fills the pauses between words. Outside the sealed room, muffled footsteps and distant voices echo faintly—a world moving on while Lyra stands trapped in suspended time. Clips reveal a shadow in the tinted hallways, movements that strain beneath the suffocating weight of regulations.

Whispers ripple among the panel members, subtle nods exchanged like covert signals. The officers lean in, their voices hushed, lips barely parting beneath stoic masks. Fragmented phrases float across the polished table: "Immediate expulsion." "Suspension as an alternative." "Institutional reputation." Lyra's jaw tightens. Her mind catalogs each possible ruin, each fracture point where her future might shatter.

Then the door opens with a slight hiss.

Major Elena Voss steps in, her presence slicing through the tension like a blade. Her gaze—sharp and unreadable—sweeps the room before settling on Lyra. She strides forward, her voice smooth and deliberate, embodying calculated control.

"There is another path," Voss begins, her palms pressed lightly on the table, fingers steepled with intent. "Expulsion would fracture the program's image at a critical moment. The academy faces external scrutiny. We need stability. So, we offer Cadet Hale a compromise: she will become the academy's public face, a model cadet, a symbol of resilience and order to the outside world."

The implication hangs heavy: represent the institution, cease unauthorized inquiries, and be the polished emblem while silence draws its curtain over the shadows.

Lyra's jaw clenches. Her fingers curl into tight fists at her sides. Her eyes flicker with a sudden, sharp blaze—not quite controlled, not quite surrendering. The silence stretches thick with barely contained fire.

She rises, her stature demanding attention as she fixes Voss with a mix of ice and fury.

"I want a private word," Lyra says, her voice low but sharp as a whip crack across the room.

Voss nods once, curt but measured. "You will have it."

An escort moves beside Lyra, leading her into the adjacent chamber—small and clinical, with the cold gleam of a polished desk and muted echoes sealing the door behind them. The larger hearing fades into a hushed reprieve as whispers volley silently just beyond the soundproof barrier.

Inside that tight space, the walls bear witness to negotiations where the stakes loom large, and the price of survival weighs heavily on every breath exchanged.

"We're offering you survival," Voss states, steepling her fingers again, her eyes gleaming with quiet authority. "You will become our symbol of stability during this crisis. The academy needs that narrative."

Lyra's lungs tighten. Anger wars with the reality she faces—the narrowing corridor of choices, each door closing behind her. "I didn't get into this program to become a poster child for silence," she retorts, her voice steady but edged with raw integrity. "I won't shut down an investigation to preserve an image. If someone's responsible for the crash, they need to be held accountable, not buried under political spin."

Voss's lips curve into a thin smile. "You're misunderstanding me. It's not about letting others off the hook. It's about your security… and the greater good."

Lyra clenches her fists, her knuckles paling as she grips the folder in her hands. "My security isn't worth trading my voice."

A silence stretches, taut and brittle, as both women measure the invisible lines of power and consequence drawn between them. Outside, the hum of ventilation systems fills the void—relentless, indifferent, eternal.

"This proposal grants you breathing room, Cadet," Voss says at last, her eyes steady. "Without it, you stand to lose everything. Think carefully."

Lyra's breath hitches. Her heart pounds like a warning siren beneath her ribs. She understands now—understands the trap, the choice between two forms of loss. Slowly, she nods. The accord settles into her bones like weight.

"Then I accept," she says quietly. Her voice carries the weight of battle-worn resignation and defiant hope, tangled as one.

Voss extends a hand—a pact sealed beneath the merciless fluorescent light.

Lyra takes it. The handshake is firm—a silent truce in the war waging both inside and out.

She steps back into the corridor, the folder bearing the academy's strictures held tightly in her grip. The memorandum's words feel like lead sliding into the pit of her stomach—promises made, freedoms surrendered, the horizon forever altered.

The hearing room remains empty behind her. The heavy knock of consequences echoes long after the doors close.

The door slides shut behind him with a cold finality. Blaze steps inside the sterile administrative office, harsh fluorescents draining color from everything—the metal desk, Sarge's weathered face, and the officer's pressed uniform. The light feels hostile, engineered to strip away any humanity from what comes next.

Sarge was already seated, his spine rigid and his eyes sharp, tracking Blaze's every movement. Across the metal table sat the administrative officer, unreadable beneath the knife-edge crease of his uniform. Without preamble, he spread an official memo across the polished surface.

Blaze's gaze froze on the words: *Negligence in oversight. Failure to maintain discipline. Formal warning of reassignment pending continued association with Cadet Hale.*

The paper was thin, and its weight was crushing.

"Look," Sarge said, his voice low and steady. "I know this looks bad on the surface, but you've got to factor in the context—Lyra wasn't sneaking around just for kicks. She was trying to keep everyone safe. The crash investigation... it's tangled and complex." He paused, choosing his next words with deliberate care. "The academy's got its fingers in too many pies. Political pressure from above, investigative pressure from below. Everyone's scrambling to cover their own backs while the real issues rot underneath. She acted on instinct, but it came from something real."

The officer's jaw tightened. "Mitigating circumstances acknowledged, Lieutenant, but protocol must be upheld. Captain Arden's record notwithstanding—" His gaze cut across to Blaze, unyielding.

"Continued contact with Cadet Hale violates direct orders. The consequences are severe."

Blaze swallowed, bitterness flooding his mouth. His fingers curled against the polished table surface, his knuckles whitening with the effort of restraint.

The officer slid a fresh document forward. It spelled out the ultimatum in crisp, merciless type: cease all communication with Cadet Hale immediately or face reassignment to a non-flying post. Or worse: court-martial.

Blaze's fingers twitched toward the paper. Each word on that memo wrapped around his chest like wire, squeezing the air from his lungs.

He rose slowly, muscles rigid, every nerve burning with the weight of it.

Sarge remained seated, but his eyes never left Blaze, tracking the storm building behind his face.

They stepped into the corridor, and the door clicked shut.

Blaze began to pace, taking short, violent strides. The stale office air clung to him, suffocating.

"The bullshit in command..." His voice dropped to a harsh murmur, almost swallowed by the hum of the fluorescent tubes overhead. "They care more about politics than people. Lyra's just trying to expose the cracks, and I get bum-rushed for trying to back her up." He clenched his jaw. "I can't just turn away. Not now."

Sarge moved closer. His hand—rough and calloused from years of flying—settled on Blaze's shoulder, grounding him.

"I get it, man. I do." Sarge's voice was steady and unwavering. "But right now, you've got to play their game. Lay low. Keep your head down. Let me watch Lyra's six. We'll find a way. We always do."

Blaze met his eyes. Gratitude flickered through the storm inside him—raw, desperate gratitude. That promise hung between them, fragile but solid, a tether against the chaos.

"You think they'll ever understand what she's about?" Blaze's voice cracked, rare vulnerability bleeding through. "What we're about? Or are we just pawns to them?"

"Maybe not," Sarge's gaze didn't waver. "But that won't stop us from moving forward—quietly, strategically. We've survived worse."

Blaze exhaled slowly. The fight inside him softened, worn down by the steady pull of camaraderie.

He reached into his pocket and drew out the formal warning. The paper crinkled softly between his fingers as he folded it along the existing creases and slid it back into his jacket. The cold weight pressed against his ribs—a silent reminder, a challenge.

Turning toward the corridor, he paused for one last look at the empty room. This was where orders were handed down, where futures were altered.

The sterile light seemed to dim as he stepped back into the hallway.

The base hummed around them, indifferent to the battles within.

Blaze's strides echoed down the corridor—purposeful, hollow, resolute.

The maintenance bay sprawls like a steel cathedral, its cavernous roof swallowing the afternoon light in a muted gray wash. Lyra slips through the yawning hangar doors. The distant clatter of tools fades into the vast emptiness. Jazz perches atop a battered crate, her legs swinging, and her sharp eyes scan the dim corners as if danger might materialize from the shadows themselves.

Sarge waits near a tangle of time-worn cables, his tall frame folded into a loose stance beneath the industrial fluorescents that hum faintly overhead. His face carries the worn stoicism of too many battles—some fought outside the cockpit, others in the maze of academy politics. When Lyra and Jazz approach, the quiet between them feels loaded, heavy with unspoken truths.

"Glad you could make it," Sarge says, his voice gravelly but calm. He drops the curtain of pragmatism before hope takes root. "Listen, kid. No matter what you think, this place clamps down tighter than a beast with a bone. Elena Voss runs this academy like a fortress. Right now, you're her biggest target."

Lyra's eyes spark defiantly, but her shoulders sag just a fraction, betraying the weariness she refuses to name. She folds her arms across her chest, her fingers curling tightly.

"You're not going to like what I'm about to say," Sarge continues. "You need to play the game—for now. Stick to the lines they've drawn. Push too hard, and they'll crush you." He leans forward slightly, his voice dropping. "Survive under their terms. Create breathing room. Then fight back when the tide shifts. Right now, fighting head-on means losing it all."

Jazz shifts on the crate, her eyes brightening with quiet fire. "C'mon, Lyra. He's right. This is just a pit stop, not the finish line." She reaches out, gripping Lyra's hand with a firm, steadying squeeze. "Don't let the fear get to you. The truth is still out there, waiting. And we'll find it."

Lyra turns her gaze to Jazz, meeting those fierce eyes brimming with loyalty. The weight of the moment ripples through her. The stubborn set of her jaw tightens, then loosens by fractions—not surrender, but a wary truce. Her voice comes low and measured.

"Fine. I'll lie low. For now." She exhales slowly and deliberately. "But this isn't silence. I'll never be silenced."

The words landed between them like a promise neither would break.

Sarge stepped forward and produced a folded note from his jacket pocket. His hands didn't waver as he pressed it into Lyra's palm. "This has names—people to avoid, notes on what you watch, and what you don't say out loud. Stay sharp." He held her gaze a moment longer. "I promised Blaze I'd watch your back. That means shielding both of you wherever I can."

Lyra's fingers closed around the paper. The creased edges bit lightly into her skin. She understood what the note meant: a map through the minefield ahead, a reminder that she wasn't alone in this. She tucked it into the pocket of her flight jacket, securing it close.

Jazz stood, brushing dust from her uniform. The bay's hum persisted like a distant heartbeat.

They moved toward the exit, their footsteps swallowed by the concrete expanse, echoing faintly and unevenly amidst the scent of oil and cold metal. The massive doors yawned ahead. Beyond them, the pale afternoon light seemed to mock the darkness they were choosing to navigate.

"Remember," Jazz murmured, drawing alongside Lyra, "we don't give up. Not now. Not ever."

They stepped out into the uncertain gray, three silhouettes dissolving into the day.

Lyra's knuckles rapped sharply on the sleek, unadorned door. It slid open, silent as a whisper, revealing Major Elena Voss seated behind a sparse desk, her fingers steepled beneath a watchful gaze. Voss's eyes held that cool, measured detachment—like a hawk eyeing its prey—yet the faint crease at the corner of her mouth suggested something akin to intrigued amusement.

Lyra stepped inside. Her boots clicked softly against the polished floor. The room smelled of cold metal and recycled air—sterile, but not uninviting.

She squared her shoulders, leveling a gaze that refused to flicker. "Major Voss." Her voice was steady, edged with fire. "I won't deny that I accessed the maintenance logs without authorization. That was my decision. But I won't apologize for chasing the truth."

A bead of sweat trickled down her temple despite the chill. Her jaw tightened. Each breath came deliberate and steady—a quiet defiance held just below the surface.

"There are safety risks here," she continued. "Real ones. And anyone responsible should be held accountable."

Voss's fingers flexed slightly. A faint smile curled at the corners of her lips. "Your resolve is commendable, Lyra. It's rare to see cadets stand their ground with such... fervor." She leaned back, and the metal chair whispered beneath her. "However, this isn't just about truth or duty. The academy is under scrutiny. Political eyes are pressuring every move we make. External pressures demand visible control and visible order." She paused, letting the weight settle between them. "Expulsion seems the straightforward route, but there's an alternative."

Lyra's gaze sharpened. The corners of Voss's mouth twitched again, thin charm spilling into her tone. "We could spare you the ruin of dismissal if you agree to become the academy's public face—the model cadet, the symbol of stability and excellence." Voss's eyes locked onto Lyra's, unblinking. "In exchange, you will cease all unauthorized investigations and all digging into this crash. Silence is key." She fixed Lyra with a gaze that barely masked the weight of the consequences behind those words.

The offer hung between them, cold and heavy as fallout dust.

Lyra's fingers curled into fists, and her throat constricted. But when she spoke, her voice remained level and controlled. "I'll consider making peace with silence, but on my terms."

"Go on."

"No forced silence on the crash itself," Lyra said. "No turning a blind eye to wrongdoers. I won't surrender my integrity for a public mask." She leaned forward, her gaze unwavering. "If I'm to represent this institution, I demand those boundaries in writing."

Voss's smile thinned, calculating and subtle. Beneath the veneer, something shifted—a grudging respect, perhaps. "I anticipated as much." She settled back into her chair. "Limited conditions, then: you will speak as the academy's model cadet, yes. But we acknowledge your right—privately—to press for safety improvements. The public won't hear of it, nor will you be completely muzzled." Her voice turned silky and precise. "Your value to us, politically and symbolically, makes your presence indispensable."

The tension curled and tightened inside Lyra's chest like a drawn wire. Suspended between hope and surrender, she weighed the alternatives: expulsion, suspension with her name dragged through the dirt, or this shallow olive branch.

She exhaled slowly.

Finally, her eyes flickering with reluctant acceptance, she extended her hand.

Voss rose smoothly, meeting Lyra's grasp with a cool firmness. The handshake lingered a fraction too long—a subtle assertion of power. "A wise choice, given the current climate."

Lyra's fingers closed around the grip, a quiet surrender spoken in a touch. The deal struck, she turned toward the door, each step measured but heavier for the newly bound chains.

The corridor outside greeted her with the soft hum of late afternoon light filtering through armored windows. The air smelled faintly of heated concrete and a distant storm, tinged with the metallic undercurrent of tension she carried inside her chest.

In her hands, she held the fresh memorandum—official, typed in cold precision. Her eyes skimmed the words: model cadet, public appearances, approved statements. The document dictated her future responsibilities, a roadmap penned by political necessity rather than personal choice.

Her fingers traced the sharp edges of the paper. Each word felt like a compromise, a forfeiture of autonomy in exchange for survival. She wanted to rage against it, to tear the contract to shreds. But she didn't. Instead, she slid the document into her uniform pocket. The weight pressed against her hip, a silent reminder that freedom carried a high price and that survival in this game sometimes meant wearing a mask carved by others' hands.

A quiet fire burned in her chest—rebellion buried but far from extinguished.

She straightened and stepped down the corridor. Her boots echoed against the polished floor, mingling with the distant clatter of the base's relentless machinery. The sterile hum wrapped around her like a shroud as she disappeared into the shifting shadows of Astra Flight Command.

A clerk's stamp thudded sharply against the thick paper. Final. Official. Lyra's fingers briefly tightened around the pen before she signed, the scratch of ink echoing in the silent Command Center.

The sheet was crisp and heavy in her hands—a formal warning etched in precise language that demanded the immediate cessation of all contact with Captain Arden. She read the words again, each one a small blade. The order didn't just separate them; it criminalized what they felt. Her chest constricted. Determination hardened alongside the fear. She handed it back, her voice clipped and steady despite the tremor beneath.

Across the base, in quarters that smelled of loneliness, Blaze sat alone. The envelope snapped open with a sharp tear of coated paper.

His eyes flicked to the typed words. Each sentence was a blow.

No communication with Cadet Lyra Hale.

Immediate compliance mandatory.

Failure to adhere will result in disciplinary action.

The weight pressed down—cold, relentless. His jaw tightened, and his knuckles blanched as he crumpled the letter, rough fibers biting into his fingers. The anger flared—hot, sharp, useless.

Slowly, he smoothed it back with care, as if erasing the wrinkles might erase the order. It didn't.

Sharp footsteps echoed in a narrow corridor lined with dull gray lockers and flickering fluorescent lights.

The late afternoon sun slanted low, casting long shadows that stretched and crawled across the cracked linoleum floor. Dust motes drifted through the harsh light like tiny ghosts.

Lyra rounded a corner near the barracks, shoulders squared, heart hammering in a tight rhythm. Blaze stepped from the opposite direction. The quiet gravity that had become his shield settled around him like fog.

Their gazes locked—collision.

The air tightened, heavy with things left unsaid and promises too fragile to speak aloud. Lyra felt it compress in her chest, stealing her breath. Blaze's eyes—fierce, unyielding—softened ever so slightly, a flicker of the weight of what he must deny himself.

Neither moved forward, caught in the eddy of their fractured connection, breath shallow and catching.

For a heartbeat, time fractured between them—regret, a bitter tang in the back of the throat; longing that ignited and burned but could not be fed; fear of what the future demanded.

The corridor's silence enveloped them. A taut thread stretched thin.

Without a word, their eyes spoke the things they dared not say aloud: the fractures between duty and desire, obedience and rebellion.

Blaze stepped back first. The stiff snap of his boots echoed with finality.

Lyra exhaled slowly. She pivoted, sending her own boots down the hall—heavy, measured. Each footfall was a surrender wound, a quiet sacrifice to the written orders now tattooed on their futures.

At the threshold of her quarters, Jazz materialized from the shadows like a ray of fierce sunlight. Her smile was sharp and knowing.

Without pause, she slipped a small, folded note into Lyra's palm—a whisper of solidarity folded into plain paper.

Lyra's fingers curled around it, and her pulse quickened.

The words inside flashed in her mind like a beacon: *Stand tall. This isn't over.*

Warmth crept beneath the cold armor of the day's despair, a flicker of rebellion—enough to steady her breath as tears threatened to spill, unchecked.

Jazz caught Lyra's eye. No words were needed; her gaze was a shield—steadfast, defiant.

Lyra blinked away the sting, her lips curving with reluctant gratitude.

The room was dim, with a single fluorescent strip peeling back shadows across the pale walls.

Lyra sank onto the edge of her bunk, the thin mattress barely yielding beneath her weight. Her eyes traced the cracked paint of the ceiling, mapping invisible paths to somewhere beyond this suffocating silence.

Across the base, in a similarly sparse room, Blaze sat on his bunk. His fingers drummed a restless rhythm against the faded blanket.

The scent of cold metal and jet fuel lingered faintly in the air—a stubborn reminder, a ghost of battles fought both in the sky and in the heart.

His mind circled the same ache. Unspoken promises unraveled in the stillness of the evening. Hope was wounded; futures were uncertain.

The simmering ember of a fight was far from extinguished.

They passed in the corridor three days later.

"I heard," Lyra's voice cut through the hush—sharp and low. "They're trying to cage us both."

Blaze's reply came raw and hoarse. "The system is crueler than any storm we've flown through."

"And yet," her eyes flashed, burning with defiance, "we're still here."

"That never changes." His voice was barely above a whisper, shadowed with bitterness and something softer—more desperate.

The crackle of tension pulsed between their words. Fear of loss tangled with a stubborn hope. Neither knew how long they could hold on.

But in the stillness of their forced farewell, the tether between them refused to sever.

Lyra's steps echoed faintly as she disappeared down the hall. Blaze stood in the narrowing light, the formal warning like a shackle around his heart.

Jazz's note rested heavily in Lyra's pocket—a quiet promise of resistance, nestled amid the cold orders that sought to keep them apart.

The Unsanctioned Flight

Blaze slips out of his quarters before the first fingers of dawn have draped themselves across the sky. The corridor is a muted tunnel, with dim lights flickering faintly above as his boots scrape quietly on the linoleum. His duffel bag, heavy and packed with intention, swings at his side, the leather whispering faint creaks with each step. Inside, he has everything he needs—everything he has decided he can't leave behind. There is no turning back now. He pauses, his fingers brushing the wall's cold metal panel to steady himself, then glances toward the flickering corridor lights—nothing stirs behind closed doors.

Outside, the air bites with the crisp freshness of pre-dawn—cool, sharp, and faintly scented with damp concrete and the lingering tang of jet fuel from the night's tail-end flights. He inhales deeply, his shoulders easing as the breeze curls against his neck, weaving through the sparse grass by the barracks. Shadows pool in the hollows between buildings, flattened and stretching like slow-moving tides of ink.

His boots tap a steady rhythm across the cracked pavement as he strides toward the cadet dormitory. The building rises starkly against the deepening sky, its windows catching the last pale gleams of night. He stops by one window, perched half a floor above the fire escape stairs, and gives two precise knocks—deliberate but soft—an urgent summons.

Behind the glass, movement stirs. A hand lifts, wiping a crust of sleep from a sharp, alert eye. Lyra's face emerges, lips parted for a moment as the window sash is eased open with a muted creak. She blinks against the chill, startled but instantly focused, her green eyes pinning him in the low light.

Blaze crouches on the narrow metal rungs of the fire escape, the coarse grit of peeling paint scraping against his palm, his breath a ghostly mist in the cold air. His voice cuts through the silence, low and clipped like a thread pulled taut.

"Meet me at Hangar 3. Five minutes. No questions."

The words carry the weight of a command, edged with a desperate kind of resolve that leaves no room for hesitation. His gaze doesn't waver, locking onto hers through the window's frame.

Lyra blinks, then sits upright, the shadows lifting from her face as determination gathers like storm clouds. Without a word, she moves back inside.

In her cramped dorm room, the soft rustle of fabric and the zip of gear punctuate the quiet. Five minutes, she estimates by the glare of the small clock on her bedside table. Her fingers work with practiced speed, pulling on flight gloves and fastening harness straps over a sleek suit that smells faintly of motor oil and ozone. Her breath lifts in shallow, steady puffs—a rhythm synced with the pulse of adrenaline threading through her veins.

In the dim corridors, she slips past sleeping cadets, careful to step lightly on the well-worn floorboards. The musk of unwashed blankets and the faint scent of pine cleaner mingle with the distant hum of air filters. She pauses briefly outside a bunk, crouching and scanning the hallway—empty. Then, like a shadow, she moves, her eyes flicking over closed lockers and faded posters pinned crookedly on pale walls.

Lyra's hands brush over the cool metal of the fire escape railing as she descends the last flight of stairs. The morning chill bites sharper here, with dew clinging to the edges of her boots, soaking her cuffs with cold moisture. The sprawling base is still and hushed, the low rumble of distant generators a faint heartbeat beneath the deeper silence.

Ahead, Blaze's silhouette stands rigid beneath the low-hung clouds, a dark contrast against the pale wash of the coming light. He glances back down the steps, his fingers tapping against his duffel.

"You made it."

Her lips curve into a breathless grin, her eyes bright with a reckless spark.

"Wouldn't miss it."

Their footsteps echo softly, slipping across the slick tarmac where droplets bead and shimmer under the weight of dawn. The towering outline of Hangar 3 looms ahead—a cavernous shadow swallowing the faint glow of the awakening world.

They move together toward the hangar's mouth, her shoulder brushing against his, close enough that she can feel the coiled tension radiating from him like heat off sun-warmed concrete. There's no certainty in this—only the sharp edge of risk and something deeper, wordless, binding them. She doesn't fully understand what he's asking of her, and perhaps that's the point. Trust tastes like copper and possibility on her tongue, like the moment before a dive when gravity hasn't yet claimed you. His jaw is set, the muscle flexing with the weight of whatever choice he's already made. She sees it in the rigid line of his shoulders, in the way his hand grips the duffel as though it contains not just gear but consequence. And still, she follows.

"Blaze, what exactly are we doing? I need details." Her voice cuts through the chill, but she meets his unyielding gaze squarely.

He shakes his head, his voice low and firm.

"No time. Just trust me."

Lyra exhales, the air tasting like rain on hot tarmac, and nods.

"Trust, huh? You're going to owe me for this."

"And I don't plan on losing."

Their eyes lock, a flicker of shared defiance sparked amid the encroaching light. Then Blaze turns, leading the way toward the hangar's yawning doors, shadows folding behind them like a secret too heavy to speak aloud.

Blaze slipped through the yawning mouth of Hangar 3. Shadows pooled thick where the cold concrete met the cavernous walls. Outside, a thin strip of blue-gray dawn crept through the open doors. Inside, the air was stale, holding its breath against the morning chill.

Lyra waited in the recesses, her silhouette a sharp slash against the darker stone. Her jaw was tight, and her fingers flexed in a controlled rhythm—the restless energy of someone who had rehearsed this moment a hundred times in her head.

Blaze's eyes flicked to the laminated patrol schedule hanging crookedly near the maintenance bay. His wrist caught the soft glow of his watch—seconds ticking in tight harmony with his heartbeat. Two minutes clear. No ground crews. No watchers.

"Window's open," he said, his voice low and clipped. He stepped toward the nearest trainer jet and swiped a borrowed keycard. The magnetic strip whispered compliance. A dull click. Access granted.

His fingers moved across the avionics console with surgical precision, erasing fingerprints—artifacts of recent logins that could trigger an automated alert the moment someone ran diagnostics. Every trace mattered. One forgotten swipe, one overlooked login timestamp, and the academy's security protocols would flag the intrusion before they had even cleared the tarmac.

Lyra kept the handheld device alive, its small screen flashing system feedback. Clear. No alarms. No trace. Her fingers twitched with eager impatience, betraying the calm she wore like armor.

"Reset complete," she murmured, her eyes sharp.

She moved into the rear cockpit with practiced grace, the metal biting cold through her flight gloves as she fastened the harness. Her shoulders were firm, honed by months of grueling drills. She ran through the checks quietly, each gauge a pulse point under the hood. The fuel tanks brimmed past ninety percent. Hydraulics whispered at steady pressure. Avionics alignment was locked true.

"Fuel levels stable," she called out, her voice measured. "Hydraulics holding. Gyro alignment nominal."

Blaze nodded without looking away from his own panel, his fingers methodically peeling back maintenance covers to expose cables and circuit breakers like veins beneath synthetic skin. One by one, he flipped switches—transponders muted, beacon lights turned to neutral. Set to invisible. Untraceable.

Lyra's hands moved quickly, her fingers dancing over a compact keyboard, rerouting internal comms to a secure, discrete channel. The low hum of the jet's awakening systems echoed through the cavernous hangar, mingling with the sharp tang of metal and the faint, oily bite of fuel vapor. The concrete floor felt cold beneath Blaze's boots, each footstep swallowed by shadows thick as spilled ink.

Her breath hitched—brief, barely perceptible.

A shadow crossed her eyes—the weight of unseen chains pulling taut beneath her skin. Expulsion. Disgrace. The academy's iron jaws closing shut. She blinked, swallowed hard, then squared her jaw. Her fingers tightened on the harness strap, her knuckles whitening for just a moment before she released it. When she looked at Blaze, her gaze was steady. Unflinching.

She steeled herself with a whisper. "Ready."

Blaze's nod was an unspoken vow—no fanfare, no hesitation.

The cockpit hatches hissed closed, sealing their world from the cavernous stillness. His fingers pressed the switch for external power. Soft growls rippled through the aircraft's frame. Hangar lights dimmed to near darkness, shadows swallowing them whole as electricity hummed alive beneath their skin.

"You know what we're sailing into?" Lyra's voice was a breath against the encroaching silence. "No one's supposed to be here."

Blaze's glance was a cool blade. "No one who matters."

Her grin was quick, tight—defiant. "Let's light it up before the bastards catch wind."

"Five minutes, tops," Blaze replied, his voice clipped. Exit routes and patrol patterns hummed through his mind. "Just enough to prove we can do this."

They shared a look—brief, electric—then settled into their roles, each movement measured and deliberate. Lyra's fingers found the controls with hungry precision. The cockpit became their shared sanctum, where instincts meshed with protocol.

The jet breathed beneath them, alive and hungry, waiting. Outside, the base lay hushed, cloaked in shadows and secrets.

Blaze finished the final system checks, confirming that signals were silenced and circuits were firm. The faint metallic click of safety pins sliding free reverberated softly in the tight space. Lyra's pulse tapped rapid rhythms against the throttle.

"Ready on your mark," Blaze murmured, his eyes flicking to the instruments.

Lyra leaned forward, her voice barely above a whisper. "Let's fly."

Outside, the hangar breathed a quiet acceptance, oblivious to the storm about to take flight beneath its iron ribs.

Blaze's fingers tightened on the throttle, coaxing the engine awake. A low rumble vibrated through the cockpit—a familiar shudder creeping into his bones. The machine's heartbeat synced with his own.

The trainer jet coughed to life beneath him, its metal joints protesting before settling into a steady hum. He eased the throttle forward just enough to nudge the aircraft off its moorings, the wheels grinding softly against the hangar floor. Shadows stretched long across the bay, swallowing the jet's dark silhouette as it began to creep toward the runway edge.

The cool dawn air bit at his exposed skin beneath the cockpit seals, mingling the sharp scent of ozone with damp tarmac. Every inhale tasted of thick anticipation, a silent promise hanging just beneath the engine's growl.

Lyra's gloved hand flicked at her helmet mic, adjusting for clarity. Her voice crackled through their private comm channel, sharp and steady.

"All systems green. RPM steady at 80 percent. Engine temp holding."

Blaze's eyes flicked to his own instruments, searching the tiny dance of needles and lights that promised life or failure. The base remained swallowed in pre-dawn stillness—no movement on the tarmac except for what they controlled, no voices crackling across the tower frequencies. Only the hush of distant waves and the occasional metallic creak of restless aircraft broke the silence. Their engines were the only defiant sound interrupting the calm.

A dim red glow swept past a nearby maintenance vehicle crawling along the tarmac.

Blaze's hand snapped to the throttle, cutting power. The jet's engine stuttered, the drone tapering off into near silence as the ground vehicle passed, its headlights slicing brief, ghostly bands through the dark.

"Vehicle approaching from the east," Blaze murmured, his voice low but clipped. "Hold."

Lyra's fingers clenched the stick, her knuckles whitening beneath her gloves. Her eyes, sharp behind the tinted visor, flicked constantly over the instruments, her jaw set tight. A pulse of unease flared in her chest, but she kept her voice calm.

"Copy. RPM dropping. Ready when you are."

The truck's taillights vanished into the night, swallowed by the maze of hangars and shadows. Blaze pushed the throttle forward again. Power surged back to the engine with a hungry growl. The aircraft rumbled beneath them, eager to break free.

He steeled himself against the bite of the morning air seeping through the cockpit seals and guided the jet closer to the runway's threshold. The lights marking the path blinked in rhythmic succession—like distant fireflies casting pale halos through the mist. He glanced up once toward the looming control tower.

Silent. Vigilant. No movement. No unexpected watchful eyes.

Blaze's hand found the stick. The throttle slid forward with intention.

"Throttle's ours," he breathed. "Let's move."

The jet lurched forward—steel and fire thrusting against the ground. A storm of sound built in the cockpit: the crescendo of turbines roaring with hunger, tires skimming the runway's worn surface. The jet tore along the strip, veins of speed pulsing through the frame, thrust carrying them beyond limits etched in countless training logs.

"Elevate," Blaze commanded, his voice rough with controlled adrenaline.

Lyra reacted instantly, her hands poised and precise on the stick. The nose rose, slicing through a blanket of cold air heavy with the salt tang of the ocean below. The earth fell away—a quilt of shadow and faint light receding beneath them.

Somewhere in the control tower, Jazz leaned forward, caught off guard as a feed flickered on her screen. An unauthorized jet was moving at an hour it shouldn't be. Her fingers hovered over the console, her heart skipping in sudden disbelief. The needle of panic nudged forward.

She resisted the urge to blare the alarm.

Jazz squinted through the grainy feed, studying the helmeted figure at the controls. Lyra's lean profile was sharp against the cockpit glow—unmistakable. A breath caught in Jazz's throat. She watched the stick movements, the precise adjustments, and the fearless angle of ascent. Admiration battled against her duty, and duty lost.

"Lyra..." she whispered, her voice barely a ghost.

Jazz lowered her binoculars slowly, her eyes never leaving the shrinking shape of the jet as it climbed past the hazy horizon. The rising dawn painted the sky in swaths of steel blue and soft apricot—the perfect backdrop for a flight stolen from the rules.

"What the hell," she mouthed, her voice barely steady, caught between admiration and disbelief.

Inside the cockpit, the silence between Blaze and Lyra hummed with electric tension. The base melted away beneath a bowl of stars fading into dawn's promise. No words broke the moment—only whispered breaths and the steady thrum of engines that bound them together in flight and unspoken rebellion.

The jet shivered beneath Blaze's hands as he eased the throttle forward. A sharp intake of breath. The roar swelled in the cockpit. His pulse thrummed in steady time with the engine's raw hunger igniting to life.

The coastal ridge—that critical boundary marking Astra's airspace—dropped away below in swaths of mist and shadow. The world shrank as Blaze drove the spear of metal straight up. Each pulse of power fed the climb. The engine's growl pounded against his chest in a steady cadence.

Behind him, Lyra's eyes darted across the gauges. Her brows knitted tight with focus.

"Engine temps are holding steady, but the mixture is rich at sixty-five percent," she murmurs, her voice taut. Her fingers dance low on the panel, coaxing the fuel ratio to leaner. The subtle hiss of valves adjusting and the barely audible click of switches create small sounds that stitch their flight's fragile rhythm together.

Blaze nods. His hands remain steady and sure as he feeds the throttle with measured pushes. His jaw tightens against the pressure building in his ribs. The cockpit hums with life—metal and flesh intertwined, surging skyward. Around them, clouds gather thick and white, billowing like ghostly pillars.

A sudden murmur escapes Lyra before the jet shudders. "Trim is drifting left. Pressure spike, maybe ten seconds out."

Blaze's fingers twitch, ready to adjust.

She is already there. Her hands flick over the secondary controls with light confidence, coaxing the yaw into balance. The stick vibrates beneath his grip—subtle tugs of unseen forces made tangible. He blends his throttle feather with her corrections, climbing toward the apex with a shared instinct born from hours of training.

The cabin contracts under gravity's relentless squeeze. G-forces press deep against Blaze's ribs. His breath comes shallow but steady. The world narrows to the green glow of Lyra's HUD, a perfect line cut across a shifting horizon.

He catches the faintest lift of her eyes—a quick lock on the horizon line, flickering like a lighthouse beam. She anticipates, counters, and adjusts before a twitch becomes a shove.

The jet jolts. Sudden turbulence rattles the frame like a warning. His muscles tense instinctively—old habits from dogfights and narrow escapes pulling at his reflexes. But before words can form, Lyra's knee nudges the rudder pedal, a barely perceptible movement that smooths their ride.

The metal's cry softens. Tension eases like a held breath released.

Blaze glances over, meeting her gaze through the smoky visor. "You read that before I felt it."

His voice comes out rough from exertion, edged with something like respect.

She quirks a half-smile, one edge teasing. "Someone's got to keep you from flying us apart."

He doesn't answer. Instead, the jet crests the clouds, bursting through a ceiling of soft ice crystals that sparkle like shattered glass caught in the dawn light. A flush of cold air seeps past the cockpit seals—sharp with ozone and salt spray. The chill prickles his skin beneath the collar of his flight suit.

Below, the sea stretches wide and pale, blurred by distance and early light.

Their breaths come harder now, lungs aching against the constraints of gear and gravity. The first climb is complete.

The jet eases into level flight, gliding over the ocean's gleam—a fragile ship suspended in an endless void.

Lyra's voice breaks the silence, low and sure. "Pressure's stable; avionics are nominal."

Blaze allows a flicker of a smile—the kind that threatens the stern captain's mask. "Not bad for a rookie."

"The rookie's got better instincts than some veterans I've seen." Her grin widens behind her helmet.

He shakes his head, amusement softening his gaze. Lyra's steady hands have matched every correction without hesitation. A reluctant respect tightens in his chest—the kind he didn't expect to feel while watching someone still proving themselves.

"Keep that up, and you'll have me eating my words."

"No risk of that," she counters, her voice carrying an edge of challenge.

They settle into a quiet rhythm, the cockpit alive with subtle clicks and soft beeps. The ocean yawns below, immense and indifferent, as the jet carves its path against a bleeding horizon.

"Ever think about how small we are up here?" Lyra muses, her voice a breath of wonder. "Just two dots scratching the sky?"

"Every day." Blaze's eyes scan the instruments, but he feels the weight of the moment in the spaces between the numbers.

She laughs—brief and unguarded. The sound fills the tight quarters with warmth. "Don't let it go to your head."

"No risk of that." His voice thickens with the ghosts of battles past and the promise of fragile alliances forged in steel and silence.

Lyra's fingers stroke the controls again—steady, precise—a dance of confidence and instinct honed through repetition and trust. "Ready for the next?"

He nods without hesitation. "Let's see what you've got."

The jet hums beneath them, its wings cutting through the thinning air as they push higher. The first test is behind them. The sky sprawls, endless and wild, ahead.

###

"Let's see what you've got." Blaze's voice cuts sharply through the cockpit comms—low, steady—a challenge buried beneath. The jet bucks as he yanks the stick hard left, banking steeply into a simulated pursuit turn. His eyes flicker to Lyra's HUD, watching her every move like a hawk circling its prey. Below them, the ocean stretches—a gleaming mirror fractured by the early dawn's breeze. The roar fills the narrow space; engines spool with hungry urgency.

Lyra grips the controls. Blaze's command fades into the background hum. Without missing a beat, her fingers shift to the primary stick, and she pulls into a rapid barrel roll. The world spins sickeningly. The horizon loops overhead—blue sky twisting around gray-winged clouds, the base's edge a distant line swallowed by sea spray and shadow. Her voice snaps through the comms, sharp and precise: "Barrel roll complete. Initiating S-turn."

Blaze recalibrates instantly, easing the throttle to feather the jet's angle of attack through the curving maneuver. His arms flex against the g-forces pressing into his ribs and shoulders. "Throttle down to thirty-five percent. Adjust pitch by twenty degrees." He half-smiles, caught off guard by her crisp tone and fluid control. The staggered rhythm of the ocean below aligns with the pulsing strain in their muscles.

Suddenly, Blaze fires a flaring cue into their HUD—a jarring burst of simulated threat that lights the cockpit screens red. "Missile lock detected. Defensive break now!"

His eyes narrow, and his voice sharpens like a razor in her ear.

Lyra reacts without hesitation, whipping the jet into a textbook break. The abrupt jolt twists the world sideways, pressure pinning flesh to metal. Then—just when Blaze expects the familiar—she throws in an unexpected upward corkscrew, a move she'd learned in secret, cutting through standard protocols.

His breath hitches, and his lips part in a quiet curse. "Damn it, Lyra. Where'd you pick that up?"

Her laugh is quick and breathless. "Some things they don't teach you in class." Years of flying off-the-books with smugglers on the outer rim had taught her moves the academy would never sanction—instincts honed in the dark, where margins for error didn't exist.

Her hands flick over the controls, precise and sure, muscles taut beneath her flight suit as the jet slices through the banked turn, spray and wind whipping past the cockpit glass. She threads the aircraft with razor-sharp precision above the jagged coastline. The sun, still low, sketches dark shadows on the cliffs and foamy surf. She dives toward the shadowed shore, then pulls hard enough to push the jet to its structural limits. A sharp crack echoes from the frame—a warning—but she holds firm, breath caught and eyes locked ahead.

Blaze watches. He beats his own pulse in time with hers. This isn't just flying; this is trust hanging on the edge of a knife. He lets her take the lead now, peeling back his throttle and allowing her to set the tempo.

"Ready for the vertical loop?" His voice drops low and steady, the unspoken question hanging between them.

Lyra's nod bobs into view on the HUD—a pixel-perfect signal. The jet shoots upward, a missile streaking through clouds of salt-kissed mist. G-forces slam into their seats like pistons, limbs trembling under the steel bite of harness straps. Blaze pulls tight alongside her, muscles burning, matching every twist and turn, every grip of the yoke.

Their eyes meet over the glare of instrument panels. In that moment, Blaze's carefully constructed walls fracture—just slightly. He sees her not as a rival pilot or a problem to manage, but as someone willing to fly into the unknown at his wing; someone he might actually trust.

The world shrinks into a synchronized dance of cold metal and burning sky. The vertical loop completes in perfect harmony. The jet tips over, sailing midday over ocean glass.

The contrail behind them flickers thin and silver, a shimmering trace of their passing carved against the earliest light. Side by side, they roll out, breath rough but smiles creeping free in rare, unguarded victory.

"Thought you might surprise me," Blaze admits, his gruff tone edged with something almost vulnerable.

Lyra's voice hums with quiet triumph amid the crackle of comms. "You've got to keep me on my toes, Captain."

He grunts, something close to a chuckle. "Yeah, well... you're making it too easy to keep up."

"Is that a compliment?"

"Maybe. Don't get used to it."

Lyra's grin is infectious, crackling through the cockpit like electricity. "You're just mad you lost the lead."

"Not lost," he replies, his voice carrying a hint of finality. "Handed over."

She snorts. "Sure, Captain."

Their laughter fades into the soft rush of flight instruments, the jet steady now, gliding through the dawn's cool embrace. The ocean below sparkles with the first golden fingers of sunlight—a quiet witness to their flight. A moment sealed by skill and something more. Something unspoken and fierce. Something that neither of them could quite name but both understood in the marrow of their bones.

Blaze nods, his fingers twitching near the throttle. His eyes, sharp as ever, scan the instrument cluster. "One more. Vertical loop. Tight recovery. Follow my count."

Lyra's breath steadies as she tunes into his rhythm. "Got it." Her fingers tap control inputs with precision, recalibrating engine mix and attitude as the jet noses up. "Climbing—engine at eighty-five percent, angle forty-one degrees, eleven seconds to apex."

The jet pitches skyward, slicing through the pale dawn like a silver arrow against muted violet clouds. Blaze's gaze flicks to the power gauges, tracking energy bleed with surgical focus. "Five seconds," he calls out, his voice clipped but reassuring. "The recovery window's tight—forty-five degrees."

Lyra's hands dance across the panel, each dial a note in their silent symphony. The horizon slips away, replaced by the dome of awakening stars melting into orange. Her heartbeat hammers in her ears, but her fingers do not stray. "Pulling through," she replies, gripping the stick with measured strength.

In this moment, suspended between earth and endless sky, Lyra feels the phantom weight of every mistake—every time she had fought command, every disciplinary review—dissolving. This isn't rebellion anymore. This is synchronicity. With Blaze, she has learned the difference between flying alone and flying *with* someone.

The jet arcs over the apex. The world flips upside down—an intimate blend of acceleration pressing against her ribs and skin, the sharp scent of hydraulics mingling with recycled air. That metallic taste clings to her tongue, familiar now, grounding. Blaze's hand joins hers momentarily on the stick, a steady reminder. Two pilots holding a fragile trust. Together, they guide the jet over the rim, their tails twisting in seamless synchronicity.

As the jet levels out, silence swells in the tiny cockpit—the kind that feels less like absence and more like closeness wrapped in machine hum. Blaze breathes out. It is quiet, heavy with meaning.

"You're the best wingman I've ever had," his voice slips over the comm, stripped bare of ceremony, raw as the rising sun's first light.

Lyra curves her lips into a grin, one corner tugging up like a crack in her guarded armor. "I never doubted you."

No sparks, no prideful boasts—just two souls exhaling truth mid-flight, suspended between metal and sky.

The ocean below unfolds like molten glass, waves catching the sun's fingers. The horizon bleeds gold and rose—dawn stealing over the sea with slow, deliberate grace. They hover there, suspended, wrapped in wordless harmony.

This fragile connection means everything now. Weeks ago, they had stood in the commander's office after that last close call—tension crackling between them, both too stubborn to bridge the gap. But up here, in the cockpit's intimate dark, something has shifted. No reprimand could touch this.

Lyra's laugh shatters the quiet, trembling and soft, as if jolted free by adrenaline and relief. The sound skims the cockpit walls, fragile and bright, a secret known only to them.

Blaze lets the air fill their silence before his voice returns—gentle now, laced with something almost like wonder. "Alright. Enough horsing around. Let's get home."

They glide together, a perfected machine of trust—each movement a heartbeat, each breath a promise carved into the sky.

They hold a long beat on the frequency, letting the moment stretch and settle between them, a tether stronger than words.

The dawn air wraps around their wings, light blooming like fire across the water below. In the cockpit's dim glow, time warps—expanded and intimate—a horizon both fragile and infinite.

No one else knows yet what has shifted here. But in the quiet pulse of synchronized motion and whispered truths, Blaze and Lyra have sealed something no rule can undo.

Blaze's voice cuts through the quiet hum of the cockpit, low and steady. "Heading zero-four-zero, descending to fifty feet. Keep it slow."

Lyra's fingers ease the throttle back, and the trainer jet shivers under gentle protest as the flaps whisper open and the landing gear thunks down, wheels ready to meet cold concrete. The air is thick with salt and faint engine oil—the base just stirring, none of the usual crews lining the tarmac yet. They skirt close to hangars and shadowed maintenance sheds, a ghost slipping past patrols Blaze has memorized like a litany.

"Flaps twenty, gear down," Lyra calls softly, her voice steady but edged with the tremble of adrenaline. The jet's nose dips just enough to keep their approach razor-thin against the rising dawn sky.

Blaze's hands tighten on the control stick, his muscles taut beneath the worn leather gloves. "Keep it on the line. Slow down, slow down—now cut power."

The roar of the engines fades to a lazy drone as they roll, coaxing the jet along the runway's edge. Outside, dim amber lights buzz weakly over Hangar 3, with shuttered doors resembling hulking beasts waiting to swallow them whole. Lyra's gloves stick slightly to the controls, her fingers tightening on the throttle as she nudges the jet closer to the centerline. Her pulse hammers in sync with the slow, grinding wheels.

A sharp scent of jet fuel mingles with the cold metal chill as they ease inside the cavernous hangar. The hangar falls silent. Only the settling hiss of cooling hydraulics and the steady drip of condensation from the wing's underside break the stillness.

Lyra breathes out, relief washing over her in tremors. Her hands shake slightly as she unlatches her helmet, tossing it aside with the careless grin of someone who has just danced with danger and lived. Blaze follows, the corners of his mouth twitching in a rare, tight smile. A laugh finally escapes him, dark and unguarded, scattering the tension like shattered glass.

"Almost felt like we earned a medal, right?"

Lyra's eyes gleam with matching mischief. "At least a court-martial." Their laughter mingles, fragile but real, folding into the cavern's shadowed stillness.

Every nerve in Blaze sharpens at the sound of boots on concrete. He goes rigid, his jaw clenching as his eyes snap toward the hangar entrance. The adrenaline that had been ebbing suddenly floods back, hot and electric. His hand instinctively moves to Lyra's arm—a warning, a brace. Caught or safe. The calculation flickers across his face in half a second.

Jazz slips through the hangar door, her face lit with disbelief and something like excitement that fights back exhaustion. Her grin is wide, and her eyes sparkle with the thrill of witnessing a reckless victory.

"That was insane—you two look like you just fought a war and won."

Her voice bounces off the metal walls, breaking the hush with warmth.

Blaze's shoulders drop slightly as he raises an eyebrow. "Yeah, well... we like to keep things interesting around here."

Jazz steps closer, lowering her voice conspiratorially. "Not a word to the brass, got it? You two break the damn routine, and I shut my trap." She's half-teasing, half-warning, but her eyes glint with camaraderie.

Lyra glances at Blaze, then back at Jazz, nodding. "Deal."

Jazz slaps Blaze lightly on the shoulder. "I still can't believe you pulled this off. I watched the feed—I thought Lyra was nuts, then you jumped in. Perfect timing."

Blaze shrugs, but there's heat behind his green eyes. "Sometimes you have to break the rules to find out what you're really good at."

Lyra hooks her arm through Jazz's as she gathers her gear. "You're just going to have to keep watching, then."

Jazz grins wider. "Hell yeah. Keep me posted if you two survive the fallout."

The moment hums with unspoken promises and cautious hope.

One last glance: Blaze and Lyra hold each other's eyes—no words, just a pulse of understanding, tethered tight by the gravity of risk and trust. The base outside stirs to life beneath the pink glow of dawn—their secret flight already slipping into legend amid the rising clatter of daily routine.

Lyra steps away first, her boots echoing softly toward the dorms, the weight of gravity suddenly heavier but somehow sweeter. Blaze lingers a heartbeat longer, his mind racing with the inevitable reckoning, before turning toward his quarters to face the long, tangled hours ahead.

Their bond, forged in silence and motion through the sky's thin edge, now hangs precariously between them—a tether neither dares to sever amid the crackling promise of what's next.

The academy's disciplinary records flickered in Blaze's mind as he walked—the citations, the close calls, the narrow margins between heroism and expulsion. They had danced along that line before, but never like this. Never quite so visible, so documented. The weight of it settled into his chest with the metallic taste of anticipation and dread, sweet and bitter mingling together like fuel and dawn air. He wondered how long the base would hum with normalcy before someone checked the flight logs. He also wondered if Lyra was counting the hours too.

In the Commander's Crosshair

The control room hums with cold fluorescent light. A pale blue glow from endless monitors paints Flight Officer Harper's face as she leans forward, her eyes narrowing behind her glasses. Outside the thick glass, dawn breaks slowly over Astra Flight Command, painting the runway in shades of bruised purple and steel gray.

The clack of her keyboard echoes in the stillness—a steady pulse. Harper's fingers dance over the controls, replaying tower footage again and again, her eyes tracing the familiar flicker of jets sliding across the apron.

Her gaze pauses.

There—between 0432 and 0447—there is a gap in the flight logs that was not scheduled. The usual rhythm of takeoffs and landings fractures like cracked ice underfoot. Every movement here follows razor-sharp schedules; a single gap is not just a slip—it is a rupture in their finely tuned system.

She rewinds the tower cam angles over the south apron. A twin-seat jet, unrecorded on the official manifest, taxis slowly from the hangar shadows. Its engine's low rumble washes out against the ambient noise, but the visual feed catches it—unmistakable. The timestamp aligns exactly with the unlogged window from earlier.

Harper's breath catches—sharp and quiet in the sterile air.

She pulls up the maintenance logs, scrolling to the after-hours entries with a practiced eye. The screen blurs momentarily as she zooms in on edited timestamps. Several entries show jagged shifts—timestamps smoothed over, and pilot-authentication logs conspicuously absent where they should be immutable.

Her fingertip hovers over the "deleted entry" icon. She knows what finding this means: an instructor, a cadet, and careers fracturing before they have properly begun. But duty demands that she look.

She taps.

Cold certainty blooms in her chest as the hidden data recovers.

The cockpit camera feed is next. She loads the file and freezes the frame. Lyra Hale's face fills the rear seat viewfinder—tense but focused. Her helmet is slightly lifted, and her eyes are sharp and bright behind a smudged visor.

Harper's brow tightens. Quickly, she tags the flight path telemetry. The lead signature pulses with Blaze's call sign, both of their presences undeniable.

Her fingers move almost mechanically now. She exports the footage into a flagged case file: video stills, telemetry overlays, and maintenance logs. Evidence woven into a digital tapestry that tells a story far louder than the coded silence of altered records.

She leans back. The chair creaks beneath her. The faint scent of recycled air mingles with the tang of coffee from the nearby break room. Outside, a jet roars to life—a harsh reminder of the stakes riding on careful protocol.

A heavy pause settles over her thoughts. Protocol demands that she report. The thought of consequences threads through her resolve like a splinter. But she has already seen the evidence. She has already crossed that threshold.

A flicker of doubt tightens in her chest, but her hands do not waver. She compiles the encrypted file with sharp, clipped movements, as if speed might outrun the weight of what she is uncovering. Passwords are layered. Access keys are locked down. There is enough evidence for an inquiry, but only the bare minimum to trigger the chain without revealing all.

Responsibility anchors her decision—a cold weight against her growing doubt.

With a final keystroke, the file closes. Harper breathes in deeply. The faint smell of solder and worn circuits grounds her. The print command whirs to life. A single sheet materializes with a soft shush—crisp and authoritative.

She folds it methodically and tucks it under her arm as she rises.

Her footsteps fall in measured cadence against the polished floor. Each stride carries the resolve of a woman balancing truth and consequence, the stillness of the early morning wrapped tightly around her like a cloak. The door slides open with a whisper. Harper steps out, the evidence pressed close—a secret unfolding, ready to challenge the quiet order of Astra Flight Command.

Commander Reynolds's office is all polished mahogany and restrained authority. She looks up from her desk as Harper enters, her eyes sharp with the weariness that comes with command.

"I've got a full set on the unauthorized after-hours movement from yesterday dawn," Harper says. Her voice steadies, but there's a tightness there—the faint edge of someone aware of exactly what she's about to set in motion.

Reynolds gestures for the tablet. She swipes through the footage, her lips pressing into a thin line as each detail registers. "Pilot authentication logs tampered. Timestamps don't align."

"No, ma'am," Harper replies, her eyes meeting the commander's with clear professionalism. "And the cockpit feed—Lyra Hale. Right there in the rear seat. The lead call sign was Arden."

Reynolds narrows her eyes. "No record. No clearance. This goes higher than a simple oversight." She taps the intercom, her voice clipped and measured. "Assemble the disciplinary panel in conference room A. Harper, this stays strictly confidential until we convene. No leaks."

Harper nods, saluting crisply before slipping the tablet into her jacket pocket. The weight of the moment settles into the set of her jaw. She turns and moves toward the door, her footsteps steady and sure, echoing down the corridor—a sound heralding the storm she's set loose.

Flight Officer Harper steps into the stark quiet of Commander Reynolds' office. The door sighs shut behind her.

The polished mahogany desk gleams under harsh overhead lights, its surface smooth and unyielding—much like the commander's reputation. Harper carries the printed file carefully. Crisp pages whisper evidence. A tablet rests beneath her arm like a silent witness to the storm gathering momentum.

She halts at attention, shoulders squared beneath her uniform, then places the documents deliberately on the desk. The sterile scent of freshly polished wood mingles with the lingering jet fuel drifting from the base corridors—a contradiction that defines this place: concrete order masking dangerous secrets.

Harper's voice cuts through the stillness, clipped and measured.

"Commander, I've cross-checked tower footage and flight logs from the dawn shift. There's an unlogged taxi on the south apron—exactly during that unsanctioned window. Pilot authentication matches Blaze's call sign. The cockpit cam confirms Lyra in the rear seat."

Commander Reynolds remains motionless, her gray eyes sharp, unmoving, and unreadable. The subtle intensity of her stare demands precision. Harper doesn't flinch.

She taps the tablet. A clip flickers to life on the sleek screen—the claustrophobic cockpit, panels alive with blinking lights. Lyra's determined profile is outlined sharply by the fortified canopy. Time stamps blink irregularly along the video's edge.

Harper points to maintenance log entries that now appear faded and altered. "Records from after hours show suspicious timestamp shifts. Pilot authentication entries were deleted outright. The pattern indicates deliberate tampering." She pauses. Her tone remains cold and clinical, but urgency rests heavily beneath her measured words. "Someone wanted this flight erased."

Reynolds wields silence like a blade.

Then she spins slightly toward the intercom beside the desk. Her voice carries a cold finality. "Summon the disciplinary panel immediately. This matter requires a formal inquiry—and confidentiality, Flight Officer. Until proceedings begin, there should be no dissemination beyond this room."

Harper's hand snaps up in a sharp salute, the motion crisp yet weighted. Her fingers brush the polished wood before folding the tablet into her palm. Her jaw tightens—muscles clenched like coiled wire—while a cold knot of responsibility sinks heavily in her chest.

"I understand, ma'am. I'll proceed accordingly."

The commander nods once. Brief. Commanding. No words of comfort. No reassurance. Just the heavy air of duty demanding answers.

Harper steels herself against the storm gathering outside this door. She steps back. Her heels click a resolute rhythm on the tiled floor. The door closes behind her with muted finality, sealing away the quiet calm of Reynolds's office.

She emerges into the mechanical hum and flickering lights of Astra Flight Command's nerve center. Around her, the familiar rhythms of base life continue—oblivious to the fracture forming within. Rules meant to be sacred are now rigorously questioned.

The command conference room feels like a steel tomb, its air crisp with urgency and cold resolve. Frosted glass panes separate the inner sanctum from the murmuring crowd pressed against the outside—cadets and instructors alike, their faces shadowed but straining forward, desperate for a glimpse of the unfolding reckoning. Commander Reynolds stands at the head of the polished mahogany table, her posture as rigid as the military decorum she embodies. She gestures sharply, summoning Captain Jareck "Blaze" Arden, Cadet Lyra Hale, Lieutenant Marcus "Sarge" Sullivan, Major Elena Voss, and Flight Officer Harper to their places around the table.

A low buzz hums beneath the weight of the moment, whispers ricocheting down the hallway: the unregistered flight, the secret choreography in the southern apron, the breach of rules that threatened everything the academy stood for—careers, reputations, the iron-fisted trust that kept them all grounded. This wasn't just an inquiry; this was a reckoning. The crowd outside leans closer, breaths fogging the glass like restless phantoms.

Reynolds lays down the first piece of evidence—prints cascading in neat stacks across the table: flight-path overlays, their jagged curves slicing the digital paper like a heartbeat recorded on a monitor. Beside them, timestamped video stills glow faintly on a tablet, faces and cockpits frozen mid-action. Maintenance log printouts, dense with code and edits, sprawl like a puzzle demanding to be solved. Her gray eyes lock onto Blaze, steady but unyielding.

"We're wasting no time," Reynolds says. Her voice cuts through the tension, sharp and unyielding. "Explain this—now."

Blaze's jaw clenches so tightly that his knuckles blanch against the table. The scar on his left cheek glints faintly in the dim light—a silent record that carries more history than words could hold. He meets her gaze without flinching. The room inhales. Silence stretches, thick and unyielding.

Harper steps forward, her tone measured and precise. "The flight logs show a plane taxiing on the south apron just after dawn—completely absent from the official registry. Maintenance logs have been altered. Timestamps have been adjusted, and pilot authentication entries have been deleted. The cockpit camera feed, which I've downloaded and preserved, confirms Cadet Hale in the rear seat. The flight-path telemetry tags Captain Arden's call sign as the lead throughout the operation."

She taps the tablet, scrolling through layers of data. The trajectory arcs glisten on the screen, smooth lines intersecting with the digital shadows.

"The edited maintenance logs indicate after-hours access to the aircraft, which was unreported to command. The cockpit feed is time-stamped precisely, synchronized against the traffic control record. All data corroborates a coordinated, unauthorized flight." Her voice does not waver an inch, though the undercurrent of gravity strains the room's atmosphere.

Reynolds strips any pretense from his expression, watching for the slightest tell—a corner of his mouth faltering, a blink too fast. Blaze remains impassive, but the stillness between them speaks volumes. She understands what that silence means. She knows the weight of decisions made in the dark.

She turns to the rest of those assembled, the duty pressing down across her shoulders like a physical force. "Captain Arden, the floor is yours. Explain in full."

The silence thickens, hanging like mist in the room as all eyes converge on a single point of expectancy. The frosted glass panels ripple with the shadowed outlines of cadets and instructors staring and listening—not just to words, but to the soul of the man standing at the crux of his fate.

Lyra's fingers twitch at her side, energy coiled beneath her uniform like a spring wound too tight, but she remains silent. Waiting. Sarge's arms rest heavily on the table, his eyes dark pools of guarded loyalty. Voss folds her hands with calculated precision, her gaze sharp enough to cut steel. Harper stands firm, the files clutched like a shield.

No one blinks. No one breathes louder than a whisper.

The room waits. Captain Arden prepares to shoulder the storm.

Blaze steps forward. The harsh white light of the command conference room casts deep shadows along his angular face. Behind him, the low hum of ventilation and the faint scratch of maps rustling fade into insignificance—swallowed by the electric stillness he brings.

His shoulders square like a man bracing for impact, eyes locked ahead, stone-cold resolve.

The room tightens around him. Crystalline tension wraps around every breathing figure, coiling tighter as he opens his mouth.

"I authorized and flew the unsanctioned sortie." His words fall like cold metal on concrete. "Lyra Hale was a passenger under my direct orders for training maneuvers outside standard protocol."

He doesn't flinch. His gaze glides across the assembled faces—commanders, instructors, officers—and ignites something between them: a quiet storm.

Commander Reynolds leans forward, her fingers stilling against the polished mahogany. Her eyes, sharp as winter steel, skim the printed flight paths, still frames from the cockpit camera, and maintenance logs laid bare. "Captain Arden," she says, her voice sharp and precise, "I want the flight's purpose—and why you kept it off the books."

Blaze's jaw clenches and releases. He matches her intensity without breaking rhythm. "The purpose was deliberate. Standard training modules lack the flexibility needed to test Lyra's ability to handle unpredictable, high-stress situations—situations I know she's capable of mastering, situations the rulebook stifles." His hands flatten against the table, fingers splayed, grounding himself in the weight of his own words. "Forty-three minutes total: takeoff, tactical maneuvers along the southern coastal test range, recovery landing. The log was omitted intentionally."

He pauses, breath drawn and held.

"I sought to protect her from repercussions tied to previous disciplinary actions. Frankly, those actions impeded necessary growth. Disciplinary probation would not have served her talent or potential."

Lyra's chest tightens. She steps forward, heat blooming in her voice. "That's not the whole story. The truth is—"

Blaze's gaze anchors her: measured, sharp but calm. It halts her mid-sentence like a hand pressed against her chest.

"Lyra," he says quietly. Command threads through that single word, silencing the murmurs rising around her. "This is not your burden."

His voice doesn't need volume; it cuts through the room like a laser, and every officer's attention snaps back to him.

"I take full responsibility. The consequences—all of them—are mine alone to bear." His hands press down hard against the cold surface, as if bracing against a rising tide. "There will be no formal punishment for Lyra. I'll accept what comes."

Lyra's jaw tightens. Gratitude flickers across her features, then frustration. Fear shadows her eyes before settling into something quieter—wordless resignation. The silent acceptance between them draws a taut line across the charged air, and Reynolds's gaze tracks it.

The room seems to shrink. The temperature drops by degrees as his confession settles, heavy as dense fog. Paper scratches. Breath held. Shallow. Waiting.

Reynolds measures him with her steel-hard gaze, unreadable and unblinking.

"No diversion," Blaze continues, his voice steady despite the swell rising in his chest. "No excuses. This is my decision, made with full awareness of the risk—to my career, to the program's integrity. I placed my trust in Lyra. I accept the consequences now falling on my shoulders."

Silence pools between them. The weight of it presses against every wall—the rupture of protocol confessed aloud by one of Astra's best pilots. Outside the frosted glass, cadets shift, their shadows pressing closer. Instructors' faces remain impassive, but their eyes flicker with surprise and grudging respect.

Reynolds finally meets his gaze. Her fingers tap once against the mahogany, deliberate and slow. "Your willingness to assume blame does not exempt the facts from review," she says, her tone clipped and pragmatic. "But your candor is noted."

Blaze lets his hands fall to his sides. The rigid strength softens for just a moment—unguarded beneath the cold fluorescent ceiling lights. His breathing steadies, the internal storm calming to something controlled but not quite contained.

He stands tall, a pillar. With palms pressed firmly against the table, he breathes slowly, steadying what remains.

The confession hangs in the air—raw and naked in its simplicity. No twisting words. No shield. Just the hard line a man draws when he's ready to bear the cost of protecting another. The cold air wraps tighter around the conference room, sealing the charge of this moment: one man's reckless choice, one woman's untold debt, and the fierce, unbreakable bond forged in the crucible of forbidden trust.

Major Elena Voss leaned forward in the sleek conference chair, her fingers tapping the polished mahogany table—deliberate, measured, like a countdown. Her sharp gaze sliced through the haze of murmurs still lingering in the room as Blaze's confession settled like cold iron.

"This is not a mere lapse in judgment." Her voice was clipped and precise, each word dropping into the charged air with weight. "Captain Arden knowingly jeopardized the integrity of the High-G program. He endangered a cadet's life for personal reasons. That is inexcusable."

She folded her hands tightly, her knuckles whitening and her eyes narrowing to slits.

"The academy's reputation depends on strict adherence to protocol. If we allow this to slide, we will unravel the discipline that holds everything together. I recommend immediate removal from all instructional duties and permanent reassignment—a safeguard for both our cadets and our institution."

Tension spiked in the room. Silent as a pressure wave, it vibrated through the sterile air. The fluorescent hum overhead suddenly felt deafening.

Across the table, Lt. Marcus "Sarge" Sullivan sat rigid, his jaw clenched so tightly that it looked as if the steel beneath his skin might crack. His eyes burned with barely masked frustration. When he spoke, the words came low but fierce, with the intensity of someone fighting to stay seated.

"With all due respect, Major, Captain Arden is not some reckless hothead; he's a seasoned ace, decorated for valor." Sarge pushed his chair back with a scrape, leaning in until his shoulders squared as if he were bracing for impact. "Yes, he broke protocol, but those maneuvers—he only pushed because he believes in Lyra, more than the program does."

His fingers gripped the edge of the table. "Look, there's a problem here: how we treat cadets like her. We're caging raw talent when we should be letting it fly. Arden's choice to protect and train her outside the rigid system wasn't selfish; it was conviction, plain and simple."

Voss's eyes flashed. "Conviction without accountability creates a hazard. We don't elevate personal missions over safety. You're defending insubordination."

"And you're blind to reality if you think blind obedience is the answer." Sarge's voice thickened with urgency, and his jaw worked. "Without instructors willing to bear the burden—willing to fall on their swords for their students—we're just teaching robots to follow orders. That's not flying; that's not leadership."

Elena's lips pressed into a thin line. "The academy's rules exist to protect cadets and the chain of command. Arden's actions fractured that chain."

"Sometimes you have to break the chain to build something stronger." Sarge leaned in closer, his voice dropping to barely above a whisper, each word deliberately measured. "Blaze isn't perfect, but he takes full responsibility. That's loyalty; that's what matters."

Their words collided like radio transmissions fractured by static. Voss countered with precise citations—policy manuals, regulations etched into the academy's foundation, and precedent cases that had ended careers over less. Her voice never wavered, and her posture never softened.

Sarge pressed forward. "If loyalty and responsibility aren't the core of leadership, what is? Dumping Arden sends a message that the academy values paperwork over people, that we don't care about cadets who need a chance to fly true."

Commander Reynolds remained motionless behind her desk, her expression etched in stone. Pale gray eyes swept across the ideological battlefield unfolding before her—Voss unyielding in her formality, Sarge raw with conviction, neither willing to yield an inch. She watched the clash unfold like a high-stakes chess match, where every move carried consequences.

The air thickened. The hum of fluorescent lights seemed to press down from above. Distant murmurs in the hallway faded away to nothing, leaving only the sharp tap of Voss's fingers on mahogany and the harsh rasp of Sarge's breathing.

Voss's voice slashed through the moment like a blade. "This isn't a trial of character; it's about order, safety, and the future of this academy. Allowing exceptions undermines that foundation."

"Order without judgment is tyranny." Sarge's hands clenched into fists on the table. "We need leaders who protect and inspire. Blaze embodies both. Don't lose sight of that."

Their eyes locked. Voss's were cold and precise, while Sarge's were fierce and burning with conviction. The ideological fault line between uncompromising rules and hard-earned loyalty lay bare between them, raw and unresolved.

Reynolds finally uncrossed her fingers. Her gaze swept across the room, lingering on both challengers before arresting the moment in steady stillness. The room held its breath. Everyone sensed the stakes—Blaze's career, the program's future, the fragile intersection of duty and humanity—all balanced on the razor's edge of her decision.

The fluorescent lights hummed on, waiting.

Lyra's hands trembled on the edge of the table, her knuckles whitening. Her breath came sharp and uneven, her lips parted as she fought to steady her voice in the sterile glow of the conference room. The murmurs from the cadets pressed against the frosted glass felt miles away—insignificant. Nothing compared to the pounding urgency in her chest.

"Please." Her voice cracked like ice underfoot. "You have to hear me. That flight—it wasn't just a reckless stunt. It was proof." She swallowed hard, her eyes glistening. "Proof that we can work. That we *do* work. Blaze trusts me. I trust him. We're stronger together. Isn't that what you've all been saying this program needs? Trust? Partnership?"

The room became tense.

Major Elena Voss's gray eyes narrowed as she stayed silent. Lt. Marcus "Sarge" Sullivan shifted uneasily, his jaw clenching as Lyra's plea refused to dissolve into protocol and official jargon. The faint hum of distant machinery buzzed ominously—like the charged air before a storm—filling the silence where understanding should bloom.

Before the fragile tension could snap, Blaze's voice cut through the quiet: sharp and steady.

"I take the fall. All of it."

His words fell deliberately, bearing the weight of iron chains. His eyes locked onto the polished tabletop as his palms flattened against it with controlled fierceness, grounding himself in the cold reality of consequence.

"That flight was unauthorized. Lyra was aboard under my command. Every move. Every risk. Mine." He lifted his gaze then, meeting Voss's stare directly. "I'm prepared to sacrifice my career to protect her. From punishment. From expulsion. From a system that doesn't yet see what she's capable of."

Whispers faltered.

Breaths caught.

The air thickened—tinged with burnt coffee and tension. Only the faint, acrid smell of spent jet fuel wafted through the ventilation, cutting through the haze. Even Voss's steely demeanor flickered in the undercurrent of sacrifice. Sarge's broad shoulders relaxed fractionally, the tight knot in his throat loosening just enough to reveal a flicker of respect. Outside, the cadets pressed against the glass held their collective breath. The sham of institutional order crumbled before a raw, personal reckoning laid bare.

Lyra's breath caught, her shoulders tensing as Blaze's steady gaze bore into her. Tears pooled and then slipped free, tracing a hot path down her flushed cheeks. Her voice wavered like a faltering engine.

"Blaze, I—"

He silenced her with a quiet, unyielding look. The lines of his scarred jaw tightened. No words were spoken, but in that stillness, the ferocity of his protection roared louder than any accusation.

From the far side of the oval table, Voss finally broke the silence. Her voice came out clipped but laced with reluctant acknowledgment.

"Captain Arden's confession complicates disciplinary proceedings. It does not erase the breach." She paused, her composed facade wavering just enough to matter. "However, the personal cost he assumes cannot be ignored."

Sarge nodded, clearing his throat. His voice was low and steady.

"Sometimes the system's rules don't account for what's right or what's needed. Blaze made a choice—for Lyra, for the program, despite the cost."

The room held the weight of their shared silence, a collective inhale stretching long and taut. The hum of electronic equipment pulsed softly, a heartbeat beneath the human storm engulfing the chamber. The frosted glass trapped the cadet observers in muted shadows, their tight lips and wide eyes betraying admiration tangled with helplessness.

Commander Reynolds rose from the head of the table. Her sharp gaze sliced through the lingering silence.

"This inquiry will take all presented evidence under advisement," she said, her voice calm but carrying a steel-edged finality. "That includes Captain Arden's admission and the circumstances surrounding the unauthorized flight." She folded her hands neatly before her, the faintest crease of concern betraying the layered burden of command. "Until further notice, we adjourn."

A subtle shiver rippled through the room, as if the invisible ash of Blaze's sacrifice had coated every spine and settled thickly around every word left unspoken. The panel dispersed slowly. Cadets still pressed close to the glass. The sight of Lyra's shoulder trembling against the cold pane burned into their memories.

The echo of silence stretched long after the final chair scraped against the concrete.

Commander Reynolds settled back. Her eyes narrowed. The room folded into stillness.

The silence thickened, sharp and expectant against the sterile light overhead.

Her voice broke the hush like steel on stone. "An official ruling will come within twenty-four hours." Her gaze landed on Blaze with all the weight of the academy's unspoken judgment. "Effective immediately, Captain Arden is suspended from all flight and instructional duties."

At the academy, suspensions typically wound through weeks of review boards and appeals. This was different. This was immediate. The academy didn't move this fast unless protocol had been shattered beyond repair.

She lets her words hang, measured and deliberate. A verdict is already lodged in stone.

Blaze doesn't flinch. His jaw tightens, and his shoulders remain square—unmoved and unyielding. Around them, bodies shift. Chairs scrape low and subdued as tension begins to unravel.

Reynolds sweeps the room with a gaze that brooks no argument. "Captain Arden will remain on base, surrender all flight credentials and access codes to security forthwith." Her fingers tap against the polished mahogany desk, punctuating the command. "He is to have no contact with cadets until the formal review concludes."

She turns slightly, directing the next words to Lyra. "Cadet Hale, return to the barracks and await further instructions. This is not a declaration of guilt or innocence. You are to maintain your position and conduct yourself accordingly."

Lyra's chest heaves. Her lips part as if to speak, but a silent command in Reynolds' gaze clips her words. Her fingers tighten on the duffel strap, and her knuckles blanch white.

She nods, tight-lipped.

The room exhales collectively. The invisible pressure eases just enough to allow movement to return. The crowd begins to disperse—scattering like leaves caught in a sudden gust, each carrying its own thoughts, judgments, and tensions.

Sarge steps forward. His hand falls heavily on Blaze's shoulder—a silent lifeline in the storm. The squeeze is wordless, thick with something deeper than solidarity. They have flown together for three years, crash-landed once in the Nevada desert, and walked out laughing. Sarge doesn't abandon people. Not ever.

Blaze meets his friend's eyes. A ghost of softness flickers across his face before hardening once more.

Major Voss shifts beside them, methodical as always. Her fingers skim across a stack of documents, rearranging and filing—a sculptor molding icy order from chaos. Her expression remains unreadable, lips pressed into a line that doesn't waver.

Blaze pulls his flight credentials from his jacket. The metal tags clink faintly in the cold air. He holds them out to a uniformed security officer waiting just beyond the doorway.

The officer steps forward, paper pad in hand. Every movement is practiced and official. He logs the surrender with a meticulous scratch of pen on paper.

The sound is unmistakably final.

Silence swells.

Cadets pressed against the frosted glass outside watch from the corridor, unheard and unseen. Faces blur against the frozen panes. The gravity of the moment settles into every bone, a silent witness to the unraveling of careers and futures.

Eyes flicker across the polished floor, between departing figures. Whispers rise softly, then dim again, caught under the authoritative gaze of Commander Reynolds. An unspoken reckoning hangs in the air, thick with consequence.

Blaze straightens. His fingers curl lightly around the thin chain of his credentials one last time before letting them fall into the security officer's outstretched hand. His green eyes, sharp and glinting despite the weight on his chest, scan the length of the room once more.

No pleas. No regrets. Just quiet, resolute acceptance.

Reynolds stands, folding her hands deliberately as she gestures for the panel to clear. The last few officers collect their things, their footsteps a slow retreat punctuated by the rustle of uniforms and clipped orders muttered under their breath.

Outside, the distant hum of the airbase continues, unaware or indifferent to the fracturing within. The unforgiving fluorescent lights buzz overhead as the door closes behind the last of them, leaving behind the cold stillness carved by duty and sacrifice.

The hallway feels impossibly narrow. The hum of distant engines falls away as Lyra rounds the corner near the hangar offices. Fluorescent lights flicker overhead, casting jagged shadows on the cold metal walls.

She smells it first—lubricant and ozone, layered beneath the acrid ghost of burnt jet fuel. Her heart thuds. Once. Twice. Each beat hammers against her ribs as she spots him.

Blaze.

He leans against the steel-framed door, shoulders squared but weighted with something the dim light cannot soften. The scar along his jawline catches the flicker of overhead fluorescence.

She stepped forward swiftly. The strap of her duffel bag bit into her palm. "How could you?" Her voice cracked, raw and trembling. "You threw everything away—your career, your reputation." She swallowed hard. "For me?"

Blaze's gaze lifted slowly—steady, unreadable. No surprise colored his expression.

His hand rose in a measured sweep, cutting through the storm in her voice. "It wasn't a choice made lightly," he said, his voice low but unmistakably firm. "I take the blame to protect you. That's the priority."

Her breath stuttered. The pent-up storm inside her broke through cracks she hadn't known existed. Tears pricked sharply at the corners of her eyes. Her body trembled under the weight of it all—the reckless flight, the broken trust, the sacrifice she hadn't wanted.

"You didn't have to do this alone," she whispered, half plea, half accusation.

Blaze held her gaze, unflinching. The seconds stretched taut, electric. In his eyes—usually guarded with the ice of a man who had seen too much—something flickered. Raw. A quiet reckoning that threatened to fracture his hardened armor.

But the mask stood firm.

"You don't have to do this," Lyra whispered, stepping closer. Her knuckles turned white around the duffel strap. The dim corridor pressed in around them like a trap—suffocating, inevitable. The disciplinary ruling had already sealed so much, and now he wanted to seal his own fate too. "Why protect me like this? What are you hoping for?"

Blaze's jaw tightened. The briefest flicker of vulnerability shuttered behind his resolve. "Because your future matters more," he said, his voice clipped and precise. "Because I won't let the system grind you down. Whatever comes after this, I'm ready to face it."

"You don't get to sacrifice yourself for me. Not like this."

Her voice broke as she stepped closer, the narrow space between them charged with everything unspoken—the weight of what they had built together, the fear of losing it, and the ache of watching him shoulder a burden meant for neither of them alone.

"I'm not asking for pity, Blaze," she said, her lips trembling. "But I can't lose you. Not when I just found someone who fights beside me."

Blaze shifted, a slow, deliberate motion that stilled her words but didn't ease the tension. "I'm not leaving you," he said quietly, almost to himself. His fingers curled into fists at his sides. "But I'm not going to let anyone else get hurt because of me."

The cold silence slid between them like shifting shadows.

A distant clang echoed faintly—a closing hangar door, marking the passage of time neither was ready to measure. Lyra's tears spilled free now, tracing cold tracks down her cheeks. She wouldn't look away. Not from him. Not yet.

Blaze's eyes flickered once more—a storm beneath steady skies.

Slowly and deliberately, he turned away. The weight of his movements dragged against the narrow hallway's confines. His footsteps fell softly, then softer, until they disappeared into the hum of distant engines.

She stood alone in the corridor: raw, trembling, exposed.

Between them now—measured not in footsteps, but in all the words left unspoken; in the quiet ache of a bond stretched thin across impossible odds; in the knowledge that sometimes protecting someone meant learning to let them go.

A Heart at War

The linoleum stretched ahead like a cold river of dull light. Lyra's boots clicked in sharp, impatient taps. Each step echoed off walls that seemed longer and emptier than they had minutes before.

She moved down the dormitory corridor, her shoulders tight, her eyes gripping every doorframe as if Blaze might emerge from one, breathing and waiting. Behind each shut door—uniform and silent—muffled voices blurred together. There was no sign of him.

Her mind looped back to the command room, to the raw fracture in Blaze's armor when he had confessed. That moment had pressed into her chest like a sudden weight. His voice had cracked under scrutiny, stripped of its usual bravado. She had seen something in him that she had never glimpsed before—a fierce, raw vulnerability wrapped in the terrible honesty of his eyes. *He's protecting me.* The memory tightened her breath and made her throat constrict.

At the academy, fraternization between cadets carried consequences. The brass didn't tolerate it. One slip, one moment of exposed weakness, and they would circle like predators. Lyra understood the cost now. Everyone did.

Shadows gathered near corners where groups of cadets huddled close, their voices low and urgent. She caught snippets drifting sharply across the hallway's chill: *Blaze, discipline, he said too much.* Heads dipped when they caught her sight, and eyes flicked away. She could taste the rumors—bitter and spreading faster than she could outrun them.

She slowed near the stairwell, catching herself staring at a cluster of uniforms. One cadet, his jaw set tight, nudged his companion into silence as Lyra passed. Their glances were quick, uneasy, and full of unspoken speculation. It felt like a wall closing in—invisible and crushing. Watchful eyes. Muted questions. A squadron on edge, measuring her with every step and every breath she took.

The memory crashed over her again. Blaze's jaw clenched so hard that it threatened to split his skin. No bravado—just devastation carved sharply in the lines around his eyes. That flicker of love tangled with fierce, raw fear. She clawed at the sharp edges of that moment, pulling it closer until her own chest tensed, her ribs tightening against a pleat of grief and something harder to name.

A ragged exhale slipped through her lips. She halted beneath the harsh glare of the fluorescent lights. The ceiling hummed a low, relentless drone that pressed against her senses. The sharp, antiseptic sting pricked her nostrils like a warning, a cold reminder of how sterile this place truly was and how alone she felt in it.

The corridor stretched endlessly. For a split second, time knotted tightly around her heartbeat, fingers tightening against her skin.

Her breath came too fast—shallow, slipping past clenched teeth in the hope that he would emerge from some shadowed doorway and stride toward her like a phantom summoned from a fragile dream. But only silence answered. It folded over the empty corridor like a cold blanket.

She stood there, planted yet restless.

One of the nearby cadets broke the quiet. His voice drifted low and careful:

"Did you hear what he said? Out there, in front of everyone... I can't believe Blaze would say something like that."

Another voice cut in—more bitter, clipped. "Do you think he was protecting her or himself? It doesn't matter now. The brass won't let it slide. They'll rip them both apart."

"And what about the no-fraternization rule? You know Commander Reynolds won't blink twice."

Lyra's head turned sharply, her eyes flashing with defiance and exhaustion.

"So, what? Are we just supposed to let them tear us down because the rules are louder than the truth?"

The corridor fell into a hush. A few cadets glanced her way, tension flickering between them like a current. One stepped forward cautiously, his voice low and careful.

"Lyra, you've got to be careful. You know what's at stake now. It's not just about you or Blaze anymore."

Her lips pressed into a thin line. The weight of unspoken warnings settled around her like ash. She turned away, back toward the shadows where Blaze might be hiding—or gone forever.

Lyra exhaled, her throat tight. She willed the pressure in her chest to ease, but it wouldn't budge. The fluorescent light above flickered once—harsh and brittle. She pressed her palm to the cool wall, anchoring herself against the surge of silent desperation that threatened to pull her under.

Her heart pounded a fracturing rhythm in her ears, loud as a siren. But there was no rescue on the horizon—only the lingering echo of a confession and a love wrapped in sacrifice.

She breathed in shallowly.

Waiting.

Hoping.

For one last glimpse of Blaze that never came.

###

The edge of the bunk creaked beneath Blaze's weight. His fingers tensed against the coarse fabric of his flight jacket. He folded it slowly—the worn leather sighing softly at the seams—before laying it carefully in a battered duffel, half-filled with manuals and flight charts.

The stark quarters swallowed him whole. Empty shelves held a single helmet, a scuffed combat boot turned on its side, and a stray pair of gloves abandoned like shed skin. The cold fluorescent light skittered across the faded carpet, casting long shadows that crawled up the walls like ghosts.

A soft knock rattled the doorframe. Sarge's head appeared, his eyes steady beneath a brush of graying hair. Without a word, he stepped inside and pressed a paper cup into Blaze's hand. Black coffee. Bitter. The scent curled between them—a ritual they had perfected in darker moments, an anchor when everything else threatened to slip away. In this room, in this silence, it meant something. It meant *I'm here.*

Blaze nodded once, curtly accepting. His jaw clenched so hard it felt as if it might crack. His green eyes flickered, dimming beneath a veil of exhaustion—and something darker.

Sarge lingered, a silent sentinel willing to share the burden without demanding an explanation. The minutes stretched, filled only by the soft rustle of fabric and the distant hum of base operations beyond the walls.

Blaze's mind circled back to the command room. The heavy silence cloaked the disciplinary hearing. The stifled whispers trailed through the hallways. He rehearsed the words he refused to voice aloud: *He's doing this for her. For Lyra.*

Protecting her. Shielding her from the tornado of consequences that would tear her apart if they were found out. The rules weren't just lines on paper; they were steel traps tightening around them. But deeper still haunted the memory of his wingman, lost because one mistake was all it took. A funeral burned into his soul. A warning carved in pain. He couldn't let history repeat itself. Not with her.

His fingers trembled slightly as he pulled his comm device from the console. The screen glowed softly, Lyra's number etched in bright blue. He stared at it for a breath. Two. Then he pressed delete.

The emptiness hummed louder than the jet engines outside.

From beneath the console, his hand brushed against something familiar—a folded photograph. He unfolded it slowly, the edges worn, the image of Lyra's fierce smile framed by wild, wind-kissed hair. The warmth in that image was a sharp contrast to the cold determination settling over him like ice water. He slid the photo into a drawer and closed it.

Soft click.

The duffel was full now, the zipper sliding shut over the remnants of promise and regret. Blaze rose, muscles taut but steady. The room's dim light caught the angular planes of his face, hollow and etched with a private storm. His hands—so steady in the cockpit—clenched briefly at his sides.

He didn't turn. He didn't linger. Absence was his shield now, the only way to keep her safe.

"Blaze." Sarge's voice threaded through the silence, low and careful.

He looked up. The ghost of a sigh brushed his lips.

"You sure this is the right call?" Sarge stepped a little further in, his eyes searching.

Blaze shrugged slowly and measuredly. "I don't have a choice. Not if I want her to fly out of this alive."

Sarge set the cup down on the bedside table, his hands slack at his sides. "Rule one, man—protect your own. You're doing it, even if it's tearing you apart."

The words hung heavy, companionable.

Blaze finally met Sarge's eyes—a flicker of something raw and unspoken buried beneath his usual stoic mask.

"Keep her off my radar," Blaze murmured, his voice rough, a steel undercurrent betraying both his resolve and his fracture.

Sarge nodded, stepping back toward the door.

"Don't forget yourself, too."

The door closed with a soft thud, leaving Blaze alone with the fading scent of coffee and the cold stillness of his quarters.

He stood still. Silence wrapped around him, thick as a shroud. Outside, the hum of jets rose and fell—a restless soundtrack to a war he had chosen to fight from the shadows.

His fingers tightened once more on the duffel strap. The weight wasn't just in the bag; it was in the spaces now impossible to fill.

Absence is the price of survival.

And he's paying it in full.

The door whispered open with a muted hiss, and Lyra stepped inside the cold briefing room. Her boots tapped unevenly over the polished steel floor, each step sluggish, like wading through thick fog. She barely lifted her eyes from the linoleum as she slid into an empty chair at the edge of the long table, the vinyl creaking under her weight. Around her, other cadets flipped through digital checklists and murmured low compliance reminders, their faces sharp and alert—so unlike hers, which were dulled and scattered. Her shoulders sagged forward, surrendering to exhaustion that gnawed beneath her ribs.

Jazz appeared beside her without a sound, a wrapped protein bar balanced in one hand. She eased it onto the table in front of Lyra, her smile a mix of encouragement and mischievous resolve.

"Hey," Jazz teased softly. "Remember that time you called your jet a 'whirring death trap' mid-roll? Commander Reynolds nearly had a stroke."

Lyra's lips twitched, a flicker of warmth breaking through the haze, but the smile came out small and brittle, as if it barely disturbed her fatigue. She glanced down at the wrapper, her fingers brushing the crinkled foil but not opening it.

Across the room, Major Elena Voss's pale eyes narrowed behind her meticulously polished glasses. She sat at a cluster of desks, her fingers tapping a stylus against a digital pad where mission reports streamed like icy rain. Her gaze sharpened with quiet calculation, tracing Lyra's slumped frame and the subtle twitch of her brows over eyes heavy with distraction. Voss had built her career on precision and results—on identifying anomalies before they became liabilities. The deterioration in Lyra's performance over the past seventy-two hours registered as a data point, a variable that threatened program metrics and, by extension, Voss's record of excellence. The cadet was undeniably brilliant, but brilliance without reliability was a liability the program couldn't afford. Voss's lips pressed into a thin line as her stylus paused, then resumed, scribbling notes in precise strokes—"deterioration in focus," "emotional strain evident."

Near the door, Flight Officer Harper stood still, her dark eyes scanning rows of data on a glowing tablet. Her jaw tightened as she flicked through simulation logs, pausing on graphs that wavered and dipped beneath expected baselines. A terse note appeared in her ledger: "Lyra Hale – performance decline consistent over the last 72 hours. Requires monitoring." Harper's fingers hovered briefly over the screen before she tucked the tablet under her arm, her stance stiff and unreadable.

Lyra shifted in her chair, her fingers flexing restlessly against the table's cold metal edge. The unopened protein bar sat like a silent challenge between exhaustion and necessity. The room hummed with low murmurs—cadets exchanging clipped observations and instructors suppressing sighs. The briefing screen ahead lit the room with a harsh electric blue, its glow painting everyone in sterile light that did nothing to warm the tightening tension pooling around Lyra like a vise.

Jazz leaned closer, lowering her voice to a whisper.

"You'll nail it today. You always do. They don't see the fire burning beneath all this."

Lyra's gaze flickered toward Jazz but didn't hold. A knot twisted in her stomach—the familiar friction between knowing what she was capable of and feeling utterly incapable of accessing it. Self-doubt crept in at the edges, whispering that maybe they were right to watch her like this; maybe the exhaustion had hollowed something essential from her that she couldn't get back. Fear spiked through her ribs, sharp and immediate. What if today was the day she finally cracked? What if the fire Jazz spoke of had already burned out, leaving nothing but ash? Her hands curled into fists on the tabletop, her knuckles blanching. The heaviness in her chest settled deeper, a dull thud syncing with the flickering screen.

"I don't feel it. Not today." Her voice was rough, nearly swallowed by the silence but charged with fragile vulnerability hiding beneath the usual defiance.

Jazz shrugged, nudging the protein bar again. "Well, at least eat. You can't fight the sky on an empty stomach."

Lyra hesitated, then finally cracked the wrapper, the crinkle unnerving in the stillness. She lifted the bar halfway to her lips, then set it down untouched.

"I just need to get through this," she said, her eyes darting to the briefing monitor, which was now buzzing softly with updated protocols and mission parameters. The words on the screen blurred against the pounding in her skull.

From the corner of the room, Major Voss's gaze sharpened further. Somewhere in a stack of data streams, a cold calculation measured Lyra's fraying edges against program standards, weighing the cost of the volatile cadet's brilliance against the risk her recent faltering posed. Voss exchanged a quick glance with Harper, who gave a subtle nod, the unspoken warning settling between them—this was a moment teetering dangerously toward a breaking point.

Lyra reached for the bar again, and the world constricted around her, each breath a struggle beneath the surface. The chairs scraped softly as other cadets shuffled papers and exchanged concerned looks, their whispering pulses hidden beneath tight lips. The air smelled faintly of cooling circuits, recycled oxygen, and the lingering sharp tang of jet fuel soaked into the walls.

She swallowed hard, her lungs catching cold air like shards, and her fingers grazed the slick tabletop as if grasping for footing against the edges of her spiraling exhaustion. The room's collective gaze pressed down, a current of expectation and unresolved questions threading its way through glances and folded arms.

"You good, Ly?" Jazz's voice was low, a tether thrown against the widening silence.

Lyra tilted her head, blinking away the blur. "I will be. Just... one thing at a time." Her voice barely rose above the murmurs.

The briefing screen blinked in a steady, impersonal rhythm, scrolling scenarios that demanded focus and split-second decisions—a dance Lyra longed to master again. The simulation was close now—closer than she wanted.

She closed her eyes for a moment, feeling the unplugged hum of her scattered thoughts. The protein bar sat unopened, a fragile promise beside the glowing blue screen. Around her, the room tightened—a steel trap of observation, doubt, and unspoken stakes—as peers and instructors watched, waiting for the cadet at the edge to gather herself or break apart.

No one said a word. They just watched.

The flight lounge hummed with half-hearted conversations and the clink of plastic cups. Lyra barely registered it. She dragged her binders and checklist onto a corner table, set them down with a hollow thud, and then pushed them aside.

The pale, sterile light above washes over her face, sharpening the lines of exhaustion and dimming the usual spark in her eyes. Her fingers hover over the cracked screen of her comm, reluctant to look anywhere else.

Jazz slides in beside her, her voice lilting with gentle teasing. "You've got that 'do not disturb' aura cranked up to full blast, Hale. You sure you're not just ignoring me?" Her grin is easy, but concern brushes through it—faintly out of place in this cold, clipped air.

Lyra barely glances up. "I just need to be alone. For now."

Jazz's smile tightens. She nods as if she understands the invisible line drawn between them. "Alright. Solo mission it is."

Around the lounge, cadets drift past. Their eyes flick to Lyra and then dart away. Whispers swell in her wake like a tide pulling warmth. The unspoken rule circles her—stay close to Blaze, and you're on your own. No touchpoints. No safe zones.

A few feet away, a group clusters loosely. One cadet quickens his pace when Lyra's eyes meet his. Another's brow furrows before she shoves a hand in her pocket and turns sharply. The space around Lyra swells with invisible distance, the kind that makes every breath feel shallow and measured. It's the price of loving someone dangerous.

Her thumb slides over the screen. She types: *"Blaze. You okay? Need to talk."* and presses send.

Then she leans back into the harsh plastic chair, watching the blinking cursor like a heartbeat.

Minutes stretch—thick and unyielding. No reply. The screen remains blank—an empty void where comfort used to reside.

Her chest clenches. A cold knot tightens inside, squeezing her breath and stirring the taste of ash on her tongue. The protein bar beside her sits untouched. When she finally reaches for it, bitterness steals all flavor. It crumbles tastelessly on her tongue, swallowed out of habit rather than hunger.

A distant roar echoes faintly beyond the glazed windows—jets slicing through the sky. Lyra envisions those engines: one faltering, hesitant, limping through clouds like her thoughts. Flying on a dead wing, struggling to stay aloft despite a world that insists on toppling her.

Jazz shifts closer, her voice lowered to a whisper, eyes searching. "You're holding it together better than I would, Hale."

Lyra's shoulders stiffen. Her fingers tighten around the comm as if squeezing it could summon an answer. She breathes shallowly. The metal tang of anxiety prickles her veins. "It's like sinking and swimming at once, but mostly sinking."

Jazz's attempt at a soft chuckle falls flat. "You've got more fight left than you think. Don't let rules or silence drag you down."

"I'm not sure the fight is enough." Lyra flicks through the empty messages again before shutting the comm down with a harsh swipe. The screen goes black. Her palm presses against it. The glass is cool—indifferent.

She doesn't turn to Jazz, but she feels the weight of the other cadet's gaze—helpless, tethered to a friend unraveling in slow motion. The lingering quiet between them tastes like regret, unsaid words, and the brittle ache of absence.

"Have you tried calling him?" Jazz presses, urgency lightening her tone.

Lyra shakes her head, her voice barely audible. "No. I'm scared to hear nothing but static."

Jazz folds her arms and exhales softly. "Sometimes silence says more than a hundred words."

Lyra's eyes glide to the smudged window. Sunlight fractures across the runway, shimmering on cold metal and concrete. Her own reflection fragments there, flickering between defiance and uncertainty. She wants to cram the pieces back together, but the edges bite sharp.

Feet shuffle nearby. Cadet voices murmur in the distance. Lyra's fingers flex, clutching empty air as a reminder of what is missing—what has been lost in the spaces between stolen glances and unsent messages.

Jazz leans back. The chair creaks. She watches without pressing further, the bonds between them taut and fragile, like a failing lifeline just beyond reach.

Lyra presses the comm screen once more, as if willing it to pulse alive.

Only darkness answers.

Her breath catches—shallow and fast—caught in the silent cadence of an inbox that remains empty.

Lyra's fingers tremble slightly as she buckles the harness straps inside the simulator pod. The seat creaks softly beneath her, the metal cold against her hands as she adjusts the visors on her helmet. The sterile scent of disinfectant and faint ozone mingles in the air, sharp and clinical, contrasting with the dull pounding in her temples. Outside the thick glass, Major Voss stands rigid, his lips pressed into a tight line. Flight Officer Harper's sharp gaze flicks between her tablet and the pod, her fingers tapping out a steady rhythm. Beside them, Sarge leans forward, his jaw clenched, eyes wary beneath his furrowed brow.

The chamber's hum builds—a low mechanical pulse syncing with Lyra's quickening heartbeat. She inhales, steadying the chaos swelling beneath her skin, but the weight of every glance, every expectation, presses in like gravity itself.

"Pre-flight checks," she mutters, her voice tight. "Control surfaces... operational. Hydraulics... green. Fuel flow... nominal." Each checklist call sounds clipped, rehearsed but hollow, as if she's drifting through someone else's script.

The virtual canopy blinks alive with digital readouts: altitude, airspeed, G-forces. Numbers swim just beyond full grasp through the fog pooling behind her eyes. Two years ago, she had nearly spiraled during a similar sequence—the memory of that near-miss still lives in her sternum, a tight knot of fear she can't quite shake. Every metric on this screen feels weighted with that history; every dial is a judge.

Afterburners engage with a muted rush. The simulated engine roar dims against the stillness, but the simulated acceleration rolls a twist against her ribs.

Lyra's fingers hover over the throttle, twitching. Then she jerks the stick forward to bank left. The pod shudders, and hydraulics groan faintly. The sequence speeds up. The digital horizon tilts sharply—the craft spins into a rapid roll.

An alert flashes on the main screen: an unfamiliar warning, one she should have seen sooner.

Her gaze flickers to the wrong gauge—a subtle misread that sends her scrambling. Colors bleed together like hot embers, and her vision blurs, distances collapsing.

A bitter edge cuts through her chest. Her jaw tightens until the muscles ache. Her hands clamp the controls like a lifeline, knuckles whitening with every frantic grip. Instead of the regulated recovery sequence drilled into her muscle memory, she plunges into reckless instinct. She yanks hard—too hard—executing a sudden snap roll forbidden by the manual.

The simulator groans. The virtual craft's tail sweeps wildly across the digital sky. The pod jerks violently. Alarms scream. Sirens snake through the chamber, cutting cold and urgent through the hum. Heart hammering, Lyra fights the looming spin as the virtual engines sputter under strain.

"Sarge to Hale," crackles a voice like a razor through the noise. "Pull up. Immediate recovery sequence. Follow emergency protocol—now."

Lyra's breath catches. Sweat slicks her palms against the joystick's cold plastic. She clamps her jaw, muscles taut as steel cables, her mind a storm of doubt and resolve. Each second stretches, minutes compressed into heartbeats.

Behind the glass, Voss leans down, sharp eyes narrowing like a hawk circling wounded prey. Harper's brows knit, fingers hovering, poised to log every second, every misstep.

Lyra twists the stick. She counters the spin with desperate precision. The pod groans under the strain. Hydraulics scream in protest. Her knuckles blanch as she forces a final, agonizing input that wrests control back from the brink. The alarms falter, stutter, then cut to silence.

The room drops into eerie quiet. The gentle click of the helmet release echoes, followed by the soft hiss of ventilation. Lyra lifts the visor, gasping, her chest heaving like a fighter just scraped back from the ropes. Her cheeks are pale, an unwelcome flash of vulnerability beneath the cold blue glow of the console.

A long moment stretches between breaths.

"Hale, that was reckless," Voss says, his voice low and sharp, cutting through the lingering tension like a scalpel. "It almost cost you everything."

Harper nods silently, his eyes hard. Sarge exhales slowly, rubbing the back of his neck, then meets Lyra's gaze with a grudging edge of concern.

"You got lucky," he says quietly. "That was too close for comfort. That recovery was borderline reckless."

Lyra presses a trembling hand to her chest, trying to still the hammering. The taste of copper lingers faintly in her mouth, and the dry air feels suddenly thick, clogging her throat.

"Rules exist for a reason," Voss adds, his voice tightening. "This isn't impulse; it's protocol or failure."

Fingers trembling, Lyra reaches toward the comm. She swallows hard.

"I know," she says, her voice rough. "I just... I had to push back, make it work." Her eyes flick downward. "I wasn't thinking straight."

Sarge leans in, his voice firm but steady.

"You won't be thinking straight if you lose control next time. Don't let it get worse."

Lyra straightens, her jaw set as a flicker of steel shades her exhaustion. The defiance comes from somewhere deeper now, hard-won and real.

"I won't."

The three observers exchange measured looks—Voss with her calculating slant of the mouth, Harper stoic but watchful, and Sarge a gentle anchor in the storm of judgment.

The pod's console hums steadily again, its digital heartbeat now calm but with the memory of chaos etched into every dial.

Lyra slips off the helmet completely. Her green eyes are wide and alert beneath the fluorescent glare—drained but defiant. The narrow escape from disaster is carved into her sinews and skin.

The silence lingers, heavy as stone. Her breath slows, and the room exhales with her.

The simulation chamber's chill presses in, a cold witness to the fierce battle waged inside a shrinking cockpit of shadow and light.

The simulator pod shudders to a halt. The machines fall silent. An ominous stillness creeps through the control room, heavy as fog. Voices thread low and urgent through the space—fractured whispers weaving around the sharp click of keyboards and the distant hiss of ventilation. Major Voss leans closer to Flight Officer Harper, their exchange loaded with calculation. "Can she recover? Is she fit to continue?"

Across the room, Sarge's steady gaze swept over the assembly, his broad shoulders squared beneath olive drab. "Lyra's got the skill—we all know that. I never once doubted it. Hell, her instincts have pulled more than one of us out of a tight spot." He paused, rubbing the stubbled corner of his jaw, his voice rough as gravel. "But this? This right here is different."

He met Voss's scrutinizing eyes. "Her focus slipped. Twice now. These aren't small lapses. They can't be ignored."

A murmur rippled through the instructors. Tension coiled tighter than the steel cables suspending the simulator overhead. Data scrolled silently across the monitors, but those numbers felt meaningless next to the weight pressing down on every chest.

Meanwhile, Lyra's boots thundered down the polished corridor outside the bay. Her breath came in jagged gasps, and her heart hammered like a siren. She barreled past clusters of cadets, her jaw clenched tight, a tremor running through her fists—not from physical exhaustion, but from the storm of humiliation burning beneath her skin. Jazz's heels scraped hurriedly behind her, her voice urgent yet tender.

"Lyra, wait—"

But Lyra didn't slow. She couldn't. Her dark eyes flashed, unyielding, as she pushed deeper into the corridor's cold fluorescent glare. The scent of polished metal and faint jet fuel lingered around her, sterile reminders of all she risked losing. Cadets glanced away as she passed, whispers dying at the sight of her storm-etched face. Isolation bloomed around her like a shadow.

From the tinted glass of the observation booth, Major Voss watched the retreating figure. A thin smile curved her lips—calculated, deliberate. There was a quiet thrill in watching someone unravel. "This," Voss murmured to Harper, her voice a razor-thin promise. "This is leverage."

Jazz called again, softer now, her voice an attempt to bridge the widening chasm. Lyra's pace never slowed. Each step was sharper, more deliberate. She slammed into the hallway's end as if trying to outrun the weight of expectation itself.

Inside the control room, Sarge leaned against the console. His eyes held a war between dread and determination—loyalty to Lyra clashing against the fear that something deeper might be wrong. Something was breaking. He pushed off the console and faced the assembled instructors.

"She's not just any cadet," he said, his voice rough with unshed frustration. "You all saw what she did before. The edge she flies on... it's why she's here. But I'm not blind. Something's broken. Or breaking." He looked at each face, challenging yet conceding. "We need to be careful. But we can't turn on her—not yet."

His words lingered, unanswered but heavy, as the door clicked shut behind Lyra. Silence stretched a beat longer before footsteps shuffled and hesitant voices resumed their low debate.

Outside, Jazz closed the gap, her breath steady as she reached for a hand that was already gone. The space between them held a silence louder than any shout. The corridor's gleam reflected Lyra's rigid back, the fight draining from her frame yet burning subtly beneath the surface. No glance backward. No pause.

The control room waited, breath held, for the rupture to either mend or shatter completely.

The lounge was almost empty, the soft hum of overhead lights coiling through the late afternoon stillness. Lyra's footsteps barely stirred the worn carpet as she slipped toward the coffee machine, her shoulders tight and her gaze fixed on the floor. The sharp scent of burnt beans lingered stubbornly in the sterile air, mingling with faint disinfectant—the scent of spaces designed to hold tension and exhaustion in equal measure.

Her throat felt raw, dry as the stale air wrapped tightly around the lounge's muted light. She reached for a cup, her fingers trembling against the cold plastic.

Jazz cornered her without a word, stepping in front of her, arms crossed firmly, eyes steady and unwilling to let Lyra pass.

Lyra froze. Her breath hitched. Silence stretched—a heavy pause packed with unsaid words and the grinding ache of every step she had taken since the simulator, since the failure that had sent her spiraling. The weight of it pressed down like a hand on her chest.

"You're not getting away this time," Jazz says softly.

Lyra can't move. Her racing heart stutters, a faint crack in the armor she has spent three days rebuilding. When her voice comes, it is fractured, barely above a whisper, yet it cuts through the silence like broken glass. "Did he ever really care? Or am I just another pawn in his career? A casualty he is willing to sacrifice?"

Her chest tightens. The tremor starts small, building in her hands, flooding through her with sudden, fragile force. Raw doubt spills to the surface, quivering on the edge of collapse.

Jazz's gaze softens but remains firm. She reaches out, catching Lyra's elbow with quiet strength. "Hey. Sit. Please." Her tone is gentle but no less commanding.

Lyra wavers, the fragility in her eyes breaking down her defenses faster than she can rebuild them. She nods, her knees unsteady as Jazz guides her toward the nearest couch, its fabric worn but welcoming.

Jazz folds a napkin between her fingers, handing it over like a lifeline. She has seen Lyra like this once before—after the academy's final assessment last year, when Lyra had come so close to washing out. It was that day Jazz learned what lay beneath Lyra's fierce exterior: not arrogance, but exhaustion from constantly proving herself; not coldness, but fear of being forgotten the moment she stumbled. Knowing this, Jazz refused to let her fall apart silently now.

"You're not the sum of their whispers," Jazz murmurs, her voice threading comfort through the tension. "You're the fire lighting up this whole damn program. Remember that roll you nailed last month? The way you pulled out of that dive when everyone else was hesitating? That's you. And yeah, Blaze—he sees that, even if he has his own ghosts dragging him down. What you two had lifted you. It made you sharper. Don't let the silence fool you into thinking you're nothing."

Lyra's inhale breaks, ragged, like the first glimpses of dawn after a long, dark night. The walls she's built tremble. They crack. Tears flood unchecked over her lashes, cold rivers carving paths down her cheeks. Her shoulders sag, shaking violently as sobs rip through her chest. The knot inside unravels completely.

The quiet lounge swells with the sound of grief unleashed—a faint creak of metal chairs settling, but no one comes near. The room holds its breath for her.

Jazz sits close, steady and patient, offering the weight of her presence like an anchor in a shifting storm. Her hand finds Lyra's wrist, fingers gentle yet deliberate, grounding her friend in the swirling sea of heartbreak.

After a long moment, Lyra raises the napkin, pressing it clumsily against her damp face. She leans forward, burying her face in her hands, her breath shallow and uneven.

Jazz's voice drops to a whisper, soft as a promise. "You're not alone. Not here. Not ever."

The room holds its hush—a fragile sanctuary wrapped in fading light—as Lyra lets the last of her sorrow bleed out, cradled by quiet companionship and whispered truths.

Lyra's comm chimes—sharp and sudden—cutting through the barracks' low hum. She answers, expecting routine. The screen blinks back tersely. Cold. A command: report to Commander Reynolds' office at 0700 hours.

No explanation. No softening.

Just protocol.

Her stomach clenches, that familiar knot twisting tighter as the words hang before her eyes. A cold pulse thrums behind her ribs, dragging everything beneath a dark tide. This wasn't routine. Messages like this didn't come without reason, and reasons at Astra always carried weight—the kind that could crater a career before it truly began.

She stares at the screen long enough for the glow to sear into her vision. Then she powers it off.

Outside, a chill wind churns through coastal shadows, rattling the windowpanes. Jet engines echo faintly—those phantom roars of departures and returns that seem to mock her stillness.

In his quarters, Blaze lies awake. The darkness wraps around him like a shroud, heavy and suffocating. Distant roars of jets drift through the walls—a rhythm both soothing and tormenting, a metronome of a life moving forward without him.

His fingers found the edge of the drawer—rough wood, cool beneath his palm in the dim light.

He pulled out the photo—folded and creased from handling. Lyra's face stared back at him, bright and undaunted, caught in a moment he had stolen weeks ago.

His thumb traced the creases—slow and deliberate—as if his touch could somehow hold her there, suspended in paper and ink, safe from the wreckage he was certain to make of anything that mattered. The ghost of her smile haunted him—fragile, fierce, everything he couldn't afford to want.

His chest tightened, and his breath caught somewhere hollow inside.

He forced his eyes shut, wrenching away from the image and the swell of longing that threatened to break him open.

Across campus, Lyra lay stiff on her bunk. The thin mattress creaked beneath her weight, each shift of her body releasing a sound like a small complaint. The empty space beside her felt cavernous—a dark absence that ached deeper than bruised pride or shattered dreams.

Her gaze traced the cracked ceiling tiles—faint stains like constellations of doubt and fear mapping out a sky she couldn't navigate.

She reached out almost habitually, her fingers curling into empty air where warmth should have been, where he should have been.

Only cold. An unforgiving void filled with whispered confessions and silent retreats. Her heart pounded—a steady rebellion against everything protocol demanded she accept. Images flickered unbidden: the rigid set of Blaze's jaw in the command room, the quiet weight behind his eyes, and every unwilling goodbye wrapped in sacrifice she couldn't ask him to make.

Outside their separate rooms, the world slept.

Inside, two bodies lay wide awake—separate, solitary, tethered by unspoken words and fractured trust.

Lyra broke the silence first.

"Why do you always pull away when I need you most?"

Blaze's voice came low, tired, almost distant across the space between them.

"Sometimes staying close means risking everything."

Her sigh cracked with frustration and something tender beneath.

"Maybe I'm worth the risk. Maybe I'm worth the fight."

"Lyra—"

"No." Her voice sharpened, trembling just enough to fracture the armor around her heart. "Don't 'Lyra' me like I'm a problem to manage."

The clench in his chest tightened.

"I'm trying to protect you—from the rules, from me."

She laughed—soft, broken, more shiver than sound.

"Rules are killers. You're not the only one scared of losing someone, but you can't keep running."

He swallowed hard. The corner of his mouth twitched—almost a smile.

"Maybe it's not running. Maybe it's the only way I know how to survive."

Her eyes glistened with unshed tears, but her voice remained steady.

"Survival doesn't have to mean being alone."

The hours stretched.

Fluorescent lights flickered in the dormitory hallways, their buzz hanging in the air like an unseen pulse. Beyond the walls, the night breathed cold and restless, carrying the heavy weight of decisions yet to be made, futures fraying at their edges.

In their separate rooms, Lyra clutched the void where hope once dwelled.

Blaze fought the war within—a war for which neither rules nor storms could prepare him.

Two hearts beat out of sync, tethered by distance and refusing to break.

The night stretched on—endless, silent, tormented.

Into the Storm

Static crackles sharply through the command center's sterile hum. A towering screen blinks crimson: CYCLONE WARNING—IMMINENT. The siren blasts. The alarm claws at muscle and bone, warbling through steel walls in an uncompromising assault that settles deep into every nerve.

Officers in gray coats clutch steaming printouts, their boots clattering urgent rhythms across polished floors as they surge toward the hangar briefing area.

Outside, rain hammers the base like fistfuls of liquid cold. The sitrep's gravity pulls cadets and instructors alike into the cavernous hangar, heavy boots sparking sharp echoes on the wet concrete. The vast space swallows their footsteps beneath the roar of rain racing down the seams of looming metal doors, streaking slick trails that mirror the tension thickening the air.

Commander Reynolds stands rigid beneath the harsh glare of floodlights, her jaw set. Eyes like sharpened steel scan the room—calculating, weighing, bearing the burden of every decision about to come from her lips. When she speaks, her voice cuts clearly through the murmur.

"All non-essential flights are grounded immediately. Only designated senior pilots are authorized for emergency patrols. Every unit will secure equipment, safeguard power grids, and prepare for worst-case scenarios. No exceptions."

Each word lands like a salvo, binding the room in disciplined awareness.

Lieutenant Marcus "Sarge" Sullivan steps forward, his presence steady amid the rising storm. He pins a roster to the whiteboard—names and assignments crisply listed. Two teams will fortify the runway barricades, one will oversee generator backups, and another stands ready at medical staging. His voice is low but firm.

"Rescue teams Alpha and Bravo, runway barricades; Charlie, generator backup; Delta, medical staging. Check your gear, communicate clearly, and expect the unexpected."

The room snaps into motion. Bars and clamps clink, and radios warm to life. Purpose threads through the chatter like electricity.

Across the briefing hall, Blaze and Lyra lean against opposite edges of the crowd. Their eyes meet for a fraction of a second—a collision of histories neither wanted to relive today, a friction that neither could quite bury, no matter how hard they tried. Then nothing. The moment dissolved as quickly as it ignited.

Blaze's jaw tightened, muscles taut beneath weathered skin. He turned away first, staring into the middle distance, his gaze a locked vault. Command and control. Always command and control, even when the walls were cracking beneath him.

Lyra's fingers clenched white around the weathered flight log, her thumb tracing nervous circles on its spine. The leather's rough edges bit into her palm—a steadying burn against the chaos thrumming beneath her skin. She didn't look away fast enough; the damage was already done.

Sarge's hand slammed a clipboard shut. The sound echoed like a starting gun in the charged space.

"To your stations. Move."

The hangar shifted into a coordinated frenzy. Rain drummed harder against the metal ribs overhead. Boots scattered with purpose. Voices rose and fell like low thunder beyond the wide-open doors, where sheets of gray mist swallowed the horizon whole.

Lyra stood just beyond the tight clusters of cadets, the cold concrete biting at her boots as the first drops of rain streaked the hangar doors. The briefing had dispersed into frantic activity, but her gaze remained fixed on Sarge, who barked orders with a low, efficient grit that cut through the rising tension of the storm. His voice boomed off the cavern walls—sandbag teams here, generator crews there, medical prep on the far side. Each command fell like a battlefield edict.

When he called for cadets to man the barricades and haul supplies, her jaw clenched tight. Her eyes darted across the swarm of bodies, catching the resigned faces of peers settling for ground duties, their boots syncing with the distant thunder. She folded her arms, a hard line tracing her silhouette. Sandbag detail? Not for her. Her pulse quickened—not from fear, but from frustration. She refused to be sidelined while this storm threatened every last sensor and missile on the base.

She stepped forward but stopped short. Jazz intercepted her near a crate, slipping a protein bar into her hand with a nervous smile.

"You're seriously going to argue with Sarge?" Jazz's eyes flicked toward the storm-darkened windows. "Commander Reynolds laid it out—no flights. You're lucky I'm hanging around like a lost drone, ready to drag you back."

Lyra ripped the wrapper off the bar. The faint rustle cut through the hubbub. She bit down, the oats grounding her resolve like concrete beneath her teeth.

"I've got to do this, Jazz." Her voice dropped to a low, steady growl. "The southern radar station has been glitching since yesterday. I logged hours on low-visibility protocols—I know that grid inside and out."

The southern relay tower monitored the cyclone's approach sector. If it failed, the base would be flying blind into the storm's teeth.

Jazz's brow knitted. "The storm's not just a breeze, Ly. It's a damn cyclone. Do you think Commander Reynolds cares about your low-G hours when a jet goes down in that mess?"

"She should." Lyra shook her head, her jaw clenched tight. Her gaze sharpened, and her fists curled at her sides. "But I'm not waiting to find out what happens if it goes unreported."

Sarge's footsteps approached—gravelly and certain. He caught the tail end of their exchange and narrowed his gaze. Inside, something twisted. He had seen Lyra's instincts prove right before. He had also held the hand of a pilot who didn't come home.

"That's a suicide run." His voice was clipped. "Orders are orders. No one is airborne. Ground crews are already stretched thin prepping for blackout. I won't authorize you to fly into this fucking mess."

Lyra straightened, stepping into the bruising gray light spilling from the open hangar door. Her hands balled into fists, her nails biting into her palms.

"This isn't just about orders." Her voice snapped like a whip. "Yesterday's maintenance logs show repeated interference. Radar blips flicker erratically around the southern grid. I caught a signal drop near the relay tower—something's wrong. If no one checks it, we're blind."

Sarge's jaw tightened. The hard lines of his face mapped decades of discipline. Something flickered in his eyes—a reluctant respect for her conviction warring with duty and dread.

He studied her for a long moment. Finally, he exhaled.

"You will get constant radio check-ins. Agreed abort altitude. Absolutely no messing with procedures."

She inhaled sharply. The cool air choked her throat for a second, then steadied her. Fingers trembling but sure, she reached into her gear bag and pulled out her flight gloves. She slid them on with practiced movements—one finger at a time, sealing them tight.

"I promise. No heroics. I'll call you every five minutes. Abort at 2,000 feet if it gets bad."

Sarge nodded.

Jazz grinned, stepping closer. "I guess your stubborn streak finally paid off."

Lyra smirked, her shoulders squaring as she turned toward the line of ready jets.

A cold gust funneled through the hangar, tangling her short hair, with wet strands plastering against her resolute face. Rain hammered against the vast bay doors with a metallic hiss, drowning out the rumble of engines powering down and the clatter of tools in preparation. The damp chill crawled up her spine. The sharp tang of jet fuel mixed with wet concrete filled her nostrils—a familiar sting that grounded her determination.

As she zipped up the flight suit, the fabric clung slick against her skin, the familiar weight folding around her like armor forged in adrenaline and grit. The seal clicked tight under her chin. Her eyes flashed with quiet fire, burning through the haze of tension.

The hum of conversations faded beneath the howling wind settling into the hangar's cavernous space.

Lyra moved with purpose, every step a beat of defiance. Her silhouette sliced through the misty haze—a spearhead carving a promise into the storm-darkened dawn. She threaded her way toward the line of ready jets, toward the throttle, toward whatever awaited in that roiling sky.

###

Sarge pressed a tablet into Blaze's hand, the device glowing faintly amid the dim hangar light. "You're in charge of evacuations and back-up power. That checklist has the details. Keep it tight."

Blaze's jaw tightens as he nods sharply. The tablet snaps into his belt clip with a practiced flick. Fingers brushing against the cold metal, he steps into the cavernous space. Diesel and hot wiring cling to the air—sharp, acrid, and alive.

The hangar stretches wide and raw, with bare concrete slick from the residual moisture of the morning's drizzle. Mechanics in blue coveralls move between rows of silent jets, their boots thudding against the stained concrete. Oil and rubber fill the air, the smell of machines waiting.

Blaze's voice cracks like a whip.

"Fuel seals—confirm all locked. Generator feed lines—double-check. Cadets, secure loose gear. Now."

His gaze snaps toward a bank of monitors on the far wall, where the flight status display is flashing. Sorties are delayed, with some still moving despite the cyclone warning, underlining the risk creeping across Astra like a predator testing its prey.

His eyes linger on the radar blips—flickering ghosts edging closer to the storm.

A mechanic's voice rises. "Got it, Captain."

Blaze doesn't reply; his attention is already sliding back to the checklist, but his fingers tap the tablet's smooth edge. His mind stretches elsewhere—toward that flare on the screen, toward Lyra.

Jazz lingers at the command desk like a coiled spring. Her eyes flicker between the radio, the screens, and the slow progress of jet prep near the ready line. One hand hovers close to the radio mic, fingers poised, while her other hand drums an anxious rhythm against the desk's scratched surface.

She watches Blaze pace the hangar like a storm tethered by obligation. The tight set of his shoulders betrays everything—that restless energy simmering beneath his calm exterior. The way he glances toward the flight status monitor, how he presses a finger briefly against his temple, and his jaw clenched tight all reveal his inner turmoil.

Jazz's gaze shifts to the tarp-covered line near the jets. Lyra's silhouette moves beneath the plastic, fighting the wind. She sees what Blaze is doing—killing time, not just working. She reads the conflict written across his body like script.

Blaze moves toward a cluster of gear near the metal lockers. His hands work quickly, strapping down cables and stowing a flight helmet in the overhead rack. The helmet's smooth curve catches the dim overhead glow.

His fingertips drum on its rim—a quiet, restless beat, like calling to the storm.

"No loose ends," he says aloud, more to himself than to anyone else. "Flight suits secured. Helmets stowed. Generator feeds sealed." His voice carries a clipped urgency that masks something deeper.

Jazz's voice cuts through, barely a murmur.

"You're killing time."

Blaze shoots her a glance, his dark eyes flickering with something unspoken.

"I'm making sure it's done right."

"You're pacing, not just ticking boxes. You can't fool me." She flicks her gaze back to the radios. "You're thinking of getting up and going after her."

He clenches his jaw. "Can't."

"Can't or won't?"

Blaze's hand tightens into a fist. The tablet barely shifts on his belt.

"The orders are clear. I'm ground support today."

Jazz's tone dips softer. "But she's out there against the storm. And you know it's not just routine."

"Exactly." His voice drops to a gravelly edge. "I can't afford to lose control again."

From across the hangar, thunder rolls through the cracked concrete and steel beams. Rain gusts through the open doors in irregular slaps. The storm presses closer—wild, angry, alive.

Blaze steps toward the hangar doors. Muscles coil beneath his jacket as he gazes outside. Rain beads on the cracked glass, distorting the rows of jets lined up like sentinels.

Under the weather-beaten tarp, Lyra's figure shifts—a ghost of motion fighting the rising wind.

Jazz approaches quietly. She slides a printed flight path map across the desk toward him.

"I hacked into an alternate comm channel," she says. "Backup frequency for Lyra. No one on the main net will pick it up."

Blaze's eyes flick to the map and then back to the shadowed ready-jet line outside.

"I don't trust the system right now." His voice is barely audible. "I need to be in the air."

Jazz's hands tighten around her tablet. "If you leave your post, Reynolds will have your ass. Your career will be over. No questions asked."

Blaze's gaze darkens. He feels the weight of the choice pressing down on him—staying here, safe and invisible, or stepping into the void and losing everything.

"If I lose her too," he says quietly, "I won't come back from that."

Jazz lets out a slow breath. She meets his stare steadily and does not look away.

"Then let's make sure she knows you're out there."

She slips a small earpiece into his palm. Her expression balances fragile determination with concern.

Blaze pockets it. The tension thickens in his throat. He blinks it away.

A sudden crack of lightning splits the sky. The runway illuminates like pale fire.

He slides the heavy hangar door open. Cold air lashes against his face with a salty sting. It soaks through his jacket and hair. The world blurs—gray rain, flickering jet lights, chaos.

Lyra crouches beneath the tarp, her hands busy on the jet's frame. Her focus is absolute despite the wind's howl.

Blaze's breath catches. His heart hammers in time with the storm's relentless beat. The hum of engines idles somewhere out of sight. Flight calls to him like a siren's song.

He steps out fully, the wet concrete cold beneath his boots. He fixates on the lone figure moving against the tempest—a silhouette of resolve carved sharply against the dark horizon.

And he knows he is done waiting.

Sheets of rain whip sideways through the wide-open hangar entrance, rattling against steel beams and pooling on the slick concrete floor. The metallic tang of wet steel clings to the air, sharp and electric. The low drone of turbulent wind grows louder, a restless beast prowling just beyond the bay doors. Inside, radio chatter crackles with tension—pilots report spikes in wind shear and squall lines that no one can ignore.

Blaze's voice cuts through the static as he answers a call about a flooded access gate. "Roger. Dispatch ground crew; seal off sector five. Use sandbags and pumps. Keep comms open." His tone is steady and controlled.

Sector five—home to a critical fuel depot—was already vulnerable, making that flood warning more than just a routine alert. The strategic weight of it pressed against his shoulders, another layer of pressure stacked on top of what already bent him.

Yet his eyes flicker again and again to a glowing blip on the radar monitor—Lyra's signature, a tiny pulse piercing the storm's chaos. The blip pulsed stubbornly and defiantly, a spark of chaos in the ordered storm. Every siren, every warning blurred past protocol and risk, dredging up that restless coil of fear he had been fighting since the mission.

He stands near the edge of the hangar. Rain-streaked light washes over the rough concrete. The storm's breath chills him, tugging at his jacket and loosening duty's grip—if only for a flicker of rebellion. Inside, orders hum, and people move like trained shadows, securing equipment, checking generators, and setting up barricades. He should be one of them—staying grounded and focused.

But the knot tightening his jaw speaks louder than protocol. Each turbulence alert drills through him like a spike; his jaw clenches, and his fists twitch along his sleeves as heat floods his hands.

The low murmur of footsteps pulls his attention. Jazz appears beside him—quiet and purposeful. She slides a folded printout across the console, the crisp paper leaning against the faded paint like a lifeline. Blaze catches it without looking, scanning the mapped flight path she has traced in neat, precise lines.

She lowers her voice, sliding the paper closer. "I found an alternate comm. Private channel... I pre-loaded it for you, if you want it." She slips a small earpiece into his palm. "Just... figured you'd want this." Her eyes flicker, searching his face for something unsaid—calm but wavering with unspoken worry.

Blaze's hand closes over the paper and the earpiece. The plastic feels oddly heavy, an anchor in the storm-tossed sea of his thoughts. His boots splash through shallow pools slick with runoff as he stows them carefully. He folds the map before slipping it into his jacket pocket.

Sarge is focused on barking out orders at the opposite end, directing rescue teams without missing a beat; he doesn't see the exchange. No one notices Blaze's hesitation, the barely perceptible shift as his priorities rearrange themselves.

The radio buzzes again—crisp commands, escalating urgency—but Blaze tunes it out. His gaze drifts past the hangar's steel skeleton, beyond the tarmac slick with rain. There, just beyond the yellow safety line, the runway stretches out, girded in storm shadows.

The first fingers of gray light slice through low clouds, sharp as the edge of a blade. They wash over Blaze's silhouette as he steps closer to the threshold, the hangar cold behind him and the tempest beckoning ahead.

His breath curls in the damp air, ragged but resolute. The rhythm in his chest is no longer command—it's something rawer, deeper. The unyielding soldier fights the pull of duty against the unforgiving tug of the sky.

Jazz's voice floats up again, softer now but steady. "She's out there. Alone."

Blaze doesn't reply; the words don't need to be fleshed out. The storm's howl swells, filling the hollow spaces in the hangar with promise and peril.

His fingers tighten once more around the earpiece tucked beneath his collar, knuckles whitening as if trying to hold onto calm itself—as if gripping a lifeline and a promise all at once.

The world narrows to the dim outline of the runway beyond the gate, the rising tempest, and the ghost of Lyra's jet threading through the weather.

He stands on the edge of everything—protocol, fear, and a choice only he can make.

Blaze's shoulders scrape the narrow doorway as he pulls Jazz inside the maintenance alcove. His voice drops to a harsh whisper, trembling with a fear he can't swallow. "I can't let her fly through this storm alone. Not with what's coming."

Jazz's eyes dart sideways, darkening under the harsh hangar lights. She shifts her weight, her jaw tight. The stale stench of oil and jet fuel wraps around them like a cold chain—but it's her sharp, cautious silence that tightens the space between them.

"Leaving your post?" Her voice drops low, her breath sharp. "Blaze, you're playing with fire. If Reynolds gets wind of this, it's career suicide. Court-martial, maybe worse. You can't just walk away."

"She can't do this alone." Blaze's jaw clenches. His hands curl into fists, his knuckles ghost-white beneath worn glove leather. His voice breaks. "If I lose her too, I won't come back from it."

Jazz's lips press into a thin line. She fights between doing the right thing and facing the inevitable, her gloved hands opening and closing at her hips. Her eyes—dark with the weight of all she knows—finally soften. She nods.

The rain drums on the hangar's corrugated roof. Thunder rumbles in the distance, a muted percussion underscoring their tense stillness.

Without a word, Jazz pulls a worn flight helmet from the shelf—matte black, scratched, and dull from use—and tosses it to Blaze. Her fingers brush the edge, then move swiftly to unzip a flight suit hanging nearby. She hands it to him, her movements economical and sure.

Blaze slides his arms through the sleeves. The fabric is cool against his skin, rain slicking the edges where his soaked hoodie shows beneath.

Jazz fishes into her utility belt and retrieves a small black earpiece. She presses it into Blaze's palm along with a folded maintenance log. Her voice lowers further, serious as a command. "This frequency is clean. Private channel—just you and Lyra."

There's something unspoken in her tone, a quiet solidarity born from too many close calls.

She pulls out a datapad, and her fingers move swiftly across the screen, altering the maintenance log's timestamps. She forges a falsified entry, stalling any tracking of Blaze's upcoming absence. A soft click seals the data. She tucks the tablet back into her coat pocket and releases a breath held too long.

Blaze folds the altered log and slides it into his flight suit pocket. He glances at the earpiece and tucks it behind his collar. The cold plastic presses against bare skin. For a moment, his hand lingers there—the weight of protocol breaking, of loyalty fracturing in one small gesture.

Outside, runway lights burn orange through the rain curtain—blurred and trembling, like his heartbeat.

Jazz watches him, her chest tight. Her lips press into that thin line again, hiding the flutter of fear she dares not voice. They have pulled each other out of tight spots before, but this is different. This isn't just about protocol; it is about trust and what they are willing to risk for each other.

"Be careful out there," she whispers.

Blaze nods once. No promises. No certainties. Just the bare acknowledgment that they both understand what this costs.

He steps away from her and pushes into the murmur of bustling life in the hangar. His jaw tightens. Resolve settles over his features like a mask.

The wet concrete beneath his boots echoes with the rhythm of urgency. Distant voices, the hiss of hydraulic lines, and damp fabric mixed with machine grease hang heavy in the air, slick with the promise of a storm.

Blaze moves through the hangar with practiced grace. He ducks past a pair of patrolling officers—shadows blurring in his vision—and slips toward the ready-jet bay.

Rows of grounded interceptors loom ahead, gleaming with cold readiness beneath dripping tarps. His boots slap against the slick concrete. Rain pelts his shoulders as wind lashes the hangar doors. His fingers tighten on the helmet strap.

The stripped-down interceptor waits for him—engines cold but primed beneath rain-spattered panels. His hands flash along the cockpit edge, touching controls as if memorizing the hum of life they still hold.

Back in the alcove, Jazz returns to her station. She hardens herself like steel forged in hidden fire. Her voice cuts sharp and clipped as she begins weaving a web of distractions across the radio frequencies. Waiting. Always waiting for the moment the storm will claim the skies.

Outside, Blaze pulls his jacket tighter around the flight suit, helmet under his arm. Rain soaks through the loose fabric, mingling with the electric tension thrumming inside him. The storm roars from distant clouds, but he moves forward, defiance carved into every step.

The doors clang shut behind him.

Sealing him in. Sealing him out. Gone before the thunder can swallow his name.

Blaze's boots scrape over slick concrete in the ready-jet bay. Rain seeps through cracks in the hangar's rusted metal door far behind him. A pair of patrol officers stride past in crisp gray coats, breath misting in the chill. A shadow slips behind a refuel truck—muscles coiling with the urgency pounding in his chest.

Thunder rumbles overhead in tight bursts.

The jet waited in the gloom, cold and silent. Its dark fuselage was dotted with raindrops that caught the harsh fluorescents like scattered diamonds. Blaze moved toward it, his eyes locked on the sleek silhouette of the interceptor idling in the shadows.

He slipped into the cockpit hatch. The familiar clank of locking harnesses filled the small space. Switches flicked beneath his fingers, and mechanical life bloomed around him.

His hands moved through the systems check—a ritual performed a hundred times before, timed to the pulse of his own racing heart.

Flight readiness lights blinked green, and sensors hummed softly as hydraulics primed. The cockpit glowed faintly with violet HUD projections.

Outside, the world narrowed to a muted static crackle.

Jazz's voice threaded through the headset like a lifeline: smooth, taut. Her tone was carefully calibrated beneath the casual surface. Her fingers over the comms initiated a volley of maintenance queries—fuel pressure, landing gear health, engine diagnostics. All routine. All designed to stall the tactical officers monitoring the base.

"Sarge, the fuel return lines look good. No surprises today," her voice hummed over the channel.

"Tower, double-check the runway lights. All clear on this end," she added smoothly, her practiced ease masking the tension threading through her words as she delayed scrutiny with flawless professionalism.

It was a fragile dance, and Jazz led with the composure of a born pilot's confidante.

Then—shrill warning tones yanked Blaze's attention back. The control tower's voice cut sharply and insistently through his headset: all flights grounded. Repeat: all flights grounded.

The grounding order pounded in his ears.

His hands didn't hesitate. Throttles clicked forward. Systems beeped a foreboding cadence. His jaw clenched as he reached for the comm mute—one flick of his thumb sealing off the world of commands and restrictions.

The engines engaged. Metal groaned in protest against the sudden roar.

A low rumble swelled beneath him.

Outside, rain hammered the canopy—a relentless percussion that blurred the gray wash beyond the glass. Lightning unspooled jagged ribbons across the churning sky, each flash carving fleeting shadows across his face.

The jet rolled forward. Tires hissed on the wet runway. The world shrank to the strip ahead, with gauges flashing warnings at the edge of his vision. His knuckles whitened against the yoke as automated flight restrictions clattered across his HUD in urgent red—each light a command to abort, to stay grounded.

Blaze pressed on.

Wind buffeted the fuselage as he pushed the throttle to the stops. Spray flew up in torrents, hurling shards of water against the canopy with stinging force. Thunder coiled behind him, a monstrous, breathing beast.

The nose lifted.

The jet shuddered through violent gusts. Shreds of cloud bit at the wingtips as the earth fell away beneath him—the base shrinking into a grid of muted lights and rain-spattered concrete. His breath came shallow against the roaring engines. He fought the yoke against sudden dips and rises, fingering the controls with desperate precision as the jet climbed hard through the first thick fingers of the storm.

Emergency warnings flashed. Air pressure fluctuated. Stall sensors beeped their insistent alerts.

His focus narrowed to the radar screen—a pulsing constellation of faint blips amid a flashing chorus of weather echoes. One blip burned brighter than the rest: Lyra's position. A white dot flickered stubbornly and brightly through the tempest's growl.

"Come on. Come on." His voice was barely more than a rasp, lost beneath the engine's roar.

Outside the canopy, lightning scythed with brutal beauty. The gray maw of the cyclone opened wide—an uneven swirl of cloud, rain, and raw kinetic fury. The storm had swept across the coastal territories, the same tempest that had scattered Lyra's last transmission. The same one that had grounded every aircraft at the base. The same one he was flying into anyway.

Slowly, the jet's silhouette dissolved into the storm, swallowed whole by the relentless pulse of wind and water.

On the radar, the single gleaming dot shrank, sank, and merged into a storm-formed constellation of uncanny light, each blip a ghost among the chaos.

The storm swallowed him whole.

###

Lyra's jet bucked against the turbulent breath of the storm, each gust a violent hand yanking at her controls as she arced skyward toward the southern sector. Her voice cut through the static—steady, but brittle underneath—like a thin line stretched tight across trembling wires.

"Position: seven-five, heading two-eight-zero. Fuel at sixty-five percent... holding steady."

A brutal roll. Weightlessness. Then gut-wrenching G-force snatched the breath from her lungs. Her tone wavered. A sharp crack threaded through her calm.

"Correction... recovering."

Outside, rain hammers the reinforced canopy like a savage drumline. Lightning splits the bruised clouds, casting erratic shadows within her cockpit.

The erratic static hisses over the radio. Instruments strobe weak warnings. Her fingers snap to a screen. Eyes narrow at the glow—unexpected radar signals dancing like phantoms beside the southern station's coordinates.

She leans closer. The readings pulse with anomalies too precise to dismiss as weather interference. Ghosts. But ghosts don't shimmer with that deliberate rhythm.

Interference. Or something worse.

"No abort," she mutters, teeth grinding against the roar, her voice low but cutting through the noise like a blade.

A flicker of doubt ignites—memories of failure, of yesterday's quiet warnings buried in maintenance logs—but steel cements her resolve. Lyra pivots her course, clipping the jet's nose toward the blinking coordinates. Her finger skims the panel, cycling through system diagnostics; disk alarms blink amber, stubborn sentinels against her defiance.

The cockpit fills with the scent of recycled air tinged with ozone. Copper blooms across her tongue—the metallic taste of adrenaline thickening and pooling. She tastes it every time she flies into the unknown. Every time she ignores the safe choice.

Inside the helmet, her mind drums on a single image—Blaze in the simulator's dim glow, his steady jaw clenched as he ran her through approach sequences. The way his eyes had lingered on hers afterward, haunted and fierce all at once. That quiet plea hidden behind his clipped commands: *Don't do anything reckless.* But his jaw had told a different story. His jaw had said: *I know you will.*

That expression roots her hands to the controls with a fierce grip, a tether against the chaos pressing in.

A violent gust catches the jet's wingtip, causing the nose to pitch down by nearly a hundred feet. The sudden plunge wrenches her stomach free, muscle and metal straining in concert as she wrangles the stick back, fighting the invisible tempest.

"Come on..." she breathes. "Steady..."

Her pulse pounds an urgent rhythm against her ribs.

Minutes stretch between rolling thunder and the scent of wet earth and ionized air sneaking through the ventilation vents. Visibility thins to muted gray, swallowing the horizon as cloud tendrils lick the fuselage. Still, Lyra claws forward, her eyes locked on the southern station's faint beacon pulsing on her HUD.

The cockpit HUD flickers again. Her jaw clenches so hard that she tastes copper anew. She relies on muscle memory now, instincts honed through countless hours battling the capricious sky.

Her voice cuts through the static, sharp with determination, each word deliberate.

"Radar readings are distorted. It could be sabotage or atmospheric interference—either way, the southern station's signal is compromised. Systems are alerting to power fluctuations."

She talks out loud, as if by naming the problem, she can wrest control back from the maelstrom.

A sudden blast of static erupts over the comm.

"Lyra, do you copy? Base here."

Her jaw tightens. She hesitates for a heartbeat before responding, swallowing the tension constricting her throat.

"Copy, Base. Signal's shaky. Proceeding on a modified vector."

"Roger that. Be advised, a cyclone is approaching fast. The return path remains open; priority is safety—"

"Understood," Lyra cuts in. "I'm running a systems check; no automated abort. I'll keep you posted."

The familiar voice behind the radio is a thin lifeline, tethering her to safety. But in this womb of wind and rain, the distance yawns wider with each passing second.

Lightning scars the sky. Instruments flicker. The HUD's horizon reference loops erratically into oblivion. Her breaths come shallow and fast, the mask pressing tight against her skin, the rubber seal warm where it touches her jaw.

She braces herself. She remembers Blaze's steady jaw. She recalls the ghost of his warning—that quiet plea hidden behind his clipped commands: *Don't do anything reckless.*

But reckless was the only move left.

Her hands tremble inside leather gloves. Fingers dig into the sticks as she wrestles back control when the jet violently bucks and jerks. The tempest twines around her craft like a living thing, snarling and relentless.

"Eyes on the horizon," she murmurs, her lips barely moving.

A sharp, piercing alarm jolts through the cockpit. The mechanical attitude indicator blinks to life amid the digital chaos. She flicks to the analog gauges, tracing the round face with desperate clarity.

Her heartbeat pounds like an erratic drum. Every fiber strains to counter the jolts that threaten to rip the jet's nose earthward.

"Stabilize. Trim ailerons," she commands, her voice steady against the crash of thunder, though her hands shake against the yoke.

Visibility blurs—cloud and rain weave an opaque curtain. Through it, the faint glow of the southern radar station pulses, a distant sentinel fighting the storm's hungry grasp.

Her eyes burn. Exhaustion lurks beneath her fierce determination, but she doesn't blink. The world narrows to the hum of engines, the stick beneath her fingers, and the fragile hope that the station holds answers. That the station holds something worth this struggle.

She banks gently. Muscles scream. Her resolve is unyielding as she fights the wind's wrath inch by inch. The jet quivers, buffeted but intact.

"Station in sight," she says, soft but sure.

The tempest's howl dims just enough for Lyra's breath to catch on the raw edge of something like victory. Her pulse slows marginally as the instruments settle, clinging to life amid the chaos.

Forward in her helmet's cool quiet, Blaze's expression anchors her—the haunted set of his jaw, the fierce fire behind his eyes. She leans into the storm, her hands unwavering.

With her eyes scanning the gray wash, she tightens her grip, leveling the aircraft by sheer will. Every muscle is tuned and taut.

The southern station's beacon flickers faintly ahead—her destination slicing through the murk.

Her voice crackles with quiet defiance over the comm's static.

"Southern radar station, locked. Holding approach."

The storm presses in around her—a shifting, living tempest—but Lyra's gaze never falters as she drives her jet deeper into the maelstrom's clutch, her eyes fixed on the fading glimmer of the beacon beyond the thickening clouds. Blaze's warning echoes in her mind, and she pushes harder into the wind.

Don't do anything reckless, he'd said.

She's done nothing but.

The comm crackles. A fresh channel slices through the storm's static like a whispered secret. Blaze's voice cuts in—low, rough, edged with the hiss of rain battering the cockpit. It slides into Lyra's ear with razor sharpness, and for the first time since takeoff, her clenched jaw loosens just a notch.

"Lyra, this is Blaze. Switching you to backup frequency now."

She jerks her head. Her eyes snap toward the source of that grounded calm amid the chaos. His voice isn't just a command—it carries weight. A tether to something steadier than the churning sky.

"Blaze—this is a no-fly zone. You don't get to call the shots up here." The bite in her words masks something else underneath: relief, fragile and stubborn.

"Orders don't keep you alive," he retorts quietly. "Status?"

Her gaze flickers to the panel. Two warning lights pulse in sickly amber, daring her to ignore them. Static bleeds into the comm. She spits the words out, brittle and precise: "Increased interference southbound. Comms cutting in and out. Backup nav flickering. Panels three and five are showing anomalies."

Her fingers dance over the switches. The cockpit flashes intermittently with warning amber. But beneath the professional recitation, her chest tightens. The instruments are failing—losing control, losing certainty—that's where the real fear resides. She locks it down, breathes through it, and keeps her voice level.

The jet shudders. Hard.

Violent wind shear clutches the frame like an angry fist. Alarms scream in her ears—a discordant wail slicing through the thunder. The nose pitches downward. The altimeter spins. Her stomach lurches with the sudden dive.

One hundred feet. Gone in a heartbeat.

She fights the controls, her palms slick with sweat. Every movement is a battle against the storm's vicious grip. The joystick bucks beneath her grasp, but her hands don't falter. A shaky breath curls past her lips.

"Level off. Slow your roll. Trim the ailerons left." Blaze's voice cuts in, steady and surgical. "You're banking too sharply. Let the wind do some of the work—don't fight it head-on."

Lyra's fingers obey, shaking but precise. She coaxes the jet back from the edge, fighting the tremors that claw up her spine as the aircraft shudders under the strain. Slowly, the violent dive eases, and the altimeter needle crawls back upward.

"Good. Hold that heading. You're at 1,500 feet. Maintain abort altitude if signals become unresponsive." Blaze's voice cuts through the wailing alarms, calmer now but ironclad.

She presses her forehead against the canopy. The cold pane is slick with rain. Ozone—sharp and electric—fills the recycled air. Outside, the world is a swirling blur of gray and white. Lightning flashes like frozen veins across the storm's roiling face.

Behind her, another presence asserts itself—a shadow in the chaos.

Blaze's jet slides into formation—an unofficial wingman carving a path through the sheets of rain. Through the jagged pulse of his radar and the glow of his position lights, Lyra feels it: the solid thrum of his support, a bulwark against the tempest. It's not just flying in formation; it's him choosing her, protecting her without saying it aloud. That unspoken bond—the one forged in crisis and trust—settles something in her chest despite the violence outside.

"Adjust two degrees starboard. I've got your six o'clock," Blaze's voice is clipped and precise. "Radar's weakening. Copy my heading changes. I'm feeding you vectors."

Lyra's breath hitches as she shifts the controls gently. "Copy. Two degrees starboard. Maintaining visual."

The sync between their machines is a fragile dance, with metal hearts pushing skyward against the cyclone's roar. Radar echoes grow faint, swallowed by the storm's tidal noise. The duo presses onward, skimming the edge of the tempest like desperate dancers.

Thunder drums relentlessly as cloud banks close in—great, gaping walls of churning vapor in countless shades of charcoal and white, their edges serrated by bolts of electric fury.

"We're running blind fast," Lyra admits, her voice tight. "Panel six is flickering now."

"Rely on instincts. I'll keep you on course," Blaze's words come through gritted teeth. "Visual cues over instruments. Trust me."

The wet roar of the storm floods the cockpit, mingling with the sharp clack of switches and the drone of engines pushed to defiance. Above, the sky boils—a churning sea of shadows shot through with stabbing streaks of jagged light. The two jets draw closer, wingtip to wingtip, silhouettes slipping into the roil.

"Stay tight. Keep formation steady. We're flying into the eye wall now." Blaze's voice is stripped of anything but relentless focus.

Lyra breathes out raggedly. Heat prickles her skin despite the cockpit's chill. "Roger. Keeping formation. You're a tough partner to follow, Captain."

A ghost of something crosses through Blaze's tone, the faintest edge of humor hiding beneath the storm's howl. "Wouldn't want it any other way."

Voice traffic dwindles, transitioning to clipped calls and terse confirmations—a language of trust forged under pressure. Thunder looms like a drumbeat to their passage, and their lights blink steadily ahead of the churning abyss.

Together, wing to wing, they plunge into the heart of the swirling tempest.

Shadows swallow them, but they don't break.

The command center buzz swells, frantic—a rising tide of urgent voices splintering the stale air. Sarge's voice booms over the radio, clipped and commanding, while Harper's low, steady updates crackle beneath the storm's growl. Their frantic shouts volley between the tower and the teams, a staccato of military precision laced with raw tension.

Jazz stands rigid beside the radar console, her knuckles pale as they dig into the worn edges of its metal frame. On the screen, Lyra's blip shrinks—a pinprick disappearing against the pulsing advance of the cyclone's maw. The interference thickens; every second the signal weakens, and with it, the base crew's grip on certainty frays. She can feel it in the room—the collective held breath, the fear that they're watching a pilot slip beyond reach.

Inside the cockpit, Lyra's world unravels in stuttering bursts of light. The digital panels strobe unpredictably; her HUD goes dark, swallowing the horizon on which she relies. Her breath catches sharply in her throat. Static disrupts her comms as she struggles to keep the jet steady, her voice breaking through the white noise.

"Blaze... my instruments—they're failing. The horizon's gone. Nothing's reliable anymore," she admits, each word laced with the raw edge of disbelief.

Blaze eases his throttle back just enough to fall behind, settling into the role he was born for—the steady hand guiding through madness. He sucks in a ragged breath, his chest tight before words come, rough with urgency.

"Switch to analog, Lyra. Mechanical attitude indicator—top left corner. Trim ailerons two clicks to the right. Steady the roll. You've got this."

His words cut through the chaos, sharp and steady, grounding her as the clouds claw at her windshield. The storm's breath hisses across the hull, a wild thing that threatens to tear them apart at any moment.

Her jaw clenches, teeth pressing into her lower lip as she wrestles with the controls. The walls of the cockpit narrow, the instruments flickering, warning lights crawling like fireflies across the dash.

She fights the jet's wild dips and shudders, the violent push of wind shear jerking the nose down a hundred feet in a sick twist. Rain thunders against the canopy, cold and insistent, mingling with the sharp scent of ozone that makes her skin prickle. Beneath the panic clawing at her ribs, something else takes hold—a harder thing. A refusal. She clamps down on the fear, forces it down into her belly, and drives her focus forward like a blade.

A crack in her voice: "Blaze... I thought... I thought you were gone. I thought I had lost you for good."

His breath caught long before his mouth moved, a weight pressing tightly against his chest. The rawness in her words splintered his guarded calm. He clamped down hard, forcing precision back into his tone—but it didn't erase the ache threading beneath it.

"Stay sharp. Eyes up. Trust the analog—only the analog. Keep it tight—I'm right here."

The world narrows further, both jets battered by the cyclone's wrath. Lightning strikes. The storm won't relent.

Ballistic gusts tear at their wings, hurling shards of rain and debris that tap and slam like a hail of invisible fists. Lightning forks illuminate the churning cloudscape in harsh bursts, shadows dancing like ghosts on the canopy. Position lights pulse through the gray wash, each steady beacon a lifeline threading through the storm.

Blaze matches Lyra's pace, flying wing-to-wing in a dance of desperate trust. Their voices crackle with terse commands and taut acknowledgments—no space for anything less than immediacy.

"Left five degrees," Blaze orders. "Hold. Comms clear."

Lyra's grip tightens on the yoke, her knuckles whitening beneath flight gloves damp with sweat and condensation. Her eyes lock on his distant winking light, a fragile assurance amid chaos.

"Holding steady, Blaze. No promises, but I'm here." Her voice strains but steadies, each word a shard of iron will.

The cyclone pulses around them like a beast in its prime, breath swirling with rain and electric fury. Inside these fragile cockpits, survival depends on a singular, ragged thread—their tether to each other, to focus, and to unspoken trust.

It's more than flying now; it's a battle of wills. The storm closes in—relentless and unforgiving—but so do they.

Lyra breathes in, tasting ozone and the bitter aftertaste of adrenaline. She pulls the controls with resolute strength, her hands a steady drumbeat following Blaze's cadence. Together, they push onward into the storm's roar—the only constant, the only certainty, and the only instruments they can trust.

When the Sky Falls

Thunder cracks through the reinforced glass. The control tower shudders. A cyclone unleashes its fury against the ridge, and the gusts come in waves—howling, battering, rattling every pane like a warning drumroll that won't stop.

Captain Marcus "Sarge" Sullivan prowls the room with measured urgency. Boots strike steel in long, purposeful strides. His voice cuts through static in rapid bursts—clipped commands fired straight into his headset. His fingers glide over the tablet's screen, and his eyes scan tactical maps quickly. Ground crews are dispatched—foam trailers unfurl, fire trucks are primed, and medical teams steady themselves, ready to sprint.

"Standby positions, East and West perimeter. Monitor runway lights. Clear all non-essential personnel. We've got debris on Taxiway Charlie—strike teams investigate now."

He stabs the tablet again. Lightning fractures the sky in jagged veins, illuminating the flags outside that snap and tumble violently in the wind.

Flight Officer Harper sits rigidly at the communications desk. Pale shadows cast by console lights carve hollows beneath her cheekbones. Her fingers flip methodically through the worn emergency protocol binder, its edges dog-eared from countless drills. She pieces together patch lines, linking medics and rescue units onto a whisper-thin hotline. Each tap of her pen marks estimated arrival times with clinical precision. Her lips press thin, and a faint crease knits her brow.

"Confirm that only essential sorties remain airborne. No exceptions. The ETA for ground support is twelve minutes. What is the status of the debris sweep?"

Her voice remains steady, calm against the growing chaos. Static hisses softly through the comms. Every second counts.

Jazz perches on a cold metal stool beside the radar monitor. Her knuckles whiten as she clutches the laminated mission sheet so tightly that it crinkles beneath her fingers. She can't look away from the flickering screen. Through the storm's chaos, a lone dot blinks steadily—Lyra's jet. That pulse feels like a fragile promise tethered to both hope and fear. Rain driven by the storm washes over the open hatch nearby. Droplets cling to the folded fabric of her jacket, cold and insistent.

She's been here before. She has watched the radar. She has waited. But never like this—not with her chest hollowed out, not with her breath catching with every crack of thunder.

"You've got this, Ly," she breathes, her voice a ghost beneath the tower's racket. "Come home safe."

Outside, visibility collapses. Sheets of rain are so thick that they blur the floodlight beams into ghostly halos. The flags lining the runway lash like wild tongues, struggling in the grip of a savage wind that threatens to tear them free. The control room crew responds—fingers dancing over consoles, increasing scanner sensitivity, hunting through the interference. Compensating. Adapting. Beeps and chirps flicker nervously on every screen.

Sarge's hand slams flat against the brushed steel console. The impact resonates. For a moment, even the hum of electronics seems to pause. His gaze locks onto the radar blip representing Lyra—a lone flame flickering against the storm's dark maw.

"Runway crews: full emergency posture. Foam and fire teams—west end, now. We don't get a second chance on this."

Jazz shifts closer to the glass. Rain-spattered streaks obscure the horizon. The distant runway lights are mere bruises under the storm's weight. Her breath fogs a small circle on the cold pane. Eyes peeled. Heart hammering out a rhythm that clashes with the wild thunder.

Harper's fingers twitch above the radio controls. Her voice cuts sharply and clearly into handheld mics and team frequencies across the base.

"Crash crews, triage point set near Hangar Five. All medical units, confirm that route clearance is prioritized. Keep the channel open."

The wind whips in shrill crescendos. The tower sways imperceptibly—a gray steel spider webbing against the furious sky outside. Sarge surveys the room, sensing the collective tension compressed into sharp, shallow breaths. With a rapid double tap, he keys the mic again. His voice tightens as if to squeeze strength from it.

"She's still out there. Keep your eyes sharp. Keep your wits sharper."

Jazz doesn't look away from the radar. She traces that single blip threading through the storm's belly. The mission sheet slips from her grasp, fluttering onto the console with a soft thump that barely registers beneath the storm's roar.

Sarge's gaze hardens. For a long, weaving second, the entire tower holds its breath with him, suspended on the edge between chaos and control.

Then, with the snap of a man taking command, the room jolts back to action, its pulse relentless, fierce, and unwavering against the wild symphony outside.

"Get everything ready for her touchdown. This is it."

Canopy glass thrums under the assault. Hail hammers the cockpit like shards of ice. The wind claws, buffeting the jet with wild, uneven breaths—each gust a punch against the fragile bubble that holds Lyra's world. She clamps her harness tighter, feeling the chest plate bite deeper into her sternum. Her breath shortens—shallow, clipped. The sharp taste of adrenaline coats her tongue, metallic and bitter. The recycled air tastes stale beneath it, tinged faintly with ozone that clings to the cockpit walls.

Fingers grip the throttle, knuckles whitening as she wills the trembling metal to obey. The jet bucks under her touch, solo on patrol—a fragile speck wounded inside the cyclone's heart. Training kicks in—the old drills, the mantras she'd repeated a thousand times to steel her resolve when the sky turned hostile.

Suddenly, lightning tears across the storm-black sky. Jagged fingers rake the windscreen with blinding ferocity. White-hot light floods the cockpit, searing through her vision and leaving ghostly afterimages dancing behind her eyelids. Her heart stutters. The instruments flicker, spasming under electric assault. Warning lights bloom scarlet across the dashboard, slicing through the haze like blood spilled across steel. The hum of power shifts. A low, unsettling thrum vibrates through the frame.

Static crackles violently through her headset—a jagged chorus of misunderstood fragments. Then, piercing through the chaos: a voice. Sharp. Deliberate. Impossible to ignore.

"Blaze."

His voice carries the weight of command, uncensored and raw beneath the storm's roar. Relief unspools in her chest—a slow exhale slips past her lips. Her grip eases on the stick, though her fingers still tremble. She forces her voice out steady, even as her heart jams against her ribs.

"Blaze, I'm here. What's my status?"

"Systems going dark. HUD's toast. Flip backup power now—got your six." His tone slices through the static, a lifeline in the blur.

Her gaze snaps to the heads-up display—frozen, cracked glass in place of data. The primary screens glitch uncontrollably, unspooling digital chaos in flickers and sputters. Fingers fumble across a cluster of switches, searching blindly for the backup power toggle. The jet bucks violently, caught in a cruel tantrum of wind and gravity. The aircraft yaws hard, skidding toward an inverted spin that drags at her senses.

The stick jerks in her grip. She wrenches the jet back from the brink, muscles straining with every nerve firing. Sweat stings her eyes. Her breath presses heavily against ribs that ache with tension. Panic claws at her diaphragm—a sharp pinch threatening to choke her. But she clamps it down, forces air into her lungs, and steadies her voice by repeating his orders aloud like a prayer.

"Backup power's on. Lights steadying... now trim... left rudder... hold."

Blaze's voice anchors her like a rock in the storm's maw, a steady pulse beneath the wild chaos. She locks onto the cadence, every syllable a tether pulling her back from the edge. The jet shudders beneath her hands. Metallic groans rip from stressed joints and strained panels. Violent rolls and relentless battering don't break her. Muscles clenched tight, she holds the line.

A sudden, ragged roll spins her through a dizzying arc. The world tips and twists in a blur of motion and sharp angles. The jet screams in protest. Raw, grinding metal scrapes against itself with a biting sound. Then—balance. She wrenches the controls with fierce hands, quelling the spin with hard-earned instinct. Her fingers are slick with sweat as she steadies the faltering machine.

"I'm with you," she radios, her voice rough but resolute.

Silence hangs heavy for a fraction of a heartbeat before Blaze speaks again. The storm rages around her—a roar and pulse against the fragile bubble she fights to keep intact.

"Lyra, listen closely. Power's stable. Now switch the gauges to analog—ignore the HUD. Altimeter needle at nine o'clock; hold steady. Heading three-six-zero."

Her fingers move automatically, flicking switches with clumsy precision. Her eyes dart to the old-school dials that blur under the flashing lightning streaks. The storm's sporadic strobe paints the cockpit in fractured shadows, warping depth and distance. She squints, her muscles taut. The cold sting of sweat trickles beneath her helmet, damp against her skin.

"Throttle at seventy-five. Trim right slowly. Breathe. Keep the airspeed above stall. You good?"

"Yeah." Her voice tightens. "Holding it. Barely."

"You're doing fine. Keep it smooth. I'm here."

The jet shudders. Wind claws at her with every gust, but the trembling fades from her hands. Her pulse slows—just enough to grasp control. Inside the confined cockpit, the scent of ozone and burnt metal lingers, sharp and biting. Sweat trickles beneath her helmet. Her fingers tense. Her heart beats a savage rhythm. She hangs on every word, every breath shared through the static line.

Suddenly, the jet jolts—a lurch that throws her backward against the harness. Instruments flicker wildly again. Warning lights bleed through the dimness. She reflexively clamps her hands tighter around the stick, the steel beneath her palms rough and grounding against the chaos.

"Steady, Lyra. We're running this one down together."

Her eyes catch a flicker in the gloom outside—gray sky fractured by jagged white bolts. Wind thrashes the fragile shell that shields her from oblivion. The storm rages, a tempest incarnate. But inside, a fragile calm takes root. Blaze's voice—steady and unwavering—is the only constant as she matches his cadence, keeping the battered jet aloft.

Silence falls between transmissions. Heavy but not empty.

"Blaze—"

"Yes."

"I'm with you."

The words hang, fragile but true. The jet trembles with relief, a shuddering breath in flight. Somewhere deep inside, a promise pulses beneath the storm's savage heart: they'll see this through, no matter what the sky throws.

Blaze's jet shudders, straining against the cyclone's furious winds. He fights to hold altitude, skimming turbulence like a tightrope walker. The HUD flickers with storm static, but Lyra's blip stays alive—fragile, but real. His eyes track her every move, reading how each gust tips her craft, noting every drift as if he could predict the unpredictable storm itself. Lightning snarls through the sky, strobing the gray clouds outside his canopy, but his focus locks on that beacon. Not just a target, but a lifeline.

"Breaker one. Flip it. No downtime." His voice remains steady, but his fingers twitch at the throttle, muscles taut like coiled steel. The words cut through the static—sharp and deliberate. Each syllable serves as a guide rope as he pulls her through the jet's failing systems. "Circuit two next. Watch the amber light. Then green. Reset when you see it. Good."

A breath hitches in the background. Faint. Steady. Lyra's voice wavers, ragged through the static but determined.

"Breaker two... reset... amber... green. Okay."

His eyes do not leave the radar trace fighting the storm. "HUD's toast. You're flying blind now. Switch to analog. Altimeter needle twelve thousand. Hold steady. Heading zero-eight-zero. A lightning flash won't help—trust me, not your eyes."

The helmet presses against his jaw, the comm line a thin thread binding them both inside the vortex. This equipment—worn and tested through a dozen crises—grounds him now. It always does. His fingers work the throttle, controls alive beneath his gloves. The jet fights back. He fights harder.

"Trim a quarter to the right," Blaze counts, slow and steady. "Throttle down to seventy-five percent. Keep airspeed above one-forty. A stall's a killer in this wind."

The jet shivers violently. Metal groans under gravity's pull. The cyclone fights every move. But Blaze does not waver. His voice pulses through the cockpit. Calm. Steady. Pulling Lyra back from the edge.

She mutters something—a breathless acknowledgment—and fires switches under his watchful eye. The engine roars, fluctuating like a beast tamed one measured step at a time. Blaze's HUD flickers again, warning of unstable pressure, but the digital tempest fades as he steers.

Every throttle tick is timed like a heartbeat. Combat the disaster. Stay ahead.

"Descending now," Lyra gasps. "I've got turbulence on the right."

"Hold your line. Ignore the jitters. Count with me—one, two, three—throttle up. Smooth."

Lightning rakes across the sky, filling the cockpit with brutal white. For a moment, Blaze sees the storm reflected in Lyra's visor. Her eyes are wide—relentless and unyielding.

"Bracing for final approach," Blaze says, his voice nearly a whisper in the maelstrom. "You're steady. I'm with you. Step by step."

"How the hell do you stay so calm in this?" Lyra's voice cracks, edged with awe and exhaustion.

"Been through worse storms. This one's just pissed off." His jaw tightens, and tension pulls at his shoulders. "Focus. You're flying us home."

"No backup. No HUD. Just you and me."

"That's right."

The jet bucks as if the cyclone will tear it from the sky. But Blaze's tone never cracks. Every command sinks into the cockpit's chaos, grounding Lyra in reality—in trust. He's a voice anchored in the storm, steady and unrelenting.

"You see the runway lights yet?"

Lyra breathes out, harshly, into her winded helmet. "Flickering… barely. But I see them."

"Good. Keep that in line. Ready the gear."

A pause. Then the steady hum of circuits reviving. The breakers worked. Blaze's eyes never stray as he counts down their descent, threading instructions through the impossible noise. His hand brushes against his helmet. His fingers tremble for just a split second—anger and fear bleeding through the calm facade. He steadies himself. She needs him to be steady.

"We're close," Blaze says, his voice a tether holding them to hope. "Throttle steady. Trim steady. I'll talk you down until the wheels touch."

Silence falls over the comms. A fragile peace amid chaos. Then Lyra responds, a sharp inhale cutting through the static as she settles herself against the storm's assault.

"You've got me, Blaze. I'm with you."

"That's all I needed to hear."

Sarge narrows his eyes at the radar screens, their flickering green lines blurring beneath the overhead lights. The old tech groans under the weight of the storm—a relic that shouldn't still be their lifeline, yet here it is, aging circuitry the only thread between a pilot and the void. Each intermittent beep echoes like a pulse in the cramped control tower. His fingers toggle between different views, cross-referencing blinking blips with last-known transponder returns, tapping an impatient rhythm on the worn tablet.

"Runway sweep—double foam coverage. Crash crews, position along the corridor. Full emergency posture now," he commands into his headset, his voice a low rumble that barely breaks through the storm's roar. His gaze locks onto the faint, erratic trace of Lyra's jet slicing through the tempest.

Harper flips open the emergency protocol binder with methodical precision, her sharp voice cutting through the static. "Med team, coordinates two-one-zero by four-zero-zero. Rescue units, establish triage near hangar seven. Confirm route clearance—obstructions cleared in quadrants four and seven."

She clips the radio mic with exacting calm, the lines of her face taut beneath the harsh fluorescent light. Thunder cracks against the tower's reinforced glass, and the smell of rain mixed with ozone seeps inside, carried on gusts that scatter loose papers across the console.

Jazz stands rigid by the observation window, the cold biting through her thin jacket. Her knuckles blanch white where they grip the railing, as if the pressure could anchor Lyra to the sky. Rain pelts her face in sideways bursts from the open hatch. Her eyes flick between the blinking data and the blurred horizon, her lips barely moving.

"Come on, Lyra," she whispers, her breath fogging the glass. "You've got this."

The words come out thin and fragile, hardly audible above the storm's howl.

Sarge's fingers flick over the console, aligning the portable approach lights once more. Harper's teams had forced them into manual override—a gamble that would either save a life or become an epitaph. The faint yellow glow pulses through the sheets of rain, struggling against the cyclone's fury. He rubs a hand across his weathered face, trying to ease the tightness in his jaw. The telemetry feed stutters, with lag worsened by the storm's interference, but the data flows swiftly to Blaze through secured channels.

"Steady now. Lights are good," he mutters, his eyes never leaving the monitor charting Lyra's descent.

Rain hammers against the glass. Wind screams around the tower's frame. Between the gusts, a distant radio crackles, footsteps echo faintly on metal catwalks, and a failing sensor keeps time with their racing hearts—a soft, insistent beep marking seconds that feel like hours.

The cacophony cuts to brittle silence. Every breath catches.

Lyra's voice crackles over the comms, thin but deliberate.

"Final approach."

The words hang in the heavy air like a stone dropped into still water.

Sarge's grip tightens on the console, his knuckles whitening as he channels every ounce of focus into the moment. He speaks crisply, each word sharp enough to cut through the tension.

"All emergency crews, action stations. Prepare for immediate response."

Harper echoes the command, already coordinating the last nerve of the rescue and medical teams. The far hangar's triage point flickers to life, illuminated by floodlights that chase shadows across the rain-slick tarmac.

Jazz's breath comes in shallow gulps. Her eyes lock on Lyra's altitude readout—flashing red-hot with urgency. The storm's howl presses against the tower's steel frame like a living thing, breathing its rage against metal and glass.

Sarge shifts his weight, fatigue forgotten. His glance sweeps the room—a constellation of faces carved by fear and duty. All their silent prayers converge on a single point in the dark sky, riding the fragile thread of Lyra's fading signal. He thinks of the last conversation they had—her steady voice asking him to trust her, the way his chest had tightened because he knew what trust meant at thirty thousand feet in a storm like this.

"No room for error," he mutters, his voice rough with resolve.

A piercing flash bolts across the wet runway outside. Floodlights blink erratically, swallowed momentarily by the cyclonic chaos. The approach lights flicker but hold their line—a beacon refusing to break.

Jazz squeezes her eyes shut, her mouth moving in a silent cadence only she hears. Her fingers grip the railing so tightly that her whole arm trembles.

"Hold it... hold it..."

A crackling buzz cuts through the fragile quiet as Blaze's voice emerges, steady and unyielding, guiding from his vantage point in the storm's eye.

"Lyra, eyes on the runway. Trust your instruments. I'm with you."

Harper's fingers fly over her console with surgical precision, relaying Blaze's words; her own voice serves as a tether anchoring the chaos.

Sarge finally exhales a slow, measured breath. His fingers release the console. The first faint silhouette of the jet appears against the rain-blurred runway—a dark shape becoming real, becoming possible.

"Here she comes," he says, his voice low but certain. "All units, ready for recovery. No mistakes."

The tower's collective heartbeat thunders in the silence that follows. Each second stretches thin—a thread between disaster and salvation. Outside, the storm rages on, but inside, every eye is fixed, and every soul is poised for the impossible landing unfolding in the sky.

"Runway sweep complete. Foam trailers in position. All crews standing by," someone reports, their voice clipped and professional.

Sarge nods, though no one sees it. His eyes flicker to the radar once more, watching that lone blip inch closer to refuge amidst the storm's wrath.

"Let's bring her home."

The world tilts and shakes, a fractured carousel spinning against the cyclone's fury. Lyra wrestles with the controls, her eyes darting between the analog dials and the fading flicker of runway lights struggling through the heavy curtain of rain. Each gauge offers a lifeline—an altimeter needle trembling, an airspeed indicator wavering—but it's Blaze's voice in her ear, steady and measured, that tightens her focus.

"Three hundred feet. Line up left. Bank two degrees... now. Hold. Throttle steady at seventy percent."

Her fingers tighten on the yoke, her knuckles paling as a gust wrenches the jet's wing like a living thing. Cold sweat beads at her temples. Rain slaps against the canopy, and hammering hail rattles across the glass like scattered pebbles against a storm door. The gusts claw sideways, pushing her off center, but Lyra fights back, willing the jet into a reluctant ballet against the tempest.

"Keep her steady, Lyra. Count with me—one, two, three, four—hold the glide slope. Eyes on the horizon, not the storm," Blaze commands, the faint edge of unspoken fear beneath his discipline binding her resolve.

Outside, runway lights blink erratically in a desperate dance, strobes flickering on and off, casting ghostly shadows across pools of water gathering on the tarmac. Cyclone winds have overwhelmed the base's aging power grid, forcing manual overrides and stretching ground crews thin. The cyclone's howl rolls over the base in a relentless growl, punctuated only by the hiss and rumble of emergency trucks poised like sentinels on either side of the runway.

Through the headset, crackling static nearly masks Sarge's deeper, barked orders to the ground crews. He stands at the edge of the floodlit runway, muscles taut beneath soaked gear, eyes scanning the downpour for every sign. Foam trailers line the approaches, their nozzles glinting with promise as Harper's clipped voice cuts through her radio from the command post.

"Clear all debris from the north corridor. Med teams are at triage point alpha. Keep the zone locked down and clear for emergency."

The cadence of her voice slices through the chaos with surgical precision.

Lyra's tires meet the slick asphalt with a shudder. The first kiss of rubber on water-slicked pavement sends tremors through the jet's frame. The nose dips as the jet threatens to hydroplane, skidding sideways over invisible puddles. Her heart thunders. Panic prickles beneath her skin, but muscle memory floods in—trained years of instinct rooting her to the task.

"Differential braking. Rudder left—harder!" Blaze's voice slices through the howl of the storm. "You've got this, Lyra."

She slams the left brake pedal down, fighting the jet's wild urge to drift. Her calf burns; her hands shake, fingers dug into the yoke like claws. The nose swings one way, then snaps back, sliding brutally along the shiny black ribbon of rain. The jet groans, metal scraping a ragged scream against the runway's hidden debris.

Breathe. Breathe.

The runway flashes past, a blurry carousel of flickering yellow and white, melting and reforming beneath the vortex of rain and wind. Lyra's breath hitches, a sudden tightness in her chest. The jet's momentum lulls, then shudders violently beneath her hands—screeching and grinding. It slows agonizingly, finally grinding to a halt inches short of the standby emergency crews, their arms raised against the storm, faces taut with tension.

Lyra's shoulders sag. The roar of adrenaline drains away like a receding tide, leaving a hollow cold behind her ribs. She leans into the control column, her trembling fingers loosening their white-knuckled grip. The storm fades to a distant roar, muffled by the fragile safety of stillness.

Static crackles to life in her ear. A broken laugh—Blaze's voice, ragged but triumphant, shattering the tension like glass.

"You did it. Damn it—you did it."

The sound releases something tight and raw inside her. Lyra lets out a shuddering breath, disbelief lacing the edges. Her gaze catches the runway lights through a veil of raindrops on the visor, the world swimming softly around the edges, blurred and uncertain but real.

"Blaze... I'm here," she whispers, her voice rough and wet with exhaustion.

"Yeah, you're with me. Always."

A sudden wave of exhaustion curls through her muscles, the storm outside still thrumming like a living thing as she settles into the quiet aftermath of survival. In that suspended moment, battered and drenched on the fragile cusp between chaos and calm, Lyra feels the weight of everything she has fought for—pressed into the damp silence, the raw scent of fuel and rain, the electric pulse of life held fast by sheer will.

And somewhere behind that voice—steady, relentless—she finds a tether, a flicker of something unbreakable amid the storm.

The emergency crews thunder across the rain-slick tarmac like a wave breaking against jagged rocks. A crew chief's gloved hand snaps the canopy latch open with a sharp click.

Inside, Lyra's chest rises and falls beneath the soaked flight jacket. Wet hair clings to her forehead. Med techs drape a heavy gray blanket over her shoulders—the fabric smelling faintly of antiseptic and earth—shielding her from the cold downpour. Her fingers are numb.

Beneath the blanket, her heart hammers against her ribs, a rhythm that has not yet found its way back to normal.

Dr. Calloway moves quickly, fingers pressing gently but firmly against Lyra's temples, eyes scanning for any flicker of concussion or cuts hidden beneath the grime and rain.

Jazz appears at the bottom of the gang ladder. Her breath catches, and tears blur her vision. The storm's roar muffles her sobs, but without hesitation, her arms reach out and pull Lyra close.

The embrace is raw and trembling, with rainwater soaking through their uniforms and mixing with tears and salt air.

"Lyra... you did everything right," Jazz whispers, her voice thick. "You kept it together... you're okay."

Lyra presses her cheek against Jazz's, her shaky breaths cutting through the silence, which is filled only by the storm's relentless symphony. Her fingers clutch the fabric of Jazz's jacket as if holding onto resolve itself.

From the west edge of the apron, Blaze bursts forward, soaked to the bone. His boots slap hard against the water-beaded concrete. Each breath is ragged, sharp bursts that propel him ahead through a protective ring of personnel. Rain streams down his face in rivulets, and his normally composed expression cracks, relief and menace burning in his green eyes.

"Sarge." Blaze's voice is low and rough as gravel. He stops only when a solid hand comes down on his shoulder.

Sarge's dark gaze is sharp beneath damp brows, his voice low but firm. "Rules, Blaze. You know I've got your back, but you're crossing lines."

The weight of those words hangs between them—Sarge's loyalty to Blaze warring against the academy's strict protocols. It's evident in the tension of his jaw and in the way his grip tightens for a fraction of a second before releasing. A silent understanding. A pact forged in years of service.

Blaze swallows hard, his jaw clenched, but he nods curtly. "I'm not leaving her alone out here."

Sarge's grip tightens for one last moment—a silent acknowledgment—before he steps aside.

The canopy swings fully open, revealing Lyra's weary frame illuminated by flashing red lights. The emergency crew steadies her as she swings a leg over the edge. She blinks against the rain, her eyes shimmering with moisture—not just from exhaustion but from a steadfast fire that refuses to dim. She squares her jaw. A faint tremor betrays the storm inside her as her gaze locks immediately onto Blaze's as they simultaneously reach for the rungs.

Silence blooms between them, a crackling current humming in the narrowing space.

Her hands—still calloused and trembling from hours of wrestling with controls and tempestuous gusts—brush against the wet metal ladder. Blaze's fingers curl around the rails, his skin raw from the grip but steady. Time tightens. The space shrinks. Two worlds poised on the edge of unspoken confession. Their exhaustion and adrenaline mingle in the rain-spattered air.

They almost reach for each other.

But the crowd surges forward. The wails of arriving command vehicles fracture the fragile moment. Red and blue lights blaze against the storm-grey sky, reflecting off puddles and wet skin. The charged silence shatters as base security and medical staff converge.

Lyra flexes her fingers one last time, squeezing Blaze's roughened hand—barely a whisper of contact—but inside, it screams volumes neither dares to voice aloud.

"Hold on," says Blaze, his voice rough. A promise is tethered in that silent grasp.

Without breaking eye contact, Lyra allows herself to be led away toward medical evaluation. Her steps are unsteady but unbroken. The sirens scream a desperate chorus as they fade behind her figure, leaving Blaze standing—breath still heavy, heart thunderous—as the storm's howl presses in around him.

Med techs cluster around Lyra, their hands steady but careful as they guide her from the soaked cockpit to the canopy's edge. The rain hammers the tarmac, relentless—hissing like steam from the wet runway. A cold bite settles into her skin, each soaked thread scraping like ice against her neck. Lyra's legs tremble, but she stands rigid, her shoulders stiffening against the storm and the pulse pounding beneath her ribs.

One of the techs drapes a threadbare, rain-dampened blanket over her shoulders. The coarse fabric scratches her bare skin, yet the simple gesture anchors her frazzled nerves—a small kindness in the chaos swirling around them. She breathes through the wet grit in her lungs and half-turns, her lips parting to form a hoarse "Thank you" toward Blaze, whose figure leans tensely against the ladder just a few feet away. The roar of engines and wind claws at the space between them, swallowing her voice.

Blaze's jaw tightens, and his knuckles turn white against the cold, slick railing.

Military protocol etches invisible lines between them—boundaries as rigid as the steel he grips. The distance is physical, and the intensity is electric. Everything forbidden resides in that space.

The security detail moves in stiff and deliberate motions, cutting through the haze like surging shadows. One officer steps between him and the jet, his voice clipped and uncompromising. "Captain Arden, stand down. This area is restricted."

He squares his shoulders, muscles coiling beneath the soaked uniform, but his eyes remain fixed on Lyra's retreating form. Each step she takes toward the triage tent carves a hollow ache deeper inside him. He fights the impulse to follow, to reach out, to shatter the invisible lines that the rules have etched between them.

One of the guards grasps his arm, firm enough to halt him but not to bruise. Blaze pulls back, his voice low and gritty. "I'm not done here."

The officer's gaze is steel-hard. "Orders stand. Now."

Jazz folds herself against Sarge, her breath hitching with ragged sobs. Rain slicks her hair to her forehead, and her eyes glisten with an unbidden mixture of relief and fear.

She clutches the laminated mission sheet so tightly that her knuckles flash white, but her attention is fixed on where Lyra disappears behind fluttering canvas walls.

Sarge's jaw sets into a tight line, the furrows on his forehead deepening under the flashing blue lights of approaching emergency vehicles. His broad hand lands on Jazz's back with silent reassurance—a promise without grand words. "I'll see this through. We all will. She's strong. We'll protect her."

Jazz nods slowly, her voice barely a whisper. "She doesn't even know how close she came."

The storm's howl begins to wane, clouds shifting like bruises across the sky. Rain softens to a drizzle, droplets catching stray beams of emergency floodlights that still dance on the slick asphalt. The sharp scent of ozone lingers, sweet and acrid, mingling with burnt rubber and cold metal. Somewhere, distant thunder rumbles its slow, fading farewell.

Blaze's gaze remains locked on the tent flap swallowing Lyra. Dim figures of med techs flow in and out of its entrance.

Time fractures.

An endless pause is suspended in the wet hush. Then the fragile thread pulls taut, and his eyes meet hers once more through the retreating fabric.

Her fingers twitch beneath the blanket. She reaches out—the movement almost imperceptible, trembling and raw. His own hands, roughened by years of gripping yokes and railings, involuntarily flex in silent echo of hers.

Two souls, battered and breathing, changed in the crucible of the storm.

The flap swings closed.

The seal is absolute. A sudden rush of cold reality floods Blaze's chest, heavy as the clouds still linger overhead. The glare of flashing command vehicles paints harsh stripes across the apron, sharp and unforgiving. Security personnel move with renewed purpose, corralling the perimeter like the close of a battlefield.

Lyra's silhouette disappears behind thick canvas. The weight of everything unspoken settles like a stone in Blaze's gut—the rules, the silence, the risk of everything still to come.

But for now, beneath the bruised sky and dying rain, an unbreakable connection holds.

In that fragile space between storm and calm, their eyes lock.

Two hearts steady.

Refusing to let go.

Aftermath

The rain thinned to a whispered drizzle. It slicked the tarmac to a gloss-black sheen beneath floodlights that cleaved the darkness into sharp pools of light and shadow. Fire hoses hissed, their serpentine lines reeling back as emergency crews wound them in with methodical precision. A final jet of water arced through the damp air, swallowing the stubborn flames that licked the edges of the charred asphalt. Engines rumbled gently. Distant shouts mingled with the metallic scrape of ambulance doors folding closed. The acrid bite of burnt fuel still hung thick, mingling with cold steam that drifted upward from puddles like ghostly fingers reaching for wind that no longer moved.

Dr. Calloway crouched beside the wrecked cockpit, her hands firm but gentle as she navigated the cramped space. Twenty years of field medicine had taught her to move with quiet authority—the kind that steadied people without words. Lyra's pale face was etched with exhaustion, her lips drawn thin, and her breath shallow but steady. Sweat clung to her temples in a soft sheen. Every muscle beneath the soaked flight suit was taut, wound tight as a spring. "Can you hear me, Cadet Hale?" Calloway's voice cut low through the storm's fading roar, insistent without being harsh.

Lyra's blue eyes flickered. Shock and sharp awareness warred within them. "Yeah... I'm here," she whispered, her voice rough—barely a rasp.

"Good." Calloway nodded to the med techs beside her. "Assist her out. Gently. She's coherent but shaken."

Hands—steady despite the chaos—reached around Lyra's narrow frame. She rose slowly from the cockpit's confines, her boots finding purchase on the ladder's wet rung. Metal bit cold against her palms. Friction fought against her slight weight as she descended, her muscles trembling with effort and spent adrenaline. Jazz slipped beside her, a drenched blanket sliding from one shoulder to the other—heavy, clinging with moisture, but warm as a shield. Jazz leaned close, her voice rough with urgency beneath the downpour.

"You did good, Ly," Jazz murmured. "No one's going to say otherwise. I'll be right there, telling them exactly what you did."

Lyra's lips twitched—a fragile curve barely there—but it was enough. Her eyes flickered with gratitude, still wide and glassy from adrenaline's sharp edge. She pulled the blanket tighter, her fingers gripping it like a lifeline amid the swirling noise. Radios crackled. Distant engines reversed. Footsteps pounded the wet tarmac.

A few yards away, Blaze stood rigid beside his jet—its skin unmarred and gleaming even under the rain's skeletal touch. The official debrief checklist lay forgotten at his feet, its sterile pages soaked and fluttering uselessly in the wind. His gaze never wavered from where Lyra was being tended. Sharp. Unyielding. But the hard set of his jaw softened in the moments when Lyra's frightened eyes met his. No formality. No protocol. Just a raw, unspoken vow—to keep her safe, to hold the storm's fury at bay until breathing became easy again.

Sarge's approach broke the fragile stillness. His heavy boots slapped against the concrete with steady assurance, each step deliberate and grounded. They were scuffed and damp from hours of rain and dirt. He placed a hand on Blaze's shoulder—a weight that came from years of shared missions and relying on each other when everything fell apart. The gesture conveyed an understanding that needed no words. "Panels are waiting," Sarge muttered, his voice low but firm, pulling Blaze back from the edge and toward the hangar's cavernous shadow.

Blaze didn't respond; he only nodded, the steel in his eyes dulling just enough to reveal exhaustion beneath the battle-hardened facade.

The moment fractured as military police arrived. Their crisp uniforms stood stark against the wet steel and blurred neon. Two officers split the scene—a forceful divide slicing through the tenuous connection between pilot and cadet. One led Lyra down a narrow corridor, footsteps echoing purposefully on the concrete. The other rallied Blaze in the opposite direction, their voices clipped with the weight of unquestionable authority.

Lyra's breath caught—half fear, half disbelief—when she looked back. Blaze stood motionless, fists clenched at his sides. Neither moved to follow the invisible line that now bound them apart. The damp breeze lifted strands of drenched hair off Lyra's forehead. Her fingers twitched toward him but settled at her side. The cold crept beneath the layers of her flight suit—not only from the rain but from the sudden, aching gulf between them.

Blaze's green eyes flickered, narrowing in silent frustration masked by the hard edge of discipline. He leaned slightly forward, almost as if to bridge the distance, but the steel grip on his arm pulled him back.

"Stay sharp, Blaze. They're not done with us yet," Sarge said quietly.

"You think I'm going to just sit through a damn panel after today, Sarge?" Blaze growled, bitterness curling through his words.

Sarge's grip tightened but remained steady. "You've got no choice. Lyra's counting on you—not to break, not to lose yourself before we see this through."

A low rumble rolled across the runway as the last emergency vehicles pulled away. The night air tasted of wet metal and ozone. A loose cable snapped against the concrete. The floodlights cast long reflections in the puddles—scattered diamonds of light, broken and dancing as military police guided them down separate winding corridors. Each step felt like a quiet indictment of orders and loyalty.

Lyra glanced back once more. Her heart hammered against her ribs like a trapped bird. Blaze's silhouette remained framed in the blur of rain and shadow—muscles rigid yet alive with unyielding resolve. Their eyes locked for a fleeting second—a silent conversation. Unsaid promises and unspoken defiance compressed into a single moment that neither would forget.

Then the corridor swallowed them both.

The wet runway stretched empty behind—a battlefield stilled, soaked, and waiting. Scattered crews dismantled their lines and disappeared into the storm's dying breath. The cold air hummed with the aftermath. Amidst it all, two figures vanished in opposite directions, tethered by fate but pulled apart by duty.

The briefing room door slid open with a sterile hiss. Lyra stepped inside, rain clinging to her uniform, her rank insignia askew on her chest. The dampness seeped cold and heavy against her skin.

Commander Reynolds occupied the head table, her sharp gaze cutting through the quiet tension like a blade. Beside her, Major Elena Voss leaned forward, her eyes steel-gray and unforgiving. Flight Officer

Harper and a junior officer sat rigid, their notebooks poised to catch every word.

"Cadet Hale," Reynolds intoned, her voice crisp and unyielding. "Explain why you initiated a solo takeoff during the storm."

Lyra swallowed hard. Her throat tightened. She drew in a ragged breath, trying to steady the rush of heat climbing her spine.

"I followed protocol as best I could until weather conditions forced my decision," she said, her voice steady but edged with rawness. "The storm was escalating too quickly. I couldn't wait for clearance."

"Were you aware that such actions contravene academy regulations?" Harper's scrutiny narrowed on her like a laser, his jaw set in a way that suggested they had clashed before. Lyra recognized that look—he had been the one to file her last infraction report.

She met his cold stare without flinching.

"Yes, ma'am. I knew. But I chose instinct over procedure."

"Why, then, did you allow Captain Arden to guide your landing despite regulations forbidding instructor communication during solo flights?" Voss picked at each word, sharp and deliberate, leaning back in her chair as if distancing herself from the answer.

Lyra's jaw clenched. Her fingers twisted in her lap like tangled wires, betraying the fear she kept locked behind her eyes.

"I was scared," she admitted, her voice steady despite the tremor beneath it. "The storm was unlike anything I had trained for. I trusted Blaze's voice over the radio—his experience, his calm. I accept full responsibility for going off protocol."

Harper leaned in, his voice dropping low and accusatory.

"This isn't the first time, Cadet. Previous reports show multiple breaches of flight protocol on your record. How do you justify repeated exceptions to the rules?"

Voss steepled her fingers, the gesture deliberate and measured.

"There is also concern about the example set. Other cadets might interpret your actions as a license to disregard orders. We cannot afford to erode discipline."

Before Lyra could respond, the door slammed open. Jazz stormed in, clutching a mess of papers soaked from the storm outside. She flung the stack onto the table with a sharp slap, water droplets scattering like glass beads across the polished surface.

"These are flight records from the last quarter," Jazz announced, her voice ringing with certainty and energy. "Lyra's consistent performance—her judgment under pressure—it's all here."

Harper raised an eyebrow but let her continue.

"I've flown alongside Lyra in simulations and drills. When everyone else freezes, she adapts. What she did today prevented worse consequences." Jazz's eyes flicked to Lyra, warm and fierce. "She saved lives. And I'll testify to that."

A moment passed. It was heavy, waiting.

Then a door clicked down the hall, and Sarge entered, his boots echoing softly against the linoleum. His presence filled the room with a calm gravity that seemed to settle over everyone's shoulders.

"I'm here to speak on behalf of Cadet Hale," he said simply, his voice steady and unhurried. "Her courage and skill—especially in unpredictable conditions—are beyond question. What happened today isn't reckless; it's survival."

Reynolds fixed Lyra with a measured gaze that seemed to weigh her entire existence.

"Final statement, Cadet."

Lyra inhaled slowly. The taste of rain and adrenaline lingered sharply on her tongue. Her heart hammered against her ribs, but she spoke with quiet resolve.

"I flew for the team, not just for myself. I know I broke the rules, but in that moment, I took responsibility—not just for myself, but for all of us. I'm ready to learn from this and prove that I'm worthy of the trust given."

Whispers glided like wind through folded papers as the panel retreated into silence. Minutes stretched taut with expectation, each second feeling like an hour.

When Reynolds reappeared, her voice balanced between stern and resigned.

"Cadet Hale, you are reinstated into the program. However, you will receive a formal warning and must attend remedial training immediately."

Lyra's breath caught, then drifted out in a long, shaky exhale. Jazz squeezed her hand—a silent lifeline in the sterile room.

The door closed behind them, leaving only the faint echo of footsteps and the distant rumble of clearing skies outside.

Blaze stands rigid beneath the harsh glare of overhead lights. The sterile room swallows him whole.

Around the long, polished table, senior officers watch with measured scrutiny. Commander Reynolds presides at the center, her gray eyes sharp as steel. Major Elena Voss sits to her left, her posture stiff and unyielding. Across the table, near the far end, Sarge leans forward, his expression tight but watchful.

The air hums with cold tension, as if the walls themselves have absorbed the weight of countless military reckonings.

A faint pulse thudded at Blaze's temple. His jaw clenched, though his green eyes did not waver.

A senior officer clears his throat and begins, his voice flat and formal, laying out each charge like a verdict already etched in stone.

"Captain Jareck Arden, you stand accused of insubordination, conduct unbecoming an officer, and breaching the chain of command by guiding Cadet Hale during an unauthorized operation."

Blaze does not flinch. He does not plead or protest. When the silence lingers, he speaks—his voice firm, controlled, and stripped of any excess.

"I accept full responsibility for my actions." He pauses. "According to regulation 34-12, paragraph seven, instructors are prohibited from direct intervention without authorization. I violated this. No excuses." His gaze flicks briefly across the faces in the room, cold and resolute.

Major Elena Voss leans forward, a calculated edge to her words. "Captain, were you aware that your decisions jeopardized not only your career but also the reputation of this academy? Did you consider the institutional consequences of granting a cadet unauthorized guidance during a critical operation?"

Blaze meets her eyes without hesitation. "I weighed the risk. I chose to act because failure meant certain death for Cadet Hale." His voice drops lower. "Institutional concerns were secondary."

Sarge's voice cuts through the tension like a low rumble. "With all due respect, ma'am," he said, his hand spreading flat against the table, "Blaze is the only pilot here who has the skill—and the calm—to handle that storm. Without him, Lyra wouldn't have made it. The man saved a life."

The room stiffens. After a long beat, Commander Reynolds nods. "Per regulation and your request, we will hear from outside witnesses." She gestures, and the door swings open.

Jasmine "Jazz" Turner strides in, her soaked uniform clinging to her frame, her eyes blazing with fierce conviction. She has trained alongside both Blaze and Lyra—this isn't just professional testimony for her; this is personal.

"Captain Arden doesn't just talk a good game," she says, setting a thick stack of flight records on the table. Her voice carries an edge of steel. "His skill and quick thinking kept Lyra alive. He has outclassed anyone else on the roster. His guidance wasn't reckless—it was the difference between disaster and survival."

Flight Officer Harper steps forward next, clipped and precise. "I have reviewed the flight logs and telemetry. Captain Arden's commands fell within extreme exigency allowances. His actions preserved the integrity of the mission and the life of a cadet when protocol couldn't anticipate the storm's fury." Her gaze zeroes in on the panel, unyielding.

Unexpectedly, Major Voss shifts in her seat. When she speaks, her voice is cooler but tinged with earnestness. "While I maintain my concerns about precedent, I can't deny Captain Arden's dedication and tactical prowess. His judgment saved lives—not just that of Cadet Hale." Her eyes flick briefly to Blaze, a fleeting acknowledgment beneath her resolve.

When the testimonies end, murmurs blanket the room. The panel retreats behind closed doors, their voices low yet heavy with deliberation.

Minutes stretch into an eternity. Under the fluorescent buzz, time fractures—every heartbeat measuring the cost of mercy against the cold mechanics of discipline.

The door swings open. Commander Reynolds returns, her expression sculpted into an unreadable form. "Captain Arden," she intones, "the board has reached its conclusion. You will not face discharge.

However, your flight instruction privileges are suspended immediately. An administrative transfer will be arranged pending further review."

Blaze absorbs the verdict like distant thunder rolling across barren plains. His shoulders square—not with relief, but with resolve. Not a flicker of protest passes his features. The weight settles deep but does not break him.

"I understand," he replies, his voice a gravelly whisper sealed with finality.

The room grows still, the verdict hanging between flickering shadows. Outside, the storm has spent its fury, leaving behind a landscape soaked and raw—a world rearranged but still standing fragile beneath heavy skies.

Blaze remains rooted, the silence pressing in as he steels himself for what comes next.

Lyra sits slumped against the cold metal wall of the empty corridor, the sting of rain still clinging to her uniform like a second skin. The fluorescent lights hum overhead, buzzing a sterile tune that digs into her nerves. Her breaths come shallow and uneven, as if the weight of the panel's verdict has carved the air from her lungs.

Next to her, Jazz sits rigid, her usual spark dimmed, her voice a hesitant whisper in the stillness.

"We got you back in," Jazz says, her fingers gripping Lyra's arm like an anchor. "I told them the truth, every last detail. They had to listen."

Lyra swallows past the dryness coating her throat, her knees wobbling beneath the too-heavy fabric. Her knees buckled, but Jazz caught her before she hit the ground, pulling her into a fierce, grounding hug. The scent of damp earth and something faintly floral clings to Jazz's jacket—a reminder of the rain-slicked streets outside, soaked but unbroken.

"You're not alone," Jazz murmurs into Lyra's hair, her voice rough but warm. "I'm right here. You've got this, no doubt."

A heavy door scrapes open down the hall.

Blaze steps into view, his frame rigid under the harsh lights. His uniform hangs straight, untouched by humidity or rain, but the invisible weight beneath those folds presses hard on his shoulders. His hands are clenched at his sides, and his jaw is set like chiseled stone. He moves forward with Sarge trailing behind, regret shadowing his tired eyes.

Silence stretches between them, sticky and thick, like sweat trapped beneath flight suits on a humid day.

Lyra's fingers curl tightly into fists, sweat mingling with cold as their eyes meet—steady and searching. The verdict looms between them, heavier than any metal in their cargo gear. Neither speaks at first; the silence speaks louder.

Blaze's lips twitch into a tired, rueful smile before he kneels slightly, dropping his height to hers without breaking eye contact. His voice lowers, rough with exhaustion yet laced with something fiercely protective.

"I'm being transferred out. There's no telling exactly where yet... but it's not good news." He swallows, as if it is an effort just to push the words out. "That doesn't change how proud I am of you. Not one damn bit."

Lyra's ribs constrict, breath caught in an invisible vice. The words she needs to say cling to the back of her throat, choking her. Instead, she reaches out, trembling fingers brushing against Blaze's. The contact is electric and brief—charged with everything they can't risk saying aloud. A quiet goodbye is whispered without sound.

"I—don't go," she halts, her voice faltering, words caught between her heart and lips.

He lingers a heartbeat longer before straightening, his shoulders squaring like a soldier preparing for battle. Sarge and Jazz exchange looks nearby, the cost of hard choices etched deep in their worn faces. Neither moves to break the fragile pause that hangs in the corridor, respecting the unspoken grief threading through the air like static electricity.

Blaze turns, the sharp tap of his boots against the linoleum creating a steady rhythm that fades as he walks with Sarge down the length of the hall. Lyra remains rooted, her eyes locked on his retreating form, the distant murmur of base activity—blips from radios, footsteps echoing, hushed voices—seeping through the walls like a heartbeat she can't quite catch.

Her fingers tingle where they touched, alive with what's lost and what might still blaze quietly beneath the surface. Hope and dread knot together, tight and inescapable, as she watches him disappear into the fading light of the corridor.

###

Lyra steps inside her quarters. The door clicks shut behind her, a hollow finality that settles in her chest like a stone.

The air tastes stale. Disinfectant lingers beneath traces of sweat, a quiet monument to long days and restless nights. Her uniform drapes from a chair, soaked and stained, the rank insignia slipping crookedly—as if it, too, refuses the weight of the day's verdict. She sets down the small duffel. Her fingers move through the unfastening without the usual spark, mechanical as a machine winding down.

Inside, essentials spill out like muted echoes: a few changes of clothes, toiletries, and a worn flight log. A life paused before it can fully resume.

She folds a shirt. The fabric is soft between her trembling fingers. His jaw tightens. The commander's words cycle like static in her mind—a mixture of relief and reprimand threading through every breath. Officially reinstated. Burdened with caution. A second chance wrapped in cold warnings. But beneath the paperwork, uncertainty coils tightly in her chest, twisting each moment with the knowledge that the fight isn't over. Every step forward is shadowed by eyes waiting for her to slip.

Her shoulders stiffen as she crosses to the window. The sprawling flight line stretches beyond the glass, wide and unforgiving. The tarmac gleams, slick with rain and carved by floodlights that slice through the creeping dusk. Jets sit like sentinels, their metallic surfaces catching glints of fading day and harsh artificial light. Maintenance crews move with practiced precision, shouted orders sharp yet distant, blending with the low hum of idling engines. Tires hiss against wet concrete. The smell hits her hard—burnt ozone and jet fuel mingling with the crisp, salt-tinged breeze rolling off the nearby coast.

Lyra presses her cheek against the cool glass. Her breath fogs a patch that she wipes away with the heel of her hand. The smooth chill contrasts with the storm raging inside her: equal parts dread and fierce, stubborn hope. Somewhere out there, her fate is being penned in cold ink and whispered behind closed doors. For now, she watches. She watches the world move on, relentless and indifferent.

Across the base, in a dimly lit barracks, Blaze moves with the same steady rhythm he applies to flying. His bunk, once meticulously arranged, now sits stripped bare. He folds the last of his belongings—a worn leather jacket creased from years of use and scattered letters yellowed at the edges—and piles them into a duffel that is too small for the weight he carries. Motor oil and leather cling to his hands, serving as quiet reminders of the vintage bike waiting in the hangar below.

At his locker, he hesitates. His fingers brush over the smooth steel door before he pulls it open. Inside rests a faded photograph, its corners worn and colors dulled by time—a snapshot of a simpler moment and a reminder of someone lost. His palm covers the face etched in memory, and his thumb traces the outline with reverence and pain. The room is silent except for the distant sounds of base life murmuring beyond the walls. Every breath feels heavy, loaded with the gravity of what he leaves behind.

He closes the locker, and the click cuts sharply through the stillness.

With the duffel in hand, Blaze shoulders the weight of the night as he steps from the room. The corridors are vacant, and a hush settles over the walls lined with peeling paint, the ghosts of old conversations lingering in the air. His boots beat out a steady cadence on the cold concrete, each step measured and each one carrying him toward a transfer that feels less like a new assignment and more like an exile.

At the dormitory window, Lyra leans closer. Her palm presses flat against the glass. Her breath catches.

A shadow moves across the tarmac—Blaze's silhouette. Stiff. Purposeful. His stride cuts toward the waiting vehicles lined up like dark monoliths soaked in wet light. The wind tugs at his jacket. She wills herself not to blink, afraid the moment will shatter if she looks away.

Behind her, the room feels distant—a small island amid uncertainty. The sterile light of the corridor buzzes faintly beyond the door, mingling with the distant base life resuming its relentless pace. Somewhere nearby, voices murmur—orders being given, futures being decided. Neither of them can escape the tide swelling around them.

She turns from the window slowly. Her eyes linger on the fading shape as it disappears toward the convoy. The rooms might fill with paperwork: schedules for remedial training, transfer orders stamped and sealed. But beneath the bureaucracy is a current—invisible, fierce. It hums in the tightening of sinew, in the silence between words left unsaid, in the ache of what has been won and what has been lost.

Lyra's fingers twitch at her sleeve hem. "Say we did all that... was it worth it?"

Blaze keeps staring out the window. "We did what we had to." His voice roughens. "Nobody was getting out without a fight."

She swallows and bites back the urge to challenge him. "Yeah, but at what cost? They could have grounded us both and ended this before it even started."

Blaze finally turns, and shadows play across the planes of his face. Exhaustion and regret mingle beneath his eyes, but there's something else—something quieter. "I'm not the one who's going to bleed through remedial classes and warnings." His jaw tightens. "You're tougher than they realize, Hale. Stronger."

Lyra meets his gaze, and a flicker of defiance ignites despite her weariness. "And you're not exactly walking away unscathed. You're just good at hiding it."

Thick silence stretches as everything neither of them wants to say hangs between them.

"That doesn't mean I'm afraid," Blaze adds finally. "Just careful."

Lyra lets out a humorless laugh and steps closer. "Careful? You taught me to fly through fire, Blaze. Don't tell me you're scared now."

He lets out a humorless chuckle, and the corner of his mouth twitches. "Maybe I'm scared of falling."

The night deepens as Lyra folds herself against the cold glass once more. Her eyes trace the contours of the still-lit runway. The floodlights cast long shadows, and jets gleam like ghostly predators waiting in the dark to chase whatever dawn might come.

The weight of what lies ahead settles over her—cold bureaucracy mixed with simmering hope. Remedial training, transfer orders, and the endless grind of rules and regulations. But beneath it all, the sky remains wide, endless, and waiting to be conquered.

As the last light fades, Lyra presses her fingertips against the glass—a silent promise to the night, to the future. The tarmac stretches out before her, lined with steel, fire, and possibility. The fight isn't finished. Not yet.

Under the Roaring Engines

The wet tarmac glistened beneath harsh floodlights. Puddles pooled like silver mirrors at every step. Booted feet shuffled restlessly along the main taxiway as jet engines rumbled overhead—a low thunder that vibrated through bone and chest.

The sky hung heavy, bruised orange and purple from the dying storm, thick with humidity and the sharp bite of ozone still clinging to the air. A breeze snatched loose papers and curled strands of hair, carrying the salty sting of sea spray inland. Voices rose and fell in hurried murmurs, faces half-lit by neon glare, eyes flicking toward the runway where shadows danced beneath taxiing jets.

Sarge stood at the fringe, his broad frame steady against the restless crowd. His jaw tightened as his gaze swept the line of aircraft rolling toward the pads. Beside him, Jazz chewed her lip, fingers clutching the strap of her flight bag so tightly that her knuckles turned white. Her eyes darted between faces—searching, always searching—for two in particular.

"Where the hell is Lyra?" Jazz muttered, her breath coming quickly.

Sarge's eyes narrowed, shadows pooling beneath tired lids. "Blaze too." His voice hung low, weighted with something unspoken. His hands balled into fists, nails biting into his palms beneath the rough fabric of his jacket.

Whispers crackled through the clusters of cadets like static.

"The disciplinary panel started just after dusk—"

"Transfer rumors are swirling. Blaze might be shipping out—"

"They're separating him. I heard it from maintenance—"

Groups stepped closer, gossip crawling across the ranks with silent urgency. Fingers pointed toward Hangar Two, where, under the harsh glow of floodlights, stood a lone figure. Rigid. A creased uniform marked by exhaustion. Shoulders squared tight against an invisible weight. The duffel at his feet seemed to anchor him to this moment—this fragmented, impossible moment.

The crowd shifted. Uneasy. Reluctant. They moved away from the whispered accusations. Cadets broke apart like frayed ropes, conversations dying before reforming in smaller circles at the edges.

Through the widening gap, Lyra emerged.

Purposeful. Unyielding. Her steps beat a steady rhythm against the concrete. Urgency ignited in the flare of her eyes as she cut a path with unerring determination. Shadows caught in the flicker of spotlights. Jaw clenched. Shoulders squared. Every line of her body was sharp enough to carve through the thick air.

Her gaze locked on the man by Hangar Two.

On Blaze.

Flames of recollection burned beneath the surface of her skin—the storm, the blackout, every element they survived grinding into her nerves. The low hum of engines filled the space between their worlds, but it couldn't drown out her heartbeat. That connection refused to fade.

Her strides carried her closer, slicing through the dispersing crowd like a comet blazing across a still sky. Focused. Relentless.

They want to push us apart, she thought, her lips pressed tight against the floodlight's glare.

But she wouldn't let it happen. Not tonight. Not ever.

Blaze leans against the cold metal siding of Hangar Two. A bulging duffel bag rests at his feet—its canvas worn and patched at the seams from years of deployments, each frayed edge a small confession of the missions he has survived. The fabric of his uniform wrinkles sharply, evidence of a night spent wide awake, tossing and turning. His jaw clenches until the grind echoes faintly beneath sun-kissed skin, fingers twitching at his sides like restless, coiled steel. Green eyes narrow into something hard and distant, fixed on the shadowed runway stretching ahead. The air thickens with damp concrete and fading ozone from the earlier storm. Nothing stirs the pilot's weathered spirit. He stands rigid, shoulders squared as if bracing against an invisible wind—a silent soldier ready to walk away from everything.

A ripple of movement courses through the clusters of cadets nearby. Low hums of whispered speculation thread between them like an electric current. A trembling voice breaks the surface:

"That's him—Blaze Arden. It looks like it's really happening."

"Transfer to West Command, right? I heard the panels didn't go well."

"Out of High-G altogether. I guess the storm changed everything."

Groups shift. Heads bend. Glances dart like waves washing over the flight line. Phones emerge, fingers hovering inches from screens, recording ghosts in their own right—moments charged with the unspoken tension of endings and beginnings. Lyra's name flickers through uncertain lips, tangled up with Blaze's fate like a web from which neither can escape.

Major Elena Voss watches from a distance, arms folded tightly across her chest. Her uniform stretches taut over toned muscles, cutting a stark silhouette against the wet tarmac. The faint scar near her temple catches a flicker of floodlight as she shifts her weight from one boot to the other. Her eyes scan with calculated precision, tracking not just Blaze but the ripple his departure sends through the academy's hierarchy. She's here to witness this unraveling, to understand what leverage the fallout might grant her. Curiosity and quiet determination harden her gaze—no warmth, only the careful assessment of a woman who counts every advantage.

Blaze seems oblivious to the swirling currents around him. Whispered rumors and lingering stares dissolve into background noise. His focus shifts only when a sharp shadow materializes between him and the dim glow of the hangar door. Lyra emerges from the spreading crowd, breaths uneven but eyes blazing with something fierce and unyielding. Her jacket flutters in the evening breeze. Her hair falls damp and tousled like the sky above. She steps forward, each footfall steady despite the weight of exhaustion pressing down on her shoulders.

When she stops just inches from him, the world narrows. The murmurs fade. The distant rumble of engines throttling in preparation dissolves into a hum. Lyra catches her breath, the sharp taste of salt and adrenaline coating her tongue, and plants herself firmly in his path. No hesitation. No retreat.

"You're not walking away," she says, her voice low and urgent.

He opens his mouth, stiff and unreadable, as if rehearsing words that never come. The air thickens with the charged silence of a storm yet to break.

"Lyra," he finally mutters, his voice cracked like dry leather, "this isn't the place."

But she doesn't flinch. "It's exactly the place." Her eyes lock onto his with a fearless intensity that makes the tension between them palpable.

Nearby, Jazz and Sarge edge closer, shadows shifting as they move through the crowd. Jazz bites her lip, fingers curling into tight fists. Sarge's jaw tightens, his eyes hard but hopeful—the kind of hope born not from certainty but from a refusal to give up. The circle tightens around them. Cadets angle their phones, eager to catch every syllable of a confrontation that spills beyond protocol and duty into the rawness of human connection.

Blaze shifts, trying again to move past her. Lyra steps forward, her boots crunching on gravel. Their breaths mingle in the crisp air. Her stance becomes both a promise and a challenge, unyielding.

"You can't run from this. Not from me." Her voice trembles yet carries steel beneath it. "We're not done. Not by a long shot."

He stares. The battle rages quietly behind his eyes—years of regret and fear fighting to keep him locked in place. The weight at his feet feels heavier now. Not just the duffel. The burden of everything left unsaid presses down like a physical thing. For a long heartbeat, they stand poised on the edge of surrender and defiance.

Sarge's voice cuts through the thickening silence, rough and soft all at once: "Let it out, Blaze."

Jazz leans in close, a whisper meant only for them: "Please, Blaze."

The world tilts. The distant drone of jets stirs in the background like a roar beneath the surface of restrained emotion. And then, finally,

Blaze exhales—not just the breath he's been holding, but the weight of a lifetime.

Lyra moves closer still. Her hand reaches out to rest on his shoulder, grounding and steady. The touch sends a ripple through him, fierce and gentle all at once—a lifeline to a future he's too scared to claim alone.

Blaze's eyes flicker upward, meeting hers with a raw honesty that shatters the armor he has worn for too long. The crowd around them blurs into a muted backdrop. The last whispers fade like ghosts on the wind.

He doesn't move. Not yet. And neither does she.

The thunder of an F-18 splits the heavy, damp air. Steel and fire vibrate through the soles of boots planted firmly on slick tarmac. The jet screams past Hangar Two—the central artery of the airstrip, where pilots and brass move like blood through a military heart. Here, protocol bends only for those willing to break it.

Lyra's eyes lock on Blaze. He stands stiff beside the yawning hangar doorway, the duffel bag at his feet forgotten. The weight of it doesn't matter. Nothing matters but this.

The crowd surges behind her. Loose. Restless. Voices fade into a nervous murmur, swallowed by the growl of engines. They sense it—the fracture forming in the command's ordered façade.

She steps forward. Her boots scrape the wet ground with a sharp crack against the concrete. An anchor. A human blockade. Planted squarely in his path, the fading orange light spills around her silhouette, casting a raw, uncompromising shadow.

"You're not sliding away from this," Lyra says. Her voice cuts cleanly through the dull roar. "Not here. Not now. Face me."

Blaze's jaw tightens. A brief twitch betrays the storm behind his eyes. The creases in his uniform catch the last light, folding his exhaustion around him like armor. His gaze flicks sideways, searching—always searching for the exit.

"This isn't the place, Hale," he mutters, barely audible over the jets' passing thunder. He twists his body in a practiced pivot meant to sidestep confrontation—practiced, perfected, cowardly.

But Lyra moves with him, taking one small step forward. Refusal burns in her eyes—a wildfire that won't be smothered.

"You're not getting past me," she whispers, hoarse but certain. The air tastes sharp with jet fuel and tension, the scent mingling with the faint copper bite of adrenaline. His boots scrape the concrete as he halts, caught between regret and resolve.

Around them, the world tightens.

Cadets edge closer, drawn by the electric charge of the moment. Phones lift between clenched fists and shaking hands. Jazz's fingers twitch, fists balling. Her throat tightens with nervous energy. Sarge's jaw hardens into a thin line, his stance spreading broad and solid, exuding a silent challenge—a warning to anyone foolish enough to intervene. At the circle's rim, Major Voss surveys the scene like a hawk, arms crossed and face unreadable. His lips twitch—half-smirk, half-warning—as he calculates the fallout like a chess master reading three moves ahead.

Another jet rockets past, steel slicing the dusk. Heavy engines snarl a relentless declaration of power, the roar crashing over them.

Lyra's words rise above the chaos like spikes of defiance.

"You act as if walking away will fix things. As if what we've fought for—the storm, the blackout, that impossible crash landing—all of it just vanishes if you don't look me in the eye." Her voice fractures on the last word, trembling but indomitable. The crowd leans in, breath held tight, eyes fixed.

Blaze's dark gaze narrows. His lips twitch under the weight of everything unspoken. He swallows hard. The silence between them thickens, suffocating.

A second passes, stretched and electrified.

"It's over, Hale," he finally spits, his voice clipped but brittle, armor cracking. "Your future's intact. Just... let it go."

Lyra's shoulders tense, her eyes flashing with raw fire. The engines drone louder, and the world around them blurs—steel and shadows. She steps closer, her breath hitching, every inch charged with the quiet ferocity of a storm ready to break.

"You think I'll just let you erase us? Let you... sacrifice us like it's nothing?" Her voice wavers, tears threatening but held hostage beneath her fierce stare. "I won't. I can't. Not after everything. Not after you."

A crackling pulse hums beneath the roar of jets.

The crowd tightens, phones capturing every sharp word, every trembling syllable. Jazz shifts her weight, her fists loosening. Sarge's eyes flicker with hope—guarded, cautious, but there. Voss remains poised, his lips pressed thin, absorbing this fracture in the façade he's worked so hard to maintain.

Blaze shifts uneasily, caught and trapped in the web of Lyra's unwavering gaze. The weight of every shared danger presses down like the sky before a storm breaks, the air electric with the unspoken, fear and hope colliding in the gathering gloom.

"Stop walking away," Lyra shouts, her voice strained but fierce over the cacophony. "Not from me. Not from what matters."

The engines crescendo, rumbling like thunder in the cracked sky. Their words hang raw and exposed, carved sharply into the fading light.

The airstrip holds its breath.

Jet engines spool, throbbing like a living beast under the brooding sky. They drown out sharp commands and whispers ricocheting across the wet tarmac.

Lyra's voice slices through the roar, raw and urgent. "Remember the cyclone that nearly tore us apart? When the storm twisted our world and we came down together, fighting tooth and nail to survive?" She steps forward, the wind tugging at her damp hair, her eyes blazing with unshed fire. "The blackout when the simulator went dark, and we had nothing but our instincts—and each other—to keep from crashing?" The engine's growl throbs louder, yet she presses on, her voice trembling with fierce determination. "The crash landing after that rogue jet went down—you didn't think I'd let you carry that burden alone, did you? Remember? We fought for each other, Blaze. For every damn second we kept breathing. You can't just erase that. You *won't*."

The crowd tightens, breaths caught beneath the mechanical thunder. Shadows stretch long and ragged over the wet concrete, as if the night itself leans in to listen.

Cadets cluster closer, phones raised, glowing screens painting faces in cold light. Some flicker with silent recordings.

Jazz bites her bottom lip, shoulders taut. Her eyes dart between Lyra's fierce defiance and Blaze's storm-darkened face. Sarge stands stone-still, jaw clenched, his usual calm a fragile thread of hope. Even Major Voss shifts, crossing and uncrossing her arms, the twitch of her brow betraying a flicker of surprise at Lyra's fearless charge.

Blaze carries the weight of a mistake that took everything from him. That knowledge hardens his jaw and locks his shoulders. His protective instinct wars against what his heart demands—a battle he has been losing since the day Lyra looked at him as if he were worth saving.

His reply comes clipped, each word sharpened like a warning. "It's over, Hale. Your future is safe now. Just let it go." His body stiffens, rigid as steel, eyes narrowing—controlled, distant. A wall rises between them. He steps around her, shoulders squared to shield, but Lyra moves too quickly. She won't let him pass. Not without reckoning.

"Done?" Lyra's breath catches, the word twisting in the electric air between them. "You think it's that simple? Like I'm just supposed to walk away from everything we've survived together?" She closes the distance until the warmth of her breath stirs the damp fabric of his uniform. Her eyes flicker—a fierce blaze tempered by a glint of raw vulnerability—as her fingers twitch, desperate to reach beyond the space they share. "You say it's over, but what about what's burning here? What about *us*?"

Blaze's gaze flickers, sharp as broken glass. The first cracks appear in his armor. "Protecting you means letting go—and you don't see it." His voice is heavy with a pain he has fought to bury. "Keeping you close only puts you in the line of fire. I won't be the reason you lose your wings or, worse, suffer." The words drop between them, jagged and unvarnished, as engines roar close enough to shake the ground beneath their feet.

Lyra's jaw tightens, and her fists clench at her sides. Then, deliberate and steady, she lifts a trembling hand to touch his arm. Her fingers curl with quiet strength, anchoring him.

"I'm not afraid to fall," she insists softly, her voice barely above the thunder but charged with fierce promise. "Not if you're holding on with me. I won't let you sacrifice what we *are* for fear. We've fought too damn hard to let this slip away."

Blaze leans forward, tension spilling from his shoulders. His breath hitches in the electric dusk. The heat of her words presses against his own fears like a flame coaxing warmth from stone.

Around them, the crowd exhales—an invisible current rippling through the onlookers. Phones lower, and whispers hush. For a moment, the only sound is the distant hum of spinning turbines and the steady pulse of two hearts caught in the glare of a demanding sky.

"You don't understand what I carry inside," Blaze murmurs, his voice cracking despite his effort to hold it back. "The weight of a mistake that took everything from me. I'm terrified that if I let myself love you, I'll be the reason you don't come home." His eyes glisten, raw and exposed, the mask of control fracturing. But he doesn't pull away from her touch. Instead, he holds on to it—shaky but unyielding.

Lyra's fingers tighten. Steady. Unyielding. "Then let me carry it with you," she whispers with fierce clarity. "Whatever comes next, we face it together. Not your ghosts. Not these stupid rules. Not even the sky itself. Together."

Jets rumble past—a brutal symphony of power and risk. But here, amidst the echoes and steel, the fierce heartbeat of their connection rings louder.

"Not yours to bear alone," Lyra says, her voice trembling but fierce. "Not anymore."

The roar of engines claws at the edges of their voices. A relentless tide of sound crashes over the tight circle gathered near Hangar Two. Sarge edges closer beside Blaze, steady as the ground beneath their boots.

His voice is low, barely pushing through the clamor. "Let it out."

Blaze's jaw clenches. Muscles twitch beneath the worn fabric of his uniform. Sarge has been with him through three deployments, two crashes, and the kind of silence that follows when you lose someone.

His steady gaze carries the weight of that history—a tacit permission to unravel the walls Blaze has been building since dawn. And then Sarge folds back into the crowd, but never far enough to let Blaze face the noise alone.

Jazz is a whisper from Lyra's side, her voice threading through the cacophony. Soft. Urgent. "Please, Blaze." Her hands clench into fists, knuckles turning white—silent encouragement, a tether pulling him toward the truth.

Blaze draws a shuddering breath. The metallic scent of jet fuel thickens the air, and the heat from the engines presses against his skin like a physical weight.

He shouts, his voice cracking as it fights against the drone of the roaring jets.

"I'm scared." His words are ragged but sharp, slicing through the noise. "I'm scared of loving you, Hale. Terrified."

Heads turn—some searching, others closing in. But the moment carves itself out, raw and exposed.

"What if I'm the reason you lose your wings?" His voice fractures. "What if my ghosts drag you down like they did him?"

His green eyes flash, and years of weight spill out with the tremble in his voice.

"My wingman... he's dead because of me."

The confession hangs heavy, mingling with the scent of hot tarmac and burning jet exhaust—a suffocating mix that tightens throats. Heat rises from the cracked concrete beneath their feet. The buzzing engines do not mute the silence swelling between bursts of bluster.

Blaze's jaw tightens, then slackens. The first tear slips free, tracing a cold track down his weathered cheek before he hastily blinks it away. His hands open and close at his sides.

His voice drops—jagged, bare. "Every time I look at you, I see what I can't protect. And fighting—it's not enough anymore. I don't want you to fight for me or with me. I want you safe."

He pauses, running a hand across his face and momentarily closing his eyes as if the weight of what comes next might crush him.

"Even if that means I have to walk away. Even if it kills me."

Faces around him soften. Breaths are held. The usual clamor is dulled by the gravity weighing everyone down. Lyra's eyes glint with determination and something softer beneath—the fierce urge not to let him disappear into that shadow.

The engines spit and growl closer, but they don't drown out the shards of pain scattering from Blaze's confession. His voice drops further.

"I'm scared, damn it. Scared that I'll be the reason you fall. That my past will chain you forever."

He finishes, his voice ragged and hollow. The last syllables are swallowed by a long, rolling thunder of jet noise as a fighter taxis by. Exhaust burns a hazy scar into the evening air.

For a heartbeat, the crowd remains breathless, caught in the space between hesitation and the grinding reality of his pain.

Then the silence stretches, thick and stunned, hanging like smoke after a fire's blaze. Residual jet engines pulse, drowning all but the sharp, raw edges of what just spilled into the open.

Lyra's fingers press into Blaze's tense shoulder, her touch steady as a lifeline. His muscles twitch beneath her palm—a silent quake she won't let settle unspoken. She meets his sharp, storm-dark eyes without flinching.

"I'm not afraid," she says, her voice low but fierce, barely rising above the hum of idling engines. She swallows hard. "Not if you're here. Not if we're together."

A ripple moves through the gathering. The tight clusters of cadets and officers begin to break apart. Shoulders slump, whispered conversations fade, and faces turn away—some flushed with shame, others blinking back tears. The weight of unreleased tension lifts, the air loosening.

Sarge's hand lands hard on Blaze's back, a grounding punch that cuts through the chaos. "Come on, man. Let's wrap this up," he grunts quietly, nodding toward the edge of the airstrip. His voice carries a rough kindness born from years of seeing too much.

Jazz slips in beside Lyra, her smile shadowed but proud as she pulls her close in a fierce, sisterly embrace. "You've got this," Jazz murmurs against her ear, the edge of a smirk teasing her lips despite the heaviness hanging over the night. The warmth of their bodies pressed together echoes hope—a shield against the cold scrutiny that lingers.

The crowd thins more deliberately now, bodies shifting like low tides retreating from the shore. Major Voss remains at the periphery, her arms crossed tightly across her chest. Her eyes narrow—fixed and unreadable—as she calculates the cost of what she has witnessed. The steady glow of the floodlights casts sharp shadows around her stern jawline. Something in her expression softens for just a moment, a flicker of recognition that the humanity before her complicates her usual calculations. Then her jaw tightens again, the professional mask sliding back into place.

The roar of engines fades. One jet after another falls silent. Quiet blankets the wet tarmac like a heavy fog. The afterburner glow casts flickering amber pools over the cracked concrete, painting Blaze and Lyra in stark light—two figures stripped bare beneath the vast, indifferent sky.

Blaze's breath mingles with the lingering chill of the night air, ragged and uneven. His muscles quake under Lyra's touch, and he allows it to settle, letting it root him here instead of fighting it. Lyra shifts closer, their shoulders brushing, a subtle promise held in their shared space. The world hushes, caught between the end of noise and the first fragile moment of something new.

"Not afraid?" Blaze's voice cracks, soft but raw—as if disbelief and hope are fighting for air inside him.

"No," Lyra replies, her voice steady yet vulnerable. "Because I'm not alone anymore."

A shudder passes through him—the kind that is not cold but a break in armor. For once, he allows it to settle.

The crowd's gaze lingers, no longer whispering, no longer judging. They are just watching two souls stripped of their defenses, standing face to face beneath the fading roar of the sky.

Sarge gestures toward the departing cadets. "Alright. Let's clear the runway."

Jazz steals one last look at the pair, her eyes bright yet shadowed. "You ready?" she asks Lyra quietly.

"More than ever," Lyra breathes back, her fingers threading tightly with Jazz's for a heartbeat.

Voss's silhouette holds firm at the edge of the tarmac—aloof and assessing. The unspoken weight of command presses on her shoulders as she turns away, her footsteps crisp on the concrete.

The silence thickens, forming a fragile cocoon around Blaze and Lyra. The night settles like dust over the flight line, where truth outshines protocol, and where two hearts break free amid the shadows of afterburners and whispered hopes.

Falling for the Ace

B laze stands a few feet beyond the edge of the airstrip, the weight of his duffel pulling against the taut muscles of his shoulder. His gaze, sharp and restless, stretches down the runway where the dying sunlight drips molten gold across the cracked concrete.

The hangar beside him shimmers—a vast glass and steel frame that traps the last amber blaze, reflecting it back in angry, fractured shards on its glossy floor. Heat shimmers off the tarmac, warping straight lines into twisted ribbons of light that dissolve somewhere past the distant lighthouse, flashing its eventual Morse code through the dusk.

From the crowd gathered near the briefing room, a ripple of movement parts—a beacon slicing through the hazy scatter of cadets and instructors. Lyra weaves across the cooling runway, her steps purposeful but still trembling with the remnants of adrenaline. The flare of their earlier confrontation still nests in the core of her breath. Her eyes pin him like a living target, fierce and unyielding beneath the harsh glow of the floodlights.

The thunder grows louder now.

Engines roar awake with an ancient, mechanical pulse—the same roar that haunted Blaze's return, the one that carried the echo of his wingman's scream through the cockpit before the radio went silent. The deep drone reverberates beneath their feet, climbing in waves to fill the chill of the evening air. A relentless, burning cadence. A drumbeat that spells duty and danger in equal measure. The sound pounds through his chest, steady and alive, matching the quickening beat of something deeper.

Lyra's fingers itch at her side, the faint, electric sting where she clutched his flight jacket earlier—a desperate attempt to anchor him before he vanished like smoke again. Her hand remains clenched tight, knuckles white against the fabric of her uniform. The tension in her grip hasn't eased and won't ease—not until she knows he means it.

Nearby, Jazz leans back against a rusted steel pillar, his expression taut as he exchanges a quick, knowing glance with Sarge. The glow from the runway casts half their faces in shadow—worry etched into the tense lines around Jazz's eyes, while Sarge's jaw clenches, steady as a rock.

Major Voss stands a little apart, arms folded over her chest like a shield. Her gaze is sharp, unreadable, and calculating even in this charged, fragile scene. She watches them both with the precision of someone weighing risk against protocol, her silence a quiet reminder that there are forces larger than their desires pressing down from above. The crowd thins instinctively, giving space, but lingers closely enough for the undercurrent of uncertainty to ripple through the group.

Blaze meets Lyra's stare. His green eyes are darkened with layers of raw emotion—vulnerability cracked open by the weight of his confession moments ago. She has uncovered something beneath his hardened surface, a glimpse of the man who carries ghosts heavier than the flight suits they wear.

There's a silent pull, an unspoken truce that arrests time around them and drowns out the distant drone of the roaring engines.

She takes a tentative step forward. The heat from the metal beneath their boots mingles with the scent of fuel and ozone, sharp and relentless. The evening sun has bled out entirely now, leaving the sky a bruised canvas of purples and grays. A breeze stirs the hem of her jacket, but her body is still, fixed like a compass needle pointing true.

"Blaze," she says, her voice rough, low, trembling but firm. "You promised me you wouldn't run."

He swallows hard. The ghost of a cracked smile tugs at his lips, edged with that reckless ember she knows too well. He tightens his grip on the duffel, the fabric biting into his palm.

"Not this time," he replies, his voice gruff but steady. "You've got my word."

Her chest rises and falls with rapid breaths. That small promise, fragile as the last whisper of daylight, hangs between them. The world narrows to just the two of them—under relentless amber light and the pulsing rhythm of engines, their own heartbeats caught up in the same hazardous cadence.

Jazz's voice cuts through the taut silence—a sharp whoop, a crack of liveliness that fractures the moment.

"About damn time," she calls from the shadows, grinning widely.

Sarge lets out a slow, approving chuckle, flicking a half-salute toward the pair. "Took you both long enough."

A faint, almost imperceptible smile flickers across Voss's face as she shifts her stance, arms still crossed but her eyes softer now—calculating respect mixing with something that might be hope, or at least a willingness to look the other way.

Blaze finally lowers the duffel, letting it rest heavily at his side. His gaze doesn't waver from Lyra's face—raw and open, the edges softened by courage and the vulnerability of fight and flight laid bare.

"They've been waiting for this all night," he murmurs, his voice low enough for only her to hear. "But it's ours now."

Lyra's hands, once clenched tight, relax marginally, though her fingers curl in a subtle invitation. The thunderous roar of jet engines continues to ripple behind them—persistent, unwavering—like the relentless drum of something much larger than the rules that started this fight.

Between the fading light and the rising engine song, these two stand locked in a quiet standstill, suspended in the fiery promise of what comes next.

The thunder of jet engines fades into a ghostly echo, retreating into silence. Around them, the air thrums only with the faint rasp of cooling metal, the sharp tang of jet fuel lingering like a breath held too long. The vast stretch of tarmac glows dull beneath the amber bleed of twilight, shadows pooling at their feet and swallowing the last flare of heat from the day.

Lyra steps forward first. Her boots scrape a nervous rhythm against the concrete. She swallows hard, her jaw tightening before her voice cracks, barely more than a whisper.

"You told me not to run from what scares me." Her hands clench at her sides. "And you promised you wouldn't run either." She lifts her eyes to his, fierce yet fragile. "I promised you. I won't ever let you go."

The words hang between them, shaky yet weighted—a fragile tether tying their tangled fears and hopes.

Blaze's gaze sharpens, narrowing like the slit of a hawk's eye cutting through the fog. He inhales the metal-scented air, and something cracks open in his chest—the old guardedness fracturing just enough to let her in. The risk of crossing this line coils beneath his ribs, a raw nerve laid bare. But beneath that fear runs something fiercer: the knowledge that turning away from her now would hollow him out completely.

One measured step carries him into her space. The distance shrinks to nothing.

Something in her light slices clean through the darkness he's carried since that fatal mission—the wild, untamed gleam of defiance and warmth that refuses to be dimmed.

Lyra's hand rises, trembling yet sure, sliding over his chest where the pulse thrums a frantic rhythm beneath her palm. Her fingers press there, riding the quicksilver tempo, anchoring him.

Blaze stands still beneath her touch, her breath hitching. She is caught between hesitation and the delicate promise of surrender. Then, a thumb sweeps lazily across the curve of her cheek, soft as smoke and just as intoxicating.

Their lips collide in the charged hush.

This kiss isn't gentle; it ignites fiercely, scorching with every suppressed desire and every bitter fear. Every fragile thread of hope tangles fast between their heartbeats. It takes them, pulling them harshly into the furious center of everything unsaid.

The world around them wobbles. The edges of dusk blur with the heat rippling from the spooling engines nearby.

The jet exhaust swirls in ethereal waves, blurring the sharp lines of their figures and wrapping them in a distortion that mirrors the elemental danger of this moment—too real, too raw, too vulnerable to ignore. They cling, as if holding on means not falling apart, as if the fierce press of lips could stave off the uncertain storm ahead.

When they finally break apart, lungs heaving and eyes searching each other's faces in the molten quiet, the hush settles again. The hum of engines has dropped into a distant murmur, a lull beneath the metallic kiss of the cooling tarmac. The air still vibrates faintly with the scent of fuel and the silent echo of promise, their future sealed in a breathless exhale beneath the dying light.

The air hums low and thick with cooling metal, the afterburner's ghost still warm beneath their boots. Between them, foreheads pressed together, Blaze breathes in the sharp tang of jet fuel and salt-blown air drifting from the nearby coast. Lyra's lashes flutter. A wry curve quirks one corner of her mouth, but her fingers press tightly against her ribs, as if trying to hold back the storm inside.

"I didn't drag us through hell for it to end in a loss," she says, her voice clipped but soft, teasing with a stubborn edge.

Blaze's gaze sharpens. His green eyes narrow against the fading light. "Then you won't," he answers, his voice low enough that it almost sounds like a promise. "I don't want to fly any sky without you."

They hold that silence for a stretch. The quiet between them breaks only when the distant lighthouse beacon turns—a steady pulse blinking through the evening haze beyond the runway's edge. The beam slashes across the tarmac, slicing through the damp night air and casting elongated shadows that flicker like warning signs beneath their feet. The light threads a fragile glow through the darkening folds of the sky.

It's a beacon, a guide against the draw of the void and uncertainty, their silent witness as they stand on the edge of uncharted territory.

The lighthouse has always been there for them both—a steadfast anchor amid the chaos of the academy, a metaphorical home beyond the rules and risks. Neither of them needs to say it aloud.

"Looks like that lighthouse has your stubborn streak," Lyra jokes quietly, her voice barely more than a breath. "Steady. Unwilling to quit."

Blaze's rough chuckle trembles between them, his breath catching before he meets her gaze again. The notion fits him too well for comfort.

Her fingers tighten around the fabric of his flight suit, pulling him a fraction closer. "Whatever comes—disciplinary hearings, gossip, the whole damn academy turning its back on us—we face it all. Together."

His throat shifts with a dry rasp. "If you fight for me as hard as you did for your wings..." His gaze lifts to meet hers. Steady. Honest. Raw. "I'll fight with everything I've got. But I've been scared, Lyra. My deepest fear? Losing you."

The confession sits heavy between them. He knows this fear roots in his past—in loss that still shadows every choice he makes. Every risk is calculated. Every moment with her feels borrowed from a future he's terrified won't come. But here, now, he's laid it bare.

The words hang in the twilight. No steady cadence. No calculated moves. Pure, unvarnished truth bleeds into the gathering dark.

Ahead, engines rumble to life. A low growl emerges from the shadows at the far end of the airfield. The sound swells with fierce inevitability, spilling forward like thunder rolling from the horizon. Hot air shimmers. Heat waves billow off spooling turbines. The pulse of power echoes in their bones—a reminder that the world beyond this fragile moment won't pause. Rules. Danger. Risk. All ready to pounce.

Still, the engine's roar doesn't drown them out.

Lyra tilts her head. Her lips part as she draws him closer. Soft. Insistent. The kiss lingers longer this time, folding them into quiet surrender beneath the darkening sky. It isn't the desperate clash of their first meeting. This is something deeper: a whispered vow wrapped in heat and hope. The faint scent of scorched fuel mingles with the salt wind—a saltier promise beneath their skin.

When they part, the night presses in. Cool. Expectant. Lyra's hand tightens over Blaze's. Calluses meet calluses. Steady. Sure. Her eyes flicker, reflecting the lighthouse's glow. Sharp. Unwavering.

"Whatever comes next," she says, her voice steady with newfound fire, "we face it as one."

Blaze draws a slow breath. The weight of their shared future settles around him like a second skin. He squeezes her hand. The unspoken gravity threads straight through the lingering heat and noise.

"We don't fall alone," he whispers. "Not this time."

Between the blaze of hot jet exhaust and the pulse of the distant beacon, they stand side by side—two silhouettes etched against the fading amber light, bound by promises forged in fire and flight, ready to chart their course through the storm that waits beyond the horizon.

Jazz's sharp whoop cuts through the fading tension like a flare in twilight. "Finally! About time you two stopped playing chicken with the sky—and with each other." Her voice crackles, bold and bright against the hum of cooling engines.

Sarge rolls his shoulders, a grin tugging at the corners of his mouth. Then he straightens, offering a crisp salute—one that indicates he's been reading this scene since the beginning. His eyes sweep the crowd, catching a dozen relieved smiles rippling through the cadets still clustered near the hangar's shadows. Somewhere beneath the grit and grind of training, hope flares in brief, glowing embers.

Major Voss leans back with her arms folded tightly across her chest, immovable as forged steel. Her gaze is like a surgeon's blade—cool, calculating, and sharply aware of every consequence their public display will stir. The academy's politics run deep and tangled; this kind of reckless truth commands wary acknowledgment, even from her. Behind the control, though, something flickers—respect, perhaps, or the weight of knowing what repercussions will follow: the chain of command questions, the political maneuvering, the careful navigation of an institution built on protocol and power. She can't deny what she's witnessing; she just has to decide what it costs.

Blaze and Lyra step away from the gathering like a tide pulling back from the shore. Blaze leads, his feet steady on the rough concrete. His duffel hangs loosely, a quiet extension of himself. Lyra follows closely, her shoulder brushing against his—a subtle tether tightening between them. They pass rows of grounded jets, their cold steel skins humming faintly in the cooling air, bathed in the last amber glow of dusk. These machines represent everything the High-G program stands for: the academy's prestige, its cutting edge, and its promise of producing pilots who can push beyond limits. What Blaze and Lyra have just done, publicly and without apology, carries the weight of that legacy.

Silent sentinels to a fragile truce with fate, the jets loom on either side.

Beneath the immense shadow of a sleek interceptor, Blaze's mouth quirks with dry humor. "Maybe it's time we rewrote the flight manual," he mutters, his voice low. "Chapter one: falling for the ace. Think they'll cover that in training?"

Lyra's laugh is warm, soft but steady against the chill air. She nudges her shoulder against his and looks up, her eyes sharp and sure beneath the fading light. "I don't plan to let this story fizzle out halfway through. Every chapter is going to be hell-bent on being worth the risk."

He catches her gaze. Green eyes narrow beneath dark lashes. For a moment, something rare bleeds through his stony calm—a softness reserved only for her. The world contracts to the space between them: the way her boldness ignites his caution, the way his restraint tempers her fire. Words stretch between them, unspoken promises heavier than the night air.

"You make it sound like we're already flying blind."

Lyra smirks, tilting her head closer, her breath mingling with his. "Maybe that's exactly what falling feels like—one hell of a free fall. But I'm strapped in tight."

Their hands find each other then—calloused, sure. Fingers lace with quiet resolve, forged through struggle and tempered by shared storms. The simple act carries battles fought, risks chosen, and a future uncertain yet fiercely claimed.

The cooling rumble of jet engines hums behind them, a soft but insistent pulse filling the space between memory and possibility. Jet fuel and ozone ride the breeze—sharp, metallic, alive—tying them irrevocably to this moment, this place where their worlds collide.

They cross the threshold into the hangar's glowing interior. Ambient light softens their outlines, wrapping them in muted gold and steel. Mechanics glance up briefly, offer respectful nods, and then return to tools and engines—the silent cogs of a machine far greater than either of them. The distant thrum of engines blends into the backdrop, a steady heartbeat heralding new beginnings.

Jazz whistles from a few steps back, breaking the quiet like a spark above dry kindling. "Y'all better keep it together now—don't make me come over there and break it up!"

Sarge's chuckle rumbles low. "Guess we're past the 'will they?' phase. Now it's all about the 'how they.'" He offers a quick salute, more tribute to survival than protocol.

Lyra catches the exchange. Her smile folds into Blaze's shoulder as she squeezes his hand tighter, anchoring herself to this moment, to him. Blaze's lips twitch into a brief smile—one reserved for no one but her. He tucks his chin slightly, murmuring against her hair, "You make it harder to keep my distance."

She tilts her head up again, her eyes fierce beneath lengthening shadows. "Good. I don't want distance. I want every damn inch of the sky with you."

Their steps slow, souls syncing to the cadence of their new path—uncertain, fraught, and impossibly alive. Hands still linked, they disappear deeper into the hangar where steel and light mingle, leaving behind a runway etched with echoes of engines and the unspoken promise of what is to come.

Epilogue

The storm had passed, but the air still hummed with the echo of engines,
as if the academy itself refused to forget what had been risked...
and what had been saved.

Lyra stood at the edge of the runway, the sunset wrapping her
in a soft, amber glow.
Blaze approached quietly, boots crunching on gravel,
heart unguarded in a way he once thought impossible.

"You're really leaving?" she asked.

"For now," he said, voice low, steady.
"Orders. A new assignment. But—"
His fingers brushed hers.
"I'm coming back. You know that."

Lyra smiled, small but sure. "I was counting on it."

For the first time in a long time,
the sky didn't feel like a battlefield.

It felt like a promise.

Final Thoughts

Thank you for stepping into the cockpit of this story—
for flying with Blaze and Lyra through danger, heat, heartbreak,
and the kind of love that demands everything and gives even more.

If this book carried you, thrilled you,
or made your heart race like a jet at takeoff,
your review means the world.
It keeps these stories in the air
and helps new readers find them.

Until the next flight—
Clear skies, steady wings, and always... follow your fire.

Review Rquest

Thank You for Reading!

Your support means the world. If you enjoyed this book, would you leave a quick review? Even one sentence helps other readers discover the story.

★★★ CLICK HERE TO LEAVE YOUR REVIEW ★★★